THE JILTED
A NOVEL

MEGHAN O'FLYNN

THE JILTED

Copyright 2017

This is a work of fiction. Names, characters, businesses, places, events and incidents are either the products of the author's imagination or used fictitiously. Any resemblance to actual persons, living or dead, or actual events is purely coincidental. Opinions expressed are those of the characters and do not necessarily reflect those of the author—sometimes, Meghan wants to punch the extra jerky characters square in the face. (And since she can't, she occasionally settles for killing them slowly.)

No part of this book may be reproduced, stored in a retrieval system, scanned, or transmitted or distributed in any form or by any means electronic, mechanical, photocopied, recorded or otherwise without written consent of the author. All rights reserved, even if you're a dirty rotten ghost.

Distributed by Pygmalion Publishing, LLC

ISBN (paperback): 978-1-947748-97-2

OTHER WORKS BY BESTSELLING AUTHOR MEGHAN O'FLYNN

∼

The Jilted

Shadow's Keep

∼

The Ask Park Series:

Famished

Conviction

Repressed

Hidden

Redemption

∼

"Alien Landscape: A Short Story"

"Crimson Snow: A Short Story"

∼

DON'T MISS ANOTHER RELEASE!
SIGN UP FOR THE NEWSLETTER AT
MEGHANOFLYNN.COM

For those who challenge evil.

> "The hardest thing to explain is the glaringly evident which everybody has decided not to see."
> ~Ayn Rand, The Fountainhead

CHAPTER 1

ABRAM SHEPHERD, PRESENT DAY

The man writhes, his body twisting against the mattress, fists clenched, face shadowed beneath the low-hanging beams of the roofline. His olive-skinned chest seeps blood from wounds I cannot heal. He licks his lips like a nervous animal, and then cries out, high and piercing, as if someone were running him through with a blade, such a guttural incantation it sounds almost inhuman. And it may be, for who's to say what is mortal and what is not? From the moment humans emerged from Earth's womb, we have carried a thread of sharpness within us, a fury that expands when we allow even the slightest hint of that agitation to catch our gaze. Because we focus there, you know, fascinated by the wickedness we see laid bare like the flesh of a lover.

That madness becomes our own. And soon it is all we see.

I clench my pipe harder between my teeth, the smoke circling my head like an herbal fog.

The man's eyes snap open and focus—for an instant only—but in that moment I see his humanity concentrated there, fixed in that tiny glint of light around the iris. "Please, Father..." he croaks in a strong Spanish accent, and his head snaps back, his spine contorts—"Father, save me, help me"—

and then his words degenerate into glottal, hopeless blubbering. "Perdóname, Padre, perdóname."

Forgive me, Father, forgive me.

I cough once, trying to clear the putrid, meaty stench from the back of my throat, but it remains despite the smoke from my pipe, the air heavy as the cross around my neck. Perhaps if I truly wore the Roman collar as I'd once intended, I would be better equipped to fight this. But even if I were a priest, no one is remarkable enough to be granted forgiveness; my deeds here are but a physical prayer of repentance.

The man moans, froth forming at his lips and dripping down his cheek to the bed like the ooze of raw egg white. I have seen this surrender before, oh so many times, but they do not all go so easily; the skin on my left leg still burns with my most recent wound. *Helen.* She fought harder than most, crying out in prayer as she fled over the lawn, red scarf flying behind her like blood spurting from a neck wound. Afterward, I could almost feel the quivering nerves beneath her flesh as if they were mine, the sharp agony as The Dark bound her in coils of hate that tore her soul from her body and dragged it to a place I cannot begin to name. It was over quickly, as endings so often are, and though I hurled my prayers into the night, I was soon alone, my only response the bitter howl of the wind.

The man bucks off the mattress now, spraying spittle against the pillow, wetting the stained green blanket. It will not be long. He has gone so much faster than the others, perhaps because the evil is thicker since Helen was taken; I can feel the violence in the air, seeping from The Dark like pollutants into a water supply.

I can practically hear the good doctor, my only friend, whispering, "You're obsessed, Mr. Shepherd. Delusional." The doctor would tell me I should stop this madness. "Go back to your wife" he'd say. But I've spent far too much of my life ignoring my calling—the past looms full of abandoned things, wasted moments I could have used more wisely.

The man's arms and legs still, though his chest heaves

with the rapid inhales of a panting dog—much too fast. Then he screams again, loud and long, and this time it is wholly and poignantly human, and my own humanity responds with a painful tightening of my rib cage. Staring at the glitter in his wild eyes, watching him go from madness, to horror, and back, my heart vibrates with such savage intensity I think it might stop altogether; I fight against this, for I am not ready to be tossed into the fiery pits with my ancestors. I know what they did—I found the journals in this old house, hidden beneath a floorboard, the pages tattered and worn. How I wish I had not read them. Because now I see fully the wickedness I am up against—see The Dark for what he is. He's been tormenting these grounds for eons, spreading malevolence like a virus, and far more will be sacrificed unless I find another strong enough to help me, someone who can lure The Dark out, so I might expel him from this place. And if I cannot weaken his hold here, I will not have the slightest chance of salvation.

The doctor may believe he can ease my burden, soften the pain of the cancer, but he cannot ease the suffering of my soul—he does not believe there is anything to fear. But he will believe. Soon he will see it too.

I can feel The Dark even now in the coldness whirling around me, though there is no open window, no earthly source for such a breeze. The man in the bed shudders then stills, his breath a thin wheeze, his shirt covered in crimson, so steeped in his own pain he cannot not see beyond the tip of his nose. So many exorcisms, and every one ends in defeat. I still hear those lost souls crying sometimes—or the wails of angels, admonishing me for my failures. Or perhaps that is my own soul, crying out in the night, reminding me that my faith is not strong enough to heal anyone.

Yet healing is not the goal. Expelling The Dark requires far more unusual methods than exorcism or mere summoning; and something far more dangerous. The demons here must be allowed to roam free and all those near will feel their presence even if they are not perceptive enough to identify that barbarous clawing at the base of their spine. I do not know what it will do to those who are able to see the evil. Perhaps they'll go mad with it, too.

I sit on the edge of the bed, and the man's eyes snap open, the fear reflected there deeper and more harrowing than the malignancy that tightens the air around us, the breeze suddenly hot as campfire smoke. The Dark is messing with us, trying to confuse me. It will not work.

"The Light or The Dark?" I ask him.

"The Light, The Light..." Blood bubbles between his lips. I press a rosary into his hand—his mother's, his most prized possession, and it is the last bit of comfort I can offer. "Go now, my son."

"No, no, Padre, no...help...help..."

I lean close to his ear, whispering, the stink of his sweat ripe in my nostrils. "I cast thee out." He coughs, and his eyes flutter closed, still and silent as if in death. Then his back arches and he shrieks—even the walls vibrate with the intensity of his screams.

I spread my hands in the air above his forehead, his fevered skin already writhing, like a nest of snakes is wriggling beneath his flesh, and though my rings do not touch him, the skin sizzles—the smell of burning fat seeps into my sinuses. My wedding band, and Justine's band on my pinky, warm, the engraved crosses inside them brighter, hotter, than the rest. It does not matter that Justine no longer recognizes me—evil remains, but love lingers too, even if it is harder to spread.

I close my eyes, feeling the room shrink and expand, the entire house breathing with me. "I cast thee out," I whisper again. "Into The Light." I lean closer and whisper the final words, once, twice, thrice.

The man shudders. I lower my hands, the flesh on the young man's head still sizzling, burning, then extinguishing itself with a staccato sucking sound. My rings are still warm against my palm. And as the breath leaks from him in one final exhale, I feel it, the thread of insanity, the demon beneath his flesh, squirming at my nearness, gnashing its horrible teeth. I know precisely how to recognize it—I brought it here. And I will send it back.

The room seems to waver, contracting once as if birthing the evil from the atmosphere. Then it is over, the vestiges of spirit vanishing like the dew evaporating from the grass in the rays of dawn.

I push myself to standing, bones aching, and hobble to the window, to that pane of glass as perfectly round as the moon outside, and I am struck with a coldness in the gut, as if I've stepped into someone else's shoes. Is this what my ancestors saw looking out this window? Tonight I peer out at another world from the one I strode through this afternoon—the front yard is empty, the grass a dusky greenish-gray beneath the towering oak, and the earth is no longer sodden with spilled blood. But my heart hammers against my breastbone, and I see Helen's red scarf in my mind's eye, hear her screams in my ears, and the *snap* of her spine, see the way it appeared as though every bone in her body was being crunched to dust, blood spurting from the ruptured shell of her chest.

Then the scene returns to normal—quiet, gray-green, empty.

But it isn't really empty. I feel the energy there, lingering in the shadow of the porch, waiting for the next soul to be lured by the force that emanates from this place.

For every slight, there must come a balancing blow. Every dark deed done must be repaid in blood.

The girl, that unfortunate girl, red scarf billowing behind her, screaming, screaming... Helen saw the madness of this world, the evil that must be quelled. Everyone does.

But never soon enough.

> "In the kingdom of the blind,
> the one-eyed man is king."
> ~*Desiderius Erasmus*

CHAPTER 2

CHLOE ANDERSON, PRESENT DAY

"I love you, you know." Victor's mouth was at her ear, his fingers tracing her lower back, the heat of him as comforting as a security blanket—his breath was like the sound of waves against the shore. During these quiet moments, before the rest of the world had awoken, Chloe could almost believe it was just the two of them, cocooned in this little tunnel of cotton, immersed in one another, absorbing each other's energy. She'd always loved Victor's spirit—it was an untamable, reckless thing that made him an enigma, mysterious and dangerous and untouchable even when she was holding him in her arms.

"I love you, you know," he said again in a low bass growl that almost sounded like purring. The hairs on the back of her neck woke up and danced.

Chloe sighed, snuggling tighter against his chest. "I know," she whispered and turned her head, ready to lock their gazes together as tightly as their limbs. But Victor had disappeared. *What the—*

The room lit up in a great flash of light, brighter than lightning, an explosion, like someone had pitched a Molotov cocktail against the wall, and Chloe tried to cry out, but there was something wrong with her throat. She raised her hands to her neck—wet, gooey, warm. All she could see was red, as if the blood vessels in her eyes had burst and coated her retinas. *Victor, help me! Where are you?* Blackness tugged at the corners of her vision, but through the crimson haze she could make out the stark white cupboards of the kitchen —*How did I get here?* Victor's wine bottle shimmered on the counter above her like a beacon of hope. She tried to push herself to sitting, but her breath left her altogether as her chest lit up again with searing, impossible pain, as if an animal was trying to tear her apart from somewhere behind her breastbone, meat and fat and gristle giving way to ravenous claws. A great sound blasted through the room like thunder. The wine bottle on the counter blew to pieces, shards of glass raining down around her, sticking to her hair, to her arms, and then...

The pain vanished.

Chloe sat up slowly, pawing at her chest, expecting to pull her hand away bloody, but there was no blood. No cuts. The room focused in pieces: The clean linoleum counter. The ruby wine bottle. Victor and Leslie, standing near her feet, but with their backs to her. And another person, a man hidden in the shadows just beyond her family, his hands on their shoulders, as if kindly guiding them away. Her heart seized. Only his hands were visible—thick fingers, skin so pale it was almost blue, but streaked with maroon from fingernail to forearm. *Blood? Or a trick of the light?*

"Come to me," a voice said from the shadows, no more than a rattling whisper. The soft heat of his words beckoned, promising a release from pain, deliverance from every horrid thing she'd ever felt, and he had her love too, he had Victor, there with him. If only she could get to the shadowed man, there would be no more misery. How she knew this she wasn't sure, but she knew it all the same. She rolled over and crawled, closer, closer—and then they were gone. The kitchen disappeared and she was lying in the bedroom once again, feeling Victor at her back, his sinewy chest, the warmth of him. "I love you, you know."

She opened her eyes in the dark created by the blackout curtains, squinting at the dusky outline of the mirrored dresser. As her eyes adjusted, she realized she could no longer feel Victor. Her back was cold.

Chloe stretched, wincing at the lumpy mattress, her heart still slamming around inside her chest, though no longer accompanied by the sharp ache she'd felt in her dream. The dream was a recurring one—all night, every night, for the last two weeks—from Victor and love, to terror, to peace, and back, until she at last hauled herself, unrested, from the mattress.

She inhaled deeply, trying to slow her heart. Victor's black-and-white photographs on the far wall—just amorphous shapes now, but she could imagine the shots of empty rooms with bursts of glare that he insisted were proof of supernatural life—always calmed her with a pure, hopeful energy she could feel from across the room. But now the mere thought of them crackled like agitated static in her brain.

Chloe rolled onto her side. Her long, silver-blonde hair tangled in her fingers, so naturally light that it disappeared against the gloomy white of Victor's pillowcase. She traced the imprint where his head always lay, pretending he was just out getting them coffee, that he hadn't left, that they were still going to get married. Victor was probably scared about that, even if he was ten years older than Chloe, but she didn't really think that was the reason he'd left. She could be wrong though—maybe he really *was* that immature. Maybe he hadn't loved her enough. She still felt the hollow space beneath her ribs as if it were an actual hole, as if Victor had literally ripped her heart from her chest when he'd taken his daughter and disappeared.

But he'd come back, with Leslie, like he had last time and the time before. He *had* to come back—he didn't have a way to support himself and Leslie without her, and unlike last time, when he'd taken her cash to pay for hotels, he'd left empty-handed. What if—

No, stop, Chloe, he just needs a break—time to get his head together. Commitment did scare Victor, she knew that, but he wasn't like her ex-boyfriend Ron who'd just left her a note: "It's been fun." It hadn't been fun. Ron was the worst kind of liar, the kind who made you believe they cared before they shredded your heart. After that she'd trusted no one, not until Victor—the only man who'd ever made her feel whole. Loneliness seeped from the pillow and tightened her rib cage. Alone again.

Alone.

She couldn't breathe.

Chloe peeled herself out of bed, wheezing, and moved the curtain aside to peer into the street. Their yoga-pant wearing downstairs neighbor stood below the window, her Shih Tzu pissing on the meager front lawn, and it felt disrespectful to the history of the place. Their apartment building was a converted three-story mansion, built in 1802, right after the Great New Orleans Fire of 1788, back when horses still roamed the streets and filled the air with the stink of manure. The surrounding farmlands had been sold off since, and from her third floor window, she could see newer apartment buildings, a grocery store, and the hole-in-the-wall bar built in renovated slave quarters that she refused to go into—even looking at it made gooseflesh pimple on her arms, like some otherworldly thing was watching her from the darkened windows. But despite the energy across the way, they'd been happy here—she'd always felt their joy as strongly as if it were alive, a tingling that blossomed into a warm, gentle softness in her chest when he breathed her name. And now... just that dreadful aching.

Chloe padded to the bathroom, the chilly air kissing her legs, though the bottoms of her feet felt strangely hot. Hormones, maybe, but she knew she wasn't pregnant—she'd had her tubes tied five years ago, when she was only nineteen.

She pushed open the creaky bathroom door and paused at the threshold, staring at the photo of Victor and his daughter that sat on the shelf beside the bathroom mirror. Leslie was smiling, her eleven-year-old cheeks still plump with baby fat. Victor's eyes were crinkled at the corners, but that dark gaze still burned through her skull and set something deep inside her on fire. A silver ring glinted from the space between his nostrils. She turned the photo to the mirror, the frame vibrating in her palm, until Victor and Leslie were reflected along with her, Victor's smiling eyes beside her own—pretending for a moment that they were a family.

Chloe forced a grin, but her hazel eyes remained sad, the purple bags beneath darker today than yesterday; even her freckles sagged. She sighed and lowered the photo to run a finger over the glass, almost feeling Victor's heat as she had when she'd awoken. Tears stung her eyes. *Please, God, just let him come home.*

She didn't want to think that he was really gone, that she'd made him do something...stupid by arguing with him. He'd come home from setting up some concert in the park, actually smiling for once, but he'd been so wishy-washy all week about their lives together, about the wedding, and she'd been snappy, on edge, unable to push aside all he'd put her through. It wasn't supposed to be like this, not with Victor—they were supposed to be secure, stable, a reliable thing amidst the stresses of modern life. She still loved him even when he was acting crazy, and maybe she loved him all the more for his flaws, for they allowed Chloe her own imperfections. She was going to help him get better. Even when he tried to convince her he was possessed, when she realized he was really, truly sick, she'd known beyond the shadow of a doubt, that he needed her.

He's not possessed. He's just sick. Possession and demons weren't real, she knew that, but when Victor's eyes flashed fire, she couldn't be entirely certain. Grandpa had made her attend church enough to consider it, lectured her at home, too: "If you worship just because you're afraid, girl, you'll worship the Devil just as easy."

Maybe she just wanted to believe Victor was possessed because she couldn't shake the feeling that she'd done something awful to make him go.

Chloe bit her lip and the skin around her mouth paled in the mirror. In high school, her counselor had said they were feelings, just feelings, that everything wasn't her fault. She hadn't fought with her mother, and Mom had still abandoned ten-year-old Chloe a week after Chloe's baby sister Hope died in her crib—the baby had made her mother lose her mind. Victor's leaving her had reopened that horrible, desolate, throbbing wound, and sown the seeds of doubt that anything could ever be good, really good, again. Why did loneliness make you feel like the entire world had turned its back? Grandpa said trials were God's way of making you stronger, but she sure didn't need any more lessons—she'd suffered enough that she ought to be the strongest woman in the world.

Chloe inhaled one shaky breath through her nose and locked eyes with herself in the mirror, letting her gaze harden from dejected to determined. She threw her shoulders back. Raised her chin. Her next exhale was far more steady. Stable. She'd be okay. Even if she never again felt the gentle tug of adoration in her breast, or the warm quiet of love in her belly, she would survive.

She jumped when she heard a click—*the front door?*—but the breath of ice against her shoulders told her it was the central air coming to life, and soon the running water in the tub drowned out the drone of the air conditioning. The hot water seared her skin as she lowered herself into it, and her hair floated around her like silver water snakes, curling over her shoulders and arms. She rested her head against the back of the tub.

Victor's gone. I need to accept that.

But he didn't *feel* gone—though her heart ached with loneliness, the air around her still held that subtle twinge of *life*, thickening the molecules against her skin, as it had every other time he'd disappeared. Would she know it the moment he made up his mind to leave for good, a sudden absence like a black hole had opened in the living room and sucked his essence away? She might.

Chloe was only six years old when a psychic had stopped her and her mother in the street—"You have great power in you," the woman said, stroking Chloe's palm with one withered fingertip. Chloe *was* special, could sense things other people never noticed, and even Grandpa had thought that was why her mother had left her. It might be true—her mother had once told her that if she'd been able to see the future, she'd have done it all differently, and she'd looked so hard at Chloe that gooseflesh prickled on Chloe's arms. Chloe might not be able to see the future, not exactly, but at least her mother had recognized she had something to offer. Grandpa just thought it should be beaten out of her. But Victor... He had seen her gifts for what they were and he was not put off by them—the day she met Victor her world had suddenly felt brighter.

Victor's passion, his art, his way of looking at the world—like it was bigger than what they could perceive, like they could latch on to it if they looked hard enough—had awoken something inside Chloe, made her feel alive, like the first time she'd gotten on a roller coaster, her heart thundering in her ears, her mouth dry with unbridled thrill. She knew what he needed. She *mattered* to him. And God knew she loved him, even now, after he'd been missing for weeks. Chloe laid a hand against her barren gut under the water, palpating her skin, practically feeling the void, but the emptiness was nowhere near as profound as the one in her chest.

She reached for the shampoo and scrubbed, trying to wash away the worry. Even if he never came back, closure mattered, right? She couldn't be stuck in this limbo forever, not knowing where her fiancé had disappeared to. Her mother, her father, she still pondered those losses when the world went quiet, still considered what she'd done to make them leave—she didn't want to wonder about Victor for the rest of her life. She shook her head. *Don't start pitying yourself or you'll never stop.* Chloe ran her fingers along the scored flesh of her back—sometimes the scars still stung as if Grandpa had split her skin only yesterday. On those days, she could still see Grandpa's irises, sunken in the folds of flesh around his eye sockets, the way his bald spot shone between his thinning gray hair, his comb-over slanting askew as he brought the belt down again, and again, and again. Grandpa always said that if you were willing to put in the work, God would help fix you, but she sure didn't think that was how God would have wanted it done.

The past is the past, we only look forward. Nothing else matters. We'll fix you up, girl, get you right with God.

Bang! Chloe sat up suddenly, sloshing water over the side of the tub. "Victor?" Was he home? A creak arose from the next room. She strained her ears, but there was no reply, only the steady hum of the cold air and the occasional drip of the faucet. She settled her back against the tub and grabbed the washcloth, heart pounding in her throat. Surely the sounds were just remnants from her dream—or wishful thinking. Chloe's muscles tightened, but she yawned and rinsed her hair. Even if the nightmare was her intuition on crack, exaggerating while legitimately trying to tell her something, she could not begin to guess what it was trying to say. Not like someone had broken into her apartment, painted the room red, kidnapped Victor and Leslie from her kitchen, and then blown up a wine bottle for fun. That'd just be silly—and even ghosts had better things to do than harass the living.

Still, the dream felt like it had to mean *something*.

Twice more she thought she heard the door creak as she sank beneath the water. Both times, her calls went unanswered.

CHAPTER 3

CHLOE ANDERSON, PRESENT DAY

Chloe walked hurriedly, picking at her blouse where the sultry October air stuck the billowy bohemian fabric to her skin. Everything was damp, the slightly cooler breeze off the water doing little to help dry her. *Thanks a lot, Louisiana.* She stretched her arms above her head.

Shh, shh.

The skin between her shoulder blades prickled, and though the noise was surely the lapping of the water, she whipped around. Three women wandered past her, tourists in shorts and T-shirts. None looked her way.

The buildings across the Mississippi River stood out against the cerulean sky, a cubist fantasy at the horizon. The sun cooked the pavement at her feet. But the sun wasn't watching her—nor was anyone on the water, and there weren't even any cars driving by. She sighed. "Highly sensitive person," that's what the counselor had called her, but intuition didn't help when it leapt into hyperdrive. *Shit.* She used to be right about these feelings almost *always*, but since Victor left she'd been consistently wrong—verging on paranoid, if she was being honest with herself. A drop of sweat rolled between her shoulder blades.

With one last rush of breeze from the water, Chloe

headed away from the banks and toward the city, the cobbled street clacking under her heels, disrupting the steady hum of the trolley. Across the way, a man playing paint cans like drums smiled at his sticks, though his eyes didn't light up. She forced a smile and crossed the street, dropping a dollar into his bucket as she passed.

Her face cooled.

To her left, in front of a tall wrought iron gate, a man in a ball cap smiled in her direction, and then, before she could react, leaned a waist-high canvas against the fence—an impressionist piece of a woman on a black background, her face a vivid, flowered skull reminiscent of the carnivalesque Day of the Dead. Nowhere was history so vibrantly displayed as in the broad strokes of the brush or the deep shadows of an old photograph where you could almost smell the past like dust in your nostrils—that was one reason she appreciated Victor's probing lens. It made her feel like he *got it*...like he *got her* in a way no one else did. She swallowed hard, and continued on.

The street felt narrower as she approached the shop, probably the lower hanging awnings on the buildings, the street lamps that leaned over either side of the road like enormous jaws ready to snap shut. *Silly.* She paused, her spine tingling...and frowned. Something *was* wrong.

Chloe examined the peeling black paint of the street lamps, the window bars, the wrought iron gates. The night before, she'd printed half a dozen posters with one line at the top: "Victor, you are loved." He'd once told Chloe that those week-long trips—staying in dingy hotels, snapping photos in the gloomy alleys, playing music on the corners—reminded him things were harder elsewhere and made him appreciate what he had. Poor Victor. Leslie's heath was so difficult to handle—her severe allergies made homeschooling a necessity. Responsibility was what overwhelmed him and made him vanish.

But he'd always come back.

And now the posters were gone. No paper fluttered from

the lampposts, not even an errant piece of tape left behind to suggest they'd existed at all. Her chest heated. The signs had brought Victor back last time, and the idea that someone had ruined that chance... She inhaled through her nose, forcing her heart to slow. *What am I going to do now?* Victor had no friends; he didn't even have a cell, guaranteeing his solitude when he craved it, and the police had never been any help to Chloe when he went missing. The last time she'd gone to the police station, the cop had taken in her lithe figure, her heart-shaped face, and told her that she deserved more, that she should settle down with someone who treated her better.

But settling wasn't a goal anyone should have—life was meant to be lived, hard. Even the word "settle" brought to mind the heavy, wet feeling of mud in a ditch. Mud didn't even try. Mud would never be happy—could never be.

But she would. One way or another, she would be. Even if she was alone.

Alone. Her chest seized and she drew her gaze from the lampposts. Beneath the awning across the street, a rabbit stared at her—brown and gray, the size of a softball when he was all bunched up, with a single patch of black on one long ear in the shape of a half-moon. The other ear was bent almost in half. Chloe drew out a single stalk of celery from the pocket of her skirt and tossed it to him, but the rabbit leapt from his corner and disappeared up the road as if she'd run at him with a broom. He'd recover and come back for it, though; rabbits were resilient like that.

She stepped under the awning of the antique shop. A year ago, the building had been a burnt-out shell, but now the single story of gray brick could *almost* pass for original, with enormous panels of glass flanking a door stained the color of thunderheads. The building had been a courthouse in 1792 when this place was built, though back then it had served plantation masters in horse-drawn buggies, and men in threadbare trousers who risked smallpox just coming into the city. She should hate that thought, the bleakness of it, but the hollow sensation of hardship that thrummed against the small of her back now felt achingly familiar: the honest pain of a rough life.

Through the glass in the front window, a jade elephant with ivory tusks stood glittering in the display light as impressive as it had been in the early 1800s when it was carved. Beside the shining pachyderm sat an elaborate baroque bronze clock, its face adorned with hand-painted porcelain numerals, though the filigreed hands were still and silent now. Further down, a silver bowl from China gleamed. And there was the thing that had drawn her to the shop: Victor's camera, front and center. She could almost see him now, snapping shot after shot, hoping to catch a glimpse of some magic, some impossible truth from beyond.

But it was not an antique, and this definitely wasn't a pawn shop. A week and a half ago, the first time she'd seen the camera, she'd thought she was mistaken, that it couldn't possibly be Victor's, but the electricity that coursed up through her shoulder when she touched it had dissolved all doubts. She didn't even need to see Victor's band name penned into the strap, or get verification from her coworker, Greg, who'd described the man he'd gotten it from as "thirties, leather jacket, bull ring stabbed through his septum."

So Victor had been there, and Victor would return to buy back his prized possession, even if she had erased the photos stored there—thank goodness Greg and Lehmann hadn't bothered to go through them; if they had, she'd have been answering questions for the cops. Just one more reason she couldn't ask the police to investigate his disappearance, not after she'd destroyed what *might be* evidence, though those photos were surely some form of avant-garde art anyway—he'd once spent three days photographing the decaying remains of a dead squirrel in the parking lot, and another week documenting the progression of a healing set of stitches on his thigh. The doctors had medicated him after that. But... Icy fingers sprouted between her shoulder blades and raked their claws over her flesh, leaving trails of electric frost. What if he'd gotten worse? What if he'd stopped taking his meds? What it he'd snapped? He needed her—he couldn't handle life all alone.

All she'd needed in return was for him to…stay.

Chloe inhaled sharply and let it out slow, like her counselor had once told her. The bell jingled as she pushed open the door and walked inside. Dust motes tickled her nose, and she squinted against the glint off the gilded picture frames. Just being here felt like giving Grandpa the finger. *The past is the past—except here, Grandpa.*

As usual, her boss sat behind the middle display case— dead center in the back of the shop. Two other glass cases stood on either side of the store, with Greg crouched behind the one on her right, only the top of his blond head visible through the glass. Lehmann's eyes were on the little wooden dreidel spinning on top of his case. Turkish, maybe, inlaid with silver, old enough to be worth a good amount, but just seeing the toy was enough to make her shudder though she didn't know why. It felt…wrong. Mr. Lehmann looked up, his eyes hard, and raised one long, thin finger to scrape at an age spot on his pasty cheek.

"Morning, Mr. Lehmann."

He nodded in reply, eyes narrowed, frown still plastered on his maw. If there was a Guinness record for scowling the longest, Lehmann would win, hands down. Chloe glanced at the window, at the camera, but resisted the urge to touch it before she started her day. They'd see her, the way she held on to it too long, the way she flinched when it vibrated in her palms—they'd figure out why the camera mattered to her, know she was hurting. When people knew you were hurting, they could get the jump on you—and hurt you more. She'd wanted so badly for Victor to prove her wrong about that. Maybe he still would.

Was it wrong to hope for the best? Grandpa might have said yes, but…screw him.

With a final nod to Lehmann, Chloe skirted the spindly little table that held a few collectables in the middle of the room and headed for the office. Nothing there but a 1900s walnut desk—Victorian—pushed against the back wall, topped with an outdated computer and a vintage hurricane lamp painted with golden flowers; almost the same setup as the office next door, except that room had a safe instead of a computer. She paged through the ledger on the desk. No in-shop appraisals on the books today, just one appointment this afternoon with a Mr. Shepherd, probably a patron of the shop or someone clearing an estate. After a death, relatives might call antique dealers to go through the house, and the appraisers got first dibs on items of value for their shops—Greg would have fun poking around the dusty shelves for things they could sell.

She headed for the showroom, glancing once at the other door down the hall—the room she still wasn't allowed in alone, the one that held the safe. The safe was a weird antique piece in and of itself: high as her waist, black as night, with a brass handle, but no combination plate or keyhole on the front—must have the locking mechanism around the side, a highly unusual feature. Old safes were once made from wood, but by 1827, tin plate and sheet iron were introduced to surround both the exterior and interior structures—but they still weren't fireproof. This one was. Though the seams were visible, clumsy, indicating more primitive methods of bonding the metals together, the safe appeared to be made entirely of cast iron—other than the metal hinges along the side—and it had nothing to identify it, not one single manufacturer's logo. One of a kind, custom made.

She assumed that weird, old safe was where Lehmann kept the most expensive pieces, though she'd only seen him go in there a few times, most recently to retrieve a little wooden jewelry box that didn't look particularly valuable, even if it was engraved. But the woman who received it had certainly glowed at the sight of the trinket. Chloe could have believed Lehmann was a softie at heart, taking special care of those items he knew had sentimental value, but the man glowered at everyone who walked in. Whatever. The guys here were just odd.

No wonder her predecessor, Helen, had left. Greg had told her Helen stopped showing up two weeks earlier, and the way he'd spoken, whispering to make her lean closer to him, to give him her undivided attention... The hairs on her arms had prickled, her muscles urging her to run. It was a little weird, maybe, that no one knew where Helen had gone. No two-week notice, no picking up her last check, just up and...vanished.

Like Victor. Like Leslie. But they hadn't really vanished. Victor had taken his suitcases—he'd packed Leslie's entire closet. It had been purposeful. Just like Helen's leaving.

At least Chloe didn't have big shoes to fill.

She emerged from the hallway as the bell jingled and a well-dressed black couple entered the shop, him in a navy suit, her in a yellow and white flowered sundress and a hat with a yellow flower. If it wasn't Wednesday, Chloe would have guessed they were coming from church, though around here it was still entirely possible. *Church leaves no time for them idle hands, girl.* Chloe nodded, and the woman returned her smile.

From behind the woman, Greg's eyes lit up like he thought Chloe was smiling at him, that strange, blissed-out gaze he had, as though he'd never seen an ounce of heartache. He looked every bit the part of an antique store employee: button-down shirt, blue pants, and this weird thing around his neck that was more like a knotted scarf than a tie. His eyes glowed violet in the dim lamplight Lehmann used to illuminate the shop. But looking the part sure didn't make Greg a more effective employee—or a more pleasant one. She frowned as he turned away from the couple and set to work rearranging already neat items in the window display. To think he was Lehmann's favorite. He even got to go into the safe. Lehmann never appeared to notice Greg's shortcomings, just sat at his perch behind the center counter, scowling at his spinning top like he hated it, but he didn't. She could feel his tension as he stared at it though, a shallow pain behind her breastbone—it felt like regret.

Chloe approached the other display case, the one along the side wall, where the woman was trailing one slender finger over the edge of the glass top. Her finger stopped, tapped. "Here it is."

"Early 1900s," Greg chirped from the window without even turning their way. "Victorian, French, eighteen karat gold, .55 karat center cut emerald, .75 karat mine cut diamond."

Know-it-all. If Greg wanted to help so badly, he could have walked his lazy butt over there and actually assisted the customer face-to-face instead of bleating like a goat across the store. Chloe forced a smile in his direction. "Thanks, Greg," she said, hoping it didn't sound sarcastic.

The woman raised her gaze to Chloe, her irises almost black in the dim lamplight. Her husband nodded but said nothing; the set of his mouth, its tight line, suggested he didn't really want that piece at all.

Chloe stepped past the wooden shelves that ran along the back wall and slid behind the case, following the woman's finger, and pulled the ring from the velvet pad. Emeralds glinted as she held it out across the counter.

"I'll take it."

That was easy. Chloe smiled as Lehmann glowered in the couple's direction. They paid him no attention; they probably knew each other already and were used to Lehmann's sour face. Most everyone who came in either called ahead or were repeat customers, or must have been, because Lehmann always had their credit card information on file—she had yet to take money in the shop.

Chloe cocked her head, glancing from Lehmann to the woman, who was now sighing with what sounded like pleasure as she slid the ring onto her finger. "Would you like a box until you can have it sized?" But Chloe knew the answer, felt the lusty, needful energy in the air like heat running over her rib cage—that ring was never coming off. "Never mind, I can tell you'll be wearing it out."

Chloe smiled and slipped the box back beneath the counter as Greg shook his head from his perch by the window. *He's just mad he can't understand people the way I can.* He probably thought she was as crazy as her grandfather had. Her first day there she'd grabbed a lamp for a customer, and it had sent electricity spiraling up her arm, something so dark and dirty she'd dropped it back on the display. Greg had looked at her like she was nuts.

The woman's gaze was still glued to the sparkling stone. The man stepped forward, scanning the case and then the tables, scratching at his barely-there five o'clock shadow with a thick sandpapery sound. Eyes narrowed. Looking for something.

Chloe turned to him. "Can I help you find—"

"Nothing for you," Lehmann snapped from the center counter.

The couple exchanged a glance, and the man frowned, tension rolling off them both in waves.

"I thought we'd both—"

"Are you sure there isn't—"

"I'm sure," Lehmann said. He nodded toward the front door and retreated to the hallway.

They must have something else on order. That was the other reason she was certain the customers had been in contact with Lehmann prior to visiting the shop—they, and everyone who came here, already had some idea of what they wanted. Chloe stepped from behind the counter. "If you've already got the charge information," she said to Lehmann's back, "we can just ship the item he's waiting for when it arrives." There was no guarantee this couple would ever return, no matter how special the piece. Even Chloe knew to finalize orders then and there—that was Sales 101.

Lehmann disappeared into the office and slammed the door behind him. By the time Chloe turned back to the couple, they were already halfway to the exit, the woman's skirt making a gentle *swish* against her thighs as she walked.

Shh. Shh.

Like someone warning her to hush.

THE REST of the day passed in a languishing haze of activity without the interruption of calls—apparently Lehmann used his personal cell for the shop phone—or a mad rush of people. Chloe organized, dusted, catalogued, and readjusted the security cameras Lehmann had her install her second day there. The first week, the security tapes had given them nothing of interest, just long hours of still and silent vases and bookcases and trinkets, even if there were moments of strange wavering static every day around midnight that ended just as abruptly. Probably glare from the neon lights on the surrounding stores, or perhaps the streetlights glittering through the front window, a daily effect of the power grid adjusting. Might be interference on the equipment itself, too, a glitch as one day shifted to the next, or even a conversion issue from the camera to the iPad Lehmann used to watch the videos—little malfunctions were probably par for the course with low to mid-grade surveillance equipment, and Lehmann refused to try another type of camera. Still, she wanted to do well so she continued to check diligently, making the most of what she had. He didn't understand. Failure wasn't an option.

Today's tape was no different from the others. She fast-forwarded through hours of footage of the silent shop and paused at the 12:00 a.m. mark when the screen suddenly went fuzzy. *Nothing to see here.* Then the shop was back again, just like before. No sign of the arsonists Lehmann had purchased the cameras to catch. Why anyone would light this place on fire she had no idea—some kind of a high school dare? But the bar down the street was more likely to spur arson attempts by any number of intoxicated morons.

Whoever the arsonists were, they'd succeeded in the past, three times if you went back far enough. And it was in her best interests to make sure it didn't happen again, at least until Victor came back for his camera. She might be able to find another apprenticeship, but this was the only place that had something Victor would return for.

Dammit, Victor. She was convinced she'd picked right this time, but she'd fucked up. Again. A vise closed around her heart, but eased when the hairs on her neck stood up, a leery ominous vibration against her spine. She whirled around to find Lehmann scowling at her and holding out a slip of paper.

"Appraisal. Shepherd plantation."

"Me?" She glanced over at Greg, whose eyes had narrowed at the paper. Greg was the one who went on these errands, not her—she'd never once been asked. Was Greg going, too?

Greg stepped forward. "I know where it is, I can—"

"Her." Lehmann shoved the slip into her palm. She nodded and pressed her lips together to stop herself from smirking at too-good-to-help-anyone Greg.

"But Chloe isn't ready yet, and—"

Lehmann cut Greg's protest short with a glare. "It's time."

Chloe's blood boiled anyway. Why would Greg think she couldn't do it? But she had to be honest with herself—Greg was right, not that it was her fault. She had just started, and though she knew tons about history in general, she'd need training to know what things were worth. Market value and historical value weren't always the same.

"She needs to get out there. She'll come back, get information and prices," Lehmann said, as if reading her mind.

Chloe drew herself up as tall as she could. "I can go now if you want." As soon as the words were out of her mouth, she regretted them—her enthusiasm hung in the air like the whine of an over-eager puppy. *Relax, Chloe.* Just because she needed something to fill that stupid hole in her heart didn't mean she had to act like an idiot.

"You'll go this afternoon. Car's out back, supplies in the trunk." The words were surely more harsh than Lehmann intended, but the fire in his eyes suggested they had come out with exactly the right level of vehemence.

Had she done something wrong, then? Maybe he knew this trip wouldn't have anything of value and he was punishing her by making her waste an afternoon in some old man's disaster of a bungalow. She hated that she had to use his car, too, but it was already full of everything she needed to transport fragile items: boxes, bubble wrap, cloth bags. Heat rose in her chest though she forced her voice to come out steady. "Okay."

The boss turned on his heel and stumped back to his office. Greg watched him go, eyes narrowed, but approached her when the office door slammed. "You get all the good gigs." Sarcastic. His frozen smile didn't falter, but his eyes tightened; Greg knew he was more qualified, that he was… better. He had an eidetic memory—he'd told her that three times already. Greg would know immediately what the items at the Shepherd house were, and what they were worth. He wouldn't even have to bring pictures back here for appraisal like she would. Hell, she'd still be using her history degree to teach slack-jawed high schoolers if Victor hadn't left his camera here in this shop.

Greg worried his bottom lip with his teeth. He stared after Lehmann.

Perhaps that was where Lehmann's anger had been directed—at Greg, not at her. And though she'd rather have punched Greg in the penis for trying to say she wasn't good enough, she reached out and squeezed his arm, ignoring the irritated vibration that tingled up through her fingertips and squeezed her heart, gently, like the ache of sorrow—she couldn't tell if that was coming from Greg or from herself.

"I'm sure he'll let you go next time," she said. But not if she could help it. It was nice to be valued, and despite his bluster Lehmann believed in her, the way Victor had.

"Maybe." Greg's voice was low.

She busied herself rearranging the items on the display case, filling the space where the emerald ring had been.

Greg's gaze bored into her forehead until she finally turned her back, Chloe still feeling the electricity of his eyes on her spine.

CHAPTER 4

CHLOE ANDERSON, PRESENT DAY

The driveway sliced through a rolling lawn, with twisted oaks on either side that reached for their partners' branches over Lehmann's car like long-lost lovers. But one tree in the side yard stood out above the rest: at least five hundred years old from its size, sparsely leaved, gnarled branches like massive fists straining against the earth, reminiscent of a lumbering orangutan. The grass beneath the tree was perfectly still, though any movements might merely have been hidden in the shadows—the waning midday sun had cast everything in front of the main house into dimness.

And what a house it was, the kind of place that made Chloe turn her awestruck gaze to the facade: mid-1800s construction, perfectly renovated, three stories of white walls and columns, and a dozen half-circle stairs stacked like the tiers on a wedding cake. The stairs led to a wraparound porch large enough that Chloe could have driven the boss's old Malibu onto it. The engine whined and she snapped her head back down, jerking the wheel when the car veered onto the grassy shoulder. She parked on the stones to the left of the stairs, leaving the trees longing for one another in her rearview.

Outside, the air was still, as though everything had

hushed just for her. Which was ridiculous. But Chloe peered back toward the trees, something tickling the back of her neck like pulses from a frayed electrical wire. Even the branches seemed to have stalled in their relentless reaching. And then the breeze picked up again, and every inch of the sloping lawn felt alive, the grass humming around her while the gentle clack of the branches overhead grated on her eardrums.

Just trees. Chloe sighed. She might believe that things existed beyond her understanding, maybe lots of things, but she sure didn't think those things, or her nerves, should control her. That was the problem—you couldn't tell intuition from stress. Or from complete and utter exhaustion. Chloe yawned, then slammed the car door so hard her wrist ached.

Still, as she climbed the front steps, the tingle on the back of her neck clawed more fiercely at her skin, though she could locate no cause for alarm here in the quiet of the old house, or in the *thunk* of the door beneath her knuckles. She knocked again, this time with the meaty part of her fist, and could hear—*feel*—the sound reverberating through the house and echoing down the drive and into the trees, which seemed to vibrate in response. Unless that was…not the wind at all. Not jittering branches, but a deliberate *whoosh*, almost like someone using a hairdryer. *Shh, shh, shh.*

What is that?

Movement in her peripheral vision made her whirl around—she didn't catch the face, just long tendrils of curly blond hair disappearing behind the ridged pillar that made up the front corner of the house. A woman? But no, shorter, maybe a teenager. "Hello?" Chloe walked over the wooden planks of the porch toward the pillar, seeing no chairs, no tables, nothing to indicate it was ever used—might as well put up a sign that said "Get The Hell Out." The desolation prickled between her shoulder blades, the uncomfortable solitude of a long abandoned battleground. But she wasn't alone—there was someone here, Chloe had seen them.

She turned the corner, calling, "Hello, I'm looking for..." The side porch was empty save for one skittering leaf. The girl must have run inside, but if she wasn't going to answer the door, why was she sneaking around? Actually, maybe she'd been told not to answer it. Victor used to tell Leslie not to answer the door if he wasn't home. *Victor.* Chloe shook her head to rid herself of the thought and strained her ears for footsteps or a door slamming, but only the rushing sound on the breeze remained—then a louder grinding noise: metal on metal. Where was *that* coming from? She headed for the far edge of the porch and scanned the backyard.

The plantation stretched out before her, the yard slanting up to a gentle hill before sloping back down. Outbuildings ran the length of the right side of the property. In the 1800s when the plantation was built, those buildings would have been used for cooking, and processing grain—or for slave lodgings. A chill crept over her, like her body was being frozen in ice, and she drew her gaze away. Places like this always skeeved her out, almost like the terrified energy of the house's once imprisoned workers remained there, waiting to be freed. But it wasn't a ghost she saw now; someone stood about two hundred feet from the back corner of the home, where a large brick structure hulked in the middle of the lawn on a dirt slab—a kiln. No way the girl had gotten down there that fast, though she might be in Chloe's blind spot just on the other side of the hilltop.

Chloe left the porch, glancing behind her once more, then walked down the center of the emerald lawn to the top of the hill and started down. No girl. Underfoot, the earth felt strange, spongey, softer than it should have been. Had it rained? The whispering grass tickled her ankles and caught the heels of her sandals like each blade was trying to hold her back.

She paused where grass met dirt. The noise had grown louder, and now it was less a grinding and more a roar, the sound of a hurricane picking up steam. The kiln was larger than she'd guessed when she was standing on the porch. The eight-foot structure appeared original to the house, right down to the hinges on the door—though having any door at all was unusual for the time period—and the entire thing radiated shimmering waves of heat into the air. God, it was huge. A small deer could easily climb inside, not that anything would purposefully leap in there to be burned to death; Chloe could feel the warmth from where she stood fifteen feet away, rolling over her skin like breath from a dragon. For someone to be using it now was impressive—while lots of people still made pottery, firing it in a primitive kiln was a lost art. It was lovely to see others appreciated its beauty, too.

The black man working mere feet from the front of the mouth-like opening seemed impervious to the heat. He wore khaki slacks and a white button-down shirt, open at the neck, his broad shoulders rippling as he kneaded a ball of pewter clay. He grabbed a tool like a rolling pin and pushed it back and forth over the blob on the long, cement table, then sprinkled what looked like broken pieces of stone or glass on the top.

She raised a hand to get his attention. The man straightened as if he noticed her, but before she could speak he opened the door to the kiln and everything around her suddenly went hotter as the oven yawned wide. He grabbed an already formed vase, set it on an enormous spatula, and eased the spatula inside. The kiln belched flame into the air, then settled, but Chloe winced in the blistering breeze as she stepped onto the dirt. The man let go of the handle and turned to face her, the fire reflecting flakes of green in his irises.

He appeared to be her age, or at least not more than twenty-five. Her heart shuddered, not because of the broad slope of his shoulders, or the shine on his umber skin, or even the rugged squareness of his jaw—it was the sheer force of his presence that rolled over her like a wave trying to pull her out to sea. Victor'd had it too, that hungry melancholy, a yearning that made you believe you were the most critical thing in his world. But that feeling lied.

The man smiled. She cleared her throat. "Good afternoon, I'm looking for Mr. Shepherd."

"That's me." He stepped back to the table and slapped down a second clay pancake, rolling the pin back and forth, back and forth. The air around them went still and heavy again, resting against Chloe's skin like a sticky wool blanket.

"I'm here from Lehmann's shop. Hope you don't mind me coming back here to find you. I saw your daughter...or... someone up there, and I—"

"It's just me here, no one else. But I thought you'd arrive earlier." He sounded amused, not irritated, but... Why did he think she'd have been here before now? She'd come right when Lehmann asked her to. And there *was* someone else up at the house. A neighbor maybe? If the teenager wasn't supposed to be there, that was a good reason to run. "Perhaps Mr. Lehmann misunderstood your availability. But don't worry." She grinned so wide it hurt her face. "I'll be taking care of your account, so we'll get it worked out—and you won't get a better deal anywhere." She had no reason to think that was true, but it seemed like something Lehmann would want her to say.

"I can't sell elsewhere, anyway. They don't want to come out here, you know." One corner of his mouth turned up, and her heart accelerated though she tried not to consider the reason for that.

"Why don't they want to come here?"

He shrugged. The silence stretched.

"So, um... Do you have some pieces to show me?" *Show me your piece? Nice one. I must be really desperate.*

He cocked an eyebrow, removed the oversized spatula from the kiln, and closed the fire-breathing door. "This way."

The air remained hot and thick—but *quiet*—as she followed Shepherd back across the lawn and up the porch steps toward the front of the house. Still no sign of the girl—she must have run home. Chloe averted her eyes from the lean lines of Shepherd's back as he pushed the front door open and gestured her inside.

The moment she stepped over the threshold, the breeze picked up again, rattling the branches until Shepherd closed the door and shut out the din. "Gorgeous," she muttered into the sultry air. Standing in the foyer was like stepping back in time.

Though the home did not boast the more elaborate moldings and plasterwork she had seen in other plantation homes, it more than made up for those shortcomings with luscious furnishings. To her right lay a sitting room with carved white columns, deep, rich area rugs, and an Empire Federal transition sofa, its wooden arms carved to resemble scales, with vibrant red upholstery and gilded legs that ended in bulbous heads—snakes, their engraved tongues lashing their own cheeks. To her left was a second sitting area, this one with a stone fireplace and shiny wooden tables with oval tops and spindly tripod legs. The mantel held a series of clay pots; some were gloriously beautiful, carved in intricate designs, but some were twisted and misshapen and crude. Had Shepherd made them all? Perhaps she was seeing the evolution of his technique. And it smelled like food here, some herbal scent permeating the foyer. Familiar, but she could not place it.

The wooden floor thunked dully under her heels as they made their way past the staircase and down a short, claustrophobic hallway to the formal dining room, where a long oval table sat surrounded by twelve ornately carved chairs. A vase of fresh lilies adorned the center of the table, along with three small artifacts: a lady's fan, a box just bigger than Chloe's hand, and a medallion the size of a silver dollar.

Sweat dripped down her spine. She hoped the dampness under her armpits wasn't showing. *He might like things original, but he could at least invest in central air.*

Shepherd gestured to the objects on the table with one finger—these must be the pieces he needed appraised.

"Any idea where they came from?" She approached

slowly, noting the pale scar across his knuckle: a jagged line, the edges puffy and thick. "Any little detail might help, if you got them from a relative or..."

"I inherited the place." He grinned. "Been in my family for generations."

Generations ago, a plantation like this would not have been owned by anyone with skin darker than vanilla yogurt. Shepherd must have sensed her confusion because he said: "Son of the plantation master...a few times removed."

"Ah." *Plantation master.* She swallowed hard. The rampant rape of plantation slaves meant that a large percentage of Americans, whether they knew it or not, had a mixed race background, though she avoided pondering that part too deeply—slavery was one of her least favorite topics of study for its brutality. The plantation must have been passed down at a later date, after land ownership for black people became legal, or maybe someone along the line had filed a suit for ownership if there were no other living relatives.

She turned her attention to the items on the table. The first was the fan, with delicate lace stretched between bands of wood and carved bone, probably from the early 1800s— she guessed Chinese export, but couldn't be certain. The small brass box beside it came from the same time period, with diamond shaped holes bored in the sides—Jali cut. Persian. The last piece was a brooch, hand-carved, the background nearly white despite its age, and bordered with intricately cut golden vines. Exquisite craftsmanship. In the center was a tiny painted image of a girl's face, probably twelve or thirteen years old, with huge blue eyes and long, curly hair the color of ripened wheat. Chloe brushed the brooch with her fingers but jerked her hand back. It was hot, too hot to have been warmed by the heat of the room. Had it been outside in the sun? *Strange.*

"This is probably from the mid to late 1800s," she said, forcing the quaver out of her voice. "Watercolor on ivory, with gold filigree—could be worth a good amount. But it might be more valuable with a backstory." Not that they couldn't get a good profit otherwise, but she would love to show up at the shop already knowing the details—before Greg could step in. "It just came with the house?"

"Found it in the attic."

Chloe reached for the fan, avoiding the edges of the brooch, bracing herself for the heat. Closer, closer... She bushed the fan's lace with her fingertips, then the engraved handle. The wood was cool. Chloe's eyes returned to the brooch again, to the girl's face. It was as if the child were looking right at her. Her hand slid away from the fan, back to the brooch, though she stopped short of touching it. "But you have no idea who it belonged to?"

"I not only inherited the house, I inherited its mysteries."

A mystery. Mysteries ate at you until you solved them—made you lose sleep imagining the worst-case scenarios until you questioned your own sanity. But solving those mysteries, uncovering the truth...that mattered.

She finally dragged her gaze to Shepherd, and his eyes twinkled like he was withholding the answer to a question she hadn't asked. The cool breeze came again, not from outside the house, or from the room, but from within her, like frost spreading outward from her abdomen. And yet this wasn't unpleasant—it cooled her discomfort, unsticking her shirt from her back, chilling her armpits, relaxing the muscles in her chest.

"We can go upstairs to the attic and poke around together," she said. "Maybe there's a clue, or something else you'd like to sell." Lehmann would be thrilled if she found more treasures, especially since this guy didn't seem to know what anything was worth.

"That won't be necessary."

Lehmann had sent her here to look at three objects? Of course, that did happen sometimes, but usually with larger pieces. She'd been hoping to spend her first appraisal excursion walking through entire rooms or the whole house, seeking out things of value.

Her hand tingled with prickly heat, and she looked down

—the brooch stared back from between her fingers, the piece vibrating in her palm. When had she picked it up?

Shepherd cocked his head, showing the lean line of his neck. "Let me know whether these items are of interest to your shop."

He was dismissing her. "I will." But her fingers curled protectively around the jewelry in her hand. "Perhaps I can take this one with me to do a little more research?" She didn't need to take it—a photo would do. But her hand clenched harder, and for a moment there was a distinct counterpressure from inside her fist—if she didn't know better, she'd have sworn the girl was trying to breathe through her fingers.

Shepherd narrowed his eyes, glanced at her hand, and nodded.

Chloe retrieved a cloth bag from the pocket of her skirt and tucked the brooch inside, then dropped the package gently back into her pocket. The bottom of her skirt fluttered, and her ankles were swathed in a sudden chill breeze, like someone running frigid fingers over her skin. It wasn't her imagination. There *was* a draft. She glanced in the direction of the breeze, where the banister on the staircase was visible through the doorway. *He has a/c upstairs and not down here?* "I'll return it to you by the end of the week," she said.

He appraised her, his expression placid, and there was something calming in the way his features showed no anger, no malice—like the peaceful smile on her mother's face as she tucked Chloe into bed in the days before the baby came.

The last days her mother was happy.

She cleared her throat. "As for the other two items, I believe our shop would be interested, but I'll have to verify the price with Mr. Lehmann."

"Very well."

Chloe took her phone from her pocket and snapped a photo of the fan and the box. "I can come back with the paperwork..." She paused when a gentle scraping sounded from the wall beyond the stairs.

He followed her gaze. "Mice. Never can get rid of them in these old places."

"Oh." She began to raise her hand to shake goodbye, but froze as a louder sound erupted above them, a grinding like a table being dragged across the floor. Definitely not a mouse. "What—"

"Nothing to worry about," he said, eyes on her. The noise stopped. "I have some workers upstairs."

Workers? There were no other cars in the driveway. She peered at the ceiling, waiting for the scraping to return, and when the air remained silent, she lowered her gaze to him. Shepherd's posture had changed, and the stiff set of his shoulders made the prickly hairs on her neck wake and dance again, more fervently. *Excitement or fear?* She'd always had the worst time telling, and that made it all the more jarring.

"I'll be in touch about the fan and the box, Mr. Shepherd." Hopefully if she came out a second time, he'd let her look around for more valuables. "And if I can find more information on your brooch, Mr. Lehmann may well be interested." Though saying "your brooch" sounded obscene—the girl felt like hers.

Chloe extended her arm this time, and when he shook her hand, his rough, calloused fingers seemed to pulse with the vehement energy of panic and something warmer, deeper, that seeped through her arm and up into her chest. She was convinced that if she stepped closer, he'd be able to sense the chasm Victor had left in her heart...and close it for her. She looked over her shoulder, toward the front yard, where the air was cooler and maybe more...breathable. "I'll show myself out." She pulled her arm back and headed for the hall without saying goodbye.

What the hell was that?

But she already knew. The energy that zipped through her now was the same as it had been the night she and Victor had outrun the police on his motorcycle, sirens fading into the distance, sweat rolling off their skin, both of them stinking of good marijuana. They'd stopped in an abandoned parking lot, and he'd fucked her against a cement post, and the skin tore from her shoulder as she came. Now, the tension—the fear—rushed through her like that same throbbing heat, lighting every nerve ending on fire. When she was nine, the school counselor had told her mom that she had a "sticky adrenaline switch." Excitement—sexual, or just plain happiness—got mixed up with panic in her head. Her first kiss had been pretty interesting; she'd started shaking and had thrown up on the guy's shirt when her heart went haywire. Stupid. And it was just as stupid that panic could feel absolutely euphoric. *Which one is this—nerves or excitement?*

The air outside felt cooler, lighter, more crisp than it had only half an hour ago. She inhaled it in great hungry gulps as she made her way over the driveway toward the car. The wind was still shouting at her, but less agitated now. And that breeze...the breeze from the upper floor. He probably did have air conditioning upstairs. Maybe that was why the workers were here.

Then why was she still so uneasy?

The skin on her neck tingled. She wasn't alone. Chloe whirled around, expecting to see Shepherd watching her, but the front door was closed. Her gaze slid over the house, above the front door overhang, up past the second story, to where a circular attic window loomed like an angry eye. Someone was there...watching. Someone who had surely been there when she'd knocked the first time. One of the workers?

A dark shape moved behind the glass, fast as the shadow of a bird, and disappeared.

CHAPTER 5

MARTHA ALTON SHEPHERD,
TWENTIETH APRIL, 1832

He's looking at me again.

I squint into the trees in front of the house, not a breath of air moving the grass. I do not see the boy, but I know he is there, hiding near the oaks along the drive, where the shadows make my spine shudder more than the rustling leaves. Underneath those trees is where the chill is strongest; it seems to seep from every corner of this plantation, great icy winds creeping from the earth to freeze my bones even in the sweltering summer. Hany, my nursemaid-turned-house-slave, and as close to a mother as I have ever known, told me the chill is restless spirits. Lord help me, I believe her.

Yet why does that same chill seep from my husband, too?

I try my best to push those thoughts aside. "Come here, boy," I call.

From behind the largest oak, the top of his little brown head appears, then a pair of eyes, so dark they look black in the shadow of the tree. He disappears again. He's been there for the better part of an hour, watching while I sweep up the porch.

His eyes reappear, and this time he steps one foot out from behind the tree, then the other, laboriously, as if he were an old man and not a child. He is so deep in the shadows, I cannot see the trouble. Then he jerks forward and catches himself against one of the gnarled branches that plunge into the earth instead of reaching toward the sky. Limping; I am sure of it.

He hobbles a few steps more to the dirt drive, and the sunlight catches his leg, the flesh mottled yellow and black and red. *A trick of the light?* But no, the skin from his knee to his ankle is gone, the meat underneath weeping pus and blood. The wound is not new. My heart accelerates, throbbing in my ears. He shall probably die within the week. I look for Hany, hoping she'll appear on the porch, her apron laden with vegetables for supper. Hany will know what to do. But the consequences for her treating the child shall be swift if he perishes—I cannot risk that she might take the blame even if this is above my bend.

I drop my broom and go to him, taking him by the elbow and leading him to the lawn in the shadow of the house. "Stay here."

He does not speak, does not nod, just stares at me blankly, eyes shining as if he would cry, had he any tears left.

I run up the stairs and into the house, closing the door softly behind me. My legs ache almost as much as my back—even my head smarts. Only a few months here, and I feel as if I have aged years. Being the wife of a plantation owner is not what I expected. From dawn until dusk I toil, doing the washing, tending ailments, managing the workers, grinding grain, making food. It is tending wounds that scares me most, for then I have life and death on my head. I should be used to this; my father is a doctor, unlike my husband, Elisha, who only fancies himself to be. I often watched Father at our plantation while he cleaned wounds, applied strips of cotton, and used the tools I cannot fathom touching myself: the sharp metal barbs for bloodletting, the long, cruel-looking blades for amputations. Too harsh, too frightening, no matter how often I saw them. Though Father did not approve, Hany showed me the herbal concoctions and salves that might heal just as well. I can almost hear her voice now: "There you go, child, but not too much, or you're like to poison someone." I never did tell Father about those secret lessons. No matter how kind they are to their workers, no master likes it when the people in his charge know how to kill him.

I take the stairs two at a time, but pause when a thick scraping sound from above rattles my eardrums. Then comes the squeal of a door—the attic. I take the last three stairs at once and fly left into the hall, ducking behind an enormous fern that Hany's placed opposite the row of windows. I do not want my husband to see me—there is something in the way his fists clench ever so slightly, the quiet flick of his tongue when he appraises me, that makes me tremble like a child though I'm well over sixteen, plenty old enough to be a wife. Even if he does not believe it yet.

From the back hall comes the thunk of one footstep. Then another.

I hold my breath. If Elisha sees the boy by the porch, he might take him for his own brand of cures, but the slaves do not seem much improved by my husband's treatments—they return with their backs hunched, their faces twisted in pain, and they jump at mundane noises. But they live. Maybe I *should* let Elisha take the boy. What if he dies on my watch when Elisha could have helped? But the thought of those cruel tools, shaving off the infected meat—perhaps death would be kinder. The boy is like to die anyway, and hurting him further… It is unkind to prolong his suffering.

Elisha appears from the narrow back hallway and pauses on the landing. His shock of white hair practically glows as he peers down the steps, squinting at the front door. He's wearing an apron, leather, stained black with dried blood, though the entire thing is so soaked and ruined I cannot tell if there are new stains hiding amidst the old. A chill slithers up my arms and wraps itself around my throat. I see him drumming his fingers on the railing, staring at the front door, but I hear nothing over the frantic pounding of my heart until he turns and walks back up that other hallway, back up the stairs. The lock on the attic door clicks.

I exhale. *Silly, silly child.* It makes no sense, my hiding. My husband has no reason to put me in harm's way; he has lost three wives before me, all in childbirth, and he cannot wish to bury another, which is probably why he refuses to touch me. I had thought he might yearn for special moments, like the ones the slaves whispered about at my father's estate, when they thought I couldn't hear. But when twilight falls, Elisha slips off to his own room or to the fields, even though I'm well old enough to give myself to him like a wife ought to. It affronts me. I am not a child, even if he seems to look at me as such.

I back the rest of the way down the hall toward my quarters, and find Hany's kit under my bed where I left it. This time I remove my shoes before padding back to the landing, then slink down the stairs to the porch. I close the front door softly behind me.

The boy is still there, staring up at the circular window above the eaves, his eyes narrowed as if he, too, heard the scraping from the attic room.

I set the bag on the porch steps. "Stay very still."

He does not move, or maybe he cannot—at the least, he cannot very well set down with his flesh peeled away, and moving his legs at all is surely agony.

I clean the wound as best I can, but the muscle meat is showing, swathes of red and brown and black, and the pus obscures any deeper gashes. On the back of his calf, one long strip of flesh sloughs off when I apply the salve. I bury my mouth in my elbow and gag. "Pray, what got to you, boy?"

He stares at the window, his entire body trembling. Maybe an animal bite, left to fester, but then surely he'd have perished already. Perhaps a burn from the kiln? What am I doing, tending this boy, when I cannot even tell what caused his suffering?

THE JILTED

I wrap the wound in strips of cotton, and still the boy does not take his eyes from the window. "Come back tomorrow so I can look again." If he's still alive, perhaps I shall have Elisha look too.

He finally drops his gaze then, but instead of looking at me, he merely hobbles down the porch steps and toward the trees where a shaded path leads to the slave quarters. I shall have to wait until tomorrow for news that the wound has festered further, or that the boy died at my hand. That the others are coming for me, to punish me. I know they despise me. Whenever I walk down to check on the workers or gather supplies, I feel their animosity, so clear it raises gooseflesh on my arms.

Perhaps they want to hurt me.

But that cannot be true—no one ever came for my father when his treatments failed.

I have always had this feverish mind.

I watch the boy until he disappears past the first row of oaks, and then I creep back inside the house, easing the door closed behind me even more softly than before. I tiptoe up the stairs, wincing at the subtle *creak* of the wood. Elisha is busy; he'll not have questions if I hide the bag now.

Creak.

A scream pierces the silence, and I startle, smashing my elbow against the railing, but I press my lips together so I do not whimper. The sound did not come from the landing, or even the second story. Elisha is in the attic, but the cry was not his.

The scream rings out a second time, shrill and full of such anguish that it stabs at my heart, and it is a man's scream, with a lower throaty quality beneath the high-pitched wail. He howls again—utter misery—and again. Panting, I continue slowly upward, toward my room, and this time I cannot hear the creaking of the stairs at all over the man's shrieking.

I am not to go up there. I will not go up there. Father used

to say curiosity ran through my veins like wildfire, but this...
I do not want to know.

I return the kit and hasten down the stairs again, the screaming following me until I close the door. I pick up the broom and carry on with my chores.

CHAPTER 6

CHLOE ANDERSON, PRESENT DAY

The prickling on Chloe's back had calmed by the time she arrived at the shop, but the thoughts lingered, irritating and persistent: Had there really been someone upstairs at the old Shepherd place? Where had the girl come from— and gone? Chloe thought she had seen someone in that round upstairs window, but maybe it was a trick of the light on the glass. She sighed. She was just stressed. Her entire world had changed over the last few weeks; the love of her life had vanished, she'd started a new job, and she hadn't been able to sleep more than two hours a night. It'd be crazier if she was totally fine. But she gripped the brooch tighter in its cloth wrapping as she walked through the front of the store, as if the ivory were her lifeline to someplace better, where Victor still loved her, where her heart didn't hurt quite so much.

Chloe settled in the office, scouring databases, looking through images for the girl on the brooch, but identification eluded her. Ivory was expensive, so the girl had to be from money, but she didn't seem to be part of the local folklore. Chloe didn't even know if the girl was local at all—she could have been from anywhere, even another country.

She frowned at the computer screen. Though she had a

general timeframe based on when the necklace was produced, she couldn't narrow it enough to help her determine who the girl was, or exactly when she'd lived. But she didn't feel like heading all the way down to the library to scour their few antique novels and old periodicals. No high-ceilinged rooms full of dust and leather and discoveries there, nothing like what you saw on television. "None of this helps, Chloe!" Victor had yelled once, eyes wild and furious. "What the fuck am I supposed to do with books on dragons and vampires when there are *real* demons here?" She'd tried to calm him, joking that if demons were as manipulative as he claimed they were, maybe they'd hidden the books themselves. Instead of laughing, he'd side-eyed the shelves, as if worried she was right. Thank God the doctor had given Victor medication to dull those voices, even if he still whispered crazy things into his pillow in the early morning hours. At least there, she could whisper back to him.

Chloe's throat tightened, and she glowered at the computer. Obsessing about him wouldn't help. Either he'd come back on his own or she'd find him, and by then she'd have a new job under her belt—maybe even a better life for them if she started doing antique appraisals and purchases independently.

She drew a finger to the brooch on the desktop and touched the girl's face, relishing the gentle burn that crept up toward her wrist, and the sensation of adoration, love—like the piece had been created during a time of easy peacefulness. Though she wasn't sold on the notion that ghosts or demons came back to harass the living, she agreed with Victor on one point: energy couldn't be destroyed—it didn't vanish. And Chloe, and other sensitive people, could sometimes feel the remnants of that energy, even if those who'd passed on couldn't interact with the real world. She pushed a handful of silver strands behind her ear and pulled the keyboard closer. The house had been there forever. Maybe researching the plantation would prove more fruitful.

So...a man named Elisha Shepherd had owned the plantation in the 1800s, during the time frame the brooch would likely have been crafted, but he had no children listed in the records, so the girl couldn't be his daughter. He'd had a whole slew of wives, but if it belonged to one of them, it'd have been from her childhood—none were young enough to match the girl on the brooch when they'd lived there. Although...marriage records after 1820 had been destroyed by a fire at the courthouse—ironically, the building where the antique store now sat. She drummed her fingers against the desktop. Maybe birth records were destroyed too. Greg had told her they had a stack of things here salvaged from the courthouse—files that had been spared from the fire thanks to the cast iron safe. He'd shared that tidbit of information one of her first days at the shop, whispered it like she should be impressed. Hopefully, she'd find something in those files that could help her, because if Greg and Lehmann didn't have them, the papers that might solve the mystery of the girl on the brooch had burned to ash years ago. She'd ask Greg later.

In the meantime, she'd dig deeper, look at Elisha Shepherd himself. But no matter what keywords she used, the information was just as sparse as what she'd found on the house and the girl—she couldn't even find a picture of him.

She did find a single image of a hanging that occurred on the plantation in 1836. An older black woman, and a slave boy who couldn't be older than four, dead, swinging by their necks from the oak tree that sat in front of the plantation, their tongues protruding between gaping lips, eyes bulging. Bile rose in her throat. Not a single spectator or slave master stood beneath the tree. Though she could find no specifics about what they had done, the caption told her the slave woman, Hany, had been hanged for witchcraft and the boy for possession—didn't all four year olds act possessed? Things like this reinforced her need for proof of the metaphysical, or at least plausibility—she believed in the supernatural, but to accept everything at face value, to decide that a child had been possessed, to hang him for it.... Chloe shuddered. No wonder that place felt evil.

The rest of the website was mostly old photographs, other plantation houses from the 1800s to 1900s, the farmland, the workers. A notation at the end clarified that they were found while clearing out a historic building on the other side of the state—a few hours out. Perhaps she'd try to contact the site owners tomorrow, see if they had any more information, though she doubted they could help her identify the girl on the brooch. If they had a photo of her, they'd have put it up already.

She clicked off. Sometimes ignorance was bliss.

But she did need to know more about the brooch if she wanted to keep this apprenticeship. If she didn't go to Lehmann with *something*, Greg would swoop in and rattle off a bunch of facts and make it look like she couldn't hack it.

Chloe wrapped and pocketed the brooch and stalked to the front room. Lehmann was behind the center case, as usual, the dreidel spinning on the glass next to his palm. He snatched it from the counter as she approached.

"Hey, Mr. Lehmann. Got a few interesting finds from Shepherd's."

Greg's footsteps approached behind her, and her back tensed at his nearness. His belly brushed against her elbow. *God, Greg, stalk much?*

She shrugged away and pulled out her phone, opening the photo app. But.... *Huh.* She turned the cell over to examine the lens—intact and clean. Yet the image was smeared, the edges glowing white as if the camera lens had been oiled. Was something wrong with her phone's camera? Or had she messed up? She should have checked the photos before she left. That stupid house with its weird noises and its broken thermostat and its creepy attic window had thrown her off balance—made her sloppy.

She ground her teeth. "I...I know what they are, but I can go back to the plantation tomorrow, get a better—"

Greg snatched the phone from her hand. Chloe backed

away from him as he said: "The fan is late 18th century, Chinese, made of bone, with silk banding and carved wooden and steel plating. Meticulously preserved. The box is Persian, brass, a Jali cut design—easy to find a home for it."

I knew that, why didn't I speak up? Chloe clenched her fists and stood on her tiptoes, squinting over Greg's forearm, careful not to touch his skin with her shirt. How could he possibly know what he was looking at? The image of the fan was blurred enough that she couldn't even make out the engravings.

Unless...had they already looked at the pieces? Did Lehmann already know what Shepherd had, and just wanted to make sure Chloe was up to the task? And... *Greg knows what they're worth.* She could see it in his stupid, smug face, just like she could tell that he wanted her to fail. The muscles in her back tightened, and she ground her teeth together so hard they squeaked.

Greg handed the phone back with a plastic smile.

She shoved it into her skirt pocket so hard she feared she might have torn the fabric. "He has another piece, too." Chloe retrieved the brooch more gently, laying it atop the cloth bag, and tilted her palm toward Lehmann. She did not extend her hand; she didn't want him to touch it, and she didn't even want Greg to look at it—though it was irrational, she almost believed he could sully it with his eyes. "American, mid-1800s, hand carved, ivory, painted with a girl's face," she told Lehmann, as steady as she could manage.

She waited for Greg to rattle off a bunch of random facts, but he only pursed his lips and drew his gaze away, toward the back wall.

Lehmann didn't seem to notice Greg's sudden silence. "Do we know who she is?"

"Shepherd didn't know, but I'll find out." And she would. She couldn't help but be curious about the necklace—it was a mystery, a little gift from the past seeking discovery, a riddle she could actually solve when the only thing she truly wanted was eluding her.

Lehmann nodded. "Greg, anything to add?" His tone was soft, almost teasing, though his eyes remained cold.

"Nope." Greg's lips were a tight, bloodless line.

He knows, he's just trying to make me look stupid and inept in front of Lehmann. Her skin crawled. "Are you sure, Greg? You look like you might be hiding something." She winked at him, to make him think she was *kinda* kidding, though she felt dirty doing it. Why couldn't he just help her? Again Greg shook his head, keeping his eyes on the back wall. *Fucking. Liar.*

She inhaled, a sharp hiss. "What about the files you saved from the old courthouse?"

"Nothing there." Greg crossed his arms, defensive.

Chloe pocketed the brooch, and the fabric at her thigh heated, or maybe it was just her rage trying to find a place to come out. "I'll look into it tomorrow myself, if you don't mind." She'd search out whatever courthouse files existed and dig into the rest of the historical record. There had to be information somewhere. *But what if there's not?*

"You'll head back to the Shepherd plantation tomorrow," Lehmann said. "See if you can find the information you need by then. As for the pieces he showed you, tell him we'll take them—I have his information on file already and he won't get a better price, not that he cares."

"Why wouldn't he—"

"He's just clearing the house. He'd give it away if it wasn't for us. And if he has questions, he can be in touch." He smirked, like she was an idiot, and her shoulders tightened.

Shouldn't she be told how this part of the process worked? How could she learn about the pricing, about market value, if Lehmann did it all behind closed doors?

"But, Mr. Lehmann—"

"Tomorrow. He can be in touch."

Greg's eyes were wide like he'd been startled by a loud noise the rest of them couldn't hear.

Lehmann grunted and disappeared toward the back rooms.

Maybe it was a test—Lehmann wanted to see how well his new apprentice could research, like being in school all over again. *Dammit.* School had never been kind. Or...maybe Lehmann just wanted to teach her in phases. That idea was more logical, and yet it didn't *feel* true.

She drew herself taller. "Sounds good," she called after Lehmann, attempting to keep her voice even, but the heat in her chest was constricting her airway. Her flesh prickled, as if she were being watched from some dark, unseen corner of the shop. Then she registered that Greg had sidled closer—too close. His arm brushed hers.

What's wrong with you, Greg?

He raised his eyebrows, and she realized she'd spoken aloud.

"Greg, it's just...I'm trying to do my job, and you're being really unkind. It's like you're trying to get me fired."

Greg's nostrils flared, and though he didn't meet her eyes, she could tell the set of his jaw had changed—he was furious. He stepped so close that she could smell something antiseptic on his collar—*Has he been drinking?*—but no, it was cleaner...like rubbing alcohol. "Chloe." He touched the small of her back, and she froze. His jaw had softened. "I just care about you."

Every cell in her body vibrated with the desire to get away from him, but she couldn't seem to make her legs work. "You have a weird way of showing it. You could maybe stop undercutting me and trying to make me look stupid."

He stepped back suddenly when the front door opened, then headed for the back room after Lehmann. She scowled at Greg's back, heart hammering. *So much for not being a jerk.*

The customer was a woman with wiry black hair streaked with the magenta of a pre-storm sunrise. She was plump, with freckled cheeks, but her eyes were surrounded by deep wrinkles—the kind a person gets if they've spent several decades scowling. Chloe forced a smile. The woman did not meet her gaze—her charcoal irises darted from one end of the shop to the other, her fingers twining together over and over as if trying to find the perfect place to rest.

"Can I help you?" Chloe asked.

"I was supposed to get something. From Helen." It seemed like a question, but the woman's voice held no inflection to indicate this. She stepped closer to the main counter.

"Helen is no longer with us, but I'd be happy to help you."

"She's…not here?"

"Are you a friend of Helen's?"

Now the woman's face transformed—her eyes went as fiery as her hair. "Not anymore."

Then why was she here? *Oh…* Was Helen supposed to be holding something for her? Chloe hadn't seen any outstanding orders, didn't even know where—

"I've got it." Greg's voice was low as he stepped beside her again, but Chloe jumped anyway. He leaned over Chloe's shoulder and pressed something into the woman's hand: a novelty button with a photograph of some boy band peering out from beneath the shiny plastic surface. *New Kids on the Block?* What the heck did that have to do with antiques?

The woman stared at the button for a moment, then brought it to her black sweater, an odd thing to be wearing—it had to be ninety degrees outside. But as the woman fastened the pin, her sleeve cuff slipped up her arm, drawing Chloe's gaze to her wrist: tiny lines, some faded purple, others angry red. Cuts. Old and new.

Greg's face was still near Chloe's shoulder, his breath hot. He inhaled deeply, then let out the smallest of sighs that might have been mistaken for pleasure in another circumstance. Was he smelling her hair? *Back up, asshole!* She shifted away, thankful her muscles were working again.

"Do we need to write her up?" Chloe asked him, trying to tamp down the tremor that was snaking up her arms. Was it Greg or this woman who was making her nervous? That's what she was feeling, right?

"Oh, I've paid and then some." The woman tapped the button once, then lowered her hand, her shirtsleeves falling to cover the slices in her wrist. "So," she said, finally meeting Chloe's gaze, "Helen's gone? Like…gone, gone?"

Chloe nodded slowly. "I guess. I mean, I just heard she no-showed and didn't come back."

"Good. That bitch deserves whatever she got." The woman smiled.

Beside her, Greg tensed—she couldn't even hear him breathing anymore, which was good, because he had the creepiest breathing of anyone on the planet.

The bell jingled, and the woman disappeared into the street.

Looks like someone spit in that lady's coffee. And…deserves what she got? What was there to "get" anyway? Helen had just quit; abruptly, perhaps, but Chloe hadn't been under the impression that something had actually happened to her.

Greg shifted closer to Chloe again, panting like a dog.

She turned her back and took a step away. Then another.

His footsteps approached behind her, following, and finally she turned to him. "Do you know her?"

Greg stood a few feet from her, his eyes on the floor. He shook his head. "No. But I always care too much." His face had lost that fabricated sheen of happiness, and his drawn mouth and furrowed brows deepened the wrinkles in his forehead—he looked ten years older. Chloe waited for him to say more, but he walked to the other end of the counter and stood with his back to her, hands resting on the glass, knuckles white, as the orange light of sunset stained the streets.

What a weirdo.

CHAPTER 7

CHLOE ANDERSON, PRESENT DAY

When Chloe emerged from the shop that evening, the celery was gone, but the rabbit was there, as always, sitting beneath the awning across the road, twitching his stained ear. She frowned. His little paws at his mouth suddenly reminded her of a plate Grandpa had once given her: white, shiny porcelain, with a vein of pale green ivy around the perimeter, and on one edge, a tiny painted rabbit with one ear raised. Why hadn't she registered that before?

"For you, Chloe, because you're quick as a bunny" he'd said. But he'd said it in jest, sarcastic, after she'd come in dead last at a high school track meet. After that Chloe had trained harder, pushed her lungs to bursting and her muscles to failing. And when she'd made the finals, her grandfather had just nodded and served her another meal on that stupid plate.

Someone moved in her peripheral vision: two doors down, an elderly black man leaned back against the building near the mouth of the alley across from the souvenir shop, rail thin like he hadn't eaten in a month. And he was staring at her, his salt-and-pepper beard bright against his dark skin, smoke curling from the pipe he clenched between his teeth. No, on second look, maybe he wasn't staring at anything in particular. His gaze was distant, unfocused, as if he were looking through the store rather than at it. Lost in thought? She turned away, her already irritable stomach clenching.

She couldn't go home, where the silence would eat at her until her belly ached worse than it did already—and she sure didn't want to feel the agitated energy from Victor's photos, the images practically leering at her, as anxiety producing as the pictures in his camera. The ones she'd erased. Chloe hooked a left and walked past a storefront filled with glittering beaded necklaces, hats, and other baubles the tourists liked, but she refused to look inside; the inauthentic dazzle made her head throb. She could tolerate some ostentatiousness as long as it reflected the life of the city. But as much as downtown Cicatrice wanted to be like New Orleans, it never would, not quite—the entire place was pretending to be something it wasn't.

Had Victor pretended too? Had their evenings, their love, been nothing more than a ruse? But no, she'd know that, sense it, she would have—she always knew when a man was screwing with her. Victor had been flawed, sick, but he was a shitty liar. And he'd needed her. He shouldn't have been able to leave.

"I feel it."

Chloe startled—*Who the hell?*—and, too late, saw the folding table on the sidewalk. She stumbled as she side-stepped it, catching her middle toe on the metal leg, gasping with pain and shock as she smashed her arm against the pole of a lamppost. The pulsing music from the bar across the way echoed the beat of her throbbing elbow. Chloe glared at the card table, then at the raven-haired woman sitting behind it, dressed all in purple, enormous silver rings on her fingers.

The woman didn't even bother to ask if she was hurt; she just glanced at the chair across from her with one eyebrow raised as if urging Chloe to sit, and then put her hands over the glass ball on the table. Her knobby fingers flexed and released—kind of like Chloe's grandfather's hands, now that she thought of it, the way he always cracked his knuckles before he brought the belt down. Her heart shuddered to life, galloping in her chest as if the psychic, too, were about to strike her.

"I feel it," the woman said again. Her eyes were unreadable, glazed over, her lipsticked mouth a black slash across the bottom quarter of her face. "That otherworldly breeze." She drew her fingers to her lips, and then her cheeks turned suddenly ashen, her eyes reflecting the blue and red from the neon bar sign across the street.

Chloe bit her lip. Should she ask about Victor? She took a step closer to the table. "I've been looking for my boyfriend and I—"

"Something dark follows," the woman said.

The Dark. The words jumped into Chloe's mind and took her breath, tightening her lungs. Her heart banged against her ribs. She drew back from the table, her shoulder blades tingling with familiarity—had this happened before?

Chloe forced a breath and squared her shoulders. This was silly. Just because she wanted to believe, just because she'd met a real psychic once, didn't mean that everyone knew what they were doing. She couldn't focus on the liars, "the darkness," the unsafe—life was never safe. If it were, kids wouldn't end up beaten bloody by those who were supposed to take care of them. If life were safe, the people you loved wouldn't abandon you. If life were safe, maybe Chloe wouldn't have been in a hurry to get her tubes tied. Safety wasn't reality—believing you were safe, that was the ultimate delusion.

Chloe hustled away from the table, leaving the woman with her hands still poised over the ball, calling something after her, but Chloe refused to slow her pace. Oldest trick in the book. What better way to get customers than to yell about evil following you around? Of course, then you would need to buy something to get rid of the supposed spirits. "And I have just the thing," the woman would have said. Chloe passed the police station, painted a gaudy royal blue, keeping her eyes on the street, but her lungs remained tight.

I either believe this crap or I don't. Which is it?

She did. She did. Energy stuck around, that was just physics. But she couldn't pay mind to a con artist peddling the occult on a street corner any more than she could believe that spirits just wandered among them, waiting to inject unsuspecting souls with evil. If that were true, Grandpa was right, and she really didn't want him to be right—then she might have to consider whether he was right about everything, and she would never believe she'd deserved what he'd done to her. She couldn't.

Chloe headed toward the bar on the corner, where the sounds of nightlife were already burgeoning behind the gentle rush of cooling breeze: the laughter of restaurant goers, the tapping of high heels on cobblestones, the occasional clop and whinny from the horse-drawn buggies that sometimes gave tours out this way. These taverns—Victor had found solace here on the nights she could not comfort him. It was a terrible way to deal with problems. She'd wanted to help him, she'd *tried*, worked hard every day to make their lives better, and still he ended up here.

Inside the pale brick building, she found wooden ceilings and a floor-to-ceiling fireplace, but despite the people milling around the street outside, there were no customers. The bartender behind the counter was bald, with an eagle tattooed over his left ear, the barbed wire designs around his forearm dancing as he wiped down the countertop. She recognized him from the last time Victor had taken off. He'd said he had no idea whether Victor had been there or not, but his beady eyes had said he knew more than he was willing to tell her—she'd *felt* it. The bartender was a liar. He was probably friends with Victor's ex. The bar suddenly felt hotter than the steaming air outside, practically blistering the skin on her cheeks. *Cheater.* No, Victor had been depressed. Confused. His stupid ex had filled his head with nonsense, tricked him, just like she'd tricked him into taking Leslie by faking illness, as if they couldn't see the neatly weeded gardens she was clearly tending outside her house—gardens more important than her own fucking daughter. This was all Stephanie's fault, not bothering to act like a parent, putting the entire burden on Victor, on Chloe.

Maybe he's banging Stephanie again right this minute.

The rage in her blood flared once more.

The past is the past, we only look forward, and nothing else matters.

I'll stop by again later this week, she thought, heading back out to the street. It was too early in the evening for Victor to show up here anyway, and he wouldn't leave Leslie in a new place while he ran off to have a drink—the tiniest bit of milk protein floating in the air and the girl would stop breathing. Some nights he'd lain in bed, his bare chest glistening in the moonlight as he stared at the ceiling, whispering to Chloe about his hopes for a cure that would make Leslie less fragile. But hoping was all he did, while Chloe took care of the bills and everything else, the same way she'd taken care of her mother, both before and after her sister died.

But Mom left too.

She shook her head. You didn't just walk away from someone because they were flawed—if you found the right person, you fixed things. The scars on her back lit up with a sharp flash of pain, then were still.

Chloe walked on, past the Cicatrice town limits and into New Orleans proper. A magician had staked his claim on the corner in front of one of the historic mansions-turned-condos in the French quarter, with balconies so intricately designed they looked like lace. On the opposite corner, music boomed from a portable CD player, and the performer—painted head to toe in silver, his torso shining against the waning light—stiffly moved one limb, then another, like a robot. She slowed her pace as she approached a group in the middle of the walk.

There was no kiosk for this tour, just a dozen people clustered together—giddy couples and a few teenagers—

where the schedule said they should be. The guide wore a straw hat, a black T-shirt, and a blue name tag: *Fletcher*. But no Victor. Her stomach sank. They used to go on at least one ghost tour a week, though she'd always paid more attention to the buildings, the elaborate balconies, the angular lines of the old Creole architecture—even the jagged glass that stuck from the tops of privacy walls like glittering knives was dazzling, as if the walls were begging you not to ruin them, asking you to stay away while simultaneously reminding you that beauty exists in the oddest of places. The last time Victor had left, he'd told her he'd spent every night on a tour like this, watching the crowd, looking for ghosts in the shadows. He'd snapped photographs of every dark corner too, though none as dark as what she'd deleted off his camera in the shop. *It wasn't what it looked like. It wasn't.* Victor was a little off, but he wasn't a psycho.

Chloe stalked to a spot behind an older gentleman in a checked shirt. The walk through the French quarter wasn't altogether unpleasant, though her clothes stuck to her and her sandals pinched harder after the first few blocks. Her injured toe stung. She focused on her feet and let that biting pain engulf the awful throbbing ache in her chest, but she looked up when a wave of needles passed over her skin. Something weird was in the air here—something angry.

"Anyone who knows the history of New Orleans knows Marie Laveau," the guide was saying; they were all stopped now in the middle of the walk, crumbling stone and brick mausoleums hulking around them. "The Voodoo Queen rests here, in the oldest burial ground in the city. Engage in your own voodoo ceremony here and you might just see her—some have even claimed to have been slapped by her spirit."

Ah, St. Louis Cemetery No. 1, that explained it—sometimes old graves made her feel uneasy, especially if the person had been a jerk. They continued on and the prickling on her skin dulled, then vanished. Chloe scanned the people who passed by them, hoping for a glimpse of Leslie or Victor, but every man, woman, and child on the walk was too tall, too old, too boring, too…not them.

Relax, Chloe. The rest of this tour will be miserable if your skin goes nuts every three minutes.

An hour later, even her toenails were sore, and each step seemed to deepen the fog that had grown thicker by the moment, the horizon now shimmering with warm, damp haze as twilight approached. Sweat dampened Chloe's hairline—her chest felt like it wanted to implode. She wiped the back of her neck as a mantra popped into her head unbidden: *great power, great power, great power*—her childhood psychic might as well have been whispering those words in her ear. Then ribbons of some voltaic energy coursed from the earth, into the pads of her feet, and up through her legs, shuddering, pulsing as it reached the base of her spine—

What the hell?

The energy faded just as abruptly. Chloe looked up to see where they'd stopped, trying to focus on something else, anything besides her trembling muscles.

The building was old, early 1800s, the bottom level done in gray brick with arched floor-to-ceiling windows. The third story looked to have been added on later—subtle differences in the style of the gray facade, a smoothness, a *newness* above the second story ridge that she could more feel than see. An elaborate ironwork balcony wrapped the second floor, and on the top level of the building, more arched windows sat waiting, the darkness beyond them thick enough to hide a person, or twenty, behind the glass. *Like the attic window at the Shepherd plantation.* The photo of the oak tree—with the slave woman's body, with the child's body, dangling from its boughs—flashed in her mind, and she shuddered.

"And here we have the infamous LaLaurie mansion," the guide said, lowering his voice theatrically so it was just loud enough for his group to hear him. "When Delphine LaLaurie and her husband moved here in 1832, they seemed the perfect addition to the neighborhood. The mansion boasted opulent furnishings, and the couple used the place to host lavish parties. Even after her husband died, Delphine continued on with these gatherings. But things were not as they seemed." His eyes gleamed as he lowered his voice still more and Chloe strained to hear him. "She was brutally cruel to the slaves who lived there; she kept her cook chained to the stove and dealt out savage beatings. But the real horror came the night a fire broke out and responders made a grisly discovery upstairs." He shook his head, drawing out the dramatics. "They found slaves, many dismembered, some strapped to makeshift operating tables, organs dumped into buckets. Some had holes drilled into their heads, sticks protruding from their open skulls—sticks that had been used to stir their brains. Most were dead, their parts strewn across the floor...but not all. Those still alive were screaming in agony, some of them practically cut in half, entrails hanging over their thighs."

Chloe wiped the sweat from her forehead. She recognized the place now. Victor had spent an entire day here taking photos, and he'd sworn he could see ghosts in the upper windows. To her it had all looked like glare, reflections from the street lamps, but they still had one of those pictures framed in the bedroom—she loved it because it was his, because he saw magic there, because it reminded her of a day they'd spent together. That had been the weekend before he'd lost his last job, when he'd tried to tell her that he was possessed by something that made him feel "not himself," and they'd fought, hard—she'd woken up bruised. But so had he. Sometimes the tough truth is that your problems are your own damn fault. She'd told him she was one step from possessing him herself so he'd get his shit together.

Maybe she really had driven him away.

The guide gestured once more to the LaLaurie house. "Many years later, they found a graveyard under the floorboards during renovations—piles of bones from her countless victims. We'll never know just how many lives Delphine LaLaurie claimed, but she remains one of the most infamous figures in New Orleans history. Some say you can still hear her victims today, stalking the halls, seeking the blood of their torturous mistress." He laughed, maniacally, wiggling his fingers in the air like a magician. *Victor* would have believed, even if their guide didn't. And heaven help her, she wanted to believe too, wanted to feel *some* reassuring presence here, something warm and comforting outside of this prickly, agitated energy. But there was only silence beyond the rustling of the group as they snapped photos, and when she moved out of their way, the squeak of her shoes was like the low, solitary wail of a lone wolf. Tonight the entire world, maybe God, had abandoned her along with Victor.

The guide's face was still lit up with theatrics, a painted-on horror that didn't reach his eyes.

Chloe snuck away as they turned to head back up Royal Street, the ache in her feet spreading up her legs. She fingered the brooch in her pocket. Why hadn't she left it at the shop? At least identifying this girl was something she could focus on—Victor was gone, he'd come home when he was ready, nothing else for her to do. Still, she peered into each bar she passed, every restaurant, every shop, and by the time she reached the park she was seething. What was she doing out here, really? If Victor wanted to crawl into his little self-despairing hole, who was she to stop him? But maybe it really was her fault. The night before he disappeared, she had yelled at him: "Sometimes you have to make hard decisions, Victor. Do you really think magical solutions will fall from the sky and make everything better?"

But he'd cried. And though she'd reached out to comfort him, he had not stopped.

Then he was gone.

Back in her tiny apartment, she tossed her sandals into the corner and slammed the door harder than was necessary, but dammit, something had to pay, and doors didn't fight back. The rattle reverberated through the house, too long, too loud—like thunder. *He's here.* And in that moment, the certainty of it wrapped around her shoulders like a shawl made of frost. It was quiet, far too quiet, and though Chloe saw nothing disturbed she felt his lingering presence like a feathery breath between her shoulder blades.

She ran to the bedroom, scanning for the suitcases, for Victor's shoes, but the floors were clear. The bed was messy but empty; Victor's pillow sat creased and tucked neatly into the corner like always. Her own pillow was bunched up beside the rumpled blanket. As she'd left it.

In Leslie's room she paused in the doorway, looking for any trace of the girl, but the purple canopy bed was empty too, the floor was empty, and the poop emoji pillow Leslie usually had propped against the back wall was still missing. The pink dresser hulked against the side wall with the blue marks that looked like flower stickers all over the surface, but Chloe knew they weren't stickers—if she approached she would see a hundred little line drawings done in Victor's hand. Her heart seized. She didn't bother looking in the closet; that would be empty, too. The room felt like someone had sucked all the air out of it.

Panting, she returned to the hallway, trying to inhale over the tightness in her chest, but the iron grip of fear—or maybe anticipation, she couldn't tell—held her fast. That cheap bottle of red wine still sat on the kitchen counter, her and Victor's favorite, but without him there it seemed heavier, thicker, and the liquid inside less purple and more black. She winced. *For us*. She'd woken to that bottle on the counter the day he disappeared. At first, she'd thought the printed words on the tag were a promise that he was going to build them a better life, get a better job, but now those words felt ominous and they hung in the air as if someone had actually spoken them aloud. The phrase was far too much like the card—*Just for you*—he'd brought home after staying a night with his ex during one of his sabbaticals. Chloe knew something had happened between Victor and Stephanie that night, even if he'd denied it. That's why Stephanie's house was the first place she'd looked when he vanished.

No one had answered the door, but she'd seen no signs

that Leslie or Victor were there, either outside or through any window she could reach. Not a single book on the floor, no clothes strewn around the living room, no bottles of Victor's pills on the bathroom sink. Just a mistake, cheating with Stephanie, just like her and Tim, a one-time mistake.

For us. The images from the camera leapt into her mind unbidden and stayed, though she tried to force them from her brain. Victor couldn't actually hurt Leslie—he'd had his moments with Chloe, sure, but after she'd defended herself he hadn't touched her again. Leslie was fine. He never even yelled at Leslie. And no one in their right mind would pack a child's clothes if something awful had happened to them, and he wouldn't take time to pack his own suitcase if he were rushing from a crime scene.

Crime scene? I'm being ridiculous.

Chloe glowered at the wine. She should throw it away, she should take it and—

A metallic crash rang through the air, and the wine bottle exploded, sending glass zinging against the white walls, the wine trickling down the backsplash like blood. *Bang! Bang!* Chloe reeled back, shielding her face, and caught her heel on the tile, and then she was off balance, falling. Her spine sang with pain as she landed on her butt on the kitchen floor. *Bang, bang, bang!* Was someone shooting? Victor didn't have a gun, did he?

She pressed her back against the wall, squeezing her eyes closed, waiting for something to strike her... The banging had stopped. *What the fuck?* Chloe strained her ears, listening for the *drip, drip* of wine from the countertop, the metal clank of someone reloading a pistol, the tiptoed footsteps of an assailant coming to finish her off, but she heard only the staccato bursts of her own breath. She opened her eyes slowly, squinting, afraid of blinking glass into her corneas.

The walls were clean. The bottle sat in its place on the counter, intact, unshattered. There was no broken glass, no spilled wine. And the room was silent. She hauled herself up, her legs shaking so badly that she faltered, and caught herself with the palm of her hand. The countertops gleamed. She couldn't catch her breath. Was she...hallucinating? She hadn't had visions this intense since the night she'd seen her mother, features clear as day, outside her childhood bedroom window, smiling at her, practically willing Chloe to invite her inside. But when Chloe had opened that window to the chill night air, she'd known it had been wishful thinking, an unfulfilled desire manifested as a waking dream.

This didn't feel the same. This felt...*real*.

Hallucinations would feel real, too.

After her mother left her with her grandfather, he'd said she was better off, that her mother had "plumb lost her mind." Maybe Hope's death had pushed her mother over the edge. Chloe could still remember peeking through the bars of the crib, her baby sister's eyes closed like she was sleeping —peaceful, if you ignored the bluish tint to her lips. She'd never heard her mother wail like that, never seen her so out of control, sobbing, muttering to herself. Maybe losing Victor was pushing Chloe into insanity too.

No. She was just exhausted—the stress of not knowing where he was and when he'd return was getting to her. She almost wished the stress was coming from within her, something internal that she could fix, but she *knew* Victor was the root of her problems in the same way she knew the sun would rise in the morning. She had to get it together, and without knowing what happened or where he'd gone, she felt incompetent to do it.

Chloe inhaled, slowly, then gagged on a faint, putrid stench, like week-old meat. The counters were clear of anything that might create such a horrid smell, but this was no hallucination; Chloe could guess where the funk was coming from. She hadn't taken the trash down to the dumpster since the night Victor left—she'd barely been home, and when she was...she'd kind of lost her appetite. Not a whole lot of trash to toss. Or maybe she'd been avoiding the things Victor would take care of, as if the moment she disposed of the garbage she was accepting that he was never coming back.

And she wasn't ready to accept that. He always said he'd never leave this city of his own free will, and he certainly couldn't just disappear. She'd pull herself together, make more posters, call around. She'd given up on the hospitals; they'd made it clear that they weren't allowed to give out patient names or information to anyone who didn't have a release—anyone who wasn't family. She could go there, wander the halls until she found him by sheer luck, but that was a long shot. Later this week, she'd call the other ghost tours. Never hurt to ask around in case he'd gone on another one recently.

She glanced once more at the bottle, dead center in the middle of the counter, lined up perfectly the way Victor always set it. She hated how it felt so damn significant, yet she couldn't bear to move it out of sight. *For us.* It felt like a note to someone besides her—some other woman. And though she tried to push the thought away, it stuck like bubblegum in her hair.

For us. The wine was Victor's. If she touched that bottle, if she moved it or disposed of it, he might not return.

It didn't make sense, but it felt true. She left the bottle alone.

CHAPTER 8

CHLOE ANDERSON, PRESENT DAY

The air around her was thick and damp, almost too heavy to breathe. Chloe wasn't immediately certain where she was, but she was standing...indoors somewhere? She blinked.

A girl—a teenager—with honeyed corkscrew curls sat in the middle of a vast wooden floor, her back to Chloe, her face turned toward the circular window at the far end of the room, perhaps staring out at the sky. Though the room was dim, cast into shadow by the silvered moon, the girl's figure was in stark contrast to her surroundings, as if she had absorbed the moonlight and glowed from within. The stillness of her posture was both complete and deliberate—a silent vigil.

Chloe wiped a hand over her sweaty brow and inhaled through her nostrils, trying to avoid the liquid stench that permeated the room—something metallic and putrid, the odor of long-rotten meat.

"Hello?"

The girl remained still, unmoving. She didn't even appear to be breathing. The only sound was a subtle hum, akin to the buzzing whine of katydids, but it was nothing so mundane as insects. She wondered if the girl could hear it. If the girl could hear at all. But Chloe knew the girl needed help—her shoulders were slouched in defeat as if she'd been hurt, the air vibrating with an old, repetitive, lonely pain. The scars on Chloe's back awoke and throbbed.

She walked toward the girl, her feet making no sound though she felt each impact—heels, toes, then heels again. The pads of her feet blistered with the heat that seemed to radiate through the wooden planks of the floor, and the fire seared through her calves and up into her thighs, flowing through her until her entire being burned with the raw agony of scorched flesh. Her heart shuddered painfully, and though she knew it was fear, panic, the heat throbbed lower, deep in her abdomen—an unrequited longing.

She gasped and lifted each foot in turn from the blistering floor. There was no evidence of injury, only the dusky white pads of her moonlit toes.

Chloe advanced toward the girl again, but this time she had no awareness of moving her legs at all, no sensation of heels hitting wood, no singeing fire—the floor glided gently by her bare feet, like standing on a moving walkway. The girl was getting closer, though, and her golden ringlets shone as if the moon itself had brushed lightning through her curls.

"Are you okay?" Chloe asked.

Now she could see the girl's hands—she was pinching at the floor as if trying to pick up a tiny object. But Chloe could see nothing but the darkened wood, and the girl was not staring up at the window as Chloe had originally thought—her face, most of it shrouded by hair, was aimed straight ahead, her eyes downcast, her brow furrowed at whatever she was watching on the floor.

Pinch, pinch, pinch against the wood. Though from behind, the darkness on the floor could be mistaken for shadow, here the wood was in sharper focus and it was obvious that the planks beneath the girl were darker than those around her; black and shiny—wet. The girl's hands were dark, too, covered in inky stains. But it wasn't ink, Chloe knew it wasn't ink.

Pinch, pinch, pinch.

Someone had hurt this girl—terribly. Chloe's scars sang again, sharper this time, and she gasped a breath from the horrid air. "Let me help you." Her voice echoed hollowly through the room. "I know you're scared, but—"

"Come to me," the girl hissed, and the words vibrated Chloe's eardrums along with that infernal buzzing, the sound *bad, evil*, and her blood raced through her veins, hot and violent, seeking escape. A dark, nasty energy emanated from the hunched form and pressed at Chloe, pushed against her skin as if trying to find a way into her marrow where it could rot her from the inside. "Come to me," the girl said again, pinching ever more determinedly at the floor, then clawing at it with her fingernails, and the grating sound was louder than it should have been—a harsh rasping that abraded the very fabric of Chloe's sanity.

"Come where?" Chloe's voice trembled despite her best efforts to steady it. *Where is the door?* But the dark was too thick to see it—the window was the only way out unless she blindly scrambled along the walls, looking for a door that might not even exist.

The girl shifted her weight, still hunched enough to hide her belly from view, but as she adjusted her legs, her yellow dress crept up over one knee, and from beneath the hem.... Chloe gagged. An organ she could not identify pulsed in the moonlight, shiny with gore. Chloe's heart beat painfully— fear, excitement, fear—and she took a step closer, her focus locked on the throbbing black thing on the wood planks, drawn as if being reeled in on an invisible fishing line. The girl's tattered dress, intact from behind, had been sliced across the front, from shoulder to sternum; every bit of flesh on the girl's chest was congealed black like someone had peeled her skin to the muscle beneath. Chloe tried to force her feet to back away, but they stuck to the floor as if frozen by black magic.

And then the wood vibrated with an energy so violent that the spell was broken, and Chloe took two steps back, away from the zinging pain, away from the evil girl, but there was nowhere else to go. She stumbled and lost her footing, crashed to the floor. But now she saw the source of the buzzing: Victor's camera, previously hidden behind the girl's knee, its shutter whirring. The buzz echoed through the dark room, increasing in decibel until it threatened to split her skull. She crushed her hands over her ears as the girl with the corkscrew curls finally turned her face toward Chloe, the moon illuminating pale cheeks, blue irises glaring from the whites like sapphire marbles in a porcelain dish. Eighteen, nineteen years old, but slight. Her forehead was disfigured along the ridge above her right eye, where a small hole glowered, smaller than a bullet wound—like someone had taken a drill to her skull. And while the left side of the girl's mouth boasted full crimson lips, on the right, the bones of her jaw glowed white in the moonlight, her teeth bared in a skeletal grin.

"Come to me," the girl whispered in a low growl that rattled around in Chloe's brain like her head was full of stones. "Come to me," she said again, louder this time, and it was not the voice of a child, or a teenage girl, or even a female at all—it was lower, thicker. Masculine. "Come to me, and the pain will vanish. Let me take the pain."

Chloe tried to breathe, but the air was too thick, too sharp, a rusty tang that clawed at her tongue and throat as if the air were made of broken glass. Her ears ached with the pressure from her fisted hands. She drew her gaze from the girl, and her heart stopped.

From the corner, a pair of glittering eyes looked down on her, and as she sat, frozen, a pale, white-haired man emerged from the shadows—stocky, his eyes hooded like her grandfather's—and the scars on Chloe's back lit up with pain, though she knew this man wasn't her grandfather. It only *felt* like him, that raw, sure, brutish energy. His hair gleamed in the moonlight, mesmerizing, a nest of fireflies. She forced her eyes away, down toward his leather apron, where strips of meat or something else she dared not consider hung from the lower hem like uncooked bacon. And yet, though her logical mind was urging her to force her eyes away, her belly did not twitch with disgust—her abdomen felt full, warm, heavy in the lustrous moonlight, the way she'd felt snuggled up with Victor on the nights he was actually happy, the nights he stroked her hair until she fell asleep.

He paused behind the girl and raised his hands, reaching —reaching for Chloe. His forearms were stained black with something wet and shiny. "Come to me."

Chloe's feet were anchored to the floor again. She wanted to listen. She wanted to go to this man, let him take her in his arms, envelop her in his warmth. But the girl was there, the girl would hurt her, the girl...

The man smiled, and the energy in the room crackled around Chloe like buckshot, and then she moved, skittering backward over the wood floor, away from the moonlight and the man, but each corner of the room felt alive with evil, unrealized nightmares in every shadow. The man lowered his arms and dropped one beefy palm to the girl's head, stroking her golden curls, gently, gently, as if trying to comfort her—he wanted to save her from something. Maybe he wanted to save them both from whatever terrors hid beyond her line of sight. But he didn't look like a hero. The man's eyes were hooded, sad, as if Chloe had betrayed him, and her heart ached with his disappointment—in his gaze she could see her grandfather, hear his sighs of resignation. *No wonder your mother left. Your father and Victor, too.*

The girl raised her eyes. Blood, glinting ebony in the moonlight, dripped from the wound in her head, down her cheek, and over the nonexistent lip to stain her teeth, and in that skeletal grimace, Chloe saw her own face, her own smile, and with that came a harsh certainty that bubbled up from the deepest recesses of her soul—a *knowing*.

The girl had done something awful. She needed Chloe's help. And the stinging energy in the air whispered that if she refused, the girl would peel Chloe's skin from her bones.

CHAPTER 9

ABRAM SHEPHERD, PRESENT DAY

Come to me.
I sit bolt upright, nearly smashing my skull against the beam over the bed, half-blinded by the familiar, malevolent horror that eats at my soul. I recognize that voice as one might sense their own body, like a twinge in the appendix, sharp and foreign, yet unmistakably your own until they rip it from your abdomen. I reach up and touch the beams of the slanted roofline, feeling the smooth surface of Justine's picture I have tacked to the wood, the one I stared at every night for a month before I decided to leave the seminary for good. Until the night I felt, like a breath of sweet breeze, that the Roman collar was worth less to me than a lifetime of her love.

She distracted me from the evil for a time. But it never stays gone.

I've always felt the wrongness around me, lurking, waiting. Others feel it too, but they rarely act. I will not be one of them. I pray Chloe will not be either. I do not want to watch her succumb like Helen did, racing over the front lawn of the plantation, with her crimson scarf flying behind her and then…her shattered backbone and her screams. Helen dreamed of that scarf, the one her mother gave her, and I felt the gentle softness where things began for her, then the torment and horror that evolved from those affections. Helen knew the scarf would be here. And she came when called, they all do—they all come to claim what's theirs, lured by what is most precious to them, afraid or not. But what is most precious to The Dark is their strength.

This Chloe...she is different from the others, different from Helen who only ran from the evil, different from the man last week who didn't even make it out to the yard, who gave up and was taken from my bed. Chloe can feel The Dark in her blood. Will she be the one to help me banish him for good?

"Another dream?"

I startle, but the doctor does not move from his chair near the circular front window. Moonlight pours in onto the wooden floor. His eyeglasses glint so that I cannot see the skepticism in his gaze, but I know it's there, as it was when I told him I shared Helen's dreams in the weeks before she was taken.

The dreams only come when the demons are close.

"Yes, another dream."

Elisha is not even hiding himself from her, nor is Martha. *That is why I need her.* This woman is stronger than Helen, than any of them, or she believes herself to be—and belief is all it takes. Belief is the stone we all crush ourselves against. I feel her energy like the teeth of a rabid beast in my breast.

The Dark feels her energy too—he's hunting now. He's hunting *her*. She is drawing him closer, like a lure, and when he emerges to take her I can finally exorcise him from this place. But she cannot know why she is drawn here or she will resist, and I will fail. Again.

The doctor smooths his already slick white hair behind one ear and the cover of his black overcoat crinkles, revealing a stain on his white shirtsleeve, a jaundiced yellow the color of bile, streaked with crimson. He worries the stain with one long fingernail. He once told me everyone needed one long fingernail, that it helped with pulling out splinters.

"You're obsessed, Mr. Shepherd," the doctor says.

Always the same words. I grab my pipe from beneath the pillow and hobble over to the window, my bones screaming at me to stop, to sit, but I do not heed their pleas even as I wince against the sharp agony in my legs. Out on the rolling lawn below, the mammoth oak shudders in the breeze, as if it too is in pain. Its leaves glisten, wet with the blood of the moon. My shirt smells musty—I've not changed it in days.

I can feel the doctor's eyes on my back. He clears his throat. "You really believe you can see into someone else's dreams?"

"I know I can." And I am worried. This woman—Chloe—she must sense that she's in danger, must feel what's coming, like a serpent slithering closer, closer in the grass. Her sensitivity will only grow as time passes, when she realizes her love is not coming back. The jilted listen better than others, for they are already seeking salvation from their heartache; yet this makes them vulnerable to madness, and to The Dark's promises. But she must thwart The Dark; it matters for many beyond her.

She might need convincing. And nothing convinces like terror. I wish love were as strong a glue as horror, but adoration, niceness, are quieter, and far easier to lose sight of.

The doctor snorts, and I can imagine his thin white mustache vibrating with the curl of his lip.

"I can feel her," I say to the window. "This isn't a delusion." But it could be—the insane rarely believe themselves to be so.

I retrieve my lighter from my pocket and squint into the far corners of the room where remnants of the past sulk in the shadows: abandoned furniture, a forgotten washtub, wood and metal and pieces of pottery that someone once loved. Their owners are long gone, vanished into the ether. But I know where the missing end up.

I turn my back to the window and stick the pipe in my mouth, watching the sage smog curl around my nostrils, obscuring the doctor's face. He emerges as if he's an illusionist appearing through a veil of smoke.

A shudder runs through my veins, so vibrant with panic that the breath leaves me for a moment. Elisha Shepherd, flesh of my flesh, is here, somewhere, his dark energy seeping through the wooden beams and through my skin, injecting my heart with cold. I cannot see him, for he is stronger than I, but I know he is here, the same way I know he comes to her in her dreams.

I feel him.

She senses him too, and I know she is capable of understanding what he is. But he is a master at hiding—he'll remind her of those things she fears most until he wishes to be seen, and then promise to remove her agony to draw her closer. Her only chance is to see him first, to tear the veil from her own eyes. Because whether she sees him or not, where she goes, he will follow. He will not rest until he takes her too.

CHAPTER 10

CHLOE ANDERSON, PRESENT DAY

The rhythmic clack of her sandals against the cobblestones competed with the hum of insects and trolley cars and the *thump, thump* of a man playing paint cans on the corner. The air smelled like moss and urine and something almost rusty. Where was the stink coming from? Not from the park—that place was as cheery as ever, paintings practically dancing with their neon greens, butter yellows, and hot pinks, though this morning their brightness seemed forced. The man in the ball cap paused, one hand on his painting, and lifted his head as if he, too, could smell the iron in the air. Then he leaned down to adjust the canvas against the wrought iron fence.

Chloe marched on. The brooch swung against the skin between her breasts. It hadn't seemed right to keep it in her pocket, and she'd felt an odd kinship with the girl since her dream—that girl had been hurt too, a victim, if only in Chloe's nightmares. Maybe Chloe was trying to convince herself she wasn't afraid of the girl, but she was, a silent, brooding kind of horror, the hushed inhale before a scream. It was irrational, but she *felt* it nonetheless. Just as she felt generally gross—sticky and *used* somehow, though that didn't make sense either. Surely stress this time.

Just ignore it, Chloe. But she couldn't.

In the dawn, she'd recognized the girl—woman?—in her dream as the one from the brooch, just a couple years older. And the rest of it...of course she'd be thinking of Victor and his camera, she'd thought of little else since the day he left. Maybe the dream was trying to tell her to block Victor out for good. But she had far too much invested, and her heart, God, her heart—she'd do anything to stop that incessant ache. She'd take Victor back, no matter what he'd done or where he'd been, let him draw her to him and whisper in her ear and bite her shoulder hard enough to draw blood, his passion spilling from his every pore as he took her, scaring her with his strength. And she wouldn't tell him to stop—she never did.

THE LITTLE RABBIT was waiting across from the antique shop, trustworthy as ever, twitching his black ear, the other bent practically to his nose. Had he sustained an injury, or had that ear always hung so low? Maybe everything felt just a little more broken today. She hadn't even remembered to bring a celery stalk, and the omission of that small kindness felt more significant than it should have—it sat like a stone in Chloe's gut as though she'd committed a grave sin.

Greg was already at the shop, dusting picture frames by the back wall. He did not turn when she entered but he stopped dusting, just for a heartbeat, before continuing to wipe each gilded corner. Lehmann glared at his little whirling top on the center case. He gestured to the iPad on the counter, accusingly, as if blaming it for some wrongdoing—or was he blaming *her* for something? She frowned. "Morning, Mr. Lehmann."

He grunted and pointed once more at the iPad, jabbing his fingertip at the screen. "Back to Shepherd's, today. It's time."

She had intended to research the brooch this morning. Not like there was some rush—the necklace was already a couple hundred years old, and Shepherd hadn't seemed to be in a hurry. "Oh, okay, I'm still looking into the girl—"

"Just go."

Her fists clenched. Why was he being such a dick? She was doing her best—she didn't deserve this. The spinning top faltered, and her gaze fixed on the toy, like all the energy in the room was being driven into the failing spin of the wood and metal as it juddered and then skidded sideways on the case. Lehmann's knuckles hit the counter, hard, as he swiped at the top and set it spinning once again. His knuckles, his knuckles—her hand suddenly ached too. *Great power.* In the back of her brain, intuition pinged, no, practically *screamed* at her as the spinning top edged closer to her over the counter. *Great power, great power, great power.* And then she could hear the psychic who'd first said those words, and Chloe was six years old again, watching the woman trace a withered finger over Chloe's palm. The psychic's eyes had glazed over, and her voice had changed, dropped suddenly, and she'd said something more...

"Great power. You have great power in you. But watch out for the dark, child, or it will be all you can see." And the woman had released Chloe's hand so suddenly that Chloe didn't have time to react before her knuckles hit the table, hard, and her mother dragged her away, dragged her...

That's why the psychic last night had felt so familiar.

Watch out for the dark, child, or it will be all you can see.

The toy top drew nearer the edge, nearer, and some vile force surrounded her, so thick she could taste the bitterness on her tongue—the top. It was coming from the top. *Don't focus on the dark, child.* But Chloe reached for the toy like her arm belonged to someone else.

Lehmann snatched the dreidel from the glass, glared at her once more, and stalked toward the back hallway.

What was that all about? Like she wasn't allowed to touch his stupid top?

The moment Lehmann's office door slammed shut, she walked over to Greg, heart hammering. He was running a cloth over an already pristine lamp, his thin fingers working—trying to be inconspicuous and failing.

"What's with Lehmann and that toy?" Her voice trembled with agitation but she coughed to cover it.

Greg dropped the rag and stepped toward her, too close—their shoes touched. "Wooden dreidel, inlaid silver, early 1900s. Turkish." His voice had the whispery quality of leaves skittering on a path.

"I know what it is. But playing with it all the time is a weird thing for a grown man to do."

"True." Greg's hands were already busy again, polishing unseen blemishes from the lamp's surface. He glanced at her, then back to his lamp. "Especially for him."

"What's that supposed to mean?"

"They called him The Enforcer." Greg met her eyes again and stopped dusting, lowering his voice so she had to strain to hear him. "He was always the last guy there, at every concentration camp, at every mass execution, making sure the orders were followed."

Concentration camps? "Wait...you're telling me that Lehmann was actually *in* World War II?"

Greg nodded, his eyes flicking to the counter and back again.

Riiight. So he was like a hundred years old? "That makes zero sense, Greg."

"I'm just telling you what I heard."

She nodded and forced a polite smile. *Looks like there's at least one thing Greg doesn't know.* But he didn't have to lie to make himself look more informed.

Now Victor...he would have understood and glared at Lehmann right along with her for being a jerk and a weirdo, instead of inventing impossible excuses. Victor would have listened to her complaints about her boss. If he hadn't left.

Her gaze came to rest on the front window display, the fan, the box and... Her mouth went dry. *The camera's gone.*

She scanned the front wall, the tables—no camera. Had Victor come early this morning? She been on time, a little ahead of opening even...

"Greg," she said, her voice shaking, "did that man come back for his camera?"

"Fujifilm X100F," Greg said. "High-end compact, resolution 24.3—"

"Did you sell it?"

Greg frowned at the spot in the front window and pursed his lips.

"The man who brought you the camera, Greg. The one you told me about with the leather jacket and"—she gestured wildly at her own face—"the ring in his nose. Was he here?"

"Nope."

Had Lehmann sold it? "Did you see anyone here with Lehmann?"

Greg's face was a mask—unsmiling, indifferent. "Lehmann has been back in his office. I've been manning the front all morning and—Hey!"

He called after her as she took off down the back hallway, but she could barely hear him. Victor's camera. She'd been certain he'd come back for it eventually, and now they didn't have it. *Please let Lehmann have brought it back here. Please let him be cleaning it or pricing it or something.* Maybe he was just photographing it or calling a potential buyer, and if that were the case, no one had picked it up yet—she could still rescue the camera and get it back to the window where Victor could see it.

But the office was empty—where had he gone? She stepped next door, to the room with the safe, and knocked. "Mr. Lehmann?"

No answer. She'd buy it if he had it here, even if she couldn't afford it—which she surely couldn't. She'd just tell Lehmann to take it out of her paycheck; she could still leave the camera in the window, lure Victor back inside, even if it wasn't for sale. She banged again on the door. "Mr. Lehmann!"

The room remained silent. If Lehmann wasn't in the open office and he wasn't in the safe room, where was he? There was no back door to this place—there had to be something in the fire code about having a back exit, but either Lehmann had never gotten dinged for it or he didn't give a shit. *Fuck!* He had to be in there—why was he ignoring her? Where was the camera? She stalked back to the front room, fists balled at her sides, but she paused when her gaze dropped to the iPad on the counter. Lehmann turned the cameras off during the day, but they had just opened—if Greg really had been here all morning, that meant Lehmann must have moved the camera last night. At the very least, she could see whether the camera had been there after Lehmann left, whether it had been stolen; if someone had broken in, that would explain Lehmann's earlier irritation.

Please don't let it be a break-in. I'll never get it back. Chloe tapped the screen to bring up the beginning of last night's recording, waiting for the black shadows to show along with the ticking timer in the bottom corner. But her heart leapt when the screen buzzed white, then solidified into a grainy black-and-white image—fuzzier than it had been at any point in the last two weeks. She squinted. *Strange.* No wonder Lehmann had been pissed when she'd come in—not that it was her fault his equipment was fucked up. But it was clear enough; there was Victor's camera, where she'd left it. Had Greg lied about selling it? Chloe ground her teeth and tapped the screen to send the image spinning forward. Nothing moved but the time, and no one appeared to spirit anything away, including the camera—there it sat, teasing her, from the front window.

But still...something wasn't right, more a feeling than anything she could see.

Chloe stopped fast-forwarding and hit play just as the screen lightened. A foggy dawn peeked through the front glass, but the glow inside... She shifted her gaze from the iPad to the corner of the shop, where the security camera was affixed to the ceiling. The attached light was free of obstruction, and the bulb wasn't burned out—Chloe had just installed it. She turned back to the screen. Now she could see the cool glow from the camera was not the only illumination in the shop; there was a subtle brightening in the room over the middle table, as if a spotlight had been trained on the vase in its center, though the smaller items surrounding the vase sat dim and dull on the tabletop. None of the lamps had been left on, or she would have gotten a very different glare on the screen—more intense. Even near the front entrance, where you'd expect the streetlights to illuminate the floor, shadows cast the wood into blackness. Her skin crawled.

Chloe paused the image and peered around the shop again, catching a raised eyebrow from Greg. She ignored him. How had everything in the center of the room been so clear, while the rest of the shop was steeped in shadow? She rubbed at the center of her chest beneath the brooch—the skin was itchy, warm.

Chloe turned back to the screen and tapped play again, squinting at the vase on the spindly little antique table: Moroccan, late 1800s, with a set of 19th century fire grenade bottles beside it. She knew those items; she'd handled them, set them on the display herself. And she knew none of them emitted light or even reflected the radiance when the lamps were switched on.

She was reaching to fast-forward past the images of the antiques when she heard it, faint but present, a gentle swoosh like a snake slithering through grass. And then, out of nowhere, a strip of dark material—*a scarf?*—appeared in the middle of the room and drifted lazily to the floor. Her gaze darted back to the shop around her, not that the scarf would be there now. Still, she scanned the tables, the displays, the dim cracks beneath the carved Louis XVI armoire. No scarf.

Chloe picked up the iPad and held it closer to her face, staring at the slash of dark gray—maybe red—against the wood floor, and turned the volume up as high as it would go. The slinky reptilian sound stopped, then started again, this time louder and more insistent. She could no longer deny its presence.

What is that?

The slithering noise morphed into crying, thin and high pitched—the sobs of a child—and then a choke, a cough. But there was no child on the screen. And then suddenly there was: Leslie. The view of the shop had vanished, replaced with Leslie's face, close up—lips gray, cheeks and brow mottled, eyes wide and staring. It was the image from Victor's camera, now in black and white. The one Chloe had deleted.

It's a fake, just pretend. Art. He would never hurt his daughter. But Chloe could feel Victor's hands around her throat—"You can't fix this!"—just because she'd tried to make everything better. He had it in him. He did.

The past is the past, the past is the past, the past is the past.

Slowly the image moved away from the camera, and fingers came into focus at the edge of the screen—two pale, bloody fingertips in one corner, as if someone were holding the photo to the camera and pulling it away. And as the picture dropped out of frame, the person behind the photo came into focus too, first a shock of white hair and then —*oh God.*

The stocky old man from her dream. White hair, stained leather apron, sad bulldog eyes. And behind him...

Victor. On his knees, arms hanging limply at his sides, his eyes wide with terror—and the scarf was now wrapped around his mouth. A low, gravelly voice vibrated against her eardrums: "I can help you. Come to me." Her nose touched the iPad screen and she jerked her face away, but her chest warmed with anticipation, the hole in her heart closing as if the hollow voice were massaging away her pain. "Come to me."

Then the image on the screen blinked and the man was gone, Victor was gone, and only the bottles and the vase remained in the center of the shop. The floor on the screen was clear too, like the mysterious scarf had never existed...

and the camera had disappeared from the window display. The pain in Chloe's chest bloomed in one searing flash of agony, then settled into a low, quiet throb. *Oh shit, oh shit, oh shit*

The man, the man from her dreams. She must have seen him before, in the past, watching her and Victor somewhere, stalking them, and now he'd taken Victor, taken his camera, and he'd found a way to pull the deleted images from the digital memory. But...blackmail? A ransom request? It didn't feel right, not at all, and yet...

She'd go to the police. It didn't matter if she had deleted the photos since they obviously still existed, and they'd be able to help her—this tape had a man on his knees with his mouth tied shut. And even if Victor *had* done something horrible—which he hadn't—jail was better than being at the mercy of some white-haired madman.

Chloe hit rewind, her hands shaking so violently that the iPad clattered against the counter. Again she heard the hissing, saw the scarf appear, heard the hiss change to a quiet crying. Then one blip of static, and the scarf disappeared into thin air, along with the camera. Her breath stopped entirely. No Victor. No photos. No white-haired man. She rewound the recording again, but the photo of Leslie did not return, nor did the man or Victor. *What the fuck?*

She rewound it again, and again, but the images stayed the same: just the scarf, there then gone. Nothing to indicate the recording had been tampered with—even the time stayed running, not a second missing. *What am I supposed to do now?* Without the recording, she had nothing to show the police. She didn't even have the camera anymore.

Chloe could believe she'd only dreamed of that man because she'd seen him somewhere on the street. But last night, she'd seen the camera in her dreams too—had she known it was missing before she'd arrived at work today? She might be intuitive but she wasn't clairvoyant. Was she?

Great powers.

Watch out for the dark, child, or it will be all you can see.

Maybe she had just imagined this video the way she'd imagined the bottle of wine exploding. Her heart throbbed wildly, her breath wheezing through clenched teeth, *please, God, don't let me be losing my mind*. No, something was happening, something real—the camera was still gone, the scarf was still gone, and scarves and cameras couldn't vanish into thin air. Was she crazy? *Where the fuck did that scarf come from?*

"What scarf?"

She jerked around to find Greg, less than three feet from her side, his expression...worried? Chloe peered back at the office and lowered her voice. "I...something is wrong with this recording." She snapped the iPad off, inhaling through her nose and swallowing the bile in her throat, but she could still hear the thin whimpering in her ears, that lonely child's cry—ominous like a threat. It made Chloe think of the girl in her dream, with half her face missing, blood dripping onto her skeleton teeth.

"What scarf?" Greg asked again.

"There was... I thought I saw a scarf on the recording." Would he have any idea what was going on? Greg was supposed to know everything, and for once she hoped he actually did. "It showed up and then disappeared."

Greg stepped nearer, so close his shirt tickled her arm and made her flesh squirm, but she let him peer over her shoulder and reach past her to tap play.

They watched together. Hissing, crying, static, vanishing scarf. No Victor, of course, but the rest of it was weird enough. At least Greg could see it. Whether the parts with Victor had been imagined—*hallucinated*—the fact that Greg could see the rest of the recording made her feel more... normal. Sane. Like she wasn't alone.

"Helen," Greg muttered, and his face was now inches from hers, a glimmer of recognition in his eyes.

Helen. Her predecessor. The one who'd stopped showing up for work suddenly and had at least one enemy in that black-eyed woman who'd said Helen "deserves whatever she got." But Chloe had seen Victor on that screen, too, implausible though it was. Her skin was writhing with something she couldn't quite put a finger on, a thorny irritation, some bit of information she'd missed—were Victor and Helen connected somehow?

She stepped away from Greg, slamming her hip into the corner of the case. "How can you be so sure that scarf is Helen's?"

"She wore a red one like it every day."

Chloe chewed her cheek. Had Helen been here last night? But what possible reason would she have for coming to the shop? Maybe she'd picked up her paycheck?

Picked up her check in the middle of the night?

"Do you think Helen...broke in?" Did she have Victor's camera? But Chloe'd seen Victor on that screen too, silenced with Helen's scarf, and his camera was gone, and that white-haired man was there with Victor, and—

Something is very, very wrong.

"We shouldn't talk about this." Greg clamped his lips together and averted his gaze.

Chloe dropped the iPad on top of the case. What the fuck was he talking about? "We shouldn't talk about what? This isn't right, this isn't normal, Greg. And now Victor's camera is missing and—"

"Victor?" Again Greg's eyes lit up with something like recognition, and Chloe steeled herself against the sinking sensation in her belly. She pushed herself off the counter and let him draw closer to her, his nose just inches away.

"You know exactly who he is, don't you?" she hissed.

"I've heard his name."

"From who?"

Greg hesitated, his eyes dropping back to the iPad.

"Greg? From who?" Realization dawned slowly, like a pot edging toward boiling, and she suddenly wanted to thrust her hand over his mouth. "Greg—"

"Helen," he breathed finally. "She went to a concert in the

park the night she…vanished. Said she was meeting a guitarist from some band she liked."

Vanished? So, Helen had disappeared the same night as Victor, after visiting the same place—that didn't feel like coincidence. Chloe's heart launched into her throat. Victor used to talk about the antique shop all the time, used to say he was coming up here to take photos—of course Victor and Helen could have been acquainted, even if he'd never mentioned her. The pressure in her throat intensified, as if she were on a leash, the collar tightening, drawing her toward the door, drawing her away from the shop. "Greg?"

He looked up from the iPad and met her gaze.

"Helen *vanished*, and nobody notified the authorities?" All this time, Greg had made it seem as though Helen simply quit. Why hadn't he been honest with her? What the hell was going on at this place?

"Why would I?" He shrugged. "She hated working here, and I think she came from money—I honestly thought she'd quit well before she did."

"I need to know where to find her."

"Chloe, we don't need to talk about this."

What kind of response is that? "Why the fuck are you being so damn cagey?"

Greg blinked as if surprised, his violet irises so dark they looked like plums, but his jaw remained tight. He looked down at his hands. "I always care too much, far too much. I loved Helen the way you love Victor." He shook his head, and when he looked up again, his eyes had lost their glassy sheen. Then he lunged at her.

She put her hands up just as Greg grabbed her shirt and dragged her to him. It was like kissing a snake, his tongue a slippery, probing icicle between her lips. She gagged, slammed her hands against either side of his chest and shoved, but he was strong, much stronger than he looked. He held her fast, touching her back teeth with the tip of his slimy tongue, ramming his mouth against hers so hard her whole face throbbed. He tasted like ash and something worse, something foul. He moaned, and she shifted her hips, drawing her leg back. Then she brought her knee up fast and smashed it into his crotch.

The moment he released her she flew backward against the counter, panting, ready to slam something, anything, into his stupid face, but the iPad was just out of reach.

"I care about you, Chloe."

"Fuck you, Greg." She wiped her mouth as if she could clean his taste from her lips and backed toward the door.

"No, wait, you need—"

"I don't need anything from anyone, especially not a spindly little asshole like you." But her chest was on fire, her breathing shallow. She needed to get the hell out of there.

"We all think we don't need anything, that we're enough as we are." His eyes went glassy again. "But everyone comes here for something."

His vacant stare unnerved her.

Greg blinked his violet eyes. "Even you."

CHAPTER 11

ABRAM SHEPHERD, PRESENT DAY

The rings on my fingers burn, the wedding bands—hers and mine—that still allow me to feel Justine's love, long after the dementia sucked away her memories of our wedding, of our childless golden years, and reduced her to a shell in an assisted living facility. Are these bands significant enough without her shared reverence? I wonder if there will be some other object for me at the end to bring me to that next place, an item I would not have expected. One that better encompasses the deeds that molded my soul into what it became.

People have always attached significance to things. To rings, to bricks, to cars, to jewelry, all mere toys to quell the weeping of their souls, but only for a moment. I know my wife does not live in these bands of metal, even if I feel her there, even if I am attached to that feeling. And it is comforting that for every negative emotion—the hateful energy wrapped around a bayonet, the panic of an abused child seeping into a beloved teddy bear—there is love, too. I can feel it in the hair combs Martha's nursemaid, Hany, carved for her when she was a child, the gentle pulsing of easy affection, though I know their love faltered long before they hanged Hany from the oak tree in front of the plantation.

I glance down at the camera in my hand and back to the building where I took it from—the old antique shop in downtown Cicatrice. The emotions shivering through my fingertips now are more vibrant even than the heat beneath my wedding rings. The owner of this camera…he is terrified. And he should be. Victor is alive, but he is not unscathed, and his horror might as well be my own—it sits like molten rock in my chest, writhing and burbling with the fervor of hellfire.

I hobble over the cobblestones, the cancer gnawing at my bones even as the artists, drummers, and T-shirt vendors blithely peddle their wares along either side of the street. My legs burn with pain, and my eyelids feel so heavy they implore me to just sit and let them droop shut. Rock and roll music pours from the bar, and even at this hour, tourists trickle from inside to finish their sandwiches and coffees on the street, laughing and pointing at the vendors, the performers, everyone acting like the person they think they're supposed to be. They don't know what's at stake.

Does Chloe?

Martha does. She's hunting the same demon I am. And if we fail, if The Dark is allowed to grow stronger, soon we will have no hope of forcing him from the plantation. And he'll be waiting for me when I die. It always seemed that one soul could not possibly carry so much weight, but evil breeds evil exponentially, in ways I never imagined as a young man. There is much I did not believe until I saw it with my own eyes.

Up the street, a woman with purple-black hair stares at me, her crystal ball in front of her, same as every day. She certainly knows something; but can I ever be sure how much she knows? How much anyone knows? The woman does not take her eyes off me until I've ducked under the awning of the next shop.

The camera's light is off, dead, but the shutter still works. *Flick, flick, flick.* An electric energy, tingling and insistent, courses through the plastic and into my shoulders, as if opening the shutter lets in fear along with light.

I peer through the lens, panning farther up the street where the restaurants are quiet, but I see nothing strange. Nothing at the other shops, either, with their brightly colored kitsch, so I bring the viewer back down the street, closer to me, looking for…

There she is. Through the lens, I see Martha standing in the doorway of the old antique shop, a trickle of red flowing over the tattered flesh of her chin. I pull away from the camera and glance up and down the street, but no one else is looking at her, not even the woman with the crystal ball; perhaps the purple-haired psychic is a fraud after all.

I flip the camera over, examining the sticker on the bottom—"Don't Be Negative"—then the words inked on the strap: "Induced Psychosis." Below that is a line drawing, hidden just under the manufacturer's tag, a tiny guitar penned in blue ink, the edges smudged.

My hackles rise, a primitive tingling at the base of my spine. The Dark is close. I put the shutter to my eye and pan back over to the shop. Martha is gone.

But she will not stay gone. I finger the orange and blue guitar sketch, and the vibration in my arm spreads through my body, shuddering, pulsing, aching.

Calling me.

CHAPTER 12

CHLOE ANDERSON, PRESENT DAY

One quick stop—in Lehmann's car it'll take ten minutes. Then I'll go to Shepherd's and do my job. This was insane, but how could she concentrate on antiques after Greg's bullshit lip-locking stunt? Worse still than his nasty tongue was what she'd seen on that iPad. Maybe the vision was just her sleep-deprived brain messing with her, but sleep deprivation didn't cause hallucinations of things you had no prior knowledge of, and she was positive she'd never seen that scarf before. The more she pondered it, the more Chloe felt like the images on the iPad were being *shown* to her by the man in the apron.

Wait. What the hell was she thinking? That man wasn't even *real*. But Helen was. And so was Victor. Maybe they were in Helen's apartment...together. She ground her teeth and drove on.

The apartment building was easy to find—newer construction, the energy there dull and flat and boring as a prairie—nestled between Chambliss and Shell, with "Helen Kowal" still on the buzzer. Chloe took three flights of stairs up and found the apartment around the corner. She rapped on the light pine door—*Will Victor answer?*—and listened to the echo. No other noises from within. No one around to ask about Helen either; the hallway was silent as a graveyard.

She knocked once more, and this time pressed her ear against the door, but she could hear only the steady thrum of her heart. *Dammit.* Did the woman still live here? *Maybe Greg stuck his tongue in Helen's mouth and the grossness chased her out of town.*

Chloe sighed. There was no way to tell whether the apartment was vacant without asking at the front office. She tried peering through the eyehole, then ran her fingers along the letterbox in the center of the door and knelt to peek inside—a beige foyer, nothing else visible from this angle.

Oh, what the hell. She straightened and turned the doorknob before she could change her mind, and *it gave*, and her heart throbbed, hard, but in that oddly excited way. Static tingled over her arms. *You're going too far, Chloe.* But she had to know.

Inside, the place was gray with dingy afternoon. Chloe kicked aside a stack of bills, advertisements, and other letters —mail from at least a week or two, probably more. Is this what happened when you disappeared and had no one to care? Greg had known Helen was gone, so had Lehmann, and neither had bothered to check for foul play. They just assumed she'd left her job, though Greg's cagey ass might have suspected more with his "vanished"—she'd have to pry further when she got back to the shop. At least the stack of bills made her heart slow; Victor wasn't here, screwing Helen, while Chloe searched for him. Not that the two of them couldn't be together elsewhere.

She closed the door softly behind her.

The foyer was standard taupe, the floors done in an oatmeal carpet that swallowed Chloe's footsteps as she made her way past a dining room and an open kitchen. To her right, a single love seat sat in front of an entertainment center, painted white and purposefully distressed—trying for antique, trying to have personality, and failing. No art on the living room walls, no pictures on the end tables, just a flatscreen TV, a pair of yellow throw pillows, and a blanket with the Mona Lisa's face on it. Huh. People didn't just wander away and leave all their stuff behind. Maybe she was prone to disappearances like...Victor. Maybe Helen was coming back.

Chloe crept down the hallway. Why was she tiptoeing? It wasn't like Helen was going to suddenly reappear after a two-week absence and catch her sneaking though the halls. But this place, like the Shepherd plantation, felt like it was watching her, as if the paint on the walls had a million lustful eyes and she was the object of their affection. Might have been residual heebie-jeebies from her encounter with Greg's slimy mouth, though.

The bedroom door was open, and inside, a basic metal bed frame held up a queen-sized mattress topped with a pale yellow duvet. No pictures on the end tables here either, no framed shots from trips taken with loved ones, no band names inked on camera straps, no bottles of wine left out for special occasions. So...what *was* she looking for? Signs that Helen had left on purpose? No...Chloe was looking for signs Helen had left *with Victor*.

Chloe opened the folding closet doors. The closet rod sagged under the weight of dress pants, gauzy tops, and long, straight skirts. On the floor, at least fifteen pairs of shoes lined the back wall, all neatly ordered on top of their original boxes. Greg was right, Helen definitely came from money. Gucci, Louis Vuitton, vibrant Jimmy Choos, all expensive brands Chloe couldn't afford, but who needed that nonsense anyway? It was ridiculous to spend hundreds of dollars on a pair of new heels—they couldn't speak to you the way a vintage hippie shirt could, wrapping you in the love and peace its owner had once felt.

She drew her gaze to the space in front of the lifeless shoes, where a single piece of luggage sat open, half a dozen shirts neatly folded inside. Looked like she had planned to take off. Helen wouldn't have left without her suitcase, though, but a girl with thousands of dollars' worth of heels might have another bag—this one wasn't even fully packed, not a single pair of pants or anything to cover her ass. Just shirts and...a single pink teddy bear, orange bloomers over its bottom, one eye missing, the ears worn and matted as if a child had made a habit of chewing on them.

Chloe scooped the animal from the suitcase. Helen had a child? But as she held the bear, the unease in her gut roiled and bubbled over like the anxiety in her stomach was trying to invade the rest of her body. The bear felt heavy in her hands, far heavier than it should, as if she could physically feel the toy's importance directly through the pads of her fingers.

Around the bear's neck, a tag read "Josie" in uneven little-kid print. Chloe traced the letters, trying to imagine the hand that had made them; pudgy little knuckles, fisting a crayon. She flipped it over—

She dropped the bear, and it landed on its face on the floor. The back of the teddy was soiled, the entirety of its back matted and crusty with a deep brown stain, and in Chloe's head, the photo of Leslie emerged, her blue lips, mottled skin—and *Victor*, Victor as he'd been on the iPad screen, scarf around his mouth like a gag, as if he were being punished. But... *Oh God*. There was no proof the scary photos of Leslie had *ever* existed any more than the stocky man in the video this morning. She remembered deleting the photos, at least she thought she did, but she could have imagined those pictures, too.

Her heart was trying to escape her chest, every thump painfully hot. There had to be some other explanation for the visions, for the photos, for Victor's disappearance. She wasn't going crazy. *I can't be.*

She backed from the closet and spun to the dresser, yanking out the first drawer and shoving aside pants and shorts, looking for anything, *anything*, that might help her—nothing but clothes. The second drawer contained shirts and a Tupperware container of costume jewelry. *Looks like Helen spent all her money on shoes.* Chloe slammed the drawer shut and moved on to the nightstands: a hairbrush, lip balm, a package of bobby pins. And in the second drawer down...a book. The cover was warm, too warm, as if the faux leather were the real skin of a live, breathing animal. A high school yearbook. She flipped it open, squinting at the tiny photos. *Helen Kowal, Helen Kowal...wait.*

She flipped back. There was another girl she recognized, a candid shot of the woman from the shop—the one with the brilliant magenta hair who'd come to pick up her *New Kids on the Block* button, the one who had clearly despised Helen: "She deserves whatever she got." She was a decade or so younger here, just a teenager lugging a saxophone case, a bit of extra weight on her, and huge coke-bottle glasses. Still, there was no mistaking that morose expression, that black hair, and her deep, charcoal eyes. The caption identified her as Joleen Young, but someone had crossed out her name and written "Skank."

Chloe's chest ached. That poor girl. Chloe could almost feel herself wandering down that hallway, judgmental eyes on her back, hearing the whispers—"Slut," "Whore"—then out of nowhere, *bam!* Fists and blood and screaming. When she was seventeen she'd come home from school after being tormented by the popular girls, and Grandpa had forced her to sit in the bathtub for three hours until he deemed her clean enough. *We'll fix you up, girl, clean your soul 'til it shines. When the Devil stops fighting you, that's when you have to worry.*

She flipped another page, then the next, and—there. The band page. Joleen sat in the back row with her saxophone, eyes on the ground. Helen Kowal was in the front, flute in hand, long, blond braid draped gracefully over one slender shoulder. Typical Barbie-looking popular kid, flanked by equally gorgeous brunettes, who were probably just as cruel to Joleen as Helen had been.

Chloe turned a few more pages but found nothing more of interest, just the usual salutations of a bunch of high schoolers getting ready to move on to the next grade. But in the very back was a faded newspaper article, worn around the edges. She sat on the bed and unfolded it. In several places the lines on the paper were blurred—water? Tears?

Car Wreck Claims Life of Cicatrice Elementary Schooler

A Cicatrice high school student might face charges after crashing her car with a classmate and the classmate's younger sister inside. Police tell *Cicatrice Today* that Helen Kowel was intoxicated when she crossed the median...

The tiny photo showed Helen with Joleen and a younger girl, eight maybe, with the same dark hair Joleen had. Was this Josie? Helen had killed Joleen's sister? And that stuffed animal... Helen had saved the toy from the wreck, then. Gross. But why be a jerk to Joleen after that, calling her a skank? Had she pushed Joleen away because she felt guilty?

But the why didn't matter; just that it had happened. Helen had shunned Joleen the second something better had come along in the form of fancy friends with their brilliant white teeth and shiny hair.

Maybe Victor had left when something better showed up too.

Chloe ran her finger over the newspaper clipping, rereading the article, narrowing her eyes at the little image of the crash itself—broken glass and mangled steel. Finally, she folded it up again and stuck it back inside the book.

Chloe had come here looking for Helen, searching for proof her disappearance was related to Victor's, but all she'd found was a record of Helen's sins and a dirty teddy bear. Yet Chloe still felt that unmistakable presence, as if Victor was hiding somewhere in this apartment, ready to leap from behind a doorway. She just needed to prove they'd known each other. And Helen had been in the park that night, the same place Victor had been... Fuck, if he'd left with Helen, if he'd left Chloe for this woman, if he was never coming back...

Her muscles sprang into action, spurred by her frantic

heart, and she only half heard the squeal of the hangers on their rod as she yanked dresses and blouses and jackets from the rack. She tore apart the suitcase too, slinging clothing to the floor behind her onto the bear, terrified that if she looked down she'd see that the toy was unstained, that it had been clean all along…that the matted blood had been just another hallucination from her overstressed brain.

A lump grew in her throat—she was choking. But she kept rummaging, her arms aching as she pushed aside clothing, makeup, and tossed things from the drawers. Sweat poured down her back, and though the pile of clothes on the floor grew, her muscles drove her on without her consent, flailing, grabbing, snatching. The drawers from the table in the hallway got heaved to the floor—nothing. But the crawling urgency at the base of her spine did not relent.

Panting, she attacked the kitchen drawers next, where silverware and knives glittered in their nesting spot, one inside the next the way Victor had always put silverware away. The world went fuzzy—the air was too thin. But something was here, she could feel it, driving her on.

On the end of the row was a junk drawer, already half open. The wood vibrated under her fingertips and she stilled. She pushed aside pens and movie tickets, slung a business card from a heating and cooling repairman to the tile floor. And stuffed into the left side of the drawer, beneath a pack of chewing gum: a flyer from a band called Gypsy Thieves, three flaming guitars across the middle. Her breath caught. "Induced Psychosis" was scrawled across the top in blue pen, with Victor's signature beneath. It hadn't been Victor's show, but he'd been there, helping another band set up in the park for some extra cash. Helen had gone there to see the band, too—and he'd signed her flyer.

The next morning they'd disappeared.

But they hadn't just vanished, no matter what Greg said—she was optimistic, but she wasn't stupid. Victor and Helen had made a plan then gone home and packed, both of them. They hadn't been kidnapped—they'd been together that night. They'd left together as soon as Chloe had fallen asleep.

Her legs trembled, and she grabbed onto the counter to hold herself upright. They'd been together while Chloe was at home taking care of Victor's daughter, then he'd come home, packed, and snuck off with the girl in the middle of the night. Her brain flashed to the image on the iPad screen of Helen's scarf, Victor wrapped up in it like he was wrapped up in Helen herself. She'd *known* he'd left her for another woman. That's what the vision had been trying to tell her. Same with the pictures on the camera—she'd hallucinated them too, maybe seeking excuses not to love him when her gut knew he'd abandoned her. Leslie was fine, off with Victor and Helen on some expensive vacation, celebrating, embracing the life that was supposed to be Chloe's.

That's what Greg was being so cagey about. He knew Helen and Victor were together—and he'd surely figured out why Chloe was so interested in that camera, why she'd asked so many questions. He knew Helen had...taken Victor. Taken him from Chloe.

Rage lit in her belly. Without Chloe, Victor would've been on the street a long time ago—he was sick, incapable of taking care of anything himself. But Helen had more resources at her disposal; it probably hadn't been difficult to convince him to leave, and Victor had always been easy to manipulate. One night, after he'd talked to Stephanie, he'd come away from the conversation convinced that Chloe was overbearing, too controlling. His ex-wife had molded him like Play-Doh in the span of a ten minute phone call. They'd fought about it for hours, worked it out, and of course, he'd finally admitted Chloe was right, that Stephanie was a jealous bitch. They'd been okay. Even though Victor was flawed, even though he sometimes heard voices that weren't there, even though Leslie was a challenge, Chloe had done all she could to help him, to save him. To save them.

And Helen had taken him from her anyway.

She staggered back to the bedroom, half expecting to see the two of them lying in bed together, Helen's head thrown back against the pillow, Victor's back glistening as he fucked her—the red scarf tied around his neck. Then she was wearing the leather apron from her visions, plunging a blade between Victor's shoulder blades, letting the blood soak her hands, and she felt that imagined blade in her own chest too, slicing her from clavicle to sternum, opening her aching heart, blinding her with pain. Victor had betrayed her. Left her, like everyone else before him. *You ain't right, Chloe, that's why your momma left you, why your daddy left you too...*

She hadn't been enough.

Why, God? Why are you doing this to me?

Chloe fell to her knees. The disheveled drawers around her, the clothes on the carpet, the knife in her hand—had she grabbed it from the kitchen? She released it, and it thunked dully against the sea of beige.

They'd gone away together.

She'd been left alone.

She shook her head, trying to erase the truth as you'd erase an Etch-a-Sketch, but the thoughts persisted.

Alone. Again.

The past is the past.

She leaned her face against Helen's bed and wept.

CHAPTER 13

CHLOE ANDERSON, PRESENT DAY

By the time Chloe trudged back out to Lehmann's car, she was more emotionally drained than she'd ever been. Everything in her wanted to go home and go to bed for a month, as if all the exhaustion of the last few weeks had suddenly cumulated as she'd stood in Helen's kitchen.

But she could do this. She could get through this. She'd succeed anyway, in spite of Victor and his new bitch girlfriend.

Quick as a bunny, Chloe...don't be a quitter...don't fail at something else. Her eyes burned. Why was she pretending she could just go to work and everything would miraculously be okay? Even if she was wrong about Helen, and she wasn't, even if Victor came home tomorrow, he *had* fucked his ex while he and Chloe were together, and he *had* left Chloe—did it matter why? *What the hell kind of idiot would take someone like that back?*

But she couldn't help it, couldn't even begin to make herself stop loving him. The compulsion to forgive him was like an itch that *had* to be scratched. She tried to force her hands to relax their white-knuckled grip on the steering wheel. When she was a kid, a therapist had told her mom that Chloe would always have trouble with attachments. So much for that—her mom was the one who'd had issues. Mom hadn't known a thing about what really mattered, couldn't possibly understand love, investment, sacrifice she'd abandoned her own daughter. She didn't understand the time it took to foster the kind of connection Chloe and Victor'd had—or that she thought they'd had.

It wasn't fair. None of this was fair. *I shouldn't have upset him.* She might as well have literally pushed him into someone else's arms. But all she'd wanted was for him to take their lives together seriously. All she'd wanted was a partner, someone who would put her first, the way she always did for him.

The unease grew as the car bumped over the old, cobbled streets. Chloe rubbed at her breastbone, but her chest still hurt. Maybe it would never stop hurting. She blinked—her eyelids felt like sandpaper. Maybe she'd never sleep again. Chloe stifled a sob as the oak trees at the Shepherd plantation closed over the car. She pulled to a spot to the left of the steps and killed the engine, breathing into her diaphragm, trying to quell the shaking in her hands. When the tremors persisted, she ground her teeth, slammed the car door, and stalked up the front steps, letting the beat of her footfalls slow the frantic drumming in her chest.

The door opened wide so suddenly that she leaped back and caught a heel on the top step. *Shit! This is how it ends for me, this—*

Shepherd lunged from the shadows inside the front door and grabbed her hand as she careened backward off the top stair. He yanked her back to him, and she crashed against his chest, painfully twisting her arm between them.

"You okay?"

"I...yeah, I'm fine." She jerked away from him, straightening her clothes, but her heart was going faster now than it had when she was climbing the stairs, and the nerve endings in her hand where his rough skin had pressed against hers were alight with heat, though his fingers were cold. It was that frosty chill that thrummed through her veins now, relieving her manic heart of its frenzied dance, like a sorcerer had reversed a spell.

"You're here about the brooch?" His lips were smiling amicably, but his jaw was tight...and broader than she remembered, stronger than the last time she was here.

Her chest burned where the necklace hung beneath her shirt—she'd almost forgotten she'd put it on. "I...I'm still looking into that." What would he think if he saw the brooch —his brooch—hanging around her neck? Her words sounded breathy, and she sucked in air over her clenched teeth to keep her voice from trembling. Why was she here again? *Oh yeah.* "I do have an update on the other items, though."

He watched her, patiently, kindly, squinting his green-flecked eyes as if he could sense she'd had a shitty day and understood her pain. *Looking* at her the way she'd always wished Victor could—Victor, that ungrateful, cheating asshole.

"Come on in."

Chloe followed him into the front room, glancing back as the door swung shut behind them, though she didn't recall kicking it closed. She adjusted her shirt to ensure the gauzy fabric still concealed the necklace and inhaled deeply, slowly.

"You seem out of sorts. Is everything okay?"

"I..." *No, nothing is okay.* "You wouldn't want to hear it. Boring work stuff." *And my boyfriend left me for another woman, and my life is shit, and I'm hallucinating.* But her heart wasn't going nearly as quickly as it should have been, and the pain in her chest had calmed to a dull ache. The stone of the fireplace practically called to her to sit beside it. *I could live in a place like this.* It'd be a lot better than going home to her apartment where Victor's photographs still lined the walls, where his energy shuddered from every frame, from every pillow. *Bastard.*

Chloe narrowed her eyes at the hearth. Strange, though, that this place calmed her at all; she'd only been here once before, and then there'd been weird noises, people watching her from the attic. Clammy skin crawling up her spine. She knew something was wrong here—she could feel it, or had felt it in the past. Had she imagined it then? Or was she ignoring it now?

If only she could ignore everything else. Loving Victor had been a terrible mistake, and emotions were nothing but trouble—she'd known that since she was a child, when the other kids on the playground had loved how easily she cried, loved to watch her shake, loved to see how long it took her to throw up so they could ridicule her. And at night, *We'll fix you up, girl,* and then the belt would sing through the air and split her flesh, the sting of it so much easier to bear than the emotional torture she endured on the playground.

Thoughts were flying though her head so quickly she couldn't latch on to any one of them. *The past is the past, the past is the past, the past is the past... Slut! Whore! You can't fix this!*

She was losing it.

Shepherd gestured to the table—to the bronze box and the fan. "What did your boss say?"

Her boss? The pressure in her chest abated. *The antiques.* "Lehmann will take them." She waited for him to ask about price, to prove Lehmann wrong, but when he just nodded, Chloe withdrew the cloth bag and wrapped the items. They were heavy in her hands, but she felt no odd vibrations, no malicious energy from those items, nothing strange at all—just like last time. She looked at Shepherd. He looked at her. *Awkward.* She opened her mouth to thank him for his business, but Shepherd turned on his heel and headed down the back hallway.

"Let's have some lemonade to celebrate." He smiled over his shoulder. Then he disappeared into the quiet dimness beyond the arch.

Lemonade? She hesitated. The sooner she could get this

task finished, the sooner she could get back to the shop. And then…well, going to her apartment right now wasn't an option, with the wine bottle, Victor's clothes, the bed they'd shared—her heart twisted so hard her breath caught, and she stared at the carved dining table to center herself. Had someone a little like her sat there once, tracing the wood, wondering where their life had gotten so fucked up? Surely. She wasn't alone in her angst—anything she was feeling, someone, somewhere, at some point in history, had been through it. And survived. Her heart slowed. She could distract herself with work later. And here, she was in the presence of a man who didn't stand too close, or try to stick his fucking tongue in her mouth without permission.

A few extra minutes wouldn't be the worst thing in the world. *The past is the past, we only look forward, and that's all that matters.* She started after Shepherd. "I can't stay long, but I guess a little lemonade wouldn't…" *Whoa.* Beyond the arch at the end of the back hallway lay the kitchen, but it wasn't a relic like the rest of the house. Or…it wouldn't be once it was completed. The woodstove and farmhouse sinks so common in 18th century plantation houses had been removed, the standard center tables replaced with an island of cabinetry topped with white soapstone. A pitcher already sat on the countertop, the ceramic thick and rust-colored, veined with the green of tarnished copper, with a molded cup of the same color and make beside it. The wall between the kitchen and what had probably been the servants' eating area had been demolished too, leaving one large, airy space, floored with a brilliant red oak that glowed orange in the afternoon light. There were no appliances yet except for an old battered fridge, and torn plaster still showed through the side walls, but the effect was breathtaking. "Nice kitchen." That was what he wanted her to say, what she was supposed to say, right? And it was nice—despite the new items within, the kitchen still *felt* old, thick with history and personality.

"Thank you." Shepherd ran a finger over the side of the pitcher, where beads of sweat rolled toward the counter, and stopped at an imperfection on the pitcher's lip. He frowned, as if disappointed in the craftsmanship.

"Wait..." She glanced out to the yard where the kiln burned bright, then back to the ceramic pitcher. "Did you make these?"

"Indeed." Shepherd grinned so wide it seemed to light the room more than the waning sun, and heat spread through her chest and into her belly, not the heat of lust so much as the anticipation of something forbidden—or maybe it was leftover adrenaline from Helen's place.

"They're really nice." Chloe peered through one of the two tall windows out into the backyard, where the emerald lawn sloped gently up away from the house, then down toward the kiln where smoke rose into the sky. If the kiln was burning today, Shepherd must have been working, but he had no sweat on his brow, nothing on his clothes to indicate he'd been stoking a fire. She peered at him again. He always seemed clean. Pure. And this kitchen...though dust motes played in the air, the room held none of the filth she'd expect of a construction zone. It was a work in progress, striving to be something better—maybe like they all were. Perhaps she could be happy, move on, be...better, too.

Oh for God's sake, Chloe. There's no fixing you.

Victor is gone. Everyone leaves.

She stopped breathing.

The past is the past.

She forced herself to inhale and let it out as Shepherd handed her the drink, and when their fingers touched, heat radiated into her hands, up her shoulders and into her abdomen where it pulsed like the deep throb of ocean waves; her intuition trying to tell her that he was safe, that he wouldn't harm her, and her heart slowed with it. She could almost hear her mother's voice in those gentle waves: *I love you, darling, everything will be okay.* But it hadn't been okay. Chloe leaned against the counter, the cloth bags with the antiques still clutched in her hand, pressing that fist against her opposite bicep so he wouldn't see it shaking.

When she looked at him again, his smile had gone fuzzy. No, his expression hadn't changed, but something was wrong with Chloe's eyes. Her vision wavered, the room undulating and then flickering like an old-school motion picture with the reels crossed, and when it stilled, the fireplace behind Shepherd was no longer clean and painted—it was dark, streaked with soot, with hooks for iron cooking pots jutting from the wall beside it. The counter had morphed into a long wooden table, and though the pitcher remained, Shepherd had vanished. She turned to seek him out, almost hitting her head on a wooden rack that was suspended from the ceiling; hanging plants—herbs?—tickled her nose. She reached up to brush the leaves away, and—

The kitchen was as before: modern, renovated, the fireplace clean and soot-free. And there was Shepherd, holding a cup of lemonade. But behind him, beside the brick fireplace, stood a girl with only half a face, the girl from the brooch, from Chloe's dream, watching her with a skeletal grimace.

"I try," he said.

"What?" The brooch on her chest burned, searing her flesh, but her limbs were frozen and she could not reach up to move it from her skin. What was wrong with her? Did she have cancer? Did she have tumors in her heart and in her brain, tumors that could cause hallucinations and this agonizing pain in her chest?

"Are you okay?"

But she could not speak. Could not move. Could not breathe. The girl from the brooch—*she's here, how is she here?*—with her chest a jigsaw of blood and bone and misshapen flesh, and in her hands, something square and black...

Victor's camera. The girl smiled with the still-intact half of her mouth, but her teeth were stained red. Shepherd could not see the girl, couldn't possibly from the way he just stood there so calmly with his head cocked, watching Chloe with concerned eyes.

Chloe could not find her breath to scream. Pain flashed across her chest as it did in her nightmares, and she staggered backward into the wall, feeling the horrid, gritty tearing of gristle beneath her ribs, though there was nothing that should be causing such agony. She clutched at her chest, gasping at the sharpness between her breasts, and when she touched the brooch, it singed her fingers, and her eardrums lit up with the sizzling sound of searing meat. She looked down in horror and ripped the brooch from her skin. Bits of flesh tore away with the necklace, leaving a shiny wound the size of a silver dollar—an enormous broken blister.

The girl came closer, and as she passed Shepherd, he jerked his head in her direction, but seemed not to notice anything suspicious from the way he turned back to Chloe. The girl was still holding the camera out in front of her, blood pooling around her bare feet. Shepherd stepped in it. *Why can't he see her?* No, him not seeing the girl wasn't the issue—*why can I?*

You're special, Chloe, you ain't right, girl. Chloe wheezed in a breath. *The past is the past, the past is—*

Now. This is now. And something was wrong with her *now*, something terrible. The girl, dear God, some organ, pink and pulsing like a still-beating heart, hung below the hem of her dress, stippled with congealing gore.

A draft licked Chloe's arms, chilly and wet, and set the hairs on her neck tingling.

The girl approached, slow, deliberate, holding the camera in front of her like an offering, but Chloe didn't want it, didn't want to look at it, didn't want to pretend this was real and not some figment of her broken brain, and still the camera called to her, drawing her attention—she could not pull her eyes away even as every inch of that camera screamed *evil, evil, evil.* Those pictures had been evil. Maybe Victor had been evil.

She really was fucked up. *Oh, God, please help me, please.*

"Chloe? Are you unwell?" Shepherd was mere feet from her, reaching his hand out too, offering assistance, but in the dim light his stance appeared too much like the stocky old white man from her dream, opening his arms to her, urging her closer, *Come to me, and the pain will vanish. Let me take the pain.*

Chloe lurched back, panting in the doorway. The girl was gone. "I...no, I'm sorry, I'm not feeling well. I have to go." She ran from the house, and around her the sun cast long shadows on the drive, turning the oak tree into a beast with long, scathing claws.

She wanted to tell herself she was being silly, that she hadn't really seen the girl, that it was just memories of her nightmare playing into the mix of light and shadow, but she could not believe that. Did she need medication, or was she seeing things, real things, that others couldn't? For she sensed, as sure as she felt the painful hammering of her heart, that these visions were more than hallucinations, or even illness—it was a certainty, burrowed deep within her...some specialness, some...*power* was awakening. *Great power.* Even the landscape felt like it was spying on her, the peeling bark of the nearest oak like the battle-torn face of a hulking demon, watchful eyes peering from the knots.

She stared at her shirt, at the small wet stain, where her burned chest wept. This wasn't a hallucination. Not intuition. This was...this was...

This is crazy. And she could almost hear Victor, his voice trembling: "Sometimes I just feel like I'm...possessed." And then: "Evil doesn't play nice, Chloe—demons possess you to take what they want."

But she wasn't possessed. Chloe didn't feel another presence inside her head...except when she was sleeping, when the nightmares tormented her, ominous and bloody and terrible. Yet she had seen that wine bottle explode during the day, seen those visions on the iPad—was this what possession felt like? No, she was still in charge here. She touched her chest again and winced at the sting. A hallucination couldn't hurt you, but...maybe a ghost could. And a ghost could probably make someone feel possessed even if they weren't. What she felt around her now wasn't just harmless energy, remnants from some long gone spirit—the depraved souls stuck around too, and they were angry. Was that what Victor had felt? What had driven him to run away? But he'd gone with stupid fucking Helen, like that bitch could protect him.

She pulled her eyes from the tree and back to the house, where Shepherd stood in the doorway, watching her approach her car. Did he seem…worried? Maybe, but normal, and healthy, and *real*, and yet in the back of Chloe's brain, something was trying to slither into her consciousness —Shepherd was dangerous. *The bloody organ, pulsing at the girl's knees.* This whole place was dangerous. *That skeletal smile, the raw meat where her breast should have been.* How could she have felt so calm, so at ease, inside that house? Goose bumps rose on her back, but the thought that Shepherd might be out to harm her fizzled into a warmth in her chest that slowly spread downward between her legs where it throbbed in time to her heart. *That Goddamn sticky switch.* She reached the car and rested a hand on the door. Breathed. Wheezed.

God, please help me, please help me.

Her lungs convulsed, her whole body quaking as if it had been taken over by the shuddering wind, every gust rattling her bones like it rattled the branches of the oaks. And when it drove that mutilated girl's face to the surface of her brain again, she didn't really care how this haunting had happened, or why—she needed to get away from it.

She wasn't a quitter, but she wasn't a fool. Chloe tossed the cloth-wrapped antiques on the passenger seat, slammed the Malibu into drive, and peeled out onto the street, heading away from Cicatrice. Sweat poured down her back as clear fluid wept from the wound on her chest. The Malibu felt different, the steering column shivering mildly, as if it had some engine issue she'd failed to notice while driving around the city. It didn't matter. If it broke down, she'd have it towed—towed any direction except that fucking plantation or her apartment or this godforsaken city. She could hire someone to drive it back to Lehmann for less than the price of a plane ticket. One of Victor's old band buddies—one lived in Ohio now, right? Yeah, someone would drive the car back here for her. And she'd start over. Victor was gone, *again*, screwing some other woman, *again*, and there was absolutely nothing in Cicatrice she ever wanted to see again. Darkness lived in this town. Somewhere else, in a new place, she'd find light.

The world whizzed by in a haze of twilight, every whine of the engine putting distance between her and the restless spirits, but a heaviness lurked in her chest, wrapping her heart in an agitated, viscous cold, as if the sludge from a winter storm had oozed across her soul and was now burgeoning into a blizzard. She'd passed the city limits, had to have, and still her heart was thrumming a frenzied beat against her rib cage, hot and electric, but the ice around the muscle would not allow her to breathe. *I can't do this. Jesus.*

She had to be losing it, and who wouldn't be?

The past is the past, we only look forward, drive faster.

Outside, the world was becoming hazy again—her eyes didn't want to focus. Every streetlight looked the same, and the road was a blur of black asphalt and double yellow lines. Where were the street signs? She should have crossed into Mississippi by now, right? Maybe even Alabama? She put her foot to the floor.

The engine purred, long and low, whining whenever she accelerated, vibrating so hard now that the steering column shook. She eased off just enough to stop the wheel from lurching around in her hands, but as the hours wore on, the fear that had catapulted her into action waned, replaced with a weary fatigue. Her eyelids grew heavy.

She should pull over, maybe find a hotel—did she even have her wallet? But all she needed was sleep and she didn't require a bed for that, not the way her eyes ached with the need to close. At the next stop—the sign too fuzzy to read—she eased the car off the freeway and into the rest area. She parked, but hesitated, peering into the night. What lurked out there beyond the trees? Restless spirits, hiding, waiting to torment her, make her suffer even more than she already had? But she didn't feel them. She didn't feel anything but the gentle heat of exhaustion.

She barely had time to turn the car off before the world went blessedly black.

CHAPTER 14

CHLOE ANDERSON, PRESENT DAY

"I love you, you know," he said into her ear, and every cell in her body melted into his voice, though his smell was wrong, saltier, muskier, the heavy scent of meat or perhaps just his sweat. She pressed her back against him, sighing. "I know. But really, you know I deserve better, right?" She did. He was a cheater. And it seemed her body was resisting too—instead of heat where their flesh touched, her back was awash with inexplicable chill, and the pressure of his fingertips against her shoulder was like being touched by a frosty glove. Yet, her heart did not mind; the peaceful calm of early morning steadied her, even when he ran his fingers along her thigh, leaving little trails of ice. But her hip felt…slippery. Wet. So did her shoulders.

"Come to me. Closer." It was a low rumble, a humming in her brain.

The icicles on her flesh spread over her thighs, down past her knees and into her toes, then upward over her hips like creeping frost, encasing her, but it washed through her chest too and stilled her frantic heart, as if every fear she'd ever had was suddenly suspended. His icy fingers snaked between her legs, and she shuddered, sighing as he spread her. She opened her legs wider.

"Nothing will ever hurt again." His breath was like an arctic wind on her neck. "I can take away the pain."

He would, she believed him. He would fix everything. A tingle in the back of her brain whispered that something wasn't quite right, but she pushed it down, ignoring the voice, relaxing into the thought-numbing cold. His fingers sank into her, and her body shook with pleasure, but even as she bucked against his fingers, the tingling in her brain intensified, begging her to pay attention to the fear, to the dread—to flee the blissful ignorance he offered, to ignore the easy path to freedom. That voice...

She rolled over, turning to him slowly, slowly, and a crackling like breaking ice filled her ears...It wasn't Victor. It was the stocky man with white hair, his hooded eyes staring into hers, the leather strap from his bloody apron slung over his shoulder...that was the wetness she'd felt—there was blood all over her back. She gagged and shivered, but she didn't stop him—*God help me*—and a part of her relished it, for that slippery wetness between her legs was the only piece of her that felt warm.

He drew his fingers from inside her and touched her bare breast, teasing her nipple, leaving a red smear over her skin.

His eyes changed then and the ice on her flesh melted, evaporated in the liquid heat of his gaze. Fire raced through her and she cried out, scrambling backward off the bed, but the ghost had her arm, his fist like a vise around her wrist, and the man's lips were moving but it was Victor's voice yelling, "You can't fix this!" and then a female voice: "You just couldn't hold on to him, could you?" And then it was her mother, screaming from this man's lips, "Why, God, why?" Chloe kicked and spit and gnashed her teeth, tried to wrench her wrist away from him, but the man's lips peeled back, and now he spoke in his own voice—"Come to me"—and he licked his lips with one tiny flick of his black tongue.

Chloe came to on the floor, carpet fisted in her hands, a tangle of sheets wrapped around her throat like a noose. *Oh God.* A dream, a dream. She ripped off the sheet and scrambled to sitting, tasting iron, and when she looked down she realized the carpet was splattered with blood, her chin sticky with it. Had she bitten her tongue? Wait.... *No.*

She looked around, at the ceiling, at the sunlight filtering through the tear in the blackout curtain—her apartment. But...she couldn't be here. She'd fallen asleep at a rest stop last night.

Her heart roared in her chest, so loudly her head pulsed with its throbbing. Yesterday, she'd seen that vision in Shepherd's house, the girl with half a face, reaching out with Victor's camera, and she'd gotten in the car... Had she dreamed all of it? *Crazy, I'm crazy.*

She scanned the room, searching, searching—there, on the nightstand, lay the cloth bag that Lehmann always put his clients' antiques in, to keep them safe, protected. She crawled to the end table and snatched it up. The items were still there, the fan and box, individually wrapped, just as she'd left them, proof that she *had* been to Shepherd's the day before; she'd gotten the antiques. She wasn't nuts.

Then why is this happening? Had the ghost carried her back here? She touched the center of her chest, feeling the cool ivory of the brooch first and then the injured skin beneath...but...

She peered down, her silvery hair shimmering against her shoulders. Her flesh was smooth, untouched, and her breath shuddered from her lungs, chest visibly trembling with the shock. Her skin had been burned, it *had* been, she'd seen it, she remembered it happening. And Chloe could still feel the driver's seat against the back of her legs, the tightness in her muscles as she'd floored the gas pedal down that dark highway. But what if everything she remembered was wrong?

The past is the past.

Except that it wasn't. In the past, she'd tried to escape, driven hundreds of miles from here, looking for a place where visions didn't slam into her like Mac trucks, where wine bottles didn't explode of their own free will, where she could finally sleep again. A place where ghosts weren't real.

She hadn't gone to sleep here last night—she'd been brought back here. Someone had brought her back. Or... some*thing*. She was trapped.

What am I going to do?

She swallowed hard, tasting metal. In her chest, the sharp ache started up again, the hole Victor left there throbbing as she made her way down the hall on jelly legs. *I'm not crazy.* The antiques were here, in their cloth bags, on the nightstand. *I'm not crazy. I'm not.*

Chloe laid the brooch on the sink and turned on the bathwater, fingering the smooth skin on her chest, shivering despite the steam. A cold sweat dripped down her back. She hadn't imagined the blistering pain from the brooch, she knew she hadn't, so had she...healed herself from the burn? As a child, she'd sometimes fantasized that her belt lashes healed sooner than others', that she had special healing powers, but she had written off that thought as an adult; no way to prove it. But she'd never had a broken bone or any other major injury, unlike most people, despite her share of scuffles.

Chloe's legs trembled beneath her—she kept her hand on the wall in case her knees decided to give out. *The past is the past...* She shut down the mantra. Sometimes panic was prudent. Sometimes panic was precisely what you should do, no matter what Grandpa had drilled into her. And she could no longer deny that she was being targeted by some being, some force greater than herself. If there was ever a time to be afraid, it was now.

The bathwater seemed to sizzle against her skin, but she forced herself into it.

I see things other people can't. I know things other people don't.

Unlike the voices Victor had heard in his head, the voices they'd medicated him for, Chloe's visions weren't *unreal*—they weren't the kinds of things a doctor could help with. She had...great power. *One of the special ones.* But tears stung her eyes.

Why me, God? Why give this power to her, this ability to

see what others couldn't, if she didn't know what to do with it?

Come to me. The words rang through her brain, almost as if in answer, so low and foreign that she had to turn to make sure someone behind her hadn't uttered them. Someone wanted her here—they were flat-out demanding it with those words. And they would keep her here, until she...what? What did they want her for? And who was it that needed her? The girl from Shepherd's house, dripping gore onto the wood, trying to give her...the camera? Or was it the white-haired man in her dreams, with his bloody fingers and stained leather apron? The man who'd promised her a release from pain, the man she'd let put his fingers between her legs. What had she been thinking? Maybe both of them were after her—but whether for good or evil remained to be seen. Either way, there was a reason, there had to be a reason.

Great power. Great power. Great power.

CHAPTER 15

ABRAM SHEPHERD, PRESENT DAY

The doctor's face is placid, almost indifferent, but I know he cares. I can see it in the twitch of his mouth as he examines the bony protrusions of my elbows, then traces my gnarled fingers spread on the kitchen counter. There is nothing to be done, though—and he straightens, the corners of his lips turned down. "I'm sorry, Abram. This must be frightening."

I nod. I am afraid, but not for the reason he believes.

The doctor is still staring at me. "Frightening though it may be, you cannot ignore it. Death comes for us all."

A prickling heat crawls along my shoulders, up my neck, and into my hair like an army of flaming lice. Is Martha standing in the corner, watching me, somewhere beyond the new fireplace? Is The Dark creeping up on me from behind, ready to cut my time on this planet short with an unearthly blade?

Time is a relative concept, especially here, where history leaches into every moment like a stain. But the closer The Dark gets, the more she feels it, the more she sees.

"Just a little more time," I say, "and I will be ready for it."

"Ready for it? What exactly do you propose to do with this time?" His words are steeped in disbelief though he's trying to be kind. What wrong can come of humoring a dying old man?

"I have a plan. As I do for everything else."

The doctor sighs. "Ah yes, you need time to tell this Chloe that darkness surrounds this place and you need her help to drive it out. And she shall think you mad, even if she doesn't realize being here will end her, as you say." The doctor raises one white eyebrow as if he agrees I am stoking my own insanity. He is not wrong.

And Chloe can think me mad all she likes, so long as she comes to assist me, though using her as bait is not the same as asking for her help. I imagine her silver hair, her gleaming eyes. She is broken; perfect for this task. I dislike the word sacrifice, but it is not wholly incorrect. Yet I am desperate. Releasing sprits from a place is not an easy task, and I cannot do it alone. God knows I've tried.

"There was a psychic, downtown. She did not seem to think I was mad." She also didn't seem to know anything—she was a fake, like most of them are.

"If you paid the vixen, she'd have told you anything. Money speaks louder than morals." The doctor shakes his head, and his spectacles wobble on the bridge of his nose. "You cannot fix anything except yourself, Abram. Live your last days in peace."

My last days—a half a year, maybe a little more, and it will be over. But eternity is worth battling for; that is why I am here. I stare at the pitcher on the counter, at the tears of condensation puddling at its base. To think I believed gutting this space would help. It was here that Martha made her most fatal mistake: She listened. She believed. She *trusted*. Trust is a funny thing, the way it can break you if it's severed; and the cracks deception tears open are hardest to heal.

I pick up the pitcher to pour a glass of lemonade but stop short—one glass is already full on the counter. Did I put it there? No, the condensation has stopped forming, and a puddle already shimmers beneath the cup—it has been here for some time. Strange. Yet many unusual things have happened since I moved into this place.

I gesture to the pitcher, and the doctor—my dear friend, my only friend—shakes his head. "You know I've tasted enough sour to last a thousand lifetimes." He has. He lost his own daughter here on this plantation, though I suspect he chooses not to remember that—denial is the only real escape from pain. Perhaps it is why he pushes so hard to convince me my plan is nothing but a fantasy. He does not want to face those dreadful, jagged corners of his own mind.

What man would, had he a choice?

I set the pitcher down, pick up the already full glass, and bring it to my lips, the liquid warm and thick, tasting of... *Iron.* I gag and spit, and blood pours from my mouth onto the counter, crimson spreading to the edges of the soapstone and flowing off, splattering onto the wood planks. On the counter, the glass teeters angrily, then falls on its side as if pushed by an invisible hand, and more blood rains down, a red waterfall.

Elisha is angry. He does not like what I am doing. He has probably been watching from the shadows, trying to decide how best to destroy me, to suck me into the darkness with him. I would never have pegged myself as someone who would ponder such insanity, but disbelief dies quickly when you have witnessed what I have. I run to the sink and turn on the tap, making sure the water runs clear before I put my lips beneath. Rinse, spit, rinse, spit. When I look up, the doctor has his arms crossed, his back against the wall. Not horrified. Worried.

He does not know; he cannot see the blood. It's as if the two of us are in our own worlds—together, but not entirely.

I turn the tap off and look at the sink, its basin dyed pink now. But then I blink and it is clear again, clean. The counter is wet, but not red. There is no dark puddle on the floor.

It is a reminder: this house does not belong to me.

As I draw my eyes from the counter to the wet but unstained floor, I can feel the change in the air as sure as the wood beneath my shoes—yes, The Dark is very near. It is going to happen. Someone else will be snatched from The Light and dragged down, down, down to be tortured. The Dark treats souls the way a toddler does toys, except The Dark knows what it is doing—he will call her, and she will answer, they always do. I only hope she survives long enough to take those final steps onto this property, luring The Dark out so I can banish him from this plane before he swallows her.

Blood must be repaid in blood. And here, in this house, the debt has been passed down like a genetic defect, hiding in the cells. For it was my blood that murdered Martha.

CHAPTER 16

CHLOE ANDERSON, PRESENT DAY

Chloe stepped over a pothole, nerves humming beneath her flesh like a thousand locusts. *Come to me...*

She inhaled, long and slow. *I can do this.* She could beat this—whatever *this* was.

The past is the past. When exploring historical events, you had to figure out what you knew for certain, what you could verify from the historical records, then go from there. Chloe's role here—the haunting—had begun when she'd picked up the brooch. But the exploding wine bottle, her dreams, those had started before she even knew about the brooch, after Victor had left. Which meant that Victor had probably felt those spirits, too, maybe run to escape them. Is that why Helen had left in such a hurry? Had she felt that agitated energy, or had she just believed Victor and followed him like a groupie?

Chloe glanced at her fingertips. Still pruney. She had sat in the bathtub for hours, listening for voices, waiting for another vision, another sign of the ghosts...but nothing. The afternoon sun had already begun to peek through the blinds when she finally dragged herself from the tub, and when she'd gone to the kitchen, the wine bottle had seemed to stare at her from the counter—it might as well have been whispering, "You failed, you tried to help, but you drove him away when he was scared, and he was *right*, you crazy piece of shit." She would have stayed home, maybe *should* have stayed home, but the ghosts probably weren't in the apartment itself—Chloe would have felt something there, she would have. The only other place that Victor had gone with regularity was downtown Cicatrice, and the antique shop was the connection between Helen and Victor. But before she started working there, nothing harrowing or hauntworthy had happened at the antique store besides the fires, and the shop had been abandoned every time it burned—no one had died in the place to leave their spirit stalking those halls. The key had to be in the people she kept seeing, the ghosts themselves.

Chloe didn't know who the man with the bloody apron was, and she didn't know who the girl was—there was nothing online about them, and she wasn't sure where else to begin looking other than...

She shuddered. Slimy-tongued Greg was the only one who might have more information about that girl, provided there was something in the salvaged courthouse records. It sounded ridiculous, illogical—after all, the morning Chloe had first brought the brooch to the shop he had said he didn't know who she was. But Chloe had felt the bristles of untruth in the air, and she already knew he hadn't been up front with her about Helen and Victor. Though he might not know too much if Helen had avoided him the way Chloe did, he sure as shit knew that Helen and Victor had been seeing one another—cheating. Greg either had the old files on the girl somewhere or simply knew more than he was saying. But it'd sure be easier for Chloe if Greg was on her side. She needed him to listen, to believe her—to help her instead of acting like a creepy asshole.

She pulled her shirt away from her skin, but sweat rolled down her back anyway, little scurrying drips, as if the madness was trying to escape through her pores. The skin on her chest had remained unburned, but Chloe knew she'd been injured—that the girl had hurt her. And those with good intentions don't cause pain. The man in the leather apron, though, the one who emerged from the shadows, who snuck into her dreams, into her bed...he frightened her, but mostly because of the blood, that ghastly apron. Chloe didn't know what he'd done to make such a mess, and maybe she didn't want to know, but he'd been gentle with the girl in her dream, stroking her hair. Even when he'd grabbed Chloe's wrist, she'd been more terrified of the voices—her mother's, Victor's—emerging from his lips. *Come to me, and the pain will vanish.* What if he wasn't lying? What if he did want to help her? What if his role here, even the girl's role here, was to find justice for a wrong done to them a long time ago? The man in the leather apron was old enough to be the girl's father—maybe they both wanted justice for her untimely death.

Chloe felt numb by the time she made it to the antique shop. Lehmann's car was there in the back lot, as always; it was like yesterday had never happened at all. She headed back around the store and startled when the bell jangled above her head.

"Hey, Chloe."

She met Greg's gaze and his eyes widened.

"Are you okay?"

No, I'm not. I don't know what to do, and I need your help despite the fact that you're jerky and slimy and rape-y.

"Chloe?" Greg raised an eyebrow expectantly.

Had he asked her a question? "I'm sorry, what?"

"How did it go with Shepherd?"

Shepherd. She'd gone over to the Shepherd place to pick up the antiques—had it been only yesterday? "Everything went fine." It wasn't fine. Nothing was fine. Her boyfriend had left her for another woman even though she'd done everything she could to make him happy, and there were ghosts trying to fuck with her, and she had burn wounds that miraculously healed overnight.

Miraculously. *Great power, great power, great power.*

Chloe's heart slowed as she produced the fan and the bronze box with shaking fingers. But though she was trembling, for the first time in her life she felt that she was exactly where she was supposed to be. Even while her heart still ached, though grief and loneliness still crawled through her chest, she had a purpose. A mission.

She was meant to fix...something. Something that wasn't her.

Greg took the box, and when their fingers brushed, she flashed back to his tongue in her mouth and had to resist the urge to spit.

"Looks good," he said, glancing at the items. But his eyes remained narrowed, as if convinced she was hiding more antiques behind her back. "Are you sure you're okay? You really look...upset."

I just like you, and I want to make sure you're okay. He'd said that. And he'd been watching her, stealing any excuse to get close to her, from the moment she'd started working here. If he was that stuck on her, he'd help her. He would. "I need your help with something."

Greg's jaw dropped, the tip of his horrible tongue showing behind his teeth.

"You were right yesterday." She hurried on, trying not to think about his mouth, about the sweaty heat of him, his weird, astringent smell. "I did come here for something. And I need help figuring out what I'm supposed to do."

He stepped closer, and though her skin crawled, she resisted the urge to take a corresponding step back. He put a hand on her elbow. "Of course. I'm happy to do whatever I can to help."

"Good." She leaned closer until she could feel his muggy breath on her cheek. "I need to know more about that girl on the brooch."

Greg shook his head and stepped away from her, but this time she grabbed his arm, clamping her hand around his spindly bicep hard enough that her knuckles ached. "You know who she is, don't you? You have her records in that safe."

His face tightened. "Listen, Chloe, there are some things you don't need to know. Anyway, it's just an old ghost story."

So it *was* a part of local folklore? Why hadn't she ever heard about it? "You don't understand, Greg," she hissed, and her grip tightened on his flesh. "This is important to me. Maybe one of the most important things I've ever done. Please, just...please help me."

He looked down at her hand, back at her face, and finally his shoulders slumped. "Martha Alton." Though she was close enough to feel the air when he sighed, his voice was so soft that she had to strain her ears. "She lived just outside the city, on the Alton Valley plantation."

Chloe bit her lip, imagining the girl's bloody teeth. A rich girl wouldn't have been tortured like that—those women were valuable property, protected so they could be married off, bear children, run the plantations.

Greg's eyes had gone glassy. "She disappeared one night. They never found her, but it was rumored she was murdered by the field hands."

"Field hands? That doesn't sound right." Dissent and uprising among abused people might be common, expected even, but a kidnapping, a murder? If the girl on the brooch was one of the few who'd died at the hands of their workers, Chloe definitely would have known from her searches—a death like that would have been famous if only for the shock value, like the horrors at the LaLaurie mansion. Unless whoever had done it had hidden her body. Missing girls were far less conspicuous than murdered ones, especially before the days of the all-seeing internet. But since it obviously wasn't common knowledge...how did Greg know about it?

"You'd think something like that would be bigger news here," she said slowly.

"Her father, Doctor Phillip Alton, died shortly after she

vanished, under mysterious circumstances," he said. "Probably self-inflicted poisoning—no one looked for her. But we came across some writings, journals from years back, that told us a little more about who she was. And yes, I have them in the back."

"What's her connection to Elisha Shepherd, the plantation owner?"

"Can't say."

"Can't? Or won't?" Her back tightened. *Shit, keep it together, you'll lose him.* "She has to have some connection to the Shepherd plantation."

"Why?"

"Because her brooch was found there..." But there were probably lots of things piled up around that house. The brooch being in the attic didn't necessarily mean anything. Except she knew it did.

"If Martha Alton and Elisha Shepherd were married, those records burned here a long time ago." Greg's eyes glittered darkly and he reached out for her, and when she took his hand, shivers climbed up her arm and into her shoulder. Greg squeezed.

"I don't understand why Lehmann would ask who she was if he already knew."

"I'm not sure he did know. That isn't his role here, and unless someone comes in for a particular item, he doesn't pay that much attention." He gripped her fingers tighter. *This guy is so desperate.*

Chloe ground her teeth. So now she had a name for the girl. But if Greg was right and Martha was killed by field hands...how did that help Chloe? For the life of her, she could think of nothing else the girl might want besides justice for her death. That was certainly enough, but it would be impossible to locate every slave on that plantation and uncover the guilty party; they'd all be dead by now, case closed, justice served. Did these ghosts expect her to use some supernatural means to find out who murdered Martha? Did they think she could? *Great powers.* Maybe that was why they'd let Victor leave Cicatrice—let Helen leave. They weren't as sensitive to the energy here, couldn't see the things Chloe could. Unless Victor and Helen were gone because they were dead. *No, the suitcases. They left on purpose.*

Chloe chewed on her cheek. "I want to see the journals." But her voice shook.

"I'm sorry, Chloe, I'm not at liberty to remove those from the safe."

She yanked her hand away from him. "I don't understand why you want to keep this from me. It doesn't make any sense! Do you need to be the person who knows everything when no one else does? You want to be special, to be—"

"It's not like that, okay? Just let it go, Chloe."

She clamped her jaw shut, fists clenched. *I'm going to hit him.* No, she needed him. She sucked in a breath through her nose and turned on her heel, heading for the office.

"Where are you going?"

"To get Lehmann to show me the journals since you won't. I'll figure it out myself." She'd read the journals and pore through old photos, here and online—with Martha's name, she should have more luck getting information, maybe even stumble upon something like she had the photos of that slave woman and the boy, hanged for witchcraft in front of the plantation.... Wait, had the slave woman...cursed that white-haired man, and Martha, too? *Fuck.* She didn't know much about witchcraft outside of the historical events surrounding it.

"There's nothing to figure out, Chloe," he called after her.

You're so full of shit, Greg.

Lehmann's office was locked. She rapped, hard—no answer. *Goddammit, Mr. Lehmann.* She knocked again, trying the knob, but it was stuck fast. Her gaze locked on the other door—the room with the safe. The one she wasn't allowed to enter on threat of...nothing. He'd just told her to stay out. And so what if he fired her? It'd be the least distressing thing to happen to her in weeks. Chloe squared her shoulders, her footsteps echoing over the wood in time to her heart, and knocked on the door to the safe room hard enough to make her knuckles throb. "Mr. Lehmann!" she called, but she didn't wait for a response—she turned the handle and pushed the door open.

The room was dark inside, no lights except for one flickering candle on the desk against the far wall, Lehmann sitting in front of it, his back to her. A blue glow shone from a tablet beside him on the desktop, the screen lit up with *Crosses and Bows*, the little blocks moving, shifting, racking up points on the scoreboard as if being manipulated by an invisible player. Demo mode, maybe? Gooseflesh, barbed and sharp, popped up on her arms, scurried over her back, raced down her legs.

Lehmann remained still, hunched over something in front of him. She gagged at the sudden heady perfume, an herb her grandfather used to grow in the front flowerbed, one that to this day reminded her of chicken pot pie. *Sage*. Was it was coming from the candle? And Lehmann...what was he doing? He didn't acknowledge her, didn't even appear to have heard her come in, concentrated as he was on something on the desktop beyond her line of sight.

"Mr. Lehmann?" She stepped closer, and the candlelit desk came into view. Her lungs seized.

Directly in front of Lehmann, dark smears of red coated the wooden desktop, nearly black in the dim light. A long piece of what looked like bloodied tissue lay across the top, a flayed piece of meat, half dangling over the edge of the desk as if it were trying to worm away from the carnage. Lehmann's hands were hidden below the desktop, but as she approached, she could see his eyes were fixed on the stains, and his fingers rested on his bloody arm... No, his fingers weren't resting, they were *inside* his arm, his probing nails clawing underneath the skin beneath some mark, a...

Tattoo. A swastika. Black, with angry corners, the edges blurred with stains of crimson. Blood wept around his prodding nails, as if he were trying to peel the ink from his flesh.

No, not as if. Not trying. He *was* tearing his skin from the bone.

Oh shit. God, no, no, no.

She backed from the desk, colliding with the safe's door. It was ajar, the cast iron black on black, too dark for her to see into the interior, but there was something on the floor just outside the open door, a child's toy—Lehmann's wooden dreidel, but the upper half was smattered with blood, the bottom resting in a puddle of dark liquid that seeped from the narrow crack between the safe's door and its bottom lip, as if there was a badly wounded creature trapped in the safe, slowly leaking its life out onto the floor. And the top itself... it was reflecting the candlelight, silver flickering with a murky opalescence that illuminated the gore and Lehmann's footprints, bloody, wet, staining the floor all the way to his seat.

Drip, drip, drip.

The crimson puddle beneath the safe was widening. She was standing in it. And when she looked down, she realized it was on her hands, too, her wrists, and all the way up her arms, though she'd touched nothing. *Oh God, oh God, oh God.* She wiped her hands, her arms, on her clothes, but her shirt was already stained and dirty, with blood and what might have been vomit, but she hadn't thrown up, had she? She inhaled so harshly that the air burned her nose, the smoke making her gag. She couldn't breathe.

God, please help me, please.

"Chloe!" Lehmann barked, but it didn't come from the desk; it came from behind her, and when she whirled around, Lehmann was standing at her back in the doorway, nostrils flaring with agitation. "Out."

She spun back to the desk, but the blood was gone, all of it, the wood lit up with lamplight now as any ordinary office would be, and though she could still smell the sage, there was no candle to produce the scent. Even the iPad had disappeared. On the left wall loomed the safe, securely closed, no hint of toys or gore or footprints or anything else on the wooden floor before it.

Her head grew fuzzy—the room wavered.

Great power. You're special, Chloe, you're special. But Chloe couldn't breathe, couldn't sleep, couldn't *live* like this. Ghosts could show her crazy shit all day, but none of the visions mattered if she didn't know what the fuck to do about them.

Chloe pushed past Lehmann and into the main room where Greg had his gaze locked on her. *Has he been staring after me this whole time? No, that's paranoid.* Maybe this was what her grandfather had been worried about all along. Maybe this was why he'd whipped her bloody every time she'd acted on feelings that weren't logical to everyone else, every time she'd been foolish enough to reveal her specialness. Right now, she'd do anything to escape these visions—she wasn't in control of her own eyes.

Maybe being possessed wasn't as obvious as she thought it would be.

A headache stabbed at her temples, throbbing along with her frantic heartbeat. She couldn't focus, couldn't think—she needed to snuff out her chaotic thoughts before her brain exploded. She wasn't safe here. She wasn't safe at home. The only place that felt safe, the only place she hadn't been accosted by visions, was in the street, where there were apparently too many people around for the ghosts to come at her. Where the undead were forced into hiding.

But they wouldn't stay hidden for long. Her chest ached from the force of her heart slamming against her rib cage. She might be able to convince herself that her overactive imagination had made Helen's disappearance into a mystery when she'd simply quit and walked away. She could maybe convince herself that Victor and Helen weren't connected after all—if she wanted to stay in denial about Victor's infidelity. And the photos of Leslie she'd seen in Victor's camera…those had been a vision too, the universe trying to tell her something, but not a literal, physical reality. But that girl, half her face missing, organs spilling out of her… Then there was Lehman, peeling the skin off his arm with his own bare hands. These visions weren't normal. It wasn't intuition. She was being haunted. *Hunted.*

Something evil had happened here, and there was a darkness, some force pursuing her, though she had no idea why. And as she pushed her way out into the streets, she had the distinct feeling that she would vanish too, just like Victor, just like Martha, unless she found a way to destroy it.

CHAPTER 17

ABRAM SHEPHERD, PRESENT DAY

Brandon Shepherd's eyes are cast downward, focused on his hands, like every day. He lays the vase on the table beside the kiln with clay-covered fingers.

"We're running out of time," I tell him.

"There has to be another way."

"You always say that, Brandon. You know there is not."

It must be here, where the ground is still sodden with blood if you dig down far enough, where the evil is so deeply rooted that time has not been able to extinguish the energy. No other place compares to the wickedness here, not even the LaLaurie mansion, with its abominable horrors—though I still feel the corruption at the LaLaurie house, it is not the stabbing agony of new wounds, but rather the old misery of events long past. Ghosts, their anguished souls, reside there. But no demons walk those halls.

The Dark lives here now.

The breeze picks up, but it blows hot, like breath from a hair dryer. I wipe my sweaty brow. Brandon nods, refusing to meet my gaze, as if he does not want her to fulfill her purpose, though this is Brandon's way—he always thinks he can protect them. He and Gregory are cut from the same cloth. Gregory has tried numerous times to keep her from the truth, to keep her from her fate, but Gregory will have no problem cutting Chloe down if she displeases him. Brandon has no choice in the matter—we all do what is necessary.

"You know it must be this way, Brandon." Chloe must face The Dark and choose The Light—if The Dark takes her first, her energy will leave him even stronger and then I'll have no chance of escape. It is a strange thing, the notion that sacrificing one powerful soul to the ether, that depriving The Light or The Dark of her energy can make a difference, but even the Devil himself gets jealous when you take something he wants. And jealousy is a mighty weakness; it has always been.

"It takes time." Brandon straightens, his irises reflecting the fire from the kiln. "She cannot think I'm trying to force her. She will not listen."

That is true of most—it is best if they think their ideas are their own. They trust themselves more than anyone else, even when doing so is utterly insane.

"The Dark," Brandon says. "His influence is strong." I know what he means. The Dark manipulates, with the dreams, and he might already have her convinced that he is not dangerous. So we must act fast. He's too strong now since he took Helen, too heavy-handed. If we are not careful, he'll rip this entire town from this plane into his.

"Maybe I'm ready for it to be over. Maybe I deserve what comes next." Brandon keeps his eyes on the flames. He does not want to do this, but he has no choice—his powers of persuasion are the reason he is here. And we both hold within us a slave master's genes along with those of the housemaids he brutalized—we were not the first, nor the last, of the slave master's line, but people do not wish to think of these things...and so they do not. They stow that knowledge so far in the darkest corners of their minds that they convince themselves they do not possess it at all. Blindness can be deliciously comforting.

Yet I cannot afford for Brandon to be blind now. His blood is more tainted than mine, and he knows it, deep down he knows, though he still does not accept his fate; I can tell by the way he cuts his eyes at me. But he is no hero, no more than I am. We need Chloe now.

"You must act quickly," I tell Brandon. For we have a demon to deal with, The Dark to thwart, and I know not how long I have to accomplish such a feat.

The Dark wants her too, and surely Chloe can feel it—his calling, his presence, will make her more skittish. More afraid. But he's pulling her closer now so that he can take her.

"I will." Brandon meets my gaze, the flecks of green in his eyes so vivid it is like he has some foreign creature burgeoning within him, ready to explode from his irises. Perhaps he does. "Tonight."

In the end, power is all The Dark craves, and Chloe is powerful whether she has realized it yet or not. And power is the one thing that will draw The Dark out.

CHAPTER 18

CHLOE ANDERSON, PRESENT DAY

Since hustling out of the shop after seeing...whatever she saw in that office, Chloe's brain had sizzled with the agitated energy of bacon spitting in a too-hot pan.

Three hours at the library had turned up nothing useful on Elisha Shepherd or Martha Alton, but had provided plenty of conflicting information on hauntings. The few things that seemed more credible—well, as credible as she could really get—didn't give her a clue as to how to move forward.

The psychology books said people hallucinated ghosts to cope with extreme stress, or when they needed another person to help them overcome a traumatic situation. But you couldn't just blister your own skin or wake up in a different place from the one you went to sleep in—a fugue state maybe? That didn't ring true, though, and Victor had tried drugs for his hallucinations—they hadn't helped. So what would? A number of sites mentioned being "more positive" to make your energy less desirable to malevolent spirits, but she wasn't being a pessimist here. She was being a realist, and she was fucking *scared*.

The paranormal explanations—the unscientific ones—were as varied as the clouds in the sky, and not much more

THE JILTED

helpful than the scientific materials. Some people thought there were numerous layers of Heaven and Hell, different planes that could interact with one another, even if people on Earth weren't aware of it. And books and websites alike suggested spirits used objects to move between these planes. The object essentially behaved as a portal, transporting the spirit traveler between levels of Heaven or Hell and Earth. It appeared that reciting prayers was usually enough to send ghosts and demons back inside whatever item they were using as a portal, though you needed to see the presence you were trying to banish, or at least know where it was—just shouting prayers into the air seemed less effective than focusing them on the entity you intended to exorcise. After that, it was as simple as destroying the object to shut these world-to-world portals, but of course, that required you to know *which* object they were using to get to your world. Was Martha using the brooch? Chloe had felt a jittery energy running through that piece from the day she'd first touched it at Shepherd's. But what would the white-haired ghost be using to travel here? It could be a lot bigger than an object, something as big as the plantation; some of the books thought you could just remove the location of a haunting—that tearing down a house, or even redecorating a room could make the ghost confused enough to move on—but the rest claimed that the meditative procedures required to release ghosts took years to learn. Chloe had no idea what to believe.

More confusing—and disconcerting—were the differences between ghosts and demons.

Some books noted unique distinctions between the two; many didn't, making it almost impossible to research properly, though demons sounded like much bigger assholes. They liked to screw with people, messing with their emotions, altering their personalities, creating areas of hot and cold in homes. She even found reports of demons sexually assaulting people, which gave her pause—she'd had that rather intense experience with the aproned man in her bed.

But almost all of the materials agreed that demons could not take human form and wander around, which meant the girl and the man must be ghosts. Not demons. Though disquiet lingered in her belly, by the time she finished reading, possession was the only problem Chloe felt she *didn't* have—her symptoms just weren't right. She wasn't being compelled to act, her personality hadn't changed, she wasn't suicidal, and her emotions weren't unreasonable—well, not for the situation. She knew these ghosts weren't inside her body, altering her movements, like a demon would, even if they were making her see and hear things that weren't there.

So much information, all jumbled in her head. Chloe's nerves felt alive, jittery, beneath the gentle brain fog induced by bone-deep exhaustion—her hands shook even as the energy from her muscles was sucked away to some secret place she had no access to. Her body was heavy, weak. The buildings on the streets of Cicatrice loomed over her as if keeping watch, and she wanted to slap the shit out of every person she passed—they all felt like they were staring at her even if they didn't meet her eyes.

The past is the past, we only look forward, and nothing else matters.

But the past affected the future whether Grandpa had believed it or not. And the past was at the center of whatever Chloe was meant to discover.

Come on, God! What am I supposed to do with this shit? Maybe she should go to church, pray for an answer, but every time she'd sat in a pew, begging for guidance, something worse had happened. She'd prayed for Ron to come back to her in high school and the next day she'd been lying in the high school hallway, covered in blood, then sitting in a bathtub with Grandpa lecturing from outside the door: "God won't give you more than you can handle, girl. We'll fix you up." At least the bloody tub had pushed Ron from her mind, if only temporarily.

She inhaled deeply, letting the muggy air filter down through her lungs. On either side of her, the street lamps flickered on, welcoming the coming night with an orange glare that bounced off the shiny bald head of the man walking in front of her. Chloe scooted around him, but he jerked his arm at the last minute, smacking his elbow into her chest hard enough that he splashed his iced blue drink onto his shirt. He transferred the cup to his other hand and shook off his fingers, then kept walking without saying sorry.

Asshole. Maybe I should push him back.

When he tripped off the curb and spilled the rest of his drink on his pants, she smirked and continued on her way.

Exhaustion had kicked in more fervently now, and the edges of her vision blurred. She blinked hard to clear it, focusing on expanding and contracting her lungs, until her tired eyes cleared. But still bile roiled in her gut. She felt...*haunted*. Bewitched. It was a subtle yet present sensation, like little clouds of static electricity creeping around her toes, waiting to strike. Everything in that moment was a mystery—a question, not an answer—and her thoughts whirled inside her head like a thousand bits of dust in a hurricane.

She was chasing the ghost of a girl torn apart by a slave—or a group of field hands. Chloe could almost believe she was supposed to...save her. But how did you save someone who'd lived—and died—more than a century ago?

A prickling sensation climbed her spine, tiny insectile feet, and she glanced behind her, shivering. The psychic from the other day sat in her usual spot, purple-black hair shining, rings glittering in the murky dusk, her eyes trained on the row of buildings across the street. Chloe had walked right by the woman without noticing her.

What if the psychic had answers? The woman's words had mirrored those of the psychic from her childhood... *Should I go back?* No, that was crazy, that woman couldn't help her—if she could actually talk to ghosts, she'd be the most popular person on the strip, with a thriving brick-and-mortar business, instead of squatting on a urine-soaked street corner belting out clichés that might apply to anyone. That woman hadn't been chosen. Chloe had.

Something dark follows, something dark...

The woman shifted, and the neon lights from the shops striped her black hair with red, as if she'd brushed it with a bloody comb. Chloe winced, and stepped from the sidewalk as the crowd swallowed up the table and the woman.

Don't focus on the dark, child, or it will be all you can see.

Chloe crossed the street and headed down the cobbled hill, and as she put more distance between herself and the "psychic," her breath returned to normal, though she was tiring. She passed another bar, then a shop that featured crystals and jewelry, then a place full of T-shirts and chicory coffee and novelty koozies. *Where am I going?* But even as she thought the question, she knew the answer—she was trying to escape. Wasn't she? If she left on foot, would that change the outcome? Probably not. And next time she might be punished. Besides, she couldn't walk away from this any more than she could have left the brooch sitting at home by itself on the dresser. It hung around her neck now, over a patch of gauze, her chest bandaged in a protective measure in case the necklace decided to blister her flesh again. This girl needed her. The aproned man did too.

Needed her. And you didn't give up just because things got hard.

But she didn't know what to do next, and had no clue where to look for those answers. Was she supposed to use the brooch to set the girl's soul free? Maybe it'd be a portal to Heaven once she figured out the "why" part; the books said some spirits merely wanted understanding, to be heard or forgiven. But Chloe had no idea what there was to forgive, or what she could say, to put these ghosts at ease. And without knowing whether the necklace was a portal or a conduit, something the girl used to communicate, Chloe was loath to destroy it. What if it ended up being the only way she could fix this?

She narrowed her gaze at a rack of Mardi Gras beads,

pink interspersed with little orange rubber duckies, and her vision wavered again. She blinked hard and dragged her bleary gaze from the shop in time to see a familiar figure emerge from the shadows up the road. Her breath caught.

Then he saw her...and cocked his head. He approached under the streetlight, his black hair glistening as if he'd been running, though he still wore his white button-down—immaculate as always.

"Mr. Shepherd?" Her eye twitched, and her face heated —*Did I just wink at him?* She glanced down to make sure the brooch was hidden, and exhaled when she saw only the fabric of her shirt and not the girl's eyes staring back at her.

"Call me Brandon." He smiled.

"What are you doing out here?"

"I might ask you the same."

"I was just getting some air." The heat in her cheeks intensified. "And you?"

He peered around, his gaze flicking to the restaurant across the way, then back to her. "I walk here every night."

Weird. Why hadn't she seen him before? But thank God he was here—she needed to ask him if she could go back to his house to look for more information on Martha Alton, and maybe on the slaves who'd died in that tree—the witch and the "possessed" little boy. The vision in Lehmann's office had made her forget all about the safe and the paperwork; she'd let it distract her, like an idiot. Maybe some spirit had even sent that vision on purpose, just to throw her off. "Doesn't that get boring, walking through the same place every day?"

Brandon cast his gaze to the sky as if pondering the question, then smiled and shook his head. "I happened upon you here. How could that be boring?" He glanced down the street behind her again, and she turned. The psychic woman was on her feet now at the top of the hill, her head bent toward a patron: a spindly old black man with a salt-and-pepper beard, smoke curling from a pipe between his teeth. Too far away to hear over the din of the passing bar-hoppers, the men and women on their way to dinner, the occasional teenager walking by with a cigarette. But her heart quickened anyway—she knew the old man. Stress was turning her brain to mush right now, but her intuition was in high gear, chirping like a ping-pong ball on a tile floor—she'd probably have a panic attack if someone sneezed too loud. Chloe ground her teeth and turned back to Brandon, and he nodded to their right, to a road off the main drag, away from that crazy woman.

"It's a nice night. Shall we walk?"

She inhaled, more slowly than before, more evenly, trying to get her shit together so she could think. The din faded behind them as she followed Brandon up another side street, the air somehow sweeter here, the sound of their footsteps and the occasional buzz of an insect loud in the sudden silence. With Victor, she would have felt the need to fill these moments with chatter, but Brandon's quiet presence soothed the awful tension pressing on her from every side, even if it didn't make her grief go away. At least with Brandon, the world seemed less intense. Or maybe that was just exhaustion. Or maybe... If she could sense the evil around her, the horrors, surely she'd sense the good as well. Maybe Brandon Shepherd was just a good guy, and she could feel it.

Brandon stopped suddenly, and Chloe skidded to a halt beside him, following his gaze to the graveyard just ahead, one far older than the cemetery near the park—if the style of the headstones was any indication—and far darker; she didn't see a single street lamp inside the gates. She'd had no idea it existed. How had she never seen this place before? Was he on his way to do a tour or something? But she saw no guides, only the graves. Shorn grass covered each plot, and every square foot of the place was free of litter, but its spotlessness clashed with the dirtiness Chloe felt hovering around it—as though an invisible grungy film had settled on her skin.

"Are you okay?" Brandon said it softly, tentatively, with concern.

She'd almost forgotten he was standing beside her. And... she'd embarrassed herself at his home the other day, freaking out when she saw Martha. She'd explain her actions to Brandon later, when her heart wasn't trying to vibrate out of her chest. Chloe shook her head and forced a breath through her nose. "Sorry. I've never been a fan of cemeteries." More than that, being here was like walking backward through the pieces of history she'd rather forget.

"There is a darkness here, that's for certain."

Wait...he feels it too? Brandon's face was drawn, but Chloe couldn't see his eyes in the dim glow of the streetlight.

"Come on," he said, already striding up the road. She matched his gait, the clap of their soles dull and hollow like hoofbeats, the streets otherwise quiet and vacant now—she couldn't even hear the music from the bars anymore, only the wind that whispered down the alley with the gentle whoosh of incoming autumn. They turned right again, down another side street she didn't recognize, and shadows crept over them like fog—there wasn't even a street lamp back here to cast its orange glow on their cheeks. But instead of being unsettling, this walk, this path, this man, felt right and normal and easy, like she was five and the world was fair and things made sense, though she had absolutely no logical reason to feel such a thing. She wasn't safe here, with Brandon, because she wasn't safe anywhere, with anyone—ghosts were after her for God's sake.

Brandon turned again, in the direction of the main drag, toward the shop and the psychic and the man with the pipe. *Is this the right way?* Yes, there was downtown Cicatrice. Maybe they should go up another block, though, to avoid the psychic. Chloe paused at the mouth of the alley—she'd seen that bearded man before somewhere, too, and it was disconcerting that her memory was failing her. But though her brain might not recall, her gut was screaming that she never wanted to see him again. The flesh between her shoulders prickled.

"You coming?" Brandon smiled over his shoulder, and her

chills calmed, just like that. She followed him out of the alley, past the little shops with their garish signage and kitsch, but they both stopped suddenly across the street from the antique store. The front window was dim, but the street lamp showed Chloe enough—Victor's camera had been replaced by the fan she'd gotten from Brandon's, the lace now amber in the glow of streetlights. Had Greg done that? An image of Lehmann's mutilated forearm leapt into her mind, and she bristled, the agitated energy of the thought vibrating over her own exposed arms, but her chest where the necklace lay felt warm—as though the brooch was less like a portal and more like a talisman, protecting her. She laid a hand over the gauze and felt the heat burn through her shirt and warm her palm, though in a pleasant way, like the first sip of almost-too-hot coffee.

Chloe drew her eyes away from the shop window, toward Brandon. He stood staring into the shop, focused as if he was blind to all else, like he had forgotten she was there. *He does feel it. He knows something is wrong here the same way I do.* "Brandon?"

She jumped as he bolted across the street and disappeared into the shadows beneath the awning of the shop. *What the hell is he doing? Is he...* The glass flickered with sudden light —*a flashlight?* She hadn't even seen him pull it out.

Was she supposed to follow him? Chloe squinted, trying to see him in the shadows near the front door, but the shop seemed to have changed in the space of a blink. The windows were gone, and the bricks, painted a clean gray just a moment ago, were streaked with soot as if the building had been recently burned. And...were the shutters gone too? A trick of the streetlight? But no...the streetlight had also disappeared, the moon glowing bright and full overhead, casting the street in the black and white of an old movie. Even the air was different. The sweet breeze had vanished, replaced with the sour stink of manure. Another vision. *Not again, not now.*

A piece of her wanted to run after Brandon, to pull him

out and drag him away with her, but her feet were glued to the cobblestones, and the muscles in her legs refused to cooperate. And again, something spindly crawled over the skin of her back like an insectile creature with a thousand legs. *I shouldn't be here, this is wrong this is—*

She choked out Brandon's name, her voice like a whispered sob; panic had frozen her lungs, too. Then there he was again, running in her direction, and at his back, inside the shop window, a yellow glare pierced the night, brighter than it had been just moments before. Lehmann must be up and about inside—did the man actually sleep here?

Halfway to her, Brandon stopped, and at his wild look Chloe reexamined the shop window. Her jaw dropped. The golden glow was not a light from *inside* the shop—it was the glimmer of flame blossoming just *outside* the window, surrounding the window frame, and creeping steadily toward the interior of the building beneath the shadow of the awning. Brandon had lit the place on fire.

Within moments—far too fast—it was a roaring blaze, licking the sky as dry tinder and hundred-year-old artifacts caught. There were other people out here, there had to be other people who had seen what Brandon had done, but Chloe could not pull her eyes away from the flames, from the shop, from Brandon's silhouette, still coming toward her— fifteen feet away and closing. His eyes glowed orange as if there were fire inside him, though that was impossible, ridiculous, and... *Oh shit.* Had he been the one to burn Lehmann's shop to the ground last year, the one Lehmann had bought the cameras to catch? But that made no sense. Why would a young, wealthy man burn down the place that was paying him for his antiques?

Her stomach lurched—the antiques were not the only thing of value inside the shop. *The journals.* The ones Greg had told her about, her last connection to Martha, her last hope of solving this... Would they still be in the safe, or were they in a drawer somewhere, unprotected? She lurched toward the shop, but the entire front was already engulfed in flame, and there was no back door through which she could run to grab the papers—even if she could get inside, she wouldn't know where to look for them. *Please let the journals be in the safe, please let them be protected until the fire department gets here.* Surely someone had called them by now.

And probably the police, too.

Chloe's gaze darted frantically from one side of the street to the other. A couple in matching tie-dyed T-shirts were deep in conversation, their backs to the shop, and with a start she realized the air was still thick with the scent of horse shit and rancid urine, as if in this one little section of the road she'd stepped back in time. Down the way, the "psychic" woman was still at her perch behind her table, hands on her ball, fingers twitching anxiously, eyes trained on the bar across the street from her—she did not seem to notice the commotion up this way. But if the police asked the woman later, she might remember them.

"Brandon, what—"

"Come to me."

Chloe's heart lodged in her throat. *Come to me.* He reached for her hand, and she jerked it away. "What did you say?"

"Come with me." His brows were furrowed, jaw tight, almost angry looking, as if he'd had some altercation beneath the awning she wasn't privy to. Brandon's eyes jittered from side to side, up and down the road, his lower lip trembling almost imperceptibly as if the burning building pained him. But he'd burned the shop on purpose—what was he so upset about?

"It had to be done, Chloe. You know it, too."

Her heart throbbed wildly. "What?" Why would they have to burn down a store? But suddenly she didn't care why he'd done it. They'd think it was her—Lehmann had been doing business with Brandon, buying up all his antiques. Brandon had no reason to go after the shop. *She* was the disgruntled employee—she'd fought with Greg and Lehmann just today, barged into Lehmann's office raving like a lunatic, then stormed out. All Brandon had to do was point his finger at her, and she'd be in jail, trapped in a fucking cell with whatever ghosts were after her. She'd have nowhere to run.

Run! Run now!

Her heart rate climbed, wild with electricity, the pulse spreading painfully through her chest and lower between her legs, where it found a steady, blissful rhythm—like the day she and Victor had broken into that haunted warehouse upstate, when they'd spent the night listening for otherworldly voices in the whoosh of the wind. Instead, they'd heard the owner of the building unlocking the front door, and they'd run out the back, panting and laughing. And when they were far enough away, he'd fucked her by the light of the moon, lying on the dead grass in an abandoned park, and she'd sworn every star was watching them, as if every ghost they'd ever sought was listening to her moaning. Now, watching the flames grow higher and brighter within the shop, putting an end to something Victor had loved, putting an end to her old life… It was fitting, really. It felt right.

The past is the past.

She grabbed Brandon's hand.

They ran.

CHAPTER 19

CHLOE ANDERSON, PRESENT DAY

The moon was watchful as they sped down the street, past one dark block after another, each road quieter and more isolated than the last. In the park, the trees waved lazily in the breeze, out of synch with the frantic throbbing in Chloe's chest. No bars or restaurants along this strip—just the occasional artist still holding out hope that someone might happen by to purchase their wares. The man with the canvases was already gone for the night.

It had to be done, Chloe. You know it, too. It made no sense. She had so many questions, but she couldn't seem to put anything into words—her thoughts were jumbled and disconnected from her vocal cords, the frenzied energy of her pulse searing through her with every heartbeat.

Run, just run.

But run where?

At the street where she normally turned right to get to her apartment, Brandon hooked a left and they slowed, still hurrying but no longer jogging, both trying to act natural as they passed another block, then a bar. This bar was quiet— aside from the jazzy saxophone when patrons opened the door, the party had not spilled into the street. But Chloe would have been hard-pressed to hear much of anything over the rushing of blood in her ears.

Was this wrong? It didn't feel wrong, though she was still panting, and her chest was too hot, and her brain was fuzzier than it had been when she'd begun the evening. Brandon wasn't breathing hard—*why not?*—but she could smell him, his clothes redolent with the stink of sulfur. The reek of manure was gone.

Up ahead, the street lamps petered out altogether, a distinct band of black where the cityscape died and the country emerged—was he heading towards his place? That had to be…two miles? Three? But she didn't have the energy to fight him on it, and she didn't want to walk back toward town alone. The coolness radiating from him was the only thing keeping her tethered to sanity.

They didn't speak until they were fully clear of of downtown Cicatrice. Here the moon shone brighter, as it had in front of the shop, when she'd seen the building already burned. Had she seen the shop as it had been in the past? Had it been a glimpse into the future? The shop had been home to enough strange phenomena for her to know the place was screwy: Lehmann trying to peel off a tattoo, and the strange blips in the video surveillance, where she'd seen Helen's scarf, where she'd seen that white-haired man in his disgusting apron. Where she'd seen Victor, gagged.

What had Brandon seen there to make him think he needed to destroy it? Did he believe the shop was…a portal? A gateway? All the information she'd read earlier was splintered now, a bag of broken glass that refused to knit together into something coherent.

The night around her wavered. Her mouth was as dry as the cotton that had probably once grown in these fields, and the chain around her throat felt heavier than before, the metal digging into the back of her neck as if it wanted to slice clean through her spine. She strained her ears for the sound of footsteps following in the darkness, and every time she turned to check behind them the anticipation of glimpsing a police car to outrun filled her with a delicious, expectant thrill that mellowed when she saw only emptiness.

"What were you thinking?" she finally asked. But the katydids buzzing in the distance were her only reply, and despite her annoyance—of course she was annoyed, she had every reason to be—her heart pulsed lower in her abdomen than it should have, the throbbing matching itself to his breath.

You don't get to stonewall me. "I deserve an explanation." Her voice had a low, throaty quality to it, and did not sound angry even to her. "You think I wanted you to set that fire, you think I…I just don't understand."

They slowed their pace further as the road narrowed, and she checked behind them again, certain that this time she'd see the glare of police lights, that she'd hear sirens giving chase. But there was only blackness. Chloe could not even see the street lamps anymore, the velvet dark around them suddenly watchful. But she felt less terrified by this and more exhibitionistic—the way she'd felt as the stars had watched her fuck Victor in that grassy park.

"We might never understand, Chloe." She startled, turning toward the deep baritone that cut the night air, his words silencing even the breeze. "Too much blood's been spilled here, far too much for logical answers." He shrugged, so nonchalantly she wanted to hit him, but the fire in her belly burned with more than rage. She knew what that sticky anger-excitement was, why it was, but she was unable to stop the steady pulsing even as her agitation grew. The sheen of sweat on his brow was glistening, and the heaviness of his breath…his exhales almost sounded like quiet moans. But she'd just seen him light her workplace on fire, and she barely knew him—she shouldn't even be out alone with him in the dark. "You're not making any sense, Brandon."

"I saw the picture."

"What pic—"

"On the camera."

Pain exploded just above her heart, so bright and hot that

she gasped and put her hands on her knees. *No it can't be.* She'd convinced herself that the photo had been another vision, based on some truth she couldn't accept—was it real, then, a tangible, physical reality? Leslie's dead gaze appeared in her mind's eye, her face mottled pasty white and pink and blue, her lips purple. If it had been real, if Leslie was dead, not off with Victor somewhere... *Dead, dead, dead.* The air wheezed from her in ragged gasps.

Maybe that's what she'd needed to discover—maybe Martha, another victim, had wanted her to expose Victor's crime. But...how had Brandon gotten the photo? The mystery tingled in the back of her mind and deep in her stomach and she gasped in a breath, trying to steady her voice.

"How did you see the picture, Brandon?"

"I have the camera."

"You took—"

"I found it."

"You *found* it?" That explained how he knew she was connected—Victor'd had photos of Chloe in the digital memory too. But she swore she'd deleted all the pictures, she was sure...

He touched her shoulder, and her heart calmed—her breathing evened. *How does he do that?*

"There are things that happen in this city that are beyond our control," he said slowly. "And the items that matter...they sometimes show up where we don't expect them. I think they show up where we're meant to be—to tell us where we need to go."

"You're trying to say I'm meant to be at the...plantation?" Then why burn down the shop? She braced her palms against her thighs and pushed herself upright, peering out into the darkness, which suddenly seemed more menacing than it had moments before, the black thick and heavy, like a hood had been pulled over her eyes. Even the moon's gray haze could not penetrate the trees or the scrubby brush in the fields around them. Yet the thrill of dangerous anticipation had softened into some deeper ache, a pleasant throb below her belly button.

He shrugged. "Some places hold on to energy in a way they shouldn't and demons feed off the energy of others—the more they feed, the stronger they become. If we can lure the evil out, give it fewer places to hide, we'll all be safer." He tucked a strand of hair behind her ear and her cheek vibrated with his touch. "You feel things like I do, Chloe."

I knew it. Brandon was special, too.

He offered his hand again. "Come with me."

She reached for him, the scars and calluses on his chilly fingers digging into the flesh of her palm, and followed him through the quiet streets, listening to the keening wind. Where were the birds? Even the katydids had gone silent. Chloe could not tell whether being alone with him pleased her or frightened her—she only knew that her heart was ratcheting up once more, throbbing in her temples. And… demons? He'd said demons, right? "I thought demons needed to like…get inside your body."

"Not all of them."

"So I could be possess—"

"No." But his face contorted as he said it, and he massaged his rib cage. "You'd know." He dropped his hand, kept his eyes on the road.

Victor knew. Realization dawned, bright and awful—Victor really had been possessed, not just influenced by a ghostly presence, but possessed by a demon, infiltrated. And those demons were still after Chloe, even if they hadn't been able to get inside her the way they had with Victor. But they were trying—they were showing up in her nightmares, invading her vision, making her see things that weren't there. Her skull ached, the sheer quantity of thoughts threatening to make her brain explode.

Ahead, the gates that led towards the old plantation glittered darkly in the brilliant white moonlight. Brandon brushed past her up the drive, his cool skin a shock against her sweaty arm, and she ground to a halt on the gravel, trying to regain her train of thought, trying to recall what she needed to do here. But thinking was difficult when the smell of him was invading her nostrils, something sulfuric and musky and delicious and so strong she wanted to bury her face in his neck and inhale him. She inhaled the sticky air instead, heady with cut grass and autumnal decay.

"Would you like some lemonade?"

"Some...what?"

Brandon gestured to the house. "A drink."

She stared at him, certain she'd misunderstood. How could he eat right now? They were being pursued, watched, stalked, and though she knew it should terrify her, light her up with nerves, with fear, the throbbing ache in her chest left no room for any emotion but a frantic yearning to draw him closer.

"I imagine you have some questions. Maybe you'd like the camera back."

"I never want to see that camera again." *That's where the evil lives.* All the hairs on the back of her neck stood. Of course—Victor and Helen had met at the shop, the epicenter of all this. Maybe Victor's camera or the shop itself were portals for whatever demon had possessed Victor and his new bitch girlfriend. And today, Brandon had burned the shop down because he thought it held on to some evil energy that was feeding those demons. *If we can lure the evil out, give it fewer places to hide, we'll all be safer.*

She raised her gaze to the house. But this was where she'd seen Martha, where the camera had shown up—where she was supposed to be. Were the demons who tortured her roaming these halls? *Yes.* She could feel it beneath the sultry air—some malicious force was coming for her, she knew it the same way she knew the moon would vanish with the sunrise. She could take the back way home—two or three miles to her apartment—but was she really willing to walk alone in the middle of the night, knowing she was being pursued by...things not of this world? She'd never seen a car here, so it wasn't like he could drive her home after he made her a fucking sandwich, and being with Brandon at least felt a little safer; maybe they should stick together, at least for the night.

Besides…she didn't want to leave either.

The old oaks were even more ominous against the backdrop of night, the sparsely leaved branches bleached by the moon so they looked like long, bony fingers clawing at the sky. Chloe glanced at the street behind them as they approached the house, staring into the blackness which swallowed their surroundings as if they were in a bubble. The attic window glared at her under the vibrant white of the moon, watching her, watching them, and every nerve ending lit up like tiny fireworks were flitting across her flesh. "Brandon—"

He turned. She met his eyes, the iridescent flakes like magnets, pulling her closer, and then she yanked him to her so forcefully that she lost her air, the throbbing in her chest intensifying when his lips met hers. *No, this is wrong, this is...*

It wasn't wrong. She melted into his arms, grabbing his hand and pulling it between her legs. The brooch heated until it was searing her flesh through the bandage.

What am I doing?

She knew exactly what she was doing. Victor was gone, and this man was special, like she was, she could feel it in his touch, in the way his fingertips teased her over her skirt. They were meant to be. The cool swirled around them as if they were in a tornado of their own making, the energy rolling from his fingertips and lighting her nerves on fire, and then she could see Victor—*I love you, you know*—his brown eyes shining, but there was blood around his lips, and—

Brandon pushed her off him, and she staggered back, stunned. He caught her before she fell, held her at arm's length.

Her face burned with the rejection. "Oh, like you didn't want it too?"

The world around them froze.

Over Brandon's shoulder, in the moonlit grass in front of the porch, stood a tall, thin man, dark skin, eyes glittering below a shock of salt-and-pepper hair. Smoke curled from his pipe as though his beard was on fire. He stared at them a moment longer, then backed up the stairs, through the door, and disappeared inside.

CHAPTER 20

MARTHA ALTON SHEPHERD, FOURTEENTH JULY, 1834

I keep my eyes closed, my inhales even, though my monthly blood seeps through the rags tied about my waist, my body wet and sticky against the sheets. I know Elisha is here, at the foot of my bed, watching. His breathing is raspy and excited, though it may be vexation—can he tell I am not being forthright after all this time? Does he know I am awake? I feel much like a prized hog being fattened for slaughter. For aught I know, I am.

These days he watches me more intently than ever—through the arch as I eat alone in the private dining room, staring from the yard as I go about my chores, even peering into my chambers after I have retired. Perhaps he can sense the deep pain within me, the throb of loneliness so wretched and vital that I fear it may kill me unless I can wall that ache off from my heart. I wish I could speak to him of my sorrow, but I am shy to trust him. He may even prefer me in this state, though I cannot for my life think of a reason for that.

Finally, I hear the clomp of his boots heading toward the door, and the creak of the knob. The *thunk* as he closes me in.

I squeeze my eyes tighter and imagine my father's hands in mine the day he told me of Elisha's proposal, recall the look on his face the day he left me here, his smile filled with such hope for my future. But no, even in my memory, seeing it now, his lips are pressed together, tight like he is worried. And soon that too will vanish from memory—already the edges are fuzzy, faded by the twisted nest of sorrow and emptiness and a deep rage I rarely acknowledge. I am ever ill at ease, like awakening from a dream, knowing the nightmare is over, but still unable to shake off that steel cuff of panic clamped around my heart. And I know not how to calm it.

Perhaps it would be different if I had a confidant in this place, just one other person to break the silence. But not a baby; I do not yearn for that, unlike other women in my position.

Does Elisha want a child? He has yet to touch me, though others have known his touch. I noticed the swell of Hany's belly mere months after we moved onto the plantation, but I was not suspicious then—the slaves are often with child. But then the child came, and it did not bear Hany's dark mahogany hue—he is the taupe of burlap, and there is only one white man here. I wonder if Hany is sharing Elisha's bed at night, while I am in my own room, crying into my pillow. She should have known better—she knows how to make the baby go, herbs that will send it quietly slipping from your body. Maybe she tried the herbs and that was what made the child so bland, so strange. The boy also has a mark on his temple, from a round hole that festered for some time after he was born; it is long healed, but whatever made that mark, whatever scars remain, the boy simply isn't right. Two years old now, he is, with bow lips always drawn up as if he's smelled something awful, and an expression so dull it is plain to see there isn't much inside his head. I caught him with a rat from the cellar last week, its head in a trap, strangling as the boy snapped one bone in its back after another, brows furrowed while he watched the creature struggle. *Snap. Snap. Snap.* I fear someday the child might try such things on a person—he might kill Hany in her sleep. After her wantonness perhaps she deserves such a fate. I do not crave Elisha's touch myself, but the thought that he has cast me aside in favor of another...it is an unimaginable betrayal.

I roll over onto the wetness beneath me, trying to get comfortable, but I cannot bear lying in it any longer. I push aside the bedclothes and stand, change my clothing, and replace the rags between my legs. I've barely heaped all the sheets in a pile when a knock sounds at my door.

I straighten. If Elisha noticed the stains when he was here, he'd have sent someone to clean up for me, but I do not need help, and certainly not from Hany—I do not want her near me, her or her bastard child. We should put him out in the field soon, and if the boy gets hurt, I shall let his wounds fester until his limbs rot off his body. He shan't be of any value then, without his limbs, and we'll have to dispose of him. Maybe I shan't even bury him, just let the coyotes deal with his remains.

The knock comes again, and I cross my arms. The door creaks open.

But it is not Hany on the other side of the door.

I've seen this one before, following Elisha about the grounds—he's Elisha's right hand, his favorite slave, the man always at my husband's beck and call. My shoulders relax some, though not all the way. The slave is older than I, but only by a few years, perhaps twenty-five, if twenty-five tougher years than most—his hands are rough, his skin calloused and scarred. But his brown eyes are flecked with green and he has a smile full of straight white teeth.

My gaze darts to the door. He's not to be up here, in the owner's quarters. It is not permitted.

"Massa Shepherd said you could help." His voice is low, shy, and he is well-spoken, not like the others. And when he meets my gaze—as the field hands do not—his eyes have a kindness to them, though that is surely resignation.

But I pause. Elisha would not let someone dangerous alone with me. He has lost enough wives, all to childbirth. A bad investment, to risk something happening to me—at least that is what I think he would say.

THE JILTED

The man lifts the hem of his tow shirt, and I back away, fearing that he shall attack—everyone says slaves are capable of it. Should I run past him, screaming for help? But then he turns, shows me his back, and I see the burns—shiny, weeping flesh, turned black at the edges where it is trying to heal. Fresh, less than a week old.

"Elisha sent you?" This feels to be a scrape of some complexity—Elisha's sent no one else to my chambers but Hany, and when he's aware medical treatments are needed he performs them himself, in the attic. But this man standing before me, Elisha's most trusted hand of all people... Perhaps Elisha is showing me that he trusts me. Or perhaps he's lost his desire to treat after what happened last week, when I heard screaming from somewhere in the yard—the long, ululating wail of a woman. Elisha came up the lawn soon after, wiping his hands on a handkerchief, fingers stained black in the moonlight. She must have suffered some complication. Perhaps he feels guilty that he could not save her.

"Yes'm. He did send me. But I can go if you like." His eyes are tight, sad—he's in pain. My chest softens; I cannot be so close to his misery and ignore it. I should take him to another room, downstairs where it would not be seen as indecent. But Elisha sent him here—my kit is here. And I realize I've not spoken to another in weeks, though the other slaves have milled around me as they always do. Suddenly I do not want to share him.

I crouch to retrieve my bag from beneath the bed, though my hands shake, and when I return to him, he is stiff, arms at his sides. I notice he has closed the door. That makes my heart quicken—it feels improper—but I ignore that tingle in my chest. *Elisha sent him.* It would be more improper to ignore my husband.

"Hold still," I tell him as I swab the wounds with salve. His skin is soft but fiery under my fingertips. I've touched no one in months either, not since a slave died after I wrapped his wounds, horrendous gashes that looked like a bear attack. But there are no bears here. He is not the first slave to die from infection, and I did try my best, but the guilt roars at me when it's quiet, filling my head with such noise—his howls of pain, the wailing of his wife—that some nights I do not sleep at all.

The slave hisses—a sharp intake of breath—when I apply the salve to the wounds on his lower back, but he remains still, holding his shirt up around his chest even when I release him and step back to wind the cloth across his abdomen. My own hands feel foreign to me. My breathing is shallow until I finish.

I roll what is left of the cotton and replace the kit beneath the bed. "You'll come tomorrow, and I'll add more."

He drops his shirt and turns, and the broad slope of his back is so muscular, so different from the way Elisha's meat sags, that I find I must drag my eyes away.

"Thank you," he says and I like his voice, the way it rumbles in my ears. Perhaps Elisha should not have let him up. I should not be so taken, anticipating tomorrow's visit with such fluttering in my belly.

As he leaves, I almost hope the injury does not heal too quickly.

CHAPTER 21

CHLOE ANDERSON, PRESENT DAY

"There's no one here," Brandon said. They stood in the shadow of the porch, every corner around the exterior of the house so steeped in dark that she could see nothing beyond where the moonlight reached.

"I saw him, Brandon. Some old guy, smoking a pipe." The man who'd been with the psychic earlier. They'd been too far away then for Chloe to see his eyes—and she was confident she'd never seen him up close—but here on the porch, with the silvered moon reflecting off his face, his piercing gaze had been...familiar. *This is so bizarre.* She crossed her arms over her chest, as if covering herself now would somehow erase the fact that she'd just thrown herself at Brandon...and he'd denied her. But she didn't even have it in her to care, not now. Had that pipe-smoking man followed them under cover of night as they'd walked to the plantation? Had he seen Brandon set the fire? She glanced back across the yard, and again at the house. If they fled, he'd surely follow them again, at least until he got what he wanted—men didn't stalk you for no reason. But what *was* his reason?

"The shadows do funny—"

"It wasn't a shadow."

He didn't know shit. Brandon wasn't special after all—

she'd just been making excuses for him the way she always had for Victor. Chloe inhaled sharply, herbal undertones filling her nostrils, maybe residual smoke from the man's pipe—*he's real, I saw him*—and reached up to her clavicle for the brooch. Nothing.

Chloe looked down. The necklace had disappeared along with the gauze, and in their place, a nasty blister the size of a quarter glared angrily at her.

"It wasn't a shadow," she said again, frantically peering out over the driveway. The stones were painted gray by the moonlight, but the landscape was dull, matte, no glint of light off a piece of metal. No sign of the brooch. If that was a portal, if she needed it to send these demons back where they came from…*shit*. Brandon was still staring at her, disbelief clear in the tightness of his mouth. "It was a *person*," she insisted. "Watching us…watching me."

"I'll look." Brandon stepped up to the front door and she followed, the chill air kissing her skin.

"You are not leaving me out here, Brandon." If demons didn't need a vessel to inhabit, they could be anywhere, just waiting to catch her alone so they could drag her to…wherever they'd taken Victor.

Alone.

The door whined open, like the start of a terrible horror movie. She pulled her shirt away from the stinging blister, and the fabric fluttered before it lay flat against her skin as if the material were possessed by the same uneasy energy that had settled in her gut like bad sushi.

They covered the downstairs by moonlight. Every room felt uninhabited before they even walked in; Chloe's breath echoed in her ears and the air tingled with the heavy, poignant emptiness she felt at graveyards. At the kitchen doorway, she braced herself for Martha, or the bearded man from the porch, to pop from behind the archway, but nothing moved in the kitchen either, save the waving shadows of the branches on the floor, dancing in the moonlight.

On their way to the second story, Chloe followed behind Brandon, the back of his shirt fisted in her palm, the old wooden staircase creaking in protest under their shoes. The upstairs landing felt uninhabited too, though here the murky air seemed alive somehow, as if it wanted to fold Chloe into the gloom. And nagging more ferociously, like a blade scraping at her nerve endings, were the doors that lined the hallway to their right, so many doors they seemed to stretch forever into the inky black. Any one of those rooms could hide the pipe-smoking intruder. Or something worse.

Chloe squinted, half expecting to see the bearded man's face emerge, but only formless shadows crouched beside the doorjambs. And the dark to her left was too thick to make out anything besides the somber blackness.

She and Brandon crept down the hall to the right, pausing at the threshold of the first door, listening. *Listening for what?* No sounds but the wind shivering against the windows and the thick groan of their own footsteps on the wood floor. The door opened slowly, the moan of the hinge making her wince, but the noise couldn't be helped. They needed to plow through, lighting this place up like a disco, scaring anything —human or demon—from the dark corners.

Inside the room Chloe ran her hand along the wall for a switch and felt only the smooth coolness of plaster. "Don't you have lights in this place?"

"Not up here."

Of fucking course.

The first room was bleached by the moon, stark shadows creating hard edges on the walls where none should exist. The only furniture was a large wardrobe that glowered at her from the back, near the window. It might have been hiding a sinister intruder had it not been open and overflowing with toys. She stepped farther inside. The floor beneath the window ledge was also covered in plush toys, and along the left wall sat a mountain of stuffed animals—old, new, some with white batting showing through loose seams. Was their voyeur hiding beneath the pile? She kicked it before she could change her mind—*impulsive, girl, that's how the Devil gets you*—but no sound arose, no yelp of pain, no breath but her own, only the gentle *shh* of the toys she'd toppled sliding to the floor. A stuffed rabbit landed on her shoe—threadbare, one eye missing—and behind it tumbled a faded yellow Care Bear with a cartoon sun emblazoned on its soft chest. Her mother had made her watch that show when she was a kid—these toys hadn't come with the house, or at least they weren't original to the plantation like the furniture. The teddy from Helen's house flashed in her mind and goose bumps sprang up on her arms. She pushed the image aside. Maybe that toy at Helen's was somehow meaningful, maybe it wasn't—she sure wasn't walking over there tonight to find out.

"Where did all these come from?" She picked up the Care Bear and the rabbit and looked closer at them. Their fur was matted and thinning—some child had loved them. But that didn't explain why they were collecting dust in this old room. A sudden chill bit at her ankles—from beneath the pile of stuffed animals—and Chloe backed away, turning to the doorway. Brandon was gone. She dropped the toys. "Brandon?"

Chloe rushed out into the hallway, but it was empty. She swallowed hard, tiptoeing down the hall, resisting the urge to shout Brandon's name again lest the bearded man hear her and come after her when she was most vulnerable—when she was alone.

Alone, alone, alone.

The next room held the skeleton of a four-poster bed, with carved wooden spindles reaching almost to the ceiling —no mattress for a trespasser to hide beneath. There was no closet to hide in either, and no wardrobe that might contain an unseen intruder. But every surface here was covered in some treasure. She stepped farther into the room, her heart racing—*What am I doing?*—but she was unable to look away. This place would be any antique lover's dream. Figurines of stone and wood that might have been Aztec shone black in the dim light, some smaller than her palm, others three feet high. An African mask lay on a table in the corner, meticulously carved to look like it had been made from an actual human skull—the size and color were the perfect shade for aged bone. *What if it's real bone?* She turned away, toward an end table that was engraved with vines and flying birds and topped with horse figurines: most glass or ceramic or porcelain, but a few looked like bronze or iron. There were so many items in here she didn't even know where to start. Brandon could make a fortune if he sold them, but they didn't feel like mere antiques—she'd been in plenty of rooms full of old stuff that didn't make her skin crawl. Were some of these portals also?

Portals for demons to come through.

She peered at the bone mask for a beat, then back at the doorway. Where had Brandon gone? Should she keep looking for the pipe-smoking man? With every empty room, each lonely hallway, she grew more certain that the man she'd seen wasn't in the house. She hadn't heard any footsteps on the stairs, and if he'd gone anywhere up here, they'd have seen him, or at least heard him. Was he a demon? Or some kind of…illusionist?

Witch. Like the woman hanged in front of the house.

Outside the room, the hallway seemed suddenly smaller, as if the walls were breathing, constricting and relaxing, along with her. Chloe held her breath, drawing herself up taller, but her back muscles ached. Adrenaline coursed through her. That man probably *was* just another vision—Brandon surely thought she was crazy.

The way I thought Victor was crazy? She shoved the thought aside.

The next room was a library, with old books jammed into tall shelves that covered every wall. Dust motes floated through the air, beams of moonlight and grime muting the colors on the book covers. The floor and draperies appeared fuzzy, too—everything was chalky looking, everything except…

The 19th century desk in the middle of the room was far from dust free, but even in the moonlight Chloe could see the difference in shading near its center, where the dust was thinner. And there, on top of the cleared section, lay a stack of books—journals. Folders. It was like they'd been left out just for her.

The first folder contained old pictures, some photographs, some sketches. She squinted at the grainy black-and-white photos first, images of the Shepherd house—it looked the same now as it had at every point in the last hundred years, right down to the shape of the drive. Even the tree looked frozen in time, watching over the house for centuries like a very old, very devoted guard dog.

Though flipping through the book gave her heart a chance to calm, the images didn't tell Chloe much that she didn't already know. Most sketches were of cotton and corn fields, tons of black workers, and just like online, no likeness of the plantation master. She paused on a photograph of a large group of female slaves, maybe thirty of them, sitting in a row in front of one of the outbuildings. Was one of them the slave who'd been hanged on the front lawn for witchcraft along with the "possessed" child? Maybe that child really had been possessed. She glanced at a short, handwritten memo beneath, numbers of males and females. The plantation had once boasted upwards of nine hundred slaves. Nine. Hundred. People. Perhaps there was a portal here for every one of them.

The next set of photos were of a different plantation, and they appeared older than the photos of the Shepherd house, though they couldn't have been—it wasn't until the early 1840s that this type of photo processing was even available. The plantation house here had white columns, smaller than those at Shepherd's, and the building itself was far more square, simpler, no circular windows or arches; the only bit of architectural interest was the triangular roof just above the front entrance. The slave quarters were visible, very close to the house, like a detached garage—far closer than she'd ever seen in her studies of the period. And scrawled in the corner: "Alton Valley Plantation."

Martha's house.

She wiped the back of her neck. Her hand came away wet.

The next several images showed the interior of the Alton plantation house: high ceilings in the foyer, but the hallways and rooms were smaller than at the Shepherd place. One ancient photograph stuck out: a somber couple standing in what might have been a library, an unfamiliar white man in a black waistcoat, his dark hair going white at the temples, and beside him a pretty blond woman who was probably his wife. Definitely not the girl from the brooch, though these could have been Martha's parents.

Chloe flipped through sketches of the grounds, of slaves picking cotton in the fields, but she paused at the last image, another actual photo taken in front of the Alton house. A black man stood beside a horse, the slave's eyes huge and lifeless. Broken. On the other side of the horse, leading it, stood a brutish white man: shoulders high and tight, face drawn beneath his shock of white hair, like he was annoyed someone was taking his picture. Elisha Shepherd, according to the scrawl in the lower corner. Cold fingers skittered up her spine. That was the man she'd seen behind Martha in her dream, the one with the bloody leather apron. The man she'd seen with Victor. The man she'd dreamed had been in her bed.

Elisha Shepherd had been at the Alton house. But he probably wouldn't have been interacting with Martha unless... Had Martha Alton married Elisha Shepherd? Greg had thought it possible, even if they couldn't prove it without the missing courthouse documents. At the time, marriages were often arranged, girls exchanged for property, holdings, status. She was so *young*, but back then...maybe not too young.

So Chloe had a husband-wife demon team after her. Good times.

She flipped the folder closed and sneezed at the plume of

dust from the table. *Huh.* A loose page sat beneath the folder: a sketch of a grave on one side of a chasm, and a robed man standing at the edge, his arms outstretched. Above the grave, a human form floated—raising a spirit from the dead? And across the bottom of the page in loopy scrawl.

> "We all go back to the root, the sins of the fathers, for eternity. Blood must be repaid in blood."

Nothing else, no instructions for raising a ghost, or summoning a demon, or hints about what those words really meant. The page shook in her hands. *Blood must be repaid in blood.* That didn't sound good, but that sins of the fathers thing couldn't possibly be true—it was her mother's fault her baby sister was dead, and Chloe sure wasn't going to take the blame for that any more than she'd take the blame for Brandon's arson stunt tonight. Or for whatever Victor had done to Leslie. No one could expect her to pay for someone else's crimes.

Chloe jumped when a floorboard creaked behind her. She whirled around, fists up, but it was Brandon, approaching her from the shadowed hallway, his eyes black in the moonshine.

"You scared me." She looked to the doorway behind him as if expecting that someone—or something—was following him. *Nothing there.* "Where the hell did you go?"

"I was looking around, checking the other rooms. I didn't find anything...but the camera's gone." But Brandon didn't look surprised—he had the expression of someone who'd ordered a tuna sandwich and gotten exactly what they anticipated.

"Does that happen often? Things going missing?" *Things. And people.*

"Sometimes. Though items show up just as often. Like the toys in the other room."

"Why do you think that is?" Did he believe they were

portals, too? Why else would he keep them? And why could he believe that toys just appeared out of nowhere but not trust that she'd seen a bearded man on the porch?

Again he shrugged, but now his face was pained, like... like he might throw up. What was he hiding? Was he sick? "I think... I don't really know. But I think there's some kind of energy field here, dark, demonic, like the plantation, the city even, is—"

"—special," she said.

"—cursed," he said at the same time.

Cursed. Her body wasn't possessed—this place was just fucked up. She touched the blister on her chest and winced. Brandon's gaze locked on hers, and her heart rate climbed again as she averted her eyes and peered into the dark corners, then out the window at the moonlit sky.

Finally, Brandon cleared his throat and gestured to the books on the desk. "I see you found the files," he said. "After you left last time, I decided to do a bit of searching. That's what I came up with."

She turned away from the window. "So Martha married your ancestor, then? Elisha Shepherd?"

He shrugged.

"And this..." She gestured to the picture on the table, the man beside the grave, and the spirit floating above. *We all go back to the root, the sins of the fathers, for eternity.* "What's this about? It says that blood has to be repaid—"

"That's...not mine."

But there was no dust on that page, though grime saturated every other surface. She stared at Brandon, and her back tensed. She didn't know him at all. Maybe he and the mystery intruder were friends. Maybe they'd summoned the demons together.

Brandon frowned. Her chest went tight, and this time his nearness did not quell it. She glanced once again at the drawing, at the spirit hovering over the grave, but whirled back at the sound of his footsteps. Moonlight streaked his brow, and his face had twisted into a grimace. Fear crawled up Chloe's spine. "Brandon? Are you okay?"

"I...yeah." He hunched over, clutching his gut.

She thought of the brooch, how she'd worn it secretly and it had blistered her, how she'd been hurting but hadn't said anything. What secrets was Brandon hiding now? She felt compelled to reach for him, put a supportive hand under his elbow and tell him, *Me too, we're in this together*, and then she could no longer smell the dust motes, only the musky scent of his skin mingling with the dread that had been seeping from her pores all night. *No, Chloe. No.* He'd already rejected her once. And also...the demons.

Brandon straightened, but this time she walked away from him, peering out the window, hands fisted at her sides. In the past, she'd have seen it as romantic, the way the grass shimmered in the moonlight, how the shiny leaves glistened as they danced under the stars. Even the shadows on the lawn might have been amorous as they swayed back and forth. But tonight, the glittering leaves looked like unshed tears, and the stark shadows were knives, ready to cut. The lawn and everything on it squirmed with the energy of a garbage bin behind the dog shelter after kill day. Maggots, and buzzing insects, and fresh death.

She wasn't going home tonight. That yard, that lawn—unseen horrors hid there, and no way was she going to risk even passing by it. The oak wasn't even reaching for the sky, towards the light, like any normal plant would—it was seeking the earth, slithering into it with every thick, gnarled branch.

Chloe returned to the table where Brandon still stared down at the sketch, his face tight. He did not move when she reached for the page with the summoner and touched it, tracing the letters, her fingers tingling, the blister on her chest throbbing. *Blood must be repaid in blood.* She turned it over. And there, on the back in tiny lettering:

"Cast thee out," from the lips of the chosen,

> the portal in hand as you speak.
> Once their name from your lips to banish,
> and thrice at a whisper to keep.

Her breath caught. Were these...instructions? You needed to hold the demon's portal and then say their name to get rid of them? And if you wanted to bring a demon here...whisper their name three times. She pulled her hand back, slowly, her fingers stinging, but her brain was on fire with a *knowing*, a certainty that she could not refute. The man she'd seen standing on the porch wasn't an illusionist or a witch—he was here, somewhere, summoning ghosts. Summoning... demons.

And Brandon had helped him.

CHAPTER 22

CHLOE ANDERSON, PRESENT DAY

When Chloe awoke it was still dark, the leaded glass of the windows splashing ribbons of moonlight onto the floor, inviting somehow, as if the light were beckoning her. She'd slept in Brandon's room—alone—with a dresser pushed in front of the door in case Brandon was a complete maniac. Strange, though—it was the first time in weeks she hadn't had some bloody nightmare, which should have been good news, but now unease mingled with the calming moon and morphed into a thinly veiled déjà vu, a nagging sensation that she'd missed something critical—seen something she could not remember.

She reached an arm out beside her, seeking heat, seeking perhaps the source of her disquiet, as if she'd find Elisha Shepherd in his leather apron lying alongside her again. The bed was cool and empty. But something called her, though not with words or a cry—it came from outside, the yearning *shh, shh* of wind trying to get through the glass...or trying to persuade her to come out.

The wind calmed.

And still something called her.

She crept from the bed, pulling the sheets around herself. The floor was positively frigid, and she shuddered as the cold crept through her ankles, up the backs of her legs and trilled along her spine like bits of sleet. She pulled the blanket tighter around her shoulders. Her toes were numb.

I should put my shoes on, walk home, get ready for work. She was still wearing her clothes from the night before. But the chill pulsed through her veins like a drug, and the scents of thick leather, old lacquer, and hidden dust moved slowly through her sinuses and into her bloodstream, massaging all the little places she couldn't touch. It was the smell of things that were real, substantial, safe—the smell of things that lasted.

Outside, the front lawn spread toward the towering oaks that stood watch over the house, the driveway creeping away like a road to nowhere in the misty dark. The moonlight shimmered on the grass and bleached the stones in the drive —a painting done in shades of ash. But despite the silvered moon, the blackness around the trees was too thick to make out much beyond the lines of the branches.

Shh, shh.

She spun to the dresser she'd moved in front of the door, convinced she'd see long, thin claws snaking between the door and the jamb as the demons tried to push their way inside—but the dresser was still there, and though she strained her eyes and peered into the inky corners, she could see nothing in the room with her. But the hairs on her neck rose. And as she turned back to the window, she caught movement from the corner of her eye, something the size of a large dog—but it wasn't a dog—shooting from the porch toward the oaks, skin shimmering gray and wet in the moonlight. It happened too quickly for Chloe to make out the animal's features, but the way it moved...it was almost like a snake, or a lizard, slinking instead of running. She drew her gaze to the side lawn and her pulse stilled in her throat.

Martha. The girl stood close to the house, wearing the fog like a burial shroud. She appeared to be searching for something, her head pivoting left and right—maybe looking for the animal. Then she took off across the lawn, past the trees where the creature had disappeared, and ran toward the backyard, blonde curls flying behind her, whole and unharmed, her dress clean and yellow and untorn. Before Chloe could wonder what that meant, the sound came again —*shh, shh*—and now she felt it in her bones instead of hearing it at all. It was calling her—*Martha* was calling her.

Her heart shuddered back to life, fear swelling in her chest. This might be important, the key to figuring out this mystery, to figuring out how to make it stop, but she'd be an idiot to face a demon alone. That's what the girl was, right? The floor was warmer under her toes as she made her way to the door and pulled the dresser aside, its wooden legs creaking. "Brandon?"

The black in the hallway was so thick he could have been standing mere feet away and she'd never have seen him. She felt her way from the doorway to the landing, listening for the sound of footsteps, the tap of someone seeking her out as she was seeking them, but she heard only the wind outside, louder than the *shh, shh* that had woken her, and more insistent, as if in the time it had taken her to navigate to the stairway, something critical had happened and angered the breeze. Something she should have stopped.

Something was wrong, something...

A pang of guilt stabbed her belly, so sudden and unexpected that she cried out, a sob catching in her throat. Her heart was breaking, but not just with the pain of loss—now the throbbing ache of grief was coupled with the sharper, searing sting of remorse, and then her déjà vu blossomed into realization: it was her fault Leslie was dead. She should have known what Victor was capable of, should have known he was possessed, should have believed him. She should have stopped him. That's why the demons were after her.

Blood must be repaid in blood.

A sound vibrated against her eardrum, a hollow grinding noise like a handsaw carving through bone. It was difficult to tell whether it came from above her, or back down that infinite hallway—the sound echoed like the sea in a conch shell, at once there, and nowhere. The hollowness in her heart spread until she couldn't feel her legs beneath her anymore. She stepped back toward the hall, intent on finding Brandon.

Then someone screamed, a man, she thought, but she couldn't be sure—the only thing she knew for certain was that this was not the scream of someone in need of assistance, not just a cry for help. This was a long, low howl of sheer terror, one that ended in the crackling sob of a person desperate to die. Someone being tortured. Someone already beyond saving. Had the pipe-smoking man she'd seen last night attacked Brandon? Was that his cry she heard?

The scream came again—yes, definitely above her—and this time she ran, no longer hesitant, feeling her way down the stairs, sweat dripping from her hairline and over her temples as she clung to the railing, running for the exit, for the evil was here, inside the house. She looked back at the upper landing every few seconds, terrified that some malevolent, torturous thing would emerge from the blackness and seek her out, teeth gleaming in the moonlight, claws dripping someone else's blood. The screams seemed to get louder as she descended, surrounding her with a chorus of terrified shrieking, not just one, but many men, many women, many children.

Chloe, you're going to let it happen again.

She was running away—running away again. But her legs would not stop. Chloe stumbled off the bottom step and toward the front door, arms outstretched, the screaming so loud now she could not hear her own footsteps, could not think, could not even breathe.

The door slammed behind her. And yet the screams followed her as she flew from the house and into the moonlit night, her bare toes catching on the cracked steps, the jagged stone slicing the pads of her feet, though the stairs had been smooth and pristine yesterday, hadn't they? When she reached the drive, the rocks cut harder, every step piercing her skin so that she was surely leaving bloody prints in her wake. But the wails had finally begun to fade into the background, sucked into the vortex of the house as if the brick and mortar were eating them. Only a faint sobbing now floated above the thin rustling of the grass. The attic window was dark, and there was nothing ominous in the trees, just low hanging wisps of fog, though she could almost imagine an evil eye in the clouds over the oak. Her skin crawled. Something was watching her.

"Have mercy, have mercy!" The scream came from the direction of the house, and when she looked up again, a feeble light shimmered in the attic window, like someone had lit a candle. Someone *was* there. Someone vile. And she'd be taken next if she didn't get out of there, and fast.

Chloe turned and ran down the driveway, toward the overhanging trees, for any property beyond these cursed acres was surely less dangerous. She clapped her hands over her ears to drown out the shrieks that were gaining volume even as she put more distance between herself and the house. *You're failing them, Chloe. You're leaving them behind.*

Her foot caught on a root at the edge of the drive—*Fuck!*—and she tumbled, arms windmilling, landing hard on her knees beside the hulking oak—the hanging tree. She tried to stand, but stumbled again. Her ankle was stuck in an enormous root that had somehow gotten twisted around her foot, like gnarled fingers anchoring her to the dirt. The ground beneath her shuddered, though not like a shudder from her own terrified body—it was as if the earth itself had hold of its quarry and was sighing with contentment. The screams wailed on.

The moon emerged from the amorphous clouds, a glowing orb, and Chloe was suddenly convinced that this was the eye she'd felt watching her when she'd escaped from the house. Now it shone through the branches, painting black lacework over her skin, as if the twigs had leapt from the leafy boughs to scrape at her very flesh.

For one glorious moment, the world stilled, the screams silenced. No noise from inside the house or around it, no movement in the branches. Nothing from the moon or the keening wind—even the rustle of the grass had gone mute.

And then... Martha, springing across the lawn from the slave quarters, her porcelain pale face intact, her dress unstained, all her organs inside her body. And Leslie was with her, her feet flying over the grass.

Chloe's breath caught—*She's alive.* She wrenched her ankle again but it remained stuck, ensnared in the roots. She screamed Leslie's name, and the girl only looked back and glared, the way she had before Chloe and Victor had moved in together, refusing to talk to Chloe, crying when Chloe tried to hug her, begging her dad not to go out with Chloe until one night he'd actually stayed home despite Chloe's protests, saying they needed to take it easy.

Take it easy? They were supposed to be a family.

"Leslie, where's your dad? Where—"

Leslie leapt up the steps. Chloe jerked at her leg again, yanking so hard she thought she'd snap the bones in her ankle, but the oak's roots did not falter. Leslie disappeared into the house. Martha climbed the steps after her, but more slowly, and then turned on the top step, staring right at Chloe. "Come to me," Martha hissed, and Chloe didn't know how she could hear the girl from so far away, but she could. She struggled against the root, the flesh around her leg already slippery with blood. *I'm coming.* This girl wasn't trying to hurt her, she was trying to help Leslie, save Leslie—maybe she was trying to save Chloe too.

Martha raised her arm and pointed at the tree. "Come to me." And then she vanished through the front door after Leslie.

The crunch of gravel echoed at Chloe's back, like the grinding shift of tectonic plates, and she twisted to peer behind her, still wrenching at her leg. But the low branches of the oak hid half the world from view—she could see nothing save for the gnarled bark, the crooked roots obscured by dirt and shadow. The wood around her leg held.

Another crunch of gravel rang though the night, and this

came from somewhere on the drive—footsteps?—just beyond her line of sight. She stopped breathing. Though she could not see whatever lurked there, she could feel it, a pulsing cold that wormed around her heart and throbbed jaggedly as if someone had wrapped her chest in barbed wire. Another miserable howl rang from inside the house as a white man emerged from the shadow of the trees, wearing the attire of another time: a long, black suit jacket, cinched at the waist, and a white shirt with a collar so high it might as well have been a turtleneck. He carried what looked like an old medical bag. *Elisha Shepherd*. Chloe froze, but Elisha did not turn her way, just walked past the trees and over the lawn toward the outbuildings. Was he...a doctor? While it wouldn't have been common practice, doctors in the 1800s did sometimes wear aprons, especially for amputations.

Where is Brandon? She peered back toward the house. The windows no longer reflected the moonlight—they were black and vacant, as if the glass had been broken out. And something was running down the brick, something viscous and dark, dribbling down the columns as if the eaves were crying tears of blood.

Then the world came to life again, and the screams from inside the house intensified even as her lungs remained clamped shut. But it was only one wail this time, not numerous victims and she could swear she recognized the voice. *Martha*. The girl was dying inside that house, someone was killing her right now—the slaves maybe, like Greg said. Why couldn't Elisha hear it? But he was gone, somewhere in the backyard—he would be too late to save her.

Chloe finally inhaled, gasping, the air thick and hot around her. She yanked at her ankle—*I'm coming, I'm coming*—and her foot pulsed with a sharp pain like she'd barked her shin. She looked down. Three other, smaller, branches were wrapped around the upper part of her calf, so fully ensnaring her that Chloe could almost believe the tree had sent fresh growth winding around her—shackles made from wooden serpents. She pulled again, tearing at the branches on her calf, but it was like fighting with a table leg—the wood was stronger than she was. Martha's shrieks echoed in her ears. Chloe pulled harder. *She's dying, she's dying, this is what I'm supposed to prevent.* The girl was up there, being tortured by whatever evil lurked on this plantation. Martha wasn't the demon—she was trying to escape the demon just like Chloe.

Again Chloe yanked at her leg, grinding her teeth. *Fuck, let go!* Finally, her foot moved, and the branches around her calf cracked with a long, low *creeeeaaaak*, as if the wood were crying right along with the ungodly wails still roaring from the house. Tears sprung into her eyes as the branch flayed the skin off her calf and raked over her ankle down to the bone. But she was free.

Chloe pressed herself to standing, and the earth undulated beneath her, rolling like a wave of soil, casting her back to the ground. And then something else was moving, shifting —the tree. Her eyes were lying to her, everything she was seeing was a lie—this had to be a dream or another vision. One of the tree's knotty roots broke free from its earthly prison in a shower of dirt and snaked toward her. As that one gained speed, another behind it burst out the same way, and then a few feet beyond it, still another wrenched itself loose, and then—

It couldn't possibly be, but it was. The branches were coming alive, and already one thin limb had coiled itself around her waist, gripping so hard her breath left her again —her ribs ached, sharply, as if they might snap. Skin tore from her knees as she wrenched the branch from her middle, easier this time, and pulled herself free, and then she was running over the drive toward the main house, toward the screaming girl—*If I get there in time, I can help her and all this will stop.* But she ground to a halt at the edge of the drive. Elisha Shepherd stood on the lawn halfway between the tree and the porch, as if waiting for her. Their eyes locked, and his gaze dropped to her ankle.

"I can make it stop. The pain." His voice sent a tide of coolness rising from groin to clavicle, stifling the panic in her chest. He was a doctor—that was his job, to take away the pain. And...the screams had stopped. Everything had gone still and silent. *Dead.* She'd failed Martha. She'd failed Victor. She'd failed Leslie too, and the heat rose again, cloaking her heart in flames as she met Elisha's disappointed gaze—the same look her grandfather had always given her. It had been Elisha's job to take Martha's pain, and he'd failed, too; he was trying to make amends. Trying to help someone else, maybe trying to find a way to save the girl in the afterlife.

"I'm sorry," she whispered, her voice trembling. *You ain't right, girl. We'll fix you up, get you right with God.* It was true, what Grandpa had said—she wasn't special. "I'm sorry, I'm so sorry, I tried, I tried!"

She ran for him, sobbing—*What am I doing, what am I thinking?*—but her feet had a mind of their own, and... She paused, and looked down. Her ankle was no longer bleeding.

He'd healed her. He'd saved her from being a victim inside that house.

Elisha Shepherd smiled and opened his arms to her. The fear in her chest vanished, replaced with the cool, easy peace of a winter morning. Love. *Love.* He forgave her, even though she'd screwed up.

Thirty feet. Twenty. But as she closed the gap, the ground beneath her feet warmed too, blistering the pads of her toes, and the remainder of Elisha's chill evaporated like steam in the sudden broiling heat. Because Elisha Shepherd was no longer alone.

Oh no.

The man with the pipe stepped beside Elisha Shepherd, then in front of the stocky plantation owner, but the men did not acknowledge one another—they were both so focused on her it was as if they were unaware of the other's presence. She tried to stop herself, but too late, and her forward momentum threw her against the bearded stranger's spindly chest, smoke enshrouding her face. "Fight," he whispered through the smog. "*Fight.*"

She pushed herself off him, looking for Elisha, her heart

frantic. The peace she'd felt moments before was gone, and she'd do anything to get it back, anything—she didn't want to hurt anymore, didn't want to be alone. *I can take away the pain.* But Elisha Shepherd had vanished.

"Help me. Please." Was she talking to this man or to Elisha Shepherd or to God? Was there anyone who could help her? Bile rose in her throat. She raised her eyes to the moon and saw Leslie's dead, mottled face, Martha's bloody teeth. "I'm sorry, I'm so sorry."

Beneath her, the earth had cooled. She blinked and lowered her gaze. To her left, the stairs were no longer cracked or broken, and the clean white columns gleamed in the moonlight—no tears of blood running down its facade. The scrawny black man with the pipe and the salt and pepper beard remained, gold flakes in his eyes sparkling even in the shadows beneath the house.

"Help, please." Tears streamed down her cheeks. "Help."

"Blood," the man whispered. "Your blood is tainted, too."

CHAPTER 23

ABRAM SHEPHERD, PRESENT DAY

Every beep of the hospital monitor barks like a drumroll counting down the swing of an executioner's axe. Those blips and whirs are supposed to represent life, but really they remind us how fragile life is, how close each of us is to that beep slowing until it's one long, droning note, signaling the end.

Auditory anticipation—the anticipation of death. And it feels especially significant in the middle of the night, when the rest of the world is hushed and still.

"You should have taken a different path, my friend," I whisper to the man in the bed. They have taken the bull ring from between his nostrils—there are a few other little holes in his face and ears where piercings presumably once went, ostentatious to be sure, but it's much too late to worry about fashion. He's come a long way since he left Induced Psychosis, and not for the better. Not toward The Light, no sir. His chart is riddled with treatment for old wounds, abuse maybe, though the files say he always denied it. Because, of course he would. No one wants to admit to that sort of thing. And I know how the demon attacked him. How it hurt him.

Has Chloe figured it out yet? Has she identified the

THE JILTED

demon that broke her fiancé, that turned him into a shell of the man she'd once loved?

"A much different path," I say, louder this time. His eyelids do not so much as flutter, and though the beep of his monitor stays strong, I know he cannot hear me. He cannot hear anything, could not even if he were awake, not with the gauze wrapped around his skull.

I PEER AT HIS CHEST, where the outlines of the bandages show through the paper-thin gown. The police probably thought they could save the girl by opening fire on him, but it was too late for her. Much too late. That poor baby. Leslie was her name, and I feel like that's critical for me to remember, as if my remembering will make her premature death any less atrocious.

"Who are you?"

I turn at the sound of a woman's voice, and have to direct my gaze downward. She's in a wheelchair. She is pretty, even with the dark circles under her eyes: frizzy brown hair that hangs to her shoulders, eyes green like the sea, a wide, full mouth. She's wearing a long black dress that just covers her feet where they sit on the wheelchair's rests. She looks so innocent, but I know she's far from it. I know by the way she wrings her hands—by her guilt.

"A friend of the family," I say. But if Victor were to wake up now, he'd deny it—this man will not recognize me when he sees me again.

They never do.

She pushes herself closer to me, the wheels squeaking, perhaps in protest of the fact that they must move her forward through this awfulness. "I'm his ex-wife—the only family he has. I'd think I'd know you."

She is the first to be curious about who I am. No one else seems to care that I am holing up with a braindead ex-rocker who is only clinging to life through the miracle of modern science. Everyone who works here is waiting for him to die so someone else can use his bed. Maybe someone with better insurance. Someone worth more. Someone who still has a chance. He's been an anomaly the entire time he's been here—no one should have remained alive after suffering such grievous wounds.

I extend my hand. "I'm sorry—I'm just a friend, but I wanted to sit with him." The lie slides out easily. She does not flinch at it, does not recognize the deception.

"No no, I'm sorry, please stay." Her voice is monotone, but she takes my hand, and her thin fingers are fiercely hot. "I'm Stephanie. I can come back later."

Stephanie. *The mother.* I've been sitting here off and on for weeks listening to the nurses whisper, listening to the police ask their questions, the detectives speaking in low tones—Victor had been a little crazy in life, were the doctors sure he wouldn't wake up and hurt someone? The doctors said he wouldn't, not because they believed he was nonviolent, but because they knew he wasn't ever getting up again. God, that poor girl, poor little Leslie. I'll pray for her later, though she does not need it. This man, though…he's tainted. There is a special place in Hell for someone who puts a child in harm's way, and no amount of praying will fix that for him now.

"I'm happy to step out so you can spend some time with him," I say, but she shakes her head.

"No, I'll come back." She turns to the bed. "I'm sorry." Her voice cracks on the last word. Her apology isn't meant for me. She still loves him, after everything, probably will for eternity, which is why she's here—she needs to profess it. Loving him was her most egregious sin, and will be part of her penance, now and forever. Every day she will suffer for it. Because no matter how sick he was, no matter how volatile he became, she would have taken him back, for she remembers him before, when he used to be happy, when he used to be sane, before the demon attached itself to him—that's who she still sees when she closes her eyes. Her sin was

THE JILTED

not acknowledging what he had become. And now it is too late for her, for Leslie—for Victor, too.

I turn to the door—it's half open. She's gone.

I set the camera on the bed by Victor's thigh, and still he does not stir, though a part of me almost expects him to acknowledge it. We each possess an item of particular significance; one that represents who we are, that lets us pool our energy into it—an item to collect our past and all its rights and wrongs within it like a treasure, and then guide us past this plane and on to the next. Some people are lucky enough to have their item be another human. But not Victor. I draw his hand to the controls and use his finger to flick the shutter open. The red light goes on. And I wait. I've charged the battery as fully as I can, and the power should last for hours, perhaps a day. But it will not take that long.

I lean closer, thinking perhaps I will be able to smell the death on him already, but I inhale only the antiseptic haze of rubbing alcohol.

"The Dark almost took Chloe," I say softly. "We may need this man later." He has a purpose there, in that other place—his life here is over. And if Chloe fails...

From the corner of my eye, I see Martha emerge from behind the curtain at the back of the room. The front of her yellow dress is soaked in blood, and every step leaves crimson footprints on the white tile. Martha is the only color in here. She closes her eyes and nods, and then I see Victor as he was that night, eyes wide with panic, blood seeping from the wounds in his chest, the back of his head behind the ear blown away, leaving a gaping, craggy hole.

I put my hands above his forehead, my rings heating, and the iron, the gunpowder, the rotten meat stink fill me. And I whisper. And whisper. And whisper thrice. An act which would not be allowed, were I a man of the cloth—it is serendipitous, perhaps, that I left. Being a priest would not have saved me, but this, this...

How odd that the only thing that might lead me to salvation requires divergence from a faith I'd once held so dear.

Victor's finger twitches against the camera's shutter, only the tiniest twitch, but it's there.

Beeeeeeeeeeeeeeeeeeeeeeeep.

I draw my eyes to the monitor, see the line has flattened at last. It is morbid, perhaps, the relief that courses through me, but we are all just seeking an end instead of living. In this room, the inflectionless drone is the music of sweet completion.

I haul myself from my seat as the nurses rush in to flank the bed, checking vitals, retrieving paddles. They know he is gone, and though he has tried to take his own life a number of times, he does not have a Do Not Resuscitate order in his chart. They will do their best, though they know they aren't really saving him for any kind of life. No matter who you are, or what you deserve, they will help you, indeed they will. That is their job.

It is not mine.

A nurse with rich brown skin races around the far side of the bed where Martha stands in her puddle. Martha does not move to let her pass, but she does not need to—the woman steps through her without knowing. She does not feel sudden gooseflesh, or a prickle of wrongness on her neck—she is one of the good ones. She will find her item, the thing that holds her truth, simply seek it out, and pass through cleanly. Easily. And why wouldn't it be easy for her? She has nothing to fear.

I flick the camera's shutter closed on my way out.

CHAPTER 24

CHLOE ANDERSON, PRESENT DAY

Chloe awoke in the dark, stretching, touching the pillow beside her and finding it empty. She opened her eyes. And bolted upright, heart in her throat.

It wasn't that there was anything amiss in the room itself, it was that it was the wrong room. At Brandon's house, the window let in the silver moonshine, but here the only window was covered with Victor's blackout curtains, the ones he'd used when he was being a lazy fuck, sleeping through the day—only a thin band of light shone through the tear in the center, from the time she'd yanked them down. Victor's pillow lay beside her, uglier than it had been yesterday. She grabbed it and threw it across the room, watching the sunlight stream in when it struck the shade. The curtains fell back into place, and the darkness returned.

Chloe leaned back against the headboard, chewing on her cheek, trying not to let the fear take root. She'd been clawing at the pipe-smoking stranger in the moonlit yard at the plantation. She'd been trapped by the serpentine roots of the old oak. But if those memories were real, she'd have injuries to prove it. She grabbed her ankle—flesh intact, no gouges—then checked the soles of her feet, but there were no slices in the pads, no injuries at all from knee to heel, just smooth, pale skin, the same way the blister on her chest had disappeared the other night. Her chest was clear, too. Had she healed overnight, or had the wounds not happened in the first place? And... *Holy shit, I saw Leslie.* But she couldn't make sense of that, couldn't make sense of anything—it was as if the dream world and the real world had all been hacked into pieces and were shuffled together in a way she didn't understand.

Chloe dropped her foot, breathing deeply. She was still looking for normal answers to a situation that didn't follow ordinary rules—what had Brandon told her last night? *Too much blood's been spilled here, far too much for logical answers. There are things that happen in that house that are beyond our control.* Beyond their control was right—she felt entirely out of control, vulnerable. But Martha and Elisha Shepherd were vulnerable too. They'd been there last night, sad, desperate, and Martha had been screaming from inside the house somewhere. Neither had come after her, neither had tried to harm her—not even when they'd seen her tangled and defenseless in the tree roots. They weren't the demons. They needed her to help them. So what demon were they running from and how was she supposed to get rid of it? Had the bearded man summoned something else, or was he himself the source of the evil?

Her legs shook as she padded down the hall toward the bathroom. *Blood must be repaid in blood.* Something about those words prodded a little spot at the base of her brain and stuck there like thorns of apprehension she couldn't expel. *Your blood is tainted, too.* The man with the pipe had said that, and she definitely *felt* tainted—even her skin felt dirty, sticky, though she hadn't done anything wrong. She didn't deserve this. Victor had, but...the demon had control over him. The demon had made him do horrible things.

And it wasn't going to get inside her.

Chloe turned on the water in the tub and stared at herself in the mirror as the room filled with steam. Her chin vanished into the fog. Then her nose. And as her eyes finally disappeared into the mist she let her gaze stray to the photo of Victor and Leslie on the shelf—her finger was already on it, tracing, tracing, the glass warming with the heat of her hand and the steam. One drip sluiced down the center of the glass and settled on the lower rim of the frame. And then the steam closed over the photo, blotting out Victor and Leslie altogether. She put her thumb over Victor's face, watched him reemerge, and frowned. Then she dropped the frame into the sink and winced at the bright clang of shattering glass. Tears smarted in her eyes. Her stomach twisted. What was she thinking? What had she done? She'd let Victor fuck up their lives. She'd watched Brandon, a man she hardly knew, set fire to her place of employment, to the place that was hiding answers about Martha. Then she'd gone home with him, as if she'd been in on it all along—at least that's what the police would think. But the cops were the least of her problems.

God, please tell me what to do now.

She swallowed her tears and sank beneath the water's surface, letting the hot liquid invade her nostrils, her ears. Blocking out the world. The water closed over her head like a tomb and she relished the pressure, gritting her teeth against the heat, forcing herself to remain under the surface. Her chest lit up with pain, as though someone was trying to drive a spike through her breastbone, but she deserved it, that misery. *I'm sorry, Victor. I should have done things differently, should have tried harder.* But Victor had done this, ultimately, even if she should have listened to him, should have foreseen it.

Thunk.

She stilled.

Thunk.

The noise was distant—it wasn't coming from the tub. She waited, straining her ears through the water for another bump, a drip, but...nothing. Her lungs burned. Hot liquid stung her corneas, but she opened her eyes, slowly, slowly, and the white ceiling came into focus, not so much as a ripple in the watery film between. And then a man's face peered over the edge of the tub—*Victor!* She tried to sit up, but the water seemed to have solidified around her, pinning her in place. Victor hovered above her, Victor, with his wild, disheveled mop of dark hair, his deep brown eyes, his...red scarf. *The* scarf. And his mouth...his lips twitched as if they could no longer remain closed, finally parting, and as she lay immobile beneath the water, drowning, a long, slow waterfall of gore slid from between his lips and into the tub, hitting the water and dispersing, obscuring her vision with red.

"Fight!"

She didn't know who uttered the word, but she heard it, deep and urgent, and she shot to the surface, sputtering and gasping hungry breaths into her aching lungs, her fingers tangling in the scarf. The moment she touched the fabric, she could smell the rusty tang in the air too, feel the stickiness of it cloying in the back of her throat. Her fingers twisted in the material and she tugged, pulling him down to her, because in that moment there was no more anger, only relief that he was finally home, it was over, he loved her, things would be okay now, she wasn't alone anymore.

"Victor, baby, I'm sorry, I'm so sorry."

He smiled, face inches from hers, lips still red with blood.

Oh, thank you, God, thank you. They'd get him to the hospital, everything would be fine.

Chloe smiled back at him, but froze as he raised a knife from beneath the outer lip of the tub, and drove it into his own forearm—

She screamed and scrambled to the back of the tub, trying to get her feet beneath her, but by the time she had righted herself, Victor was gone. She was alone.

But the water in the tub was still pink. She sat in the bathtub, shivering, dripping, staring at the door, straining her ears for anything that might indicate another presence in the apartment, but the only sound was the click and whoosh of the air conditioning, the *tick, tick, tick* of the water from the edge of the tub to the tile, and her own frantic breathing. She swallowed over the lump in her throat. And when she raised her hand through the dissipating mess, a long, thin string of mucusy gore clung to her fingers, gelatinous and maroon and viscous, like a crimson tapeworm.

Off, get it off! She skittered from the tub so quickly she almost fell over the edge. The doorway wavered and her heart rate exploded, her entire body trembling as she waited for another vision to emerge, a demon, something that, this time, would surely drag her screaming to her death. *Please, no, not again.*

She blinked hard, and the bathroom solidified.

Tears in her eyes, Chloe looked back at the filthy water. Her skin was still slick with Victor's blood. The towel hook snapped from the wall and clattered against the floor as she scrubbed the blood from her hand, attacking the drips that had collected on her legs and—she stopped, panting. The towel was clean. She was clean. But grief tugged at her, weighing her body down. Though she couldn't verify whether the spindly bearded man was a vision or a stalker, the other figures in her visions—Martha and Elisha Shepherd—had died decades before. Leslie was dead also, with those blue lips. Now she'd seen Victor with blood pouring from his mouth—was he dead too, then? *Of course he is.* Maybe she'd already known it—that's what the horrid, crackling electricity from the photos was trying to tell her. She wasn't fighting for a Goddamn relationship anymore, or even for his life—she was fighting for her mind, for her soul.

Her stomach lurched, and she lunged at the sink, vomiting bile and something gray she didn't remember eating. Her stomach heaved again and she gripped the edges of the sink so hard her palms ached, her gut trying to force the horribleness from her body. But this purging was no help for her brain, where thoughts raced about like snowflakes in a winter storm—every time she tried to get hold of one, it melted before she could examine it. Her stomach cramped again, then settled.

I have to make this stop.

She rinsed her mouth, trying to slow her heart. Last night she'd been ready to blame Brandon for summoning demons, but he wouldn't have burned down the shop to get rid of them if he'd brought them here. Brandon had tried, but he'd been wrong about the place...or maybe he'd been right about the store being a portal and wrong about the technique. Either way, it hadn't worked, because though the shop was gone, the horrible energy lingered, as powerful as ever. And it *was* powerful. Vicious. Martha and Elisha Shepherd were running from this greater horror, maybe the same one that was after her. Was their demon the same demon who had possessed Victor, who had forced him to take Leslie's life? But if that were the case...

Chloe straightened. Was the demon *here*, in this apartment? She thought she would have felt the malicious energy within these walls before Victor left—during the time he'd claimed he was being possessed—but she'd been trained to ignore her intuition, the energy in the air, her entire life. She was listening to her instincts now, though...so what *was* she looking for? A demon needed...a portal. If she could feel her way through this place, if she could find the portal the spirit was using, sense its energy, maybe she could banish the demon for good. And though she'd found a million different instructions online for banishing a demon, the words she'd seen at Brandon's, scrawled on the picture of the man raising a spirit, felt like her best bet. Hold the portal, say their name once, right? She just...needed the name. *Fuck.*

Her fingertips were numb as she tucked the towel tighter over her breasts and opened the door to the hallway. On her way to her bedroom, the pads of her feet were neither hot nor cold—she felt no tingling anywhere on her skin. Numb. Disconcerting when her entire goal was to *feel* the place out. The bed looked the same as always, Victor's pillow still lying on the floor beneath the window where she'd tossed it. She grabbed her pillow—nothing beneath. The comforter came next, then the sheets, until all of it was a pile on the floor. Normal.

What did she think she would find in the sheets? A severed head for the demon to emerge from? She sighed and checked under the mattress anyway, then moved on to the furniture. She opened the dresser drawers as she'd done at Helen's—though less frantically—rifling through clothing, feeling for anything amiss, but there was no tingle, no vibration, no static coursing through her palms, nothing. Victor's T-shirts were next, then the top dresser drawer where he kept spare guitar picks and flyers from shows, back when he used to have a band, before he'd sold the guitar, back when he used to believe there was money in music. She touched each guitar pick on the dresser, each roll of film Victor had left, ran her fingers over the photos on the wall, waiting for static to leap up her arm, showing her that *this* was the item that mattered, but even the photographs stayed cool, dull. Dead. The closet? She ran to it and flung the doors open, but nothing felt suspicious—or even looked suspicious. The suitcases were missing, but she'd known about those. He'd taken them the day he left. Pretty organized for a guy who had just killed his daughter while under the influence of demonic possession.

Though... She eyed the clothes on the floor, the near-full drawers. Victor wasn't particularly trendy and didn't have a large wardrobe—had he not taken his clothes with him? Had he known he wouldn't need them because he planned to hurt himself after what he did to Leslie?

Maybe he'd put Leslie's body in the suitcase instead. No, she was too big to fit.

Not if he cut her up first.

Sounded like something a demon might do. A shiver ran up her spine, from her lower back to the nape of her neck, and she grabbed Victor's robe from the floor and put it on, knotting the belt tightly. So Victor took one suitcase with Leslie's body in it, and another bag with her clothes? Why pack at all for a kid you'd murdered? That thought had lulled

Chloe to sleep many nights in the last few weeks, and even now, when she actually believed the photos were true, that something had happened to Leslie... It still made no sense to pack clothes for a dead girl.

She headed for Leslie's bedroom, ignoring the barren bed and the empty end tables, and flung the closet door open. Her mouth went dry. Leslie's suitcase was there, on the top shelf of the closet. Chloe had looked in here, but she'd shut the door when she realized the clothes were gone. She hadn't checked for the case. Chloe grabbed the handle—was it heavier than it should have been? Something clogged her throat, and she wheezed as she hefted the suitcase from the shelf and lowered it, slowly, the silver clasps glinting in the light from the window. One of the latches was smudged with something brown. Her heart seized.

Oh God, what if she's in there? Could a demon use...a dead body to creep into their world?

Chloe set the case on the ground and unclicked the first latch, unable to draw breath, unable to force her hand to the second latch, where brown splotches coated the spring. *It's just soda, or marker, or food Leslie spilled. If it were blood, it'd be black, or maroon, or even just a darker brown.*

She brought her hand to the second latch and touched the stain.

The metal was cool, dull—not even a spark of static. She pressed the mechanism to release the latch and grabbed both sides of the case, drawing it open, slowly, slowly, wincing in anticipation.

The case was empty. Her breath left her in a whoosh, but that didn't help slow her heart.

Chloe closed the case and shoved it back into the top of the closet, but stopped at the noise echoing in the silence—metal on wood. Something else was up there. She ran her fingers over the top lip of the shelf and pulled down...Leslie's iPad? *Crosses and Bows* danced on the screen. *Strange.* Leslie had said she'd lost it. Victor couldn't even afford a ring for Chloe after buying that damn device, and Leslie hadn't appreciated the sacrifice, had tried to blame Chloe for the missing tablet, when she'd... hidden it purposefully so she could blame Chloe? Little bitch. The girl had been jealous, maybe, but it wasn't fair, not at all.

There had to be something here Chloe had overlooked. She replaced the tablet and strode to the dresser—pink with silver handles, sketches of guitars and unicorns and dragons inked onto the front facade in Victor's hand, along with some cruder drawings that Leslie had done herself. They'd spent a whole afternoon in here, "decorating." Chloe laid a finger on a dark, nasty scribble on the side, layer upon layer of black Sharpie. It had once been the face of a dog, the only picture Chloe had added to the dresser. Leslie had made it disappear.

The dresser drawer squealed open and Chloe plunged her hands inside, but it was empty. So was the next drawer, and the next—empty but for the old band flyers that lined the drawers instead of newspaper.

All of Leslie's clothes were gone, not just a weekend's or even a week's worth. He'd taken none of his things, and all of hers? But there was no way Leslie's entire wardrobe, let alone her pillows, would have fit in Victor's suitcases. Even if Victor had shoved Leslie's things in garbage bags, he wouldn't have spent an hour walking back and forth to Helen's car with all Leslie's stuff in the middle of the night. Chloe certainly would have woken up for that.

She slammed the last drawer shut with enough force that the dresser teetered on its back legs before righting itself. More questions, no answers, and she'd found nothing that felt the least bit agitated, nothing like the brooch, nothing that seemed like a portal. Though...what if Leslie's things were in that room at Brandon's, with the toys of other children? God only knew what had happened to them. She should go back—and now that she knew Brandon's arson stunt hadn't helped, they could make another plan. Not like there was anyone else who could help, anyone else she could trust. Shit, maybe she should ask the damn psychic on the strip.

Bang!

Chloe startled, leapt backward away from the dresser. *Bang!* The noise rang through the apartment again—*the kitchen.* She ran from the bedroom, out into the hallway, falling to her knees at the entrance to the kitchen when three more shots—they had to be gunshots—rang out in succession.

Bang! Bang! Bang! The shots kept coming, deafening her, but the kitchen was normal, the wine bottle intact, and the door, the front door... Bile rose in her throat. Helen, as gorgeous as she'd been in her yearbook photo, stood stock still in the doorway, hand on the knob as if she was either entering or trying to leave. Her blond hair curled down her back like spun gold, her blue eyes wide, staring into the kitchen with a look of unbridled horror. Chloe turned, but she could see nothing amiss, nothing—

Bang! Bang!

The wine bottle exploded, showering the countertops and backsplash with ruby liquid and chunks of something wet and gelatinous, gray peeking through the garish red, like tiny bits of...brain. And still Helen stood, unmoving, eyes on the river of claret flowing over the tiles.

Had Helen made the wine bottle explode? Was *she* the demon?

Of course she'd done this. The woman was evil, killing her friend's sister, bullying Joleen in her time of grief, stealing other women's boyfriends. Either Helen *was* the demon, or was possessed by it, but Chloe didn't care which. This woman had ruined her life.

Chloe scrambled to her feet—*I'll fucking kill you myself*—but didn't even take the first step forward. She didn't have to. The man in the leather apron approached from the hallway behind Helen, wrapping his hands over her shoulders, gentle, then squeezing, squeezing, and Helen's eyes widened. But she didn't struggle—she stood like she was in a trance, drugged, ignorant of whatever horror she'd seen moments ago in the kitchen.

"I'll fix it, girl. I'll fix it for you."

Elisha locked eyes with Chloe.

He's here to help me, he wants to help me.

His fingertips were at Helen's temple, blood welling around his nails, and then he drew his hand down like a claw, over her cheek to her jawbone, fingernails peeling strips of flesh from her face.

Everything had frozen, even the blood in Chloe's veins; her emotions had gone numb. But that lonely pain, that horrible solitary ache—that was gone. Elisha drew his fingernails back to Helen's forehead again, then scraped them down once more, slicing over her eyebrow and past the round part of her cheek, and Chloe averted her eyes, staring at Helen's neck, at the blood trickling toward the woman's shirt. And now Helen moved, not her arms or legs, but her mouth—it was tensing and flexing, the exposed muscles of her jaw working as if she was trying to tell Chloe something.

But Chloe didn't want to listen. This woman was a demon, this woman had stolen her boyfriend, this woman had killed her friend's little sister, this woman…deserved it. She deserved anything she got.

"Come to me," Elisha said, the rattling bass vibrating her marrow, and the numb frost that had encased her muscles thawed enough to let her step closer. Elisha smiled. "Come to me."

She took another step, watching Helen's eyes, the dull blue haze in one, the other coated in a shiny red film. Chloe reached for Elisha's hand; his fingers were slick.

"I can make it all stop, I can help you." His lips weren't moving. Why weren't his lips moving, why—

Blinding, searing pain shot through her chest, something thick like gristle tearing beneath her ribs. Chloe stumbled backward and grabbed the counter.

He was supposed to help her, to take her pain. It shouldn't hurt. "Please leave." That's what she was supposed to do, right, to make it stop? No...what had the picture said? Say their name, his name. Thrice...no...once to banish. Was that right? "Elisha Shepherd." He cocked his head, the way Brandon did, and the sudden resemblance in their manner was so striking it made her stomach turn. "Please go, God, help me, please help me." Her voice was a strangled whimper now, barely loud enough to reach her own ears, but... someone had heard her.

The man vanished along with Helen. The kitchen was clean, the wine bottle intact.

But the energy was still thick enough to slice with a blade.

"What do you want from me?" she whispered. Tears stung her eyes. "What the fuck do you want?"

Air hissed through the A/C unit. Chloe stared at the wine bottle. Grandpa always said that if you were willing to put in the work, God would help fix you. *We'll fix you up, girl.* And though she'd spent an awfully long time feeling the slash of the belt instead of the peace of God's grace, she sure needed to believe in something now. And no God or Devil would keep harassing her without cause—without some purpose.

She'd been going with the flow, blindly, hoping some clue would reveal itself and guide her in the right direction, but she wasn't lost at all. Martha and Elisha were trying to show her, trying to get her to understand that Helen was the enemy—Elisha could have hurt her the other night, or killed her just now, but instead he'd showed Chloe that he wanted to hurt Helen as much as she did. The wine bottle went fuzzy in front of her eyes.

I hear you guys. Helen, or the demon inside her, had either possessed Victor or made him lose his mind, and though she wasn't entirely sure why, this spirit was after Martha and Elisha too. Was this demon...old? Had it existed, perhaps by another name, back when Martha and Elisha Shepherd lived, maybe been responsible for Martha's death? It made sense— clearly demons weren't limited to a human lifespan. But whether this demon had left for a time or had long been banished from this plane, or whether it was a new demon altogether, it was certainly here now.

Chloe hadn't seen many stories about a demon coming back and harassing the same person over and over, which meant if she found a way to banish it, she should be free. So...what would this demon's portal be? An item associated with Helen? Maybe something in Helen's possession when the demon came into this world. The scarf? She hadn't seen it at Helen's apartment and she had no idea where else to begin looking. But this wasn't just about Helen; the demon hadn't sought Chloe out directly—Martha and Elisha were the ones harassing Chloe. If she sent Martha and Elisha back where they came from...would Helen follow? *Will I be free then?*

Either way, the portals were the key—she'd start with whichever ones she could find. Martha's was probably the brooch, but she had no idea what Elisha's was. Would she know it when she touched it? There had to be a better way than touching each of a thousand items at the plantation.

Maybe there was.

The shop. Though the antiques might have been destroyed, she should still be able to read the writings, the journals Greg had mentioned, *if* they'd been in the safe. And if Chloe could learn what was important to Elisha, maybe she could figure out Elisha's portal. Maybe Greg's creeper ass even knew where Helen's scarf had ended up, in case she needed that or some other item to send Helen back where she came from. And Greg was probably standing in the ruins of the antique store right this moment.

Chloe hauled on her skirt, then her blouse. She'd go to the shop first. Even if the old files had burned in the fire, even if she didn't get to see any of those old journals, even if the antique store was just ashes, maybe she'd find something...*feel* something.

Energy couldn't vanish any more than a person could.

CHAPTER 25

MARTHA ALTON SHEPHERD, TWENTY-
FIFTH DECEMBER, 1835

Hany stops at Elisha's table and pours him water. I clench my fists on my knee, the corset beneath my dress digging painfully into my ribs. Elisha knows of my fury. He must. I banished the boy to the outer buildings along with Hany, hiding them far from my view, lest that hot and prickly rage in my gut consume me as I go about my chores. But Elisha instructed Hany to return to the house, or so I suspect. I've not asked her, and yet here she is, and she'd not defy her orders—someone gave her permission.

I tear my gaze from them and look to the other slaves milling about the room. It is plain to see they are not in a celebrating mood. Even those drinking with the other masters are not smiling—their backs stay straight and tight. One of them keeps looking at the stairs as though he fears the banister may jump from its spindles and beat him.

Or perhaps this is my own feverish imagination. Some days are so steeped in dread that it is hard to see through to the other side of them, and today my chest aches relentlessly, despite the flickering Christmas candles set along the mantels and tables, despite the stockings, lumpy and filled with candies, despite the other ladies in the sitting room, comely in their gowns of silk and jewelry that sparkles in the candlelight. The lace that peeks from my bodice may appear just as festive, but beneath it my heart is cold, painful. Nineteen years old and already I have near completely forgotten what joy is.

"I still cannot believe it," Annabelle says, her blue eyes glittering, a smirk at the corner of her mouth, full lips ripe for tattle. She's a handsome woman, and she knows it. Their plantation is ten miles from here, over the hills, the nearest one to us—if she lived closer, would she hear the screams from the attic at night, the way I can? "Trash," she says, shaking her head.

I peer across the room to the man Elisha is sitting with—stiff-postured and gray-haired, with a black waistcoat and a cane the color of ripe cherries. His wife isn't here—she will never be back. Only a fortnight ago, she bore the babe of a field hand. They sold the child, I heard, a little tan boy with curly black hair and his mother's eyes. Perhaps one day I shall see the boy passing through here, just another hired hand, but I'll guess his lineage by the shape of his brow. Perhaps I shall hug him and tell him how sorry I am that he was torn from his mother. Or perhaps I shall just smile and send him on his way, then retire to my chambers to cry for him and for what could have been.

Elisha finally glances my way, and I wither under his familiar sneer, though the rest of him is still foreign to me. I crave but one man, the only man from whom I receive affection, kindness. Adoration. He used to come to see me at least every other day at Elisha's behest, bringing word of the other workers—he was their unofficial spokesman. And I was glad of it, the information as well as his nearness. He never looked at me with pity, as Hany does, or with fear, as do the other slaves. But his eyes hold a profound sorrow that even now speaks to the deepest recesses of my soul. He has become my best friend—my only friend. The night Elisha slapped me for sending Hany away, *he* caught me in the kitchen, sobbing against the huge stone fireplace, aching with pain and loneliness. He touched my shoulder—but one small, innocent touch. "Come to me," he said, and I did, lost in his care for me, in his kind voice, in his brown eyes, the irises flecked with green.

"A whore," Caroline whispers, but her hips are the widest of any of us—she has five children to her name, though only three babes survived infancy. And she cannot prove the lineage of the ones she put in the grave, for at least one died in the womb, before its skin bore any color at all.

"I heard they did not sell him," Annabelle says, raising an eyebrow. "I heard the master of the house ordered his skull crushed with a rock."

My lungs seize.

"They ought to lynch the father, teach them all a lesson," Caroline says, and they both nod.

God, what have I done? I blink back tears. The night I lay with him under the harvest moon, his calloused fingers probing the soft recesses of my body, I cried too, but they were not the tears of loneliness and abandonment and sorrow I've wet my pillow with nearly every night since I arrived here.

I am in love. I do not dare to think it, I do not want it to be, yet there it is, all bubbly, spilling out over my heart. It is not even the tingly feeling that matters, but the other deeper, realer part; and somehow it is greater even than my fear.

I swallow hard against the bile rising in my throat. I need to get away from the plantation.

"Martha, dear, are you all right?"

"Yes," I say, but my voice shakes. These women would string him up for looking at them too long. "A little tired, is all." They would string me up, too, if they had their way—for my belly is already fluttering with new life.

"Mm-hmm." Caroline looks at me knowingly and my heart stops.

I could ask Hany for the herbs to wash it out of me, to kill it, but even the thought of this child brings me more joy than I have felt in the last three years combined. Yet I know what happens to those who choose this path. That this man, the only kindness I've known in recent years would be sold, or swing from a tree, be snuffed from existence—it is too much to bear. And I cannot shake the feeling that my fate would be far worse than simply being cast aside.

I shift in my seat, trying to ease the ache in my ribs. My father would not allow me to be hurt, no matter his disappointment. I am his only daughter. The scandal might destroy us, but it is in his best interest to care for me, to keep me safe; I know more now about tending a plantation. He might allow me to return home. It is unlikely, but hope has never been a burden, and the fact that I have any faith left in me is a miracle—and so I stoke it, embrace it.

I stare at the candles, and dare to hope.

CHAPTER 26

CHLOE ANDERSON, PRESENT DAY

Chloe stared at the antique shop, her mouth dry as ash. On the walk over, she had steeled herself for the destruction: a burned-out facade, cracked windows, an irreplaceable collection of history blackened and then soaked by a fireman's hose, everything waiting for her to stand, to listen, to feel the air for the slightest vibration on the breeze. But not in her wildest imaginings had she pictured this.

The bricks were clean, right up to the roofline. Intact windows reflected the morning sun. It was as if the fire had never happened.

Her stomach twisted so painfully that she had to fight the urge to throw up. If she'd imagined the fire, what else had she imagined? There was no way to know for sure, no way to prove whether she was psychic or insane. She'd figured that out long ago, from the twitters of her classmates—how difficult it was to prove that you're not crazy.

Chloe forced her feet forward, and the bell above the antique shop door announced her arrival. Lehmann stood at the center display case, his dreidel spinning on the glass near his left hand, the toy red and bloody, but when she blinked it was normal. *Normal.* Just like everything else but her. Around went the top. Around, around, around.

Greg hailed her from his post near the front window. "Morning," he said with a huge plastic smile. "I'm glad you're here."

Her brain felt frazzled, jumpy, like her gray matter was being zapped by a thousand jolts of static electricity—but that's what she was here to feel, right? That energy? But where was it coming from? She scanned the front windows, the floors—everything was intact, right down to the dust on the edges of the display tables, and no one piece jumped out as being especially significant. She'd touched most of those pieces in the past, anyway, and none had called to her like Martha's brooch had—which meant Elisha's portal was probably not here at all. So what was making her hackles rise? The entire store? Surely demons weren't just wandering up from Hell and into the shop, then straight out through the front door to terrorize the living.

Lehmann raised his hand to scratch at an age spot in front of his ear, and one tiny corner of black from his swastika tattoo peeked from beneath his shirt—a tattoo just like the one in her vision, the vision that had made her forget about the journals.

Chloe steeled herself. She was not going to ignore any more potential clues because she was distracted—the demons might be the ones throwing these visions at her, to confuse her and keep her from fulfilling her purpose here. She swallowed over the lump in her throat and approached Lehmann. He looked furious. *Why does he hate me so much?* And Greg, too…wasn't right. The muscles in Greg's neck were corded, his mouth set in a grimace. His knuckles were white around a crystal vase.

She stood taller. "I need to see the journals—the papers related to the Shepherd plantation, to Martha Alton."

The vase in Greg's hands wobbled, but he caught it before it crashed to the floor. Lehmann looked back down at the spinning top. "Greg, come get them for her." Then he grabbed his toy, stalked off to the back room, and slammed the door, leaving her staring after him.

"Don't do this," Greg said behind her, his voice suddenly strained. "Please." It was the whispered plea of a child hiding in the dark, trying to reason with a...monster.

She whirled on him. "I just want to see the writings you told me about." If she could figure out how Martha and Elisha had gotten here, then she could send them away. Unless..."Do you know where Helen's scarf went?"

"Scarf? No." Greg kept his eyes on the wall. "Trust me, you don't need to know any of this yet." He put up a hand when she started to protest. His lip trembled. "Don't do this," he said again. "I love you. Brandon doesn't."

Her mouth dropped open. That's what all this was about? He was jealous of Brandon? "You don't even know me."

"Neither does he."

What the hell was he talking about? She was trying to escape supernatural creatures—love had nothing to do with it. "I'm not dating Shepherd." She crossed her arms. "Not that it's any of your business."

"I'm really not sure you need—"

"Fuck you, with your 'not sure'!" She was yelling at him. "Get the Goddamn journals!" Her fists clenched—she'd hit him in the mouth if he tried to deny her again.

"Fine," he spat. He looked anything but fine. His lips were pressed so tightly together they were white, the muscles in his jaw working. He headed for the back, leaving her standing in the middle of the shop, alone, feeling like maggots were writhing on her skin.

LEHMANN'S OFFICE felt smaller than it ever had, or perhaps it was simply the enormity of the task before her. She had the journals. If she found nothing here, then what would she do? Just go back to the plantation and hope that some antique felt *extra* special? Search for the brooch again? Was it even possible that she'd be able to locate it? Her stomach sank as she pored over the first few sheets—ledgers, old pages from the courthouse. Greg had been right: there was nothing on the marriage between Martha Alton and Elisha Shepherd, and nothing else of any use to her.

She set the ledgers aside. The journals beneath were water-stained, the covers cracked, bindings broken. Inside, the pages were yellowed with age, and creases obscured some of the line drawings and made the words impossible to see clearly, though she could still identify the subject matter: male and female cadavers in various stages of dissection, and separate diagrams of muscles, bone, and organs. Meticulous. On the third page, a flayed jaw jumped out at her, the connectors between muscle and bone fastidiously shaded. But this sketch showed the subject's full face: a woman, with her eyes wide open, not closed as you'd expect of a cadaver. In her mind's eye, Chloe saw Helen standing in her doorway with half her face peeled off, gore running down her neck and onto her shirt. Chloe shuddered. Looked like Elisha Shepherd was a doctor, as she'd suspected, and it appeared he'd been operating on cadavers to hone his skills. Oh... maybe the medical bag she'd seen him carrying last night was his special item, his portal—maybe even the leather apron. She'd look for those things first.

But the drawings...she ran a finger over the woman's jaw, her fingertips buzzing—could the journals be the portal? The vibration wasn't like the bright, insistent tingling of Martha's brooch, far from it; every cell in her body urged her to run from the dark, broody energy that seeped from the pages, oozing into her fingers. She snapped her hand back. Had the shop itself been so threatening to Brandon, or was it these books he'd been trying to destroy with the fire? But if Brandon had wanted them burned, why not just light them up at the plantation? He had to be the one who'd given them to the shop—wasn't like Greg had found these journals in the old courthouse.

And something else nagged at her: the handwriting looked so much like what she'd seen at Brandon's, in the captions beneath the pictures of slaves in the fields, the words on the sketch of that robed man at the gravesite, summoning a spirit from beyond. Had Elisha Shepherd drawn those pictures? Maybe he'd written the words: "Blood must be repaid in blood" and the instructions for banishing and summoning a spirit. She flipped to the next sketch, dropping the page as fast as she could to avoid the vibrations from crawling into her palm. This one was cruder but clear enough: the black subject here did not appear to be a cadaver —the wounds were bleeding, thick, dark channels cutting a line from the injury to the edge of the sheet. The drawing was of the torso only, with a deep gash down to the rib bones; someone with thick white fingers was applying salve to the injury with their fingertips. The notations were too blurry to read, though Chloe guessed it was instructions on wound care.

The next page was too damaged to make out. Chloe turned to the middle of the journal where the wear and tear seemed less intense, and her blood ran cold, but not in the pleasant way she'd experienced with Brandon—this chill was painful, icy-sharp, crawling over her as if the entirety of her flesh was a just-waking limb. Why was she so upset? There wasn't even a picture here, just writings, but the words felt as if they might jump off the page and attack. She cringed as she read details of a tubal ligation procedure, professional and precise: the slicing of the abdominal wall, the location of the uterus and ovaries, the tiny print noting: "Abdominal wall feels tougher than that of a white, but organs are in a normal location."

Had he expected them not to be? Most doctors of the time were well aware that both black and white had the same insides—that's why they experimented on their slaves in the first place. Wasn't like they were doing it to advance the medical treatment of the slave community.

She flipped to the next page, and the frost stabbed her gut like tiny icicles. There was only one sketch: a slave woman, her skin filled in with jerky pencil scribbles, held down by what might have been leather straps or rope, the lower half of her torso an open pit like the Operation game Chloe and her mother used to play. But the woman's arms strained upward, muscles flexed, and her eyes were wide with misery—she'd been conscious. A faceless person wearing Elisha Shepherd's apron stood above her, hand *inside* her severed belly. *Oh fuck.* Was that how he'd done the tubal ligation? He hadn't used anesthesia? She'd read that in her history classes—the masters thought slaves didn't feel pain—but she swallowed hard to dampen the nausea. She had always avoided delving deeper into that, still didn't want to know. But maybe she should have paid more attention.

Chloe turned to the next page, riveted like someone driving past a bad car accident—not wanting to see, but unable to look away. This page had a photo, an *actual photo* of a little girl, five, maybe less, her mouth open in a silent wail, her round cheeks shiny with tears, tied upright to a chair with leather straps looped around her shoulders and her midsection. She had some kind of fist-sized growth near her temple. Elisha Shepherd stood behind her, brows furrowed in concentration, with what looked like a hand-cranked drill, the tip shoved deep into the mass. Chloe's own temple throbbed once, sharply, bile sour in the back of her throat. Below the photograph: "Protrusion has grown as part of skull, though only on outside; brain intact where instrument pierced through." And a smaller notation—"forty minutes"—in the margin.

Forty minutes? Was that how long it took the child to die? She couldn't have lasted long once Shepherd pierced her brain with a hand drill. *I hope she died faster than that—maybe she passed out.*

Somewhere outside the office, in the front of the antique shop, the clang of breaking glass rang through the air—Greg wasn't okay with her looking at these and now she could see why. He thought he could protect her from the horror, but he didn't know that these ghosts had come to her, didn't know about the demons. Her heart hammered a frenzied rhythm in her ears, but she turned the page, inhaling through her nose to avoid retching.

Scrawled on the top: "It appears the outermost layers are the only ones affected by the malady." The photo on that page, another real picture, was of a burly black man with a cuff on his neck and thick chain wrapped around each extremity and bolted to the legs of a shallow metal sink the size of a modern bathtub—Chloe had never seen one like it before. Along the sides hung strips of what looked like…skin. The man's abdomen was a wide swath of exposed tissue, shiny, though the only light source appeared to be a large window at the far end of the room—a blurred circle of white. In this image, Elisha Shepherd held a fillet knife, his forehead knitted, his hand hovering with the blade in mid-peel, separating another strip of skin from the man's rib cage. *Outermost layers*…some kind of cancer? Scar tissue? She retched, and recovered.

Elisha Shepherd, the man she'd seen at her apartment, the man who'd been in her bedroom, the man she'd had visions about—he was a madman. And she'd felt calmed by him. What was wrong with her?

He'd tricked her. This wasn't about Helen…unless the demon inside Helen used to be inside Elisha Shepherd. But this felt bigger somehow, the energy now throbbing through her so violently she could not take a breath. Demons might be crafty, but the Devil…He had a million tricks. She'd spent every childhood church service hearing about it as she sat next to Grandpa in that pew, and she felt that memory shuddering through her bones now: the vibration of the choir and the deep, resonating bass of the pastor, and the evil, underscoring all of it, the reason for them to be there, the thing they were collectively fighting.

Fight. *Fight*.

She turned the page, wanting to ignore it, wanting to run, but she needed to keep going, to see, and the energy crackled around her like lightening as she dropped the next page, then the next. She stopped flipping. Another black-and-white photo. The girl—Martha. Every cell in Chloe's body was riveted to the page, connected to this book by some cosmic power that would not allow her to draw herself away.

Martha was in the washtub, mouth open like she was moaning, her arms and legs strapped down on the outside edges of the tub. Black blood dripped from her calf to the floor. The room was dark, hazy, as if in shadow, though the dozens of little glowing pinpricks could be candles. Elisha Shepherd was kneeling between Martha's legs, one bloody fist grabbing her knee, forcing it outwards, the other hand hidden between her thighs—and from this angle it looked like his arm was *inside the girl* to his forearm. And the notation: "When taken from the womb, the bastard moved but once before we slit its throat."

The bastard...a child? Wait, was this an abortion? *Fuck*. Martha had either married Shepherd or had been sent there for an abortion gone wrong, but either way, it had backfired. Elisha Shepherd was a brutal man. A man who had reduced Martha to a shattered, bloody husk. Who had yanked out more than just a fetus.

She squinted, forcing herself to look closer, to *see*.

The washtub was the same one from the photo of the chained man, but she couldn't locate the circular window in this shot—it must have been nighttime. And though she'd not seen the washtub before today, she knew the window, the floor, the sloping lines of the roof...knew them from the dream she'd had, the one with Martha sitting, bleeding, pinching invisible things from the wood. Martha had tried to show her this place. Martha had tried to tell Chloe where she'd died, where the evil energy was concentrated. Where a demon, or the Devil himself, had bled her life onto the floorboards.

Chloe slammed the journal closed, trying to shove the horrific picture from her mind, but Martha's leg, black with blood, and the horror of everything else she'd seen was seared into her brain so completely that each blink brought back images of suffering, the mouths of victims gaping with fear and pain. And that chained man, his skin torn off in strips, eyes open—she could practically hear him screaming, begging for his life, or perhaps begging Elisha Shepherd to end it.

No...she *could* hear him. And not only him.

From somewhere in the front of the shop, the wails began, just as they had last night at Shepherd's house—low and steady, then crescendoing, a cacophony of voices, like a machine with broken gears, screeching and scraping and grinding. But Chloe could discern individual voices, too: a woman's shriek, like a bark, short and sharp and panicked, every exhale an exclamation of astonished pain; the longer, raspy wails of an infant who had been left to cry far too long; the thunderous bass of the men's voices, the choked gasps for mercy, and then their voices, too, increased both in volume and in pitch, no longer the sheer terror of anticipation but the agony when all your worst fears have been realized, when the pain of living has far superseded the fear of death. And yet they were still alive, screaming, crying, shouting. And below it all, that grinding machine-like sound—*a bone saw?*—and the vibration of it shattered her balance, sending her to her knees on the wooden floor.

"Please! Stop!" She was shouting too, trying to project her voice above all the others, but that only magnified their crescendo. And piercing through the screaming, sharp like a hypodermic needle, a hiss: "Blood must be repaid in blood." Then Martha was in the corner of the room, one arm lifted, pointing at the desk. She was missing half her face again.

"What do you want from me?" Chloe screamed at her. "Just tell me, please, I'll do anything to make this stop!"

The bloody organ at Martha's knee pulsed, then twisted as though something was inside it, writhing. Around them the miserable human voices undulated like the merciless crashing of waves in a storm.

I don't want to be special anymore. Please leave me alone.
Chloe closed her eyes, scrambling blindly backward toward

the door, arms up as if to protect her ears, her face, from absorbing the madness, or maybe to avoid Helen's fate, flesh peeled from bone—*The Devil wears many faces.* Grandpa used to say that, and she believed him now. *Say her name, once, banish her.* "Leave, Martha." Chloe's voice trembled. "Leave."

"Blood must be repaid in blood," Martha whispered again.

Then, as suddenly as it had begun, the screaming stopped, and the silence smacked into Chloe with the force of a truck. She lowered her arms and opened her eyes, gasping as though her lungs had been suctioned closed. *Blood must be repaid.* But it wasn't like she could force a demon, let alone the Devil, to pay for his sins. She crawled from the wall and pulled herself up on the desk chair, holding on to the desktop as if it could tether her to reality.

There had to be a way to banish the evil back to Hell. For it didn't matter whether she was fighting Elisha Shepherd, Helen, or Martha, or some combination of whatever demons had possessed them—she was desperate to send them away. And Martha *had* vanished, Chloe had *made her* vanish by saying her name, just as she had made Elisha Shepherd disappear along with Helen at the apartment. But they wouldn't stay gone—they'd just come back through whatever portal they'd used the first time, unless she destroyed that too.

Chloe's entire body was shaking. The demons kept coming back, to *her*, to her energy. Her fingers ached from gripping the desktop, and she tried to force her hands to relax.

She needed to lure the evil out so she could see it, focus on it—the books had said that. And there was only one thing the demons wanted.

Demons feed off the energy of others, and the more they feed, the stronger they become.

She'd have to let the demons feel her energy, her power, let the evil...come to her. *Come to me.* And once the demons were out in the open where she could focus her energy back on them—maybe during another vision—she'd force them back to Hell where they belonged, one at a time if need be. Now, without the screams shattering her concentration, she recalled the poem from the back of that sketch—*Cast thee out, from the lips of the chosen, and then say their name, just once. Cast thee out*—she had to say that too, right? And she needed to find the items, the brooch, the medical bag, whatever portal they'd used to get here. And she would find them. Then she'd wait. She wasn't sure how she could be so certain that these items existed at all, items critical to this process, but she knew it, *felt* it, the same way she knew something lurked at the old Shepherd plantation, deep within its bowels, some malevolent energy still roaming around long after those who lived and suffered there had died. Chloe had felt it the first day she'd been there. Even the stuffed animals at that house felt cursed. Her gaze dropped to the journals, closed now, and icy fingers raked her spine. The plantation was where these horrors had taken place. The plantation was where the blood had been spilled, where the energy was focused. The portals were at the plantation, not the shop. The demons were there too.

A sharp pain, like the one that attacked her in her nightmares blossomed, and she put her hand over her breastbone as if doing so could keep her heart inside—her hand came away wet. She winced, looked down. The blister from the brooch was back, weeping clear fluid onto her fingers, though there was no sign of the necklace.

You're bad, Chloe, we'll fix you up, girl, get you right with God.

The blister on her chest stung, and wept, and her heart ratcheted up though she couldn't tell if it was anxiety or pleasure, and it didn't matter, not now. She wasn't bad. She was going to help Brandon get rid of these demons—she was going to save herself. *I'll show you, Grandpa.* She'd show them all.

CHAPTER 27

CHLOE ANDERSON, PRESENT DAY

The fear tasted like rust on her tongue but it spurred her onward, toward the plantation,
her heart throbbing from her throat to her groin, her knuckles white on the steering wheel. Though she might not be sure what the demons had used to creep into their world, Brandon certainly wasn't clueless—no way. He'd have known what had happened at the plantation, about the torture, and he'd set the antique shop on fire to get rid of the evil in Elisha Shepherd's journals, hadn't he? He might have been wrong about the journals being the portals, but in case he wasn't, she had the journals in the backseat, hidden inside cloth bags. She might get fired when Lehmann realized she'd snuck them out through the front door, but that was the least of her worries.

Right now, she and Brandon needed to pool their experiences, learn what hadn't worked in the past, and figure out what the demons had used to get here so she could banish them. Though Brandon hadn't succeeded in destroying the shop, he had to have a reason to *believe* it would be effective. He'd probably tried other things in the past as well—lighting a building ablaze wasn't generally a first choice. If she could discern the portals by process of elimination they could save time, too, and it felt like time was running out—any vision, any attack, could be the one where they finally decided to take her. But at the moment she didn't even know whether each demon had their own portal, or if they were all using one. Or they might be the same demon, if Grandpa was to be believed. *The Devil wears many faces.*

She parked away from the tree, out of reach of its branches; something was hiding there, she knew it, no matter how crazy it sounded. The breeze cooled her fiery cheeks as she peered across the lawn, frowning at the outbuildings, the wide expanse of grass, the trees beyond. Questions whirled like a cyclone in her brain, but the tingling in her gut told her she was exactly where she should be, and it was about fucking time she trusted that without question.

Come to me.

"Chloe?"

She jumped. Brandon stood at the base of the stairs, hands in his pockets, his head cocked. "I wasn't expecting you."

"I...we need to talk." A shaky breath shuddered through her lungs, but she kept her fingers pressed against the car door, as if once she let go, any surreal, impossible thing could happen. *Stop stalling, Chloe.* She glanced sideways at the tree and her grip tightened further. "Last night, after the fire, I woke up in my apartment. You were right about the demons and we need to figure this out, maybe search for a different way to banish them..." She forced her fingers off the car door and the breeze on her palms felt like frost.

He raised a brow as if uncertain what she meant, but then his face softened. "I did wonder where you went last night."

I bring up demons and that's his only response? But her shoulders relaxed, and she realized she'd been worried he'd be skeptical—after all, he hadn't seen Martha when she was right next to him, and he'd suggested the man she'd seen on the lawn was a shadow. And whether he was a skeptic or not, she needed his help. And he needed hers. "This isn't really about last night, not completely. I...I've been having visions. Of Elisha Shepherd, the man who used to live here. Your ancestor."

His face did not change, but he stepped backward up the steps and waved her into the house—yeah, this would definitely be a "sit down inside" conversation. Instead of pausing in the foyer, she headed for the dining room, the hollow *thunk* as he closed the front door like the beat of some ancient drum. The table was empty besides the vase of lilies that were as healthy as they'd been her first day here, but this time no necklace waited for her on the tabletop, and she suddenly missed the brooch as one might miss an amputated limb. The wound on her chest tingled. That piece had... power. They needed to find it. She touched the blister on her chest—still wet and stinging.

Brandon stood across from her, his probing gaze locked on her face. "Tell me about these visions."

"Like last night, the fire—"

"That wasn't a vision. I was there too."

"No, I went to the shop today—the place is fine. There was no fire."

He shook his head. "Something is messing with your mind."

"I... No, it's not me. Last night, something messed with *us*, screwed with your fire. Maybe the demons...intercepted it somehow." It wasn't like demons just fixed up the shop every night between eating the souls of child brides and making wine bottles explode. Chloe stared at the table, unable to meet his gaze, but her calves prickled at an unseen breeze... from upstairs. Something was calling her. And still Brandon remained silent. Did he not believe her? "We should go over everything we know about what happened here—there's a reason these demons are coming back, showing themselves to me. And we need more information if we want to get Elisha and Martha to leave." She finally raised her eyes to his.

Brandon's mouth hung open. "Martha?"

"I've...seen her too." *I sound just like Victor: "I'm possessed, Chloe. The demons in my head say the most awful things, late at night when I'm trying to sleep."*

Brandon's eyes narrowed, but she stumbled on, the words pouring from her lips. "You're already aware that Elisha tortured slaves here, literally took them apart—and he killed Martha, the girl from the brooch." She was talking too fast, much too fast. The chill on her legs intensified, gripped her, almost felt like long, cold fingers were trying to pull her toward the steps. "But what we don't know is what they're using to get back—"

"Elisha didn't kill anyone." Brandon shook his head, calmly, but his exhale was harsh, as if someone had hit him in the belly. "It was the field hands."

"He did, I saw him do it." Hadn't she? Or had she just seen Elisha trying to abort the child, and assumed he'd done more because of the other horrors in that journal? No, no, he had written that he'd killed the kid—*the bastard moved but once before we slit its throat*—so surely he hadn't let Martha just walk away. He was a maniac.

"How did you see?" The sharpness in Brandon's voice made her pause. "In a...vision?"

"The journals at the shop."

"What journals?"

He had to have brought them to the shop—how else would Greg have gotten hold of them? Not like Elisha Shepherd would have made them public. But one of Elisha's heirs—Brandon—could have found them and decided what to do with them. Unless...

"You really don't know what I'm talking about?"

Brandon shook his head.

Last night on the lawn, she'd lost the brooch—it had disappeared clean off her neck. What if something had *taken it* off her neck? Could demons do that? And if so, maybe Martha herself had moved the journals to the shop. Or Elisha had. But why the shop, why would they...

THE JILTED

Greg's words leapt into her mind: "They called him The Enforcer. He was always the last guy there, making sure the orders were followed."

Wait, was that why Lehmann took care of every interaction himself—he was handing out portals to unsuspecting patrons, giving the demons a way into their world? Lehmann was probably a demon too—or just possessed by one. And that was definitely enough motivation; now Brandon trying to burn down the shop made sense, if he'd wanted to stop her boss from spreading these portals around. But once those items were sold, the demons in them roamed free—destroying the shop wouldn't help her escape the monsters that were after her now.

"I keep seeing Martha," she blurted. "I need to figure out why so I can send her back where she came from, along with Elisha. Helen too."

Brandon's scowl softened, his eyes widening in shock. "Can you talk to them?"

Not "No, you can't" or "What the hell do you mean?" That hadn't taken much convincing. "I...no, I can't really talk to them." He frowned, but she pushed on. "That isn't the issue I'm worried about now—there are *real* demons here, roaming around. We need to find a way to get rid of them." And in her head it was Victor's voice, screaming, "What the fuck am I supposed to do with books on dragons and vampires when there are *real* demons here?"

Brandon was still frowning, but in a way that looked pained. "What if I take you there? Can you talk to her then?"

"Take me where?" She must have been staring through him because when she refocused her gaze, he was no longer across from her on the other side of the table. She turned and saw him at the bottom of the stairway already, his hand on the railing. He caught her eye, then started up the stairs without a word.

The higher they climbed, the colder the air became. She steeled herself, as if tensing would keep the demons from sneaking into her brain—but surely they'd have done that already if they were able. Yet Victor's voice still whispered, "The way they talk to me, they make me feel like someone else, someone not myself. Someone bad."

Brandon paused on the first-floor landing. To their right were the bedrooms and the library that Chloe had explored the night before. To their left, a long hallway stretched away from them, with windows that overlooked the front lawn and cast yellow sunlight on the doors across the way. How had that hall been so dark last night with the moon full outside? It was almost like something in the house had... chosen what to show her. Chosen what to conceal.

Directly in front of them was a third hallway, far narrower than the others—even the doors looked thinner, flimsy, almost. Had she even seen this hall last night? She followed Brandon past a tiny room with a bed in each corner and then past three closed doors, to the end of the hall—to an oak door with a large metal lock...on the outside. Trying to keep people out, or trying to keep something in?

Brandon pulled a key from his pocket. The lock snapped with a metallic clank and he opened the door to reveal...not a room at all. The attic stairway, steep and dark and claustrophobic. As they ascended, the temperature rose, and Chloe wiped at her neck, but not before tiny beads of sweat dripped under her blouse and down her spine. The air was barely breathable near the top, no breeze from an open window, no fan, nothing. And...the place was enormous. It spanned the entire length of the house, with exposed beams overhead, and every inch was littered with furniture: tall, skinny armoires, turn-of-the-century tables, antique rifles, vintage area rugs, and larger things hidden behind drop cloths, though those could have been stacks of smaller items —unless they'd brought larger furniture up in pieces, there was no way they could have hefted them through that narrow stairway. The only light came from the round window at the front of the house, the window she'd noticed her first day here, when she'd been sure someone was watching her. Maybe someone had been. Someone not of this world.

But that window...

This is it. The place from Elisha Shepherd's experimentation journals. This was the place Martha had died. Shit, maybe Martha's bones were hidden beneath the attic floorboards, and that was what the girl had used to sneak back into their world. If a brooch could be a portal, surely your own freaking body could.

The skin on Chloe's back crawled like it wanted to shimmy right off her bones and run away. The attic seemed to be getting smaller every moment she stood there, and even the dust motes, spinning lazily in the sun, looked like they were contracting, drawing closer to one another, moved by an unseen force. She focused on the outer reaches of the room, where a bed was tucked against the eaves, the mattress atop a low, antique bed frame, oak spindles barely protruding above a stained green blanket. Why would an old mattress still be made up with sheets? The crawling intensified, over her arms, down her back. Brandon didn't sleep up here—she'd seen his bedroom. So who did this belong to?

Brandon headed for the shadowed back wall and returned carrying...the brooch. "Found it outside." That rang false and her heart jittered along with her flesh.

Chloe held out her hand, but he did not drop it into her palm—instead he clenched it in his fist, and her shoulders tightened with an irrational, but unmistakable, rage. A demon hadn't taken it—Brandon had.

It's mine, it isn't his.

But it *was* his.

"This is where Martha was when she..." Brandon nodded to his closed fist. "Can you see her now? Is she here?" So he knew about Martha—he already knew the demon was there. Did he know about all of them?

Chloe squinted around the room, but aside from her and Brandon, it was empty. "No."

"But you know she's here?"

Again Chloe paused, concentrating, but she could feel nothing outside the unease still prickling over her skin. Her face burned. "I...I'm not sure."

He turned away from her and sighed.

Her jaw clenched, the crawling sensation evaporating in the heat of her agitation. It wasn't Chloe's fault the demon girl wasn't here. Brandon was acting like Victor did when he'd mess with her, pretending she wasn't all that great to appease Leslie with her stupid tantrums.

She stared at Brandon's back. *Turn around.* But he didn't. He stayed facing the window, hands clasped behind his back, brooch in hand, unmoving, rapt, as if there were a parade out there only he could see. Wait...maybe he *could* see something she couldn't. Why else was he avoiding her gaze? Guilt?

Guilt. It rang true. It *felt* true, too, like a little burst of fire in her gut. "Did you do this, Brandon? Did you summon them?" She almost hoped he'd say yes—if he had summoned the demons, surely he could make them leave.

His shoulders tightened. "Of course not," he said to the window, voice low. "You can't bring someone back—that's not how any of this works, and even if I could 'summon' a spirit, the last person I would ever summon would be Elisha Shepherd." He spat the name out, and his voice was sharp, furious. So he knew that guy was a dick—Elisha must be harassing him too.

And this is where the answers are. She let her eyes drift, tried to sense the air around her as she used to sense the energy in Victor's photographs from across the room.

The rug.

Her heart rate increased as she fixed her gaze on the area rug in the center of the floor, the fibers yellowed with dust and age. Chloe knelt beside it and peeled the corner back. It suctioned to the floor, then came loose with a tearing sound, and she stood, flinging it away to reveal the floor beneath.

In the sunlight, the stain was not solid black like it had been in her dream. It was about five feet across, and deep brown as though someone had spilled ebony lacquer, and striated with charcoal-colored veins that followed the grooves of the wood. *Martha died here. Right here.* The floor had soaked up her blood like a sponge. Chloe knelt beside the stain once more, knocking, prying at the boards around the stain, carefully avoiding touching the gore. There were no gaps, no hollow sounds, nothing to indicate a secret compartment beneath might be hiding the girl's body—or anything else vital.

She closed her eyes, feeling the sweat on her skin, the dust in the air. The demons had shown her this place in her dream, but to what end? Would they have done so if they thought she could use it to harm them? Of course not. And now that she'd found the place, now that she was sitting beside the spot where Martha had been killed, she felt... numb. Nothing urged her to pry up the floor—no anticipation, no connection to Helen or Martha or Elisha Shepherd, no *knowing*.

She opened her eyes as Brandon stepped away from the window, casting a shadow over her and the stain.

"Never been able to clean it right."

"Sorry?" She could not pull her gaze from the floor.

"Tried to wash it. Some stains don't come out."

"Yeah." Her eyelids felt heavy. What was she missing? She inhaled once, deeply, focusing on the little hairs on her arms, on the tingles along the back of her neck. Chloe sat back on her heels, hugging her knees, and finally dragged her gaze around the room behind her: a table, a dresser, a pile of old books...

Six feet in front of the far wall, opposite the window, stocky wooden feet poked from beneath an enormous muslin cloth. She squinted at the legs, at the small protrusions just above the wood floor. Were those bolts? Yes, the legs were bolted to the floor. *Bolted.* She dropped to her hands and knees and crawled closer, feeling every splinter of the wooden floor beneath the pads of her fingers, seeking some hint of connection—a touch of static, a single vibration—but the wood was merely warm from the heat of the room.

She reached for the nearest leg, the metal bolt rusted and useless, but when she touched the wood, a grinding noise began in her head in time to a vibration in her palm, the steady *cshh, cshh* of a handsaw on wood. It mattered, this piece. She hooked her fingernail under the corner of the bolt and—

Fuck! Her entire body shivered like she'd been electrocuted, and she leapt up, flew backwards, and stumbled, slamming her hip against something that felt like a knob. *What the hell was that? Faulty wiring?*

You know what it was, Chloe.

Not electricity. She'd never once seen a light on in this place.

She grabbed the corner of the drop cloth covering the piece of furniture and tugged, sending a plume of dust into the air. Something clattered to the floor behind her. She dropped the cloth.

The washtub, she'd known it all along. The one from the photos, with bolts that had once held shackles at each of the four corners, a jagged line of black snaking across the lower edge, probably the remains of something once alive. Up close she could see the ridges where they'd welded the tub together and the bulging seams looked a little like...those on the safe at Lehmann's shop—imperfect, odd. *Unique.* Had workers here made both? Her heart was trying to explode from her chest.

Inside the tub, a thick leather restraint lay coated in dust as if it had been there since the day the washtub had been covered, but there shouldn't have been dust, not if it had been beneath the drop cloth. And tucked underneath, as if the leather were bleeding, a scarf, like the one she'd seen in the surveillance videos at the shop. Helen's scarf, but half obscured by a thick layer of grime.

Pain radiated from her rib cage to her sternum. Helen had disappeared just weeks ago—how had that scarf gotten so nasty? Was it Helen's portal? The questions vibrated like a tuning fork in her brain.

But… The hairs on Chloe's neck tingled as a thought settled at the forefront of her mind. She turned to Brandon. "How did you know Martha died here, Brandon?" He had sure played dumb earlier about the journals.

The world went still, the quiet suddenly electrified, like the silent, thrumming energy of a storm cloud before a lightning strike. Brandon had not moved from his place in the center of the room, his attention fixed on the floor.

"Brandon? You had to have known about the journals if you knew she died here. You had to have seen Elisha Shepherd's…those drawings, the photos."

He kept his gaze on the floor, on the stain. "I heard about it. I should have told you who she was."

She. Martha. He was just like Greg, holding things back. How could she help if these assholes refused to tell her anything? Not like they were going to do it themselves—they were both incompetent. "Why didn't you tell me?"

"I was ashamed."

Ashamed? "You don't need to be ashamed of anything that happened to her—just because your ancestors did some horrible things, that's not on you."

"But don't you see? Of course it is."

"That doesn't make any sense." Unless he felt guilty about something he'd done recently. Had he been possessed and done something awful, like Victor had? In the washbasin, the scarf called to her to touch it. "What about that scarf, Brandon? What happened to Helen?"

He did not answer.

"Did you kill her Brandon?" *Maybe for being an evil bitch?* She glanced at the attic door, suddenly wishing she were nearer to it.

"No, no…I cared for her," he said, the words heavy with sorrow. "I didn't see her go, didn't see them do it, but…she's not coming back." He winced as if the thought physically pained him.

"What happened to Helen?"

"They took her." His eyes glazed as he looked beyond her,

at the back wall, or maybe the washtub, and the world around them shrank with the air in her lungs. The demons had taken Helen. Martha and Elisha Shepherd had... possessed her, bled Helen's energy dry like they had Victor's. And if Brandon knew that for a fact, really knew…"Did you bring the demons here?" Was that why he felt guilty? Had he gotten Helen killed? Gotten Victor killed?

His eyes widened. "I didn't do any of this! I want them to go away—that's why I burned down the shop." He finally met her gaze. "This is way bigger than me, way bigger than any of us." His shoulders slumped forward in defeat. "Blood must be repaid in blood," he whispered. "That's why I'm cursed."

What? Was Brandon saying that because his ancestor had been a murderer, the demons would come back until they'd killed whoever was left of his bloodline?

"But why are they after me?" she asked.

"You have a stronger energy than most…ah, shit." He doubled over, grabbing his ribs, his face contorted in pain.

Great power. "Brandon, what's wrong with you?"

He was still bent over, clutching his side. His gaze dropped to the stain. "I used to think that everything I did, the bad things… I thought I did those things to survive. That I had no choice. But there's always a choice. And someone has to pay." He looked up, his eyes glassy. "I have to pay. It has to be me." His lip trembled; he still clutched his gut. "But it won't end with me. Anyone complicit, they'll take."

Chloe didn't have a blood debt, but she was guilty, even if Victor was guiltier. But she wasn't going to be another hapless victim like Helen.

An inexplicable chill rolled from Brandon then, curling around her like mist, slowing her heart to a sluggish throb. She exhaled, almost surprised her breath didn't fog in the sudden cool. "We have to figure out how to get rid of them— maybe an exorcism kinda thing. Those pages here, in the library—"

"'Cast thee out,' from the lips of the chosen, the portal in hand as you speak. Once their name from your lips to banish, and thrice at a whisper to keep." Brandon's voice shook as he recited it.

But listening to it out loud, it all seemed too simple. Like a...trick. The air was growing thinner, harder to breathe, and her knuckles ached from gripping the edge of the washbasin, but they no longer tingled—whatever energy had been there had dissipated. This wasn't Elisha's portal; this was just a piece of furniture so steeped in misery that it struggled to contain the anguish.

Brandon inhaled deeply, peeling his fingers from his body. "We should search the outbuildings," he said, but there was something strained, almost sinister beneath his words, and it felt like a breath of scalding air on her skin. Her blood coursed faster, hotter through her veins.

Chloe glanced toward the window, the circle staring back at her like an evil eye. She shuddered—everything in her gut was telling her to stay away from that yard. But...was it because there was something dangerous outside? And even if it was dangerous, was it somehow vital to her goal of banishing the demons? Things worth doing weren't always easy. *God won't give you more than you can handle, girl.*

When she drew her gaze to Brandon again, he was back to staring at the stain on the floor.

"You think we'll find Elisha's portal out there?" she asked slowly.

He shrugged, mouth drawn, and the gesture seemed reluctant, even sorrowful, the way you'd shrug when someone asks what kind of snacks to bring to a wake. *Who cares, no one wants food anyway.*

Brandon raised his head and narrowed his eyes, but he nodded. "I think you feel it out there too, don't you? The tension? There's nothing like that up here."

The tension...he was right. Her distrust cooled. Brandon wouldn't try to hurt her—he needed her. And he knew it. She waited a moment, peering once more into the dark corners of the attic, and when Brandon made no move to leave, she hit the stairs, her skin crawling with the feeling that something in that attic was about to reach for her with ravenous claws. The impression was still with her when she reached the second floor landing. And why not? This was the house where Elisha Shepherd had conducted his experiments. The whole place was soaked in horror, and panic, and death.

Brandon was right. Some stains don't come out.

CHAPTER 28

CHLOE ANDERSON, PRESENT DAY

The first outbuilding Chloe and Brandon came to was a ramshackle old house. Slave quarters: one long room, with walls of rotting boards and dirt floors, and an indentation in the center that was probably used as a fire pit for cooking, or to warm the house in the winter. She kicked at the earth with her sandal, blackening her toes. Nothing here that could have been used as a portal. *Like it would be that easy.*

But though her fingertips detected no vibrations in the walls or the dirt, the energy in the air remained thick, and more needling than inside the plantation house, as if the breeze might whisper memories from the past if she listened hard enough. *We shouldn't be out here.* That thought rang through her brain, a mantra on repeat, but she couldn't rule out that Brandon was right for looking around—he was the only other one who could feel the energy in these places, too, who knew what they were looking for, who'd even believe they could find a demon portal and use it. And he was the only one who would help her if demons actually came to take her energy like he'd warned. *Demons feed on energy, and the more they feed, the more powerful they become.* But how would that even work? Would they suck it out of her like a vampire?

Or would they simply crush her like the tree had tried to? How much would it hurt? She swallowed over her dry tongue.

Two more buildings yielded the same—dirt floors, wood walls, no sign that anyone had been there since the structures had been abandoned, no antiques or other items on the ground. "Why don't you tear these down?" Chloe asked.

Brandon shrugged and didn't answer.

They entered the next building—the same, dirt and stones and brick walls. Brandon didn't even appear to be investigating now; he was just standing there, toeing the dirt, eyes on the entrance. As if...waiting for something. Was he just assuming she'd be able to see something he couldn't, the way he'd thought she could talk to Martha? She scowled at him until he headed out the door.

What the hell is his problem? He more than anyone should want to find the portals quickly so they could get rid of the demons here. *Unless he knows there's nothing to find.*

The path to the kitchen outbuilding was overgrown with dewberry vines that tugged at her sandals and caught on her bare toes. She winced at the briars around her ankles, but kept moving, feeling nothing sinister in the plants' stalks, just inconveniently placed thorns. This building was easily five times larger than the others. An enormous brick hearth with a wide open mouth flanked one side, the waist-high counter boards blackened by long ago flames. The floor was dirt, like in the living quarters, but here there were benches built along the far wall that might have doubled as extra counter space. Again, the energy was dull, flat, dead.

The power she'd felt in the house, the drive to investigate, had fully dissipated—no matter what Brandon thought, no matter what she might have felt in the past, nothing lurked out here now. Chloe sighed, the weight of exhaustion dragging on her as she glared at the brick. They should go, search the rest of the house for the apron, the medical bag, something significant to Elisha. At least she knew where the brooch was. "I think we should head back to the house." She stalked to the doorway. "We'll go grab that brooch, maybe see if we can find Elisha Shepherd's medical bag. Do you know which bedroom was his?"

Brandon pursed his lips, eyes darting back and forth, his own energy stiff and…anxious? Could he see something she couldn't?

"Brandon, are you okay?" But he wasn't, she knew he wasn't—she could suddenly feel his fear like the spines of a cactus against her arms.

"We should look a little more." His voice shook, almost imperceptibly.

She frowned, her heart thundering in her ears. "I… There aren't even any more buildings to search."

He looked at the ground, then back to the doorway. Then he walked past her without another word. *What the fuck is he doing?*

She followed him over the grass, up the hill, toward the house, his breath harsh in the still air. "Brandon?"

He walked faster.

"Brandon!"

As they came even with the porch steps, she closed the distance between them and touched his arm, and the static where their skin kissed made him turn.

"I know you're scared," she said. "I am too. But if we can find whatever it is that Elisha Shepherd needs to—"

"Elisha Shepherd needs you, Chloe," he whispered, and the words cut her, cut through her frantic heartbeat and into the cool quiet in her gut. This time when her heart accelerated, she could not tell if it was with the desire to run, or the desire to crush her body against his.

"You can't let him take you, not the way he took Helen." He winced and moved nearer to her, then placed his hands on her arms, gently, kindly, and she felt herself drawn closer, the energy from his skin cocooning her the way Victor's used to—that careful, quiet serenity she hadn't felt since he left.

The demons wanted to possess her, feed off her energy— she knew this already. *Not today, assholes.* Her heart vibrated so forcefully that she'd have been shocked if he couldn't hear it—there was something in his eyes that pushed at her, trying to emerge, a secret waiting to be born. "Do you know where the portal is? What we need to make them leave?"

"I need you to help me," he said. But that wasn't an answer and they'd just spent an hour wandering around and he hadn't done a damn thing to help her. Her frustration was palpable, oozing between her shoulder blades and tightening her muscles.

"I have to help myself." The words came out before she registered her intent to speak, but they weren't untrue—she'd spent her life trying to help other people, and what if she didn't have much time left to figure this out? So far all he'd done was try to burn down the shop—and failed—follow her around like a lost puppy, and take her on pointless excursions into buildings that were clearly useless to them, places that hadn't held a single thing they needed.

"I see." Brandon's eyes had gone hard. He released her, staring behind her at the tree. Her hackles rose and she turned to follow his gaze, peering into the shadows beneath the oak, watching for some demonic creature to emerge, but saw only sparse green grass. Moss covered the base of the trunk. The dirt was smooth, as though it hadn't been disturbed in years, but the memory of being held immobile by the weight of a snake-like branch made her shudder. *What is he looking at over th—*

The wind blew, rustling the leaves just enough that the light glinted off something nearer the drive, in the green beside the limestone... *It can't be.* She took a step forward, squinting, her heart hammering, intuition sending barbs up her spine, and then the energy in the earth was propelling her forward against her will. Victor's camera—she'd know it anywhere. She broke into a run, the stones flying beneath her shoes, when she snatched the camera from the earth, her fingertips vibrated so savagely that the strap rattled against the plastic case. Beneath her shoes, the dirt simmered as if rousing itself from a deep sleep. She retreated, clutching the camera, but the energy in this thing felt *alive*, dangerous, like trying to hold onto a live alligator—all scales and claws and teeth, one wrong move and it'd take you down. *Get it away.* And though her hands were clenched around it, though her muscles did not want to release it, she forced her fingers to obey and threw the camera, listening to the plastic crackle as it split against the driveway, the tree's branches waving in the meager breeze above.

Shh, shh.

The sound prickled over her eardrums and continued down her spine, leaving a trail of needled skin on her back though she wasn't sure what had made the noise. She couldn't breathe. A nasty energy from the yard repelled her, pushing her toward the car, toward the shop, her apartment, anywhere else, but she didn't want to get in the car either—she didn't want to be alone, not with those journals, not when the air itself had sprouted ears, listening to her breathing, just waiting to pull the last inhale from her lungs.

Shh, shh.

She edged back again, toward the house, squinting down the drive. They shouldn't stay out here—it wasn't safe, it wasn't safe at all.

"We have to go inside, Brandon." With the energy it took to expel those syllables, she might as well have been screaming them. Her fingers were still tingling. Her chest remained tight. But panic spurred her muscles into overdrive and she finally turned.

He wasn't behind her—the lawn was empty. No, not empty...

Shh, Shh.

Oh, fuck me. Rattlesnakes. Dozens of them between herself and the house, blocking her path to the car, cutting off her access to the yard. And they were slithering steadily toward her, the only sound the whisper of their bellies on the dirt and the sickening rattle of their tails.

Shh, shh.

Where is he, where the fuck is he? She backed up slowly,

toward the tree, but still they slithered closer, closer. When she glanced back at the drive she realized they had gathered there too—there was nowhere to go, nowhere but the oak. Could she climb it? Would the tree...kill her if she tried?

"Brandon!" But it was a squeak. Her lungs wouldn't work.

She took another step backward, another, and then her back was against the tree and—

The world disappeared, everything spinning as if she were caught in a tornado as gray as the sky. And her chest —*God*. Pain exploded through her rib cage, radiating out from a point above her heart, and on its heels came another stab under her ribs, and another in her left breast, like her flesh was tearing beneath a blade, the agony so white-hot and poignant that it drove every other thought from her mind. "Come to me," someone whispered in her ear, and then she was being lifted, snatched away from the pain, out of the hole, away from the tree trunk, strong arms beneath her armpits, and circling her ribs. She jerked her hand to her chest to stop the gush of blood and felt...nothing. No wounds. Just the frantic throb of her heart beneath her shirt.

What the fuck was that?

She still couldn't breathe, and there was something wrong with her eyes—the world had gone dark. She fought the arms around her, wriggling and punching, clawing with her nails, until she fell to the earth. Chloe scrambled back, readying herself to kick or bite, whatever she had to do to fend the demon off, anticipating the hard grip of a hand, a blow to the head, the prick of rattlesnake fangs in her calves, but... nothing happened. There was no pain and no sound, not even the *shh, shh* of rattles.

She wheezed in a breath and blinked hard, trying to force the world back into focus. The grass was gray-green, clear— no snakes. But why was it so dark? Brandon was standing on the drive, illuminated by moonlight, staring at her with his mouth twisted in sorrow or maybe guilt. He couldn't have heard her calling to him, but he'd known. He'd pulled her away from danger, taken her away from...the tree.

She looked back. The oak stood silent, unmoving, silvered in the moonlight, but the icy fear remained, deep in her abdomen. It had been daylight just moments ago, she was sure of it.

Brandon offered her a hand, and she grabbed his arm as if he was her lifeline in a sea of horrors.

"You have to help me," he said, pulling her to standing, and she balked—*No, you need to help, you have to fix this.* "It's the only way for us to get out, Chloe. For you to get out." And then he reached for her face and drew her to him. His lips were soft but cold, trembling as if her fear had seeped into his flesh, uniting them in panic.

He traced her lower back, palpating her scars like he could massage the old wounds away. She leaned into him as a memory played in her head, a street on a sunny day—and she was six, sneaking from her house, back toward the psychic on the corner to let the woman finish her reading, ready for the psychic to tell her how special she was. But the psychic was sitting with a different child now, a little boy, stroking his palm with her withered fingertip.

"I sense a great power, boy. There's great power in you."

That woman wasn't a psychic. She was nothing but a con artist, just like her mother'd said. The rage spread from her belly like a leaping brush fire, engulfing her heart, warming her lips where Brandon's mouth touched them. Psychics were liars, all of them, even if they stumbled into the truth sometimes—for Chloe *did* have great power. Didn't she? Or was she wrong?

She jerked back from Brandon and he from her, as if they'd been repelled in the same instant. But the moment their lips parted, she felt an aloneness deeper than she had ever felt, a powerlessness that seemed to rush at her from every corner of her being and wrap her heart in such misery that she thought it might stop beating. Maybe she wasn't special at all. Maybe she just wanted to be. Maybe Brandon was the one who was special, and she felt drawn to that specialness, to the urgent, extraordinary heat of him.

He took a step back. She followed him, grabbed his arm, and the pressure in her chest abated, though her pulse throbbed lower in her abdomen, harder. His touch allowed her to breathe.

"Come to me."

She hadn't seen his mouth move, but her body was already listening, aching, and she pulled her shirt over her head, the chilled air hardening her nipples beneath the lace of her bra—when had the breeze taken on that icy edge? But even as she stepped to him again, her intuition was sparking, telling her...his voice was the one she'd heard this whole time. Brandon had been calling her here. When the demons had sought her out, he'd beckoned her to him, trying to offer her protection from their evil. And she wanted that protection, wanted to be sucked into his vortex where nothing else could harm her.

"Come on out, boy, I won't hurt you." A female voice. Who had said that? Her gaze darted to the house, to the tree, to the yard behind Brandon, but no one was there and when he whispered near her ear—"Inside"—she pressed her body against him, harder than before. The landscape around her felt a little strange, wavery and wrong, as if she were walking in someone else's dream and could only see their world through a gauzy haze. She blinked.

Brandon stared, his eyes locked on hers, so rapt with attention it was as if he'd forgotten where they were, but his eyes were not the ones that concerned her, for she felt something else, some*one* else, watching them. She raised her gaze to the window above—*Did something up there just move?* Gooseflesh rose along her back, and she shuddered, but Brandon didn't notice; his mouth was on her shoulder, at her neck, leaving trails of wetness along her throat, on her clavicle—he froze and jerked back, his gaze on her chest. She looked down. The brooch was back again, resting between her breasts. *How—* Brandon's breath came faster as he ran a thumb over the ivory and lifted it between his fingers. And though she knew she hadn't put it on, it felt as though it belonged there.

"We'll fix you up, girl, get you right with God," but the voice was real, not in her head, and her breath caught, like she'd see Grandfather standing there, belt in hand. But she saw only Brandon's face, his earnest eyes. He dropped the necklace, and where it touched her flesh, it burned, actually sizzled against her skin. She cried out, and Brandon captured her mouth and pulled her closer, harder, and the roughness of his touch mixed with the stinging between her breasts, warming all the cold places that hadn't been touched in far too long. Victor had been so distant some nights, as if she hadn't been enough to stir his desire unless she'd just fucked his friend, or slapped his face, or yelled at Leslie.

"Skanky bitch." It was the jeers of the girls from school, their voices sharp with hate. And another voice, too, with a soft southern drawl, whispering, "A whore, trash," but this voice she did not recognize—it wasn't her memory, she realized. It was a glimpse into someone else's life.

She clutched onto Brandon as if he could keep her from falling into the abyss inside her mind. *Come to me.* Was that her thought, or another voice? It didn't matter, not now, as he led her up the stairs to the front door. All the eyes, the voices, the ominous presence of this place, the ghosts and demons and blood vengeance, made her heart throb, electric and delicious, every ounce of fear redirected into that soft place low in her belly. She jerked around one final time, but she could see nothing but the trees and the old oak, massive and still and silent. The pulse between her legs throbbed harder, more painfully, maybe because of the fear rather than in spite of it.

The brooch burned, and when she reached up to touch it she could feel pieces of her blistered skin stuck to the metal backing. Brandon's hand on her wrist was tight, but not nearly tight enough as he led her down the hall and—*Jesus, it was cold*—up the stairs.

"Listen."

The word came unbidden—*from my ears, not my head, not my head*—and every creaking floorboard felt like a thunderclap inside her. The air smelled of sage and soot, but that might have been Brandon, the fire from the shop still clinging to him like a jilted lover who refused to leave.

He pushed open the bedroom door and pulled Chloe in behind him then released her arm, and the absence of that pressure on her wrist was too cold, too lonely. Thin beams of moonlight shone on the floor, jagged gashes against the shadows, the bed looming against the back wall. Brandon stopped in the center of the room and turned to her, his shirt practically glowing, his face shiny in the moonlight, his gaze locked on her chest—on the brooch. On that other girl? She unclasped her bra and let it slide off her shoulders.

Goose bumps prickled on her arms as she stepped close enough to smell the herbal tang of his sweat—sage, definitely sage. His tongue in her mouth wasn't hot and angry like Victor's, but cool and demanding, and she demanded right back, exploring him, listening to the tinny clatter as one of his shirt buttons hit the floor. His muscles were hard, firm, *stable*, but when she ran her fingers over the ridges on his abdomen, the skin was rough—there were divots in the flesh under her fingers, many little indentations, and when she pulled back, he wouldn't let her look; he grabbed her arms and shoved her against the door so hard it shuddered with the force of the impact. Liquid heat rolled through her abdomen. Brandon dropped to his knees and jerked her skirt down over her thighs, the material tearing somewhere in the back, but she had no time to consider it—his lips brushed her stomach, then lower, lower, until he was between her legs, kissing her there the way he'd kissed her mouth. She clawed at his hair, and he lifted one of her knees onto his shoulder and fucked her with his fingers.

Heat radiated through her toes, up into her head, spreading into every pore and crevice, erasing everything else. "Faster, Goddamn you." Her voice sounded foreign to her, but she grabbed his shoulders, digging her fingernails into his flesh hard enough to draw blood. "Fuck me." Victor would have blushed, would have stopped, but Brandon covered her mouth with his, and Chloe bit his lip, tasting his blood on her tongue.

He grabbed her thighs and lifted her, her legs around his waist, and her back smashed into the doorframe again as he slammed into her, her scars singing as if they were being ripped open—Victor was such a fucking pussy. "Harder, motherfucker," she wheezed.

He jerked her off the wall and carried her to the bed, still inside her, threw her down on the edge, and then moved, slowly then faster, his fingers at her nipples, pinching her, scratching at her rib cage, drawing blood, just like how she used to beg Victor to touch her. She raked her fingers over the hardness of his abdomen—scars, definitely scars, like he'd been whipped, like the ones her Grandfather had left on her own back.

"Hit me," she whispered.

He smiled. Then his hand was zinging through the air, the sting against her cheek stunning her, blinding her for one hot moment, and it wasn't Brandon fucking her anymore, but Victor, and he was hitting her like he used to, slapping her hard but not hard enough. She lashed out, hitting back, hands closed into fists—now it was Brandon again, Brandon fucking her—but Brandon didn't whine, unlike Victor, who'd ducked and cried like a little bitch the night he'd come home from fucking his ex, and she'd whirled around and nailed him in the face with the skillet. She'd paid to fix his broken teeth; the only thing she regretted about the incident was that it was a cliché.

"You deserve this." A woman's voice, and Chloe's heart lurched as she craned her neck, seeking the source of the words, but she saw nothing but the moon painting inky branches on the walls. It wasn't Martha's raspy whisper, or Leslie's high-pitched whine, or even Shepherd's growly bass. *It sounds like...me.*

She had said that to Victor. After she'd hit him. And he

had cried and nodded because he knew she was right. He had deserved it.

Brandon rose above her, wiping blood from his lip.

The throbbing between her legs quickened. She strained her face off the bed and bit at his chest, clamping his nipple between her teeth until she tasted metal, and thunder rang in her ears and behind her closed eyelids she saw the bottle of wine—*For us, for us, for us.*

I wrote it. I wrote the note on the wine.

The realization hit Chloe so suddenly that it expelled the air from her lungs with a force like she'd been hit in the gut. She gagged as the thick, rancid stench of rotten meat invaded her nostrils.

Chloe's eyelids fluttered open and Brandon's room was gone, the plantation was gone, and the light was so bright it was blinding—they were in her apartment, her kitchen, and she was spread eagled on the counter, Brandon fucking her, while the wine toppled to the floor with a crash so violent she felt the shudder in her marrow.

And Martha was with them. The girl stood by the far end of the island, her back to them as if she was embarrassed, but Chloe would know those curls and that yellow dress anywhere, especially with the bloody mess dripping down the backs of the girl's legs. The rotten meat stink was stronger now. Brandon gripped her hips harder, thrusting into her as the pressure built within her and her head cracked against the countertop as he slapped her again, her nails digging into his back.

That smell she'd noticed wasn't from the garbage, it never had been. Martha turned, her broken face twisted with rage, and the blister on Chloe's chest throbbed in time with her heart. Then the girl snarled, a tiny sliver of lip peeling back from her teeth—three were missing on the right side, the same as Victor's had been after Chloe'd smashed him with the skillet. "He's mine," Martha hissed.

The girl pointed to a spot on the other side of the island, just in front of the refrigerator, and even as Chloe's body jolted with each thrust—*in, out, in, out*—she stared behind the counter where Martha stood, unmoving, patiently waiting for Chloe to *see*. A pool of blood grew beneath the girl's dirty bare feet. But it wasn't Martha's blood.

In, out, in, out... Chloe's gaze followed the creeping stream of red until she saw...the shoes. *In, out.* Victor's boots. *In, out.* And then the rest of him, lying facedown in front of the refrigerator in a crimson lake while she was getting fucked on the counter, and... Beneath his still form protruded a blood-soaked elbow—another, smaller body. Leslie? *In, out, in, out.*

Her vision went red, and in her chest something tore open, something that should have hurt, but instead it felt like gulps of water after a workout—a release, pleasure slaking her rage. She hadn't felt such joy since high school, when she'd turned the whispers—"Slut, whore"—into screams, when she'd run at the freckle-faced instigator, the girl's eyes widening as Chloe rammed a pen into her neck, piercing her once for taking Ron from her and once for talking shit. The hot blood had coursed over Chloe's fingers and wrists until someone pulled her off. She saw Grandpa's face that night, belt in hand—"We'll fix you up, girl, get you right with God"—saw him forcing her down into the bathtub, the wounds on her back still singing, spatters of that bitch's blood staining her hands to the elbow. Grandpa thought the steaming water would cleanse her, but instead her rage had bubbled brighter and hotter until it had consumed the very last of her respect for him.

In, out, in, out, in, out.

No...wait. These bodies in the kitchen weren't right. The images of Leslie that Chloe had seen in Victor's camera were gruesome, but not bloody. Martha was...lying to her. Lying about all of it. *Demons are tricky. Demons are liars. If you worship just because you're afraid, girl, you'll worship the Devil just as easy.*

The raw muscles in Martha's jaw twitched, trying to smile. The air had gone furiously hot, as if Martha herself were a star, about to obliterate them all in a surge of flame. Martha turned away from her and again pointed at the floor—

Victor was gone. The blood was gone. But when Chloe looked up, the Formica was still crimson, and the cabinets against the far wall were pock-marked with what looked like bullet holes. But then she blinked, and that disappeared as well. Brandon stilled between her thighs.

"You have to help me, Chloe," he whispered. "The portal's in the safe at the shop, and you have to go there, destroy it. Burn it. It has to be you." He grimaced, moaned as if in great pain, and then he moved his hips, once, twice, again, again, and trembled, his heat spreading through her abdomen. Chloe stared at Martha's broken face, but she could not scream, could not speak, for deep within her, every muscle was quaking, her insides spasming around him. She threw herself backward as Brandon's fingers dug into the skin of her hips. Ice shuddered through her flesh. Her eyes locked on Martha's flayed jaw, and she rode out the waves of orgasm, smiling when the girl looked down.

Then he was gone. The girl was gone.

She was alone, quivering on the moonlit floor of her kitchen—everything intact, nothing broken, no blood, no bodies. But she was cold. Gooseflesh pimpled her arms. In the breeze from the air conditioning unit, the note on the wine bottle rustled from the counter, the paper fluttering
—*For us, for us, for us.*

CHAPTER 29

ABRAM SHEPHERD, PRESENT DAY

The pain circling my rib cage is as sharp as daggers, as though all the hateful energy in the world has been condensed and deposited into my chest.

Martha is standing at the foot of my bed, and my muscles tighten, electricity zinging from ankle to neck. I force the tide of nerves down, burying it beneath a wall of logic—she will not harm me. She wants me here, for if she did not, I would be gone already.

"Time's up," she says. For me, or for someone else? I push myself to sitting.

A drop of blood falls from her chin to the floor with a tiny *splat*.

Before I am able to swing my feet to the floor, she is gone, but the energy in the room remains vibrant and palpable. There has been some invisible shift in the atmosphere, impossible to ignore—the energy crawls over my skin like a swarm of angry beetles.

"You seem to be struggling, Abram." I startle as the doctor emerges from the shadows at the corner of the attic, his hair slicked back and shockingly white against his black vest and overcoat, now ash gray in the moonlight. He doesn't appear to notice my disheveled state, the bony knobs of my legs jutting from beneath the sheet. "What is it?" he says. "Shall I administer something, perhaps a sedative, or—"

"No, no. It's Martha again."

The doctor's lip trembles, slightly, but it is there. He is angry. He does not like it when I call her that and he cannot see her, not yet; he still believes me to be hallucinating. And in truth, Martha, the girl she once was, left long ago after paying her penance here—now her shell is just a vessel for something greater. We do not trust what we do not recognize, but we will follow a wolf that wears a sheep's clothing. And Martha wants them to follow her. To see what life really is before she takes them. She wants them to know why they are being punished, showing them that their souls are more foul than they believe, forcing them to admit that within every living thing runs a vein of evil. For those who recognize that brutality for what it is, there can be nothing more terrifying than their own existence.

Mine is no exception. Even Brandon is afraid despite his obstinacy; he has spent his life following orders, and is finally fed up, it seems. He does not want to lie, does not want to lead Chloe astray, does not want to keep doing wrong. That horrid tingling in the gut we feel when we do something unsavory is multiplied a thousandfold for him—such poignant remorse is cutting, a razor's edge against the flesh. But if Martha said the time was up, it means Brandon has finished his part, given Chloe the final piece she needs to see the truth, probably sent her to The Enforcer. Which is a relief; I was not sure Brandon would follow through. It is impossible to know what any demon will do when you summon it to walk among you, unbound by earthly vessel.

I struggle to stand, and my left femur groans as if it wants to snap. I grit my teeth and stagger to the middle of the floor, to the wood in front of the now uncovered washbasin, where my pipe shines in the moon's beam. How my pipe got here, I do not know.

"It will happen again tonight." Though I try to keep my body still—*Oh, how every movement pains me*—I shudder.

Tonight. I cannot fail again. I retrieve the pipe and clench it between my teeth, then limp past the doctor to a small table, where a covered box rests. I have the herbs beneath the bed, my words readied upon my lips, and... I lift the lid. The rabbit is hidden in shadow, but I can make out his silhouette, the crook of his bent ear. He is ready, too. If things go wrong, I'll need all the blood, all the energy I can get to finish this—to answer my calling and wait for the pain to finally cease for good.

The doctor's eyebrows furrow behind his little round glasses. "You need to rest Abram. As your friend, I pray, you cannot go on like this." He sighs again, sadly, from his position in the center of the room, and I cannot help noticing he stands right on top of the wood that's soaked in old blood, the marred boards hidden beneath the rug. He worries the stain on his shirtsleeve with one long fingernail. He rubs at his chest too, at the tiny pocket that should contain the brooch, a picture of his daughter—a family heirloom he cherishes above all else. And when he is called to collect the item, he'll recall what happened here, too, in all its grisly detail. It is a process, this enlightening, and no slave owner passes through this plane unscathed, though their suffering varies. I suspect the doctor will get off lighter than others if his treatment of me, a black man, is any indication. But he is not innocent—none of them are.

"I am afraid." My voice is barely a whisper, though I do not tell him I am less afraid of death and more afraid of Elisha. The name rolls over my skin like ice, and the air pulses, shiny and angry. Elisha does not suffer here; he relishes this pain. He will be here forever, gaining strength from every soul he acquires. My only hope is to dampen his power so that he cannot take my soul when my own time comes.

"I understand you are scared, Abram." He nods, face twisted in sympathy. "But there is nothing to be done."

Will I know when it is my time? The doctor does not know his own end is near; he believes he's here to treat me.

Perhaps the doctor will cry, weeping, begging to remain here, to atone. Perhaps it will be a simple chiming of a clock—time is up, and poof, he's gone. Maybe there will be a fight, the wheels of that great machine beginning to turn before he's ready, and he will be carried along like a rodent caught in the cogs, trying to wriggle free, and failing.

The rabbit scuttles about and settles.

"I do not want to leave this place." My stomach ties itself in knots as I replace the lid on the box again, plunging the rabbit into blackness.

"Now, Abram, you know you cannot stay forever. The malady is quite bad—I have seen cases like this before and they did not end well."

Did not end well. He means I am dying but that is not the end I fear. I want to believe that any good I do here will spare my soul, but I am not naive enough to think it is certain. I am the last living relative of the Shepherd family, the last living relative of the man who murdered the doctor's daughter. And blood must always be repaid in blood.

Phillip Alton is still watching me, awaiting my response.

"I know, Doctor. I know."

The doctor shakes his head sadly, then walks toward the window and sits in the wingback chair on that wall, his legs lit with the moon's beam, his face hidden. "We both know there isn't much choice in how the journey ends." Again, he is speaking about something else, a physical death, while my meaning is deeper—I know the true process of dissolution lasts far longer than a lifetime. It is disconcerting that I cannot see his eyes.

I sigh, reaching for my lighter, and watch the flame catch on the sage leaves in my pipe. When I look up again, the doctor is gone. His glasses lie in the chair beneath the window, dusty and cracked. There is no sound but the whispered breath of the wind against the eaves.

But I am not alone.

This I know better than anyone.

CHAPTER 30

MARTHA ALTON SHEPHERD,
FOURTEENTH FEBRUARY, 1836

I awake with the taste of iron on my tongue, the attic floor hard beneath me. Oh, and another day comes. The sun is too high to be morning, but I do not care enough to creep to the window to discern the glow.

Elisha came last night, again with that wild look in his eyes, as he has each evening for two weeks now—since the day I meant to depart and he dragged me by the hair to this attic. And still my love does not so much as call to me from the other side of the door. Perhaps he is already dead.

My body still aches from where Elisha made me lie still while he prodded all my most tender places, pinching, hurting. I did not resist—I never have, not since the night he tied me down for refusing. That night, he beat me with the leather straps he takes to the slaves when they've displeased him, like I was an old dog worthy of no better. Perhaps he believes this to be true. And every day that my letter to Father goes unanswered, the panic grows along with the life in my womb.

No one is coming to help me. Maybe Father never received the letter at all. I gave it to Hany, but perhaps she betrayed me—or perhaps Elisha found her and took it before she could deliver it.

How could I have believed she would make it to Father? How could I have believed she would even want to, after how I treated her, banishing her to the fields to be whipped like an animal?

I shift my weight, and pain sears my insides, deep and sharp. Now I know why the women scream in the field, why Elisha returns wiping his bloodied hands on his handkerchief. But those women have never returned. Perhaps I, too, am doomed to vanish.

Is it awful to wish this pain upon someone else? To pray that he takes a woman in the field instead? Do not misunderstand—I shan't like to see anyone harmed, but the ravages he bestows upon me tear at my heart as much as my body. I hear the cries of the slaves at night now, when I hobble to the window. I am ashamed I've never listened before. I might have helped ease their suffering, back when I was able to do anything besides lie here and watch the sun cast shadows on the floor. Could I ever have registered their pain before having the same done to me?

No. Until it was mine, I was blind to it.

It is disgraceful. I am disgraceful.

And in more ways than one. He knows now that I am with child—I am too far along to hide it, and I have seen that dark glitter in his gaze as he appraises my belly. Perhaps he is trying to convince himself that it is not true. Maybe he seeks a solution, but I do not want one. My child is the only thing that means anything to me. Well, the child and its father, though the thought of him makes my heart seize. My one comfort is the knowledge that Elisha does not know whom I've lain with, but he shall get it out of me, I know he shall. He'll pinch until he's wiping my blood from his fingertips, until I am no longer strong enough to resist him—I have always been weak, eaten by pain and loneliness. I should have done better. Now I fear it is too late to rectify the wrongs done—but what shall be my punishment?

I stare at the wooden beams of the roof as afternoon wanes, the long shadows shifting ever higher on the walls.

THE JILTED

And as darkness creeps into the room and soaks my skin in dusk, I finally close my eyes.

I awake to shouting from below.

Has my love returned? That is my first thought, my hope; he said if Elisha found us out, if he thought Elisha would hurt me, he'd light a fire at the courthouse, get them to pay attention to him. He said he'd make sure someone knew, that someone would save me. Even if they beat him. Even if they dragged him behind a horse, he said, they'd at least bring him back to the plantation to his master, and they'd discover what was happening here, and I could scream, and I would...live.

I drag myself to the attic window and peer into the night, at the solemn blackness in the distance. The front lawn is alight with torches, though most are stuck in the ground—I see perhaps twenty men, all white. Masters. And in that flickering yellow glow, I can make out a shadow...a noose. No, two nooses, hanging from the old oak tree. Even from here I can feel the glow of the blazing torches on my flesh. He's going to hang me. Me and my love.

But the other masters surely will not let him kill me. They know my father, or know of him—they'll not sit back while Elisha hangs his wife no matter how awful my sins.

Or will they? Men are animals when they fear they've been wronged—those men might wish to make an example of me as a warning to their own wives.

Elisha steps into my line of sight directly below the window. Until this moment, he has stayed hidden in the shadows of the porch, hidden as he has been our whole marriage—I felt the evil, but I did not see it. Maybe I simply chose not to believe it.

Elisha gestures to the front porch, beckoning to someone I cannot see, and my stomach heaves. I am going to watch my love die first.

I shut my eyes, but as the jeers begin, I open them, for who am I to close my eyes yet again to the suffering of another? I've turned my back for too long.

But it isn't him. And then I register the words they are chanting, shouting in chorus: "Kill the witch! Kill the witch!" Who are they talking about?

The boy comes first.

Hany's son, almost four and curious but also clearly terrified, his little arm jerking back with seizure-like thrusts, his feet dragging as the men pull him toward the tree. Two other men drag Hany beside him. I choke on my own vomit, rancid and awful.

"Kill the witch!"

Hany isn't a witch. Hany has never done anything even remotely like witchcraft—just because she knows how to concoct a lifesaving potion, or a life-ending one, doesn't make her...

No, this is not about witches. This is... Elisha found the letter. He wants to kill them—he wants me to watch them hang. And whatever lie he told the jeering crowd was obviously compelling.

"Kill the witch! Kill the witch!"

The boy opens his mouth and cries out, and though I cannot hear him over the crowd, I can guess his words by the movement of his lips: "Mama!" My heart wrenches. Despite my vengeful thoughts against the boy, I do not hate him. I hate my husband. Oh, dear Lord, what have I done? None of this was Hany's fault—Elisha forced himself upon her, and how could I have blamed her for that? I just felt...lost. Angry. I am no better than my husband.

But I am. I found love growing out of hate. How can death be the punishment for love? And yet it is. Hany's love for me drove her to take that letter—now she and her son will swing for it.

I run for the attic door, slamming my fists against the wood, bloodying my knuckles. It doesn't give. The washtub is clearly too big for me to lift and use as a battering ram, and there is nothing else here, no stones, no tools—Elisha keeps his things with him. I race for the window again, frantic, screaming "It's my fault, it's mine!" but no one below me even pauses, intent as they are on the tree, on the rope, on the child, his tiny feet scrambling back, trying to get to his mother. They kick him back into place below the noose. Hany grabs for him, maybe trying to comfort him, maybe pleading with the men to let them be, but I cannot see her face or her mouth, just her arms as she flails toward her child.

The crowd parts. The noose goes around the boy's head. Claude—that is his name. And Hany beside him, so close they can each smell the fear of the other, her throat already circled with rope, and she is screaming, crying out for her son. No one but me screams back, my voice echoing off the attic walls, a frantic wail that might belong to someone else. They cannot hear me. No one can hear me.

The men below tug, fast, on the other end of the lines, and the ropes whizz over the tree limb, pulling Hany, pulling the boy, both of them stumbling backward toward the tree, crying, screaming, eyes wide with terror. I batter my fists against the glass, my words unintelligible even to me, but that matters little—my voice is drowned out in the chorus of jeers echoing through the night. The boy is flying, his little legs kicking, the old, healed scar on his temple probably throbbing as the noose forces blood into his head. Did Elisha explain that scar to these men, tell them what experiments he ran on the boy? For surely that's what happened to the child, I can see this now. But no, of course he didn't tell them, not any more than he told them why he is really stringing Hany up, why he's stringing the boy up. He wants to make sure the boy tells no one about me, about the letter they tried to take to my father—to save me. And the way the men are chanting —"Kill the witch!"—they must believe the boy to be as much a demon as his mother. They do not see the demon standing beside them, smiling up at the tree.

Hany's feet leave the ground. They both grapple with the ropes, their hands at their throats, their fingers slashing at the nooses, at the skin of their necks, as if there were any hope.

It is over faster than I expect. The boy stops moving first, his little hands falling to his sides, his face going slack. Hany seems to feel her son's surrender, for she stops kicking her feet and releases the rope at her neck. She reaches for her son, finds his hand, squeezes it.

Her eyes bulge out horribly—I can see her glassy stare from all the way up here. She stops moving. Finally, she lets go, her hand dropping to her side, the child swinging with that final release.

I choke and gasp, clutching at my abdomen. "I'm sorry, I'm so, so sorry."

When I open my eyes again, Elisha is staring up at me, and in his gaze I see no anger or sadness, nor the indifference I am used to from him. He raises an eyebrow. And grins, the flames flickering against the shine of his teeth.

Then he turns away and nods to a man across the circle from him—Brandon. *Oh, my love, no.* If I have to watch him swing, I know my heart will cease to beat. And yet…there is no way out, is there? It is too late for us. Elisha points to the window and nods.

My heart soars—my love has a plan. Brandon has a secret way out. My love is going to save me.

But as he starts toward the house, he is already crying.

Crying. So he has lost hope already. I bang against the glass and the heavy supports around it, barely feeling the bones in my fingers break—the glass does not—but the men are already dispersing, some leaping on their horses, their jeers and drunken howling drowning out any sound from above.

I slide down the wall, splinters digging into my shoulders and the pads of my feet and the backs of my thighs, but I do not feel the pain from that either. Is there any physical sensation that can rival this terror?

For I fear I will soon know a pain that supersedes all else. Elisha would not summon my love to be present for no reason—Brandon is his most trusted helper. He needs him to help with whatever he has planned for me, something I shall not stay still for. There will be no prodding, no pinching, nothing so swift as a hanging. I cannot breathe.

A steady *thud, thud,* sounds upon the stairs, rising.

I clasp my hands together, but I cannot remember the prayers, cannot hear the words my father used to speak. All I hear is the panic in my heart.

"Please, God, help me."

The door lock clinks. The hinges squeal. Brandon enters first, paled by the moonlight, and though I stare at him, urging him to grace me with just one comforting gaze, he refuses even to look at me. His face is stained with tears and sweat as he sets something down—a candle, thick as my arm. Then three more.

Look at me!

I jump when Elisha steps in and locks the door behind him. He is already wearing the apron, stained with the blood of lost souls. Brandon bends, lighting the wicks, and the room brightens and flickers yellow. Elisha's eyes dance.

"Take her to the tub."

I press my back against the wall, and when Brandon grabs my wrists, I stare at him—this cannot be happening. He wouldn't, he couldn't—

Together they lay me in the metal washbasin. I fight, but I am not strong enough, not nearly—shackles clank shut around my wrists. My ankles.

"Hold her."

Brandon's tears fall on my forehead. The straps already prevent my movement—Elisha does not need Brandon. He's torturing my love, too. But then... Elisha knows Brandon loved me? And Elisha did not hang him?

Brandon grabs my hands, and I feel the love there, the gentle adoration edging beneath the pain, and then Elisha is slicing away my undergarments, stripping my dignity along with the cloth. The blade catches my skin.

"Please, God, please."

Elisha kneels between my knees. I look into Brandon's eyes. "Tell my father I love him." And the most incredible pain sears through me, a bright and vicious agony, tearing me apart as though my child is clawing through my insides with knived fingernails. I scream, but it does not dull the misery. Brandon squeezes my hands and then I am falling, the black clouding my vision, but it is not over—it will not be over for a long time, until I am begging God to take me from this place.

"Tell our baby I'm sorry." The words are coming too slow—I feel the clumsy way they leave my lips. The light dims, and I can no longer hear Brandon's sobs, I can no longer feel his hands on me. I can no longer feel the tub.

"Take the picture, boy," Elisha says from somewhere far, far away, his voice fading in my ears.

Dear God, have mercy on my soul.

CHAPTER 31

CHLOE ANDERSON, PRESENT DAY

The pavement almost steamed as Chloe tore down the road, away from her apartment, her footfalls eliciting a groan that might have come from the earth or from her own lips. The breeze was sticky, the air hot on her face, and the blanket of fog was heavy, too, wrapping the horizon to her left, smothering any lights from the distant homes across the Mississippi River. As she headed away from the water and toward downtown Cicatrice, the cobbled street clacked under her heels, much too quickly, disrupting the steady hum of early morning business people getting ready for the day, though they shouldn't have been there, not now, not when the world was black. Was it afternoon? Evening? The world around her was as dark as if it were midnight.

The man with the drums smiled at his sticks, and she almost smiled back until she realized he wasn't looking at her, maybe couldn't even see her in the moonlit dim. The man with the canvases set his pieces against the wrought iron fence and he smiled, too, then turned back to his task before she could react—and how could he see his paintings? There weren't even any streetlights around him, just the wide expanse of the cemetery in the background…was the park still there at all? She listened for the patter of Martha's feet, for the whir of the camera's shutter, for a whisper on the breeze. But she heard nothing, felt nothing, smelled nothing —she'd gone numb. Even moving her eyes seemed too much effort, and the darkness made it impossible to see the details of her surroundings anyway. *Demons. There are demons here.*

But Brandon had told her how to fix this. *Burn it.*

"'Cast thee out' from the lips of the chosen, the portal in hand as you speak. Once their name from your lips to banish, and thrice at a whisper to keep." She whispered it now, twice, trying to convince herself she'd remember what to say when the time came. Lehmann wasn't going to hand the portal over; he kept it locked up for a reason, and Brandon knew that, which was why he'd tried to burn the place down. Maybe he'd figured he'd go back and pull the portal from the ruined safe the next day. Could she whisper the words from the room outside the safe, send the demons through the cast iron walls into the portal inside? No, the rhyme had said "portal in hand." She would try to remove the portal and banish the demons first, but if she couldn't, she'd just destroy it as Brandon had said—he was the only one she could trust.

She wished he hadn't vanished before she could ask him what the portal actually was. That would have helped, but the tingling at the base of her spine said she'd know it when she saw it. *It has to be you.* Was destroying the portal a matter of her being...strong enough? If she couldn't do it, maybe Grandpa was right about her. *You're quick as a bunny, Chloe.*

Fuck that. She would burn that bitch into the ground.

The street with the antique shop loomed ahead, but...the store was black as a tomb inside. Bile rose in her throat. The windows were dark, empty—no vases or fans, no cameras or brass boxes. No signage outside, and no street lamps either, though there should have been, and the facade was different, too, the outer walls dingy gray in the moonlight. Abandoned, the way it had been when she'd watched Brandon try to light the shop on fire, and though the architecture was the same down to the bricks, she could feel the differentness, the... agedness. Was the safe even in there? She might be too late.

Chloe touched the rickety doorframe, no door at all—*this is not right*—and stepped over the threshold into the pitch darkness beyond, and—

What the hell? She blinked at the sudden brightness, squinting at the display tables, the vases, the glass bottles, the brass boxes, the fans. Greg glanced at her from his usual spot by the window, the way he always did—placid, reserved. Something in her chest lurched drunkenly, and she peered back outside, expecting the glow of sunlight through the windows—*the shop is open, it has to be daytime*—but the sky was still black. No streetlights either, though the lamps inside cast the room in a yellow haze.

Greg appraised her. His eyes weren't really violet as she'd always thought—they were blue, and striated with slashes of red that ran through the irises and toward the outer white like a spider web. He looked…sick. *Diseased*. Had he always been that way?

Distract him, then get to the safe. "What…time is it?"

He put down the fan he'd been playing with and turned fully toward her. "You shouldn't be here," he said, and his voice was low, rumbling, the growl of an angry tiger. His gaze had changed too—a tightness that looked like sorrow but felt like rage.

He was one of *them*. A demon, after her energy, wanting to possess her. She backed toward the hall. "I'm just going to talk to Lehmann," she said, her eyes burning with unshed tears.

The office door was locked, which meant she'd found Lehmann; thank God he wasn't in the room with the safe. No sound from behind the office door though—should she be worried he'd hear her? *Like I need something else to freak out about.* It'd be over soon enough. She crept to the next door and slipped inside.

The room seemed smaller than it had ever been, the safe on the wall a thousand times more imposing, though she could discern no actual difference in size. She tried the safe door—locked. Of course it was. She ran her fingers along the side, feeling for a a combination plate, a place for a key... Nothing. *What the fuck?* No wonder Brandon had lit it on fire to destroy it—the cracks around the safe door weren't even wide enough for a crowbar. But flames might weaken the seams.

She bit her lip and exhaled her frustration. If the fire thing didn't work she'd learn how to build a Goddamn bomb and pray the portal inside stayed intact long enough for her to send a demon or two back to Hell.

The iPad with the phantom *Crosses and Bows* game was no longer on the desktop. She opened a drawer, searching for paper—the drawers were empty. What sort of office desk didn't have office supplies? But then again, she'd never looked. She'd never had a reason to—she'd just assumed desks came equipped with that stuff. That meant all she had was a Zippo, a bottle of lighter fluid, and a stack of Post-its—the only kindling she could find at home—and one lone paperclip from the back of the second desk drawer.

She pulled the lighter out anyway. If she started the blaze on top of the metal safe, it would likely peter out before it caused real damage. Would the desk burn? Maybe, but by the time it seared through the varnish she'd be overcome by the smoke. She wished she'd left the journals here—at least then there'd be kindling—but the journals, along with the car, were probably still in Brandon's driveway, surrounded by snakes. *Fuck.*

She flicked the lighter—it didn't light. She tried again, and this time the flame caught, but it was weak, so weak that when she lowered it against the wood, the tiny flame barely blackened the corner—what the fuck was this thing made of? She turned to the safe itself, running a finger over the seams. Even if she lit all the Post-its, it wouldn't be enough. Setting the Zippo aside, she uncapped the lighter fluid and turned the bottle over onto the safe, taking special care to soak the seams—if the safe was going to falter, it'd be along the cracks.

The heady aroma of the lighter fluid was making her

dizzy. She held her breath.

When the bottle was empty, she snatched up the Zippo, and flicked it. Nothing happened. She tried again. The flint ground, snapped, but did not ignite. *You've got to be kidding me.* She tried again, and again, but the flame refused to light and she couldn't spend all night in here—day—whatever. Eventually Lehmann would show up. Maybe he'd kill her when he realized what she was doing.

The paperclip. She'd start an electrical fire—that might even be better, harder to extinguish. All she needed was one spark to catch the lighter fluid, and the safe would ignite too. Hopefully.

Chloe knelt, searching beneath the desk for a plug, but the wall was smooth. *Come on, you bastard.* Sweat dripped into her eyes. She ran her fingertips along the baseboard. Nothing. She pulled her head from beneath the cave under the desk and peered at the lamp, its bulb shining brightly, and then followed the cord to where it hung behind the desk. This time when she crawled beneath the desktop, she pressed her hand behind the backboard and as far up as she could, seeking the outlet the cord was plugged into. Where was that cord, *where is it?*

There!

She grasped the cord between two fingers and followed it down to—

To nothing. It wasn't plugged into anything. And yet the light remained on.

Demons feed on energy, and the more they feed, the more powerful they become. This place was a virtual power grid of bad vibes.

"The safe should open for you now."

Every nerve ending leapt, and Chloe scrambled out from under the desk, banging her head on the edge of the desktop.

Lehmann stood in the doorway, his gaze on her, and for once he didn't appear agitated—just blank, bored, as if he discovered women crawling beneath his desk every day. "I have what you're looking for."

She stared at him, then at the safe. Why would he give her anything? Was this a trick? *Demons are tricky—they are liars.*

Her muscles tensed, every fiber of her being ready to run past him from the room—but she couldn't leave. If she did, this would never end; if she failed now, her life was over anyway. She could *feel* the finality creeping up, the same way she had watched the light outside die, everything around her steeped in harsh, strained energy like the pressured applause after one last encore. Tonight was it for Chloe. She was out of chances.

Then Lehmann was gone, the office door closed, but the safe—the door was ajar, though she hadn't seen Lehmann open it. The walk to it was longer, dimmer somehow than it should have been, as if the lamp had suddenly tarnished, or maybe it had pulled its light away from the hulking iron door to avoid seeing what terrors lurked inside. Every step echoed around her, hollow, foreign, and the walls themselves were strange, too—in her peripheral vision they blinked, one moment brick, painted gray, the next black and soot-stained, but when she jerked her head in that direction, the walls were blank again, white. Like a projection screen running a faulty film roll.

Do it, Chloe. She had to get it over with. Heart thundering in her ears, she appraised the thing: black, cast iron, the top reaching to her waist, and though she remembered spraying it with lighter fluid, had smelled the stink, there was no wetness on the top of the safe—the smell had vanished too. Energy coursed through her, intuition calling her, every cell in her body screaming at her that this was why she was here. Chloe touched the handle and jerked her hand back. It was hot, searing hot, the whole thing reminding her of the wood-burning iron stoves people once used to heat their homes.

Please, God, if I ever needed you, it's now.

If you worship just because you're afraid, girl, you'll worship the Devil just as easy.

She inhaled once, a sharp hiss through her nostrils, and grabbed the handle, letting it burn her palm as she yanked the door open, steeling herself for some horrifying scene, a mass of clawing demons ready to scrabble free. But there was nothing inside but a circular white item the size of a small Frisbee on the bottom shelf. A plate? She frowned.

Chloe bent and picked it up, and the heat burned into her fingertips and palm, but the pain was less intense now—nerve damage? She gritted her teeth. The plate was white porcelain, a vein of pale, green ivy circling the perimeter. On one edge sat a tiny painted rabbit, pudgy front feet at his mouth, one black ear raised, the other cocked low over his eye.

Her throat. Something was around her throat. But when she reached up to touch her neck, she felt nothing but her own clammy skin.

For you, Chloe, because you're quick as a bunny. But in her mind's eye, her grandfather was smiling, kindly, and his eyes looked sincere, as if he wanted to make her feel better, as if the gift had been supportive all along. But it had been a tease, hadn't it? Because she'd lost, *she'd lost*, and how dare he try to make light of it?

She swallowed hard, failed, gagged. She couldn't breathe. What did this have to do with anything? The demons were messing with her and she couldn't get sidetracked by every distraction. But the words echoed in her head so loudly—*quick as a bunny, quick as a bunny*—that she could think of nothing else.

Quick as a bunny.

She looked down at the plate again... *The hell?* It was full of cookies, chocolate chip, with extra sugar glittering on the top. *Nope, not today, Satan.* She was in an antique shop, not a freaking bakery, and if she could make cookies appear she'd surely have been using that talent her entire life. Yet the treats felt as familiar as the plate, something she'd seen before, though she could not recall where. This wasn't a hallucination, wasn't a vision—this was a memory. But where—

The cookies vibrated on the plate, then began to change,

shivering as if alive, little pores bursting open and weeping blood. Chloe's hands shook, but her fingers held tight to the dish. *I know these, I know them, I...* The red drips hit the porcelain, worming like maggots, each shimmying toward the others, the stain spreading, writhing like ravenous slime seeking the outer edge of the plate, seeking her fingers—

She dropped the plate, and for a moment time slowed, the cookies lifting from the surface along with the red mess that undulated like Helen's scarf, all of it suspended in the air. Then the dish fell, the cookies fell, and the blood splattered on the wood floor, and the floor opened beneath it, the wood planks yawning wide, spreading like a mouth waiting to be fed. Chloe scrambled backward, tripping and skittering like a crab until her shoulder hit the opposite wall. But already the floor was groaning, the boards knitting back together as she watched, leaving no clue that the plate had ever existed.

Oh no. If that plate was the portal... Frantically she scanned the room for the lighter fluid, for the Zippo, but they were gone too, so she whispered Martha's name, Elisha's name in turn, hoping it wasn't too late, hoping she could still banish them, though her confidence was fading fast. She wasn't strong enough to deal with a place where the floor could swallow you whole, great power or not. The room wavered, pieces of the wall beyond the safe crumbling before her eyes—was this it? Was this how it felt before the demons took you away? *No, fuck this, no.* She didn't give a shit about banishing demons—she didn't care about anything besides getting the fuck out of there. Now.

Chloe heaved herself to standing and raced for the hallway, stumbling into the wall opposite the office. The brick was changing colors again—gray, black, gray—as if the lights were being turned on and off and on again, but they weren't. The only glow came from the front room, where the main shop blazed yellow with lamplight.

Lehmann was behind the center case, spinning his top, but he stepped around the glass counter when he saw her, his face puckered as ever—less than six feet away. "She's ready now, right Greg?" He did not take his eyes from Chloe's face. The toy spun on the glass.

"She is," Greg said from the window display. "Too bad. I really thought she was the one. But I always do."

They're insane. "I have to go." Her voice was high-pitched, frantic, the invisible noose around her neck tightening again. Because as much as she didn't get it, didn't grasp what was happening here, she felt the horror like a thousand needles pricking her flesh. She forced a breath as she edged away from the counter.

"Not so simple, just to go," Lehmann said. "I'm here to finish the jobs no one else can." He raised his arm to scratch at his cheek, and the swastika tattoo glared black and fresh from beneath his shirtsleeve. "Don't fight it so hard," he said. "You'll be back."

Finish the jobs... The Enforcer. She believed that, God help her she did. But whose orders was he enforcing? Satan's? The Devil's. *Elisha Shepherd.* "I have to go," she said again. She took another step backward, around the little display table and toward the door, and Lehmann dropped his gaze to the top. Still spinning.

But now Greg stood just to the side of the door, his back to her, staring at the dark sidewalk outside, and that blackness hid untold evils—were the dangers she knew better, safer, than those she couldn't see? Greg shifted in her peripheral vision, dropping his arm to his side. *Oh God.* A braided rope trailed from Greg's fingers to the floor, like thick shoelaces woven together—like a noose. Her insides turned to jelly. He was going to hog tie her, bring her to Elisha to...feed on?

"You don't have to do this, Greg. We're friends, right?" The words came out an octave too high, not that it mattered how her voice sounded. Greg wasn't anyone's friend, he was possessed, he was one of them, but she'd been able to steer Victor even when he was out of his mind—she was stronger than they were. *Special.* She forced a smile, but Greg refused to look at her. He spoke to the blackness outside.

"Our lives amount to nothing more than the sins we've committed against others. One lifetime for every soul I took." He fingered the rope as if praying the rosary. "I wish I could serve what I was accused of in life. Those who stuck me with the lethal injection only knew of four." He tugged the rope taut. "I just wanted them to love me. But they didn't. I thought you'd be different." Greg chuckled, but it was a melancholy sound that made bile rise in her throat. "Lehmann will be here for a million lifetimes," he said. "Flip a switch, dig a mass grave, that's all it takes to fuck up eternity." Greg finally turned from the door, and Chloe reared back, her hip slamming into the little spindly table, vases and carved glass crashing to the ground. *His chest, his—* Where Greg's chest had been, tentacle-like protuberances reached out, elongated, slunk slowly down toward the floor with a hissing noise like tearing paper.

"Brandon will be here forever, too," Greg said. "The master of the house made him do it, so maybe it's not fair, but justice isn't always fair. All those women, every wife the master had...he wanted to see what their insides looked like, whether every baby would shine dark or if any would emerge as pale as he." Greg wound one length of rope around his thumb, then another. "And he could rid himself of each wife in turn while keeping their dowries of land and slaves. Childbirth was an excuse no one would question."

Chloe's head spun. Was Greg saying that Brandon had been forced to get Martha pregnant? And Elisha's other wives? But that made no sense, Martha had died long ago, and Brandon was, Brandon was...

"Any idea how long *you'll* be here, Chloe?"

The past is the past, we only look forward, and nothing else matters. She was frozen. *Run. Run.*

Her vocal cords loosened just enough for her to croak: "I can change!" And in her mind's eye, she was screaming it, the slashes of the belt hot and fresh on her back, burning, and then Victor was walking out the door and she was shouting, "I can change, I won't hurt you again," but he wouldn't listen, even though they were a *family*. It was never too late, not for Chloe, she was special, she could—

Greg's tentacles reached the wood, and slithered toward her with a *shh, shh* noise like a hissing snake. "We evolve, the longer we're here," Greg whispered. "We see the truth. But time doesn't make us less cruel. And you'll be here until you see what you really are." One tentacle touched her ankle, slimy, hot, and she leapt back into the glass display case at the side of the shop.

"Just because other people can't learn, doesn't mean I can't." Could she make it past him into the street?

"I have nothing else for you here," Lehmann said from behind the center counter, and she glanced over, trying to keep them both in her line of vision. And then her boss, a dour man, a man of morose expressions, pulled his lips into a grotesque smile so wide it split his face in half, like he'd been sliced from one ear to the other. His teeth had grown too, lengthened into glistening, needle-sharp triangles, a jack-o-lantern come to life. From between his front teeth, a forked tongue hissed, and flicked into the air as if scenting her fear.

Fuck. This.

She ran, stumbling over broken bottles and shattered vases, scrambling through the debris of cursed things, leaping around Greg's slimy, squirming body parts that had no place on a human, not at all. She bolted past the threshold into the night, and glanced over her shoulder, expecting to see tentacles reaching for her, or the toothy maw of an otherworldly beast, but the shop was dark again, burned-out, the window glass missing, a jagged shard clinging to one corner of the encasement. The moonlight showed only rubble inside. But the scene was not quiet and still, for the soot was creeping, slowly expanding like the blood pooling on the plate, crawling over the brick of the shop, enveloping it, as if the building were trying to erase itself.

Brandon had been wrong. It would do no good to light it up again—the place had burned down long ago. Maybe they'd never rebuilt it at all.

CHAPTER 32

CHLOE ANDERSON, PRESENT DAY

The demons were coming.
The cobbles seemed intact, though—no shimmering spots appeared that might open up and swallow her, no tentacles reached from the manholes to pull her, screaming, into the sewers. But the buildings...they weren't right. Across the street, the vibrant bauble store had changed; worn bricks, no paint, and no windows, and the usual white awning had been replaced with a chiseled wood sign that said "Blacksmith." The sidewalks, street meters, street lamps —they'd disappeared too, and there was a stench in the air, the thick, musty odor of horseshit. The atmosphere was changing around her, weighing on her shoulders, compressing her lungs.

They're trying to trick me. Which way? *Just run!* She could almost feel Lehmann's needle sharp teeth sinking into her ankle, but when she jerked her head back to the antique shop, it was still a burned-out shell, blackened and crumbling. If she crossed that threshold again, would the shop be intact, Lehmann waiting behind the counter with his jack-o'-lantern grin? Or would the entire place stay dark, the rooms reeking of ash and decay?

Greg thought she had something to learn here, but she

hadn't done anything to deserve this—she had great powers, but that wasn't her fault. *I'm special, I'm special, I'm special.* Even when everyone told her she was bad, that long-ago psychic's words had always calmed her; if, that is, she pushed aside the memory of that little shithead boy, the one she'd seen with the psychic the next day. He wasn't special, not like her. Neither was Victor. But Brandon... Brandon was.

She ran up the road, toward her apartment, though it hadn't felt like home since Victor left. Maybe it hadn't been home then either—he'd always wanted her to be different, to deny who she was, just like Grandpa. She'd never been good enough.

But Brandon didn't think she was bad. And Brandon could help, would help, but she was so far from the Shepherd plantation, and even now the demons were probably creeping stealthily up the street to drag her back to that shop. And if she went to the plantation...would Elisha Shepherd be waiting for her? Would Martha?

It has to be you.

At the intersection, Chloe turned toward the park, panting, her hot tears mingling with sweat that dripped from beneath her hairline and dampened her shirt. Here, too, the buildings were not right, but she couldn't look at them, couldn't pay attention to brick and cement when there were monsters to hide from. The man with the drumsticks, the man she saw every morning, had a smile so bright it glowed in the moonlight, and she cried out—"Help me! Please!"—but he kept his eyes on his hands, smiling at his sticks, not at her, never at her. She turned away, toward the artist in the ball cap, his posture relaxed, just moving his pictures, setting up a life, a passion she'd never found, never had. She ran toward him as he leaned another picture against the fence, threw herself into him, half tripping over the cobbles—it was like slamming into a wall. He did not falter, did not stumble, did not even *look* at her.

"I think I'm sick. I need a doctor."

He reached for another painting, eyes on the canvas.

"Please, sir, please..." She grabbed for his arm, clawed at his flesh. He rubbed his forearm absentmindedly then flicked a leaf from the canvas.

This man couldn't feel her—couldn't hear her. But Brandon could. Maybe he was the only one.

Come to me. Come to me.

She had to go back to the plantation.

CHAPTER 33

CHLOE ANDERSON, PRESENT DAY

The miles between downtown and the plantation were overrun with creeping vines, thorns, and grass, but the trees showed her the way, the turns to take. Her neck ached from checking behind her so many times. Was Lehmann there, just out of sight, creeping through the brush, ready to chomp those fangs around her neck like a many-toothed animal trap? And what would happen if he did get her? Would it...hurt? *Demons.* Of course it would. Disbelief tugged at her, but just because she didn't want any of this to be real didn't make it false. The night was ripe with spying eyes—she felt them peering at her from every inky shadow and the panic throbbed in her chest, and in the tight space behind her esophagus, and between her legs.

You ain't right, girl, you ain't right.

We'll fix you up, girl, get you right with God.

The plantation driveway was longer than she remembered, and every thud of her shoes on the dirt shuddered into her bones, like the footsteps might vibrate hard enough to liquefy her marrow and send it seeping out through her pores. Lehmann's car wasn't there where she'd left it—of course it wasn't. Above, the branches of the oaks crackled together like they were laughing at her.

She paused in the drive, listening, watching. The old house was dark, but a light glowed from somewhere deep in its bowels, a dull orange barely registering at the front windows. No sounds of life, not even the caw of a night bird, though her throbbing heart might have been too loud for any other noise to pierce through—even the chittering laughter of the trees seemed to have ceased, as if the world were holding its breath. Anticipating. Gooseflesh attacked her neck, and she spun, looked behind her, for—Lehmann? Monsters? But she saw only the dark, twisted canopy of the trees. She could feel the demons though, sense Lehmann's presence, as surely as she had seen him at the shop. Lehmann wasn't going to let her get away so easily—he was The Enforcer. *Making sure the orders are followed.* The dark chaotic energy of madness twisted through her veins, and she fled up the steps of the plantation house, yanking on the handle to the front door, but the wood stuck fast. She pounded on the oak. No sound from inside.

She should run, but she'd tried, hadn't she? And she'd ended up right back where she'd started.

You ain't right, girl.

I can change, I can fix this. The demons would come here, looking for her, but she'd banish them, she'd whisper their names and cast them out and pray hard for them to leave her alone, and Brandon at least had the brooch, but Brandon... *Oh dear God where the fuck is he?*

Her knuckles ached as she assaulted the door again, pounding as hard as she could with her fists, one of her hands leaving a greasy dark mark on the wood—*blood?*—but even then she didn't stop.

A hiss of breath at the nape of her neck flooded Chloe with ice. Her head filled with images of Lehmann's split face, the wriggling tentacles emerging from Greg's abdomen, and she whirled around, bloody fists cocked and ready to fend off some hideous otherworldly creature. But no snake-like protuberances slithered toward her, no flensing claws waited, poised to tear her organs from her gut. Just the trees, branches rustling in a breeze she could not feel. And the nearest oak seemed...closer. Everything seemed closer. Distorted. The trees weren't just arched—their branches curved so sharply downward that they appeared to be tumbling over, leaves smashed beneath the weight of the lumbering wood. Even the path between the trees was cocked and twisted—and shorter than before?—as though the world was caving in on itself. And when she turned back to the house, the door bulged toward her too, hinges creaking. *Oh shit.*

Chloe stumbled off the porch, but as she turned to the drive, the tree nearest her slid closer, perceptibly, *it did*—it wasn't just the branches shuddering in the breeze, or her eyes playing tricks on her, not this time. *All* the trees were moving, creeping on downward-thrust branches like gorillas on their knuckles, the wood squealing and popping and grinding, the air redolent with the scent of green moss, decaying leaves, and some unnamable filth.

She ran toward the backyard, away from the trees, her feet slapping the lawn, making a sound less like shoes on grass and more...wet. Dense. Meaty, like a fist hitting a man's chest. And as she emerged past the tree line, she saw the light across the yard—the flames.

Was Brandon down there? Someone was—a dark shape stood before the open mouth of the kiln, smoke from the fire rising into the starlit night, gray against the black sky.

Thorns tore at her ankles. The earth felt as though it were breathing, and while she could not see them, she could almost feel vicious jaws at her heels, ready to snap her up. She scanned the yard, frantic—no trace of Lehmann—and ran harder.

Halfway down the hill she slowed—it *was* Brandon at the kiln, shovel in hand. He stood with his face toward the fire, in silhouette, but even from a distance she could see that his clothes were tattered and soaked in blood. The side of his face was disfigured, swollen across the forehead, his eyebrow torn off, and beneath his cheekbone the flesh was unrecognizable, like roadkill that had been picked apart by scavengers. He scooped another shovelful of something—wood chips, maybe—from the pile at his feet and heaved it into the kiln.

"Brandon!" she screamed at him, but he did not acknowledge her. She cried his name again, picking up her pace. "Brandon!"

Still he did not turn. He bent and scooped again as she reached the lower part of the hill, but as he righted himself, Chloe skidded to a halt, and her blood froze despite the blistering fire. Elisha Shepherd strode from behind the kiln, cool eyes glittering in the flickering light. He smiled at her.

"Come to me."

Her feet were rooted to the earth, but her nerves softened, urging her closer to him. What was wrong with her? With Brandon? Elisha was a demon, possibly the Devil himself, but Brandon just scooped more fuel from the pile—he didn't even seem to know Elisha was there. He couldn't be very special if he couldn't feel that evil. Not like Chloe
—*Great power, great power, great power.*

But she didn't want to be special anymore. She wanted to go home to Victor, to be a family. Her life with him and Leslie hadn't been perfect, but at least it had been a place where dead men didn't walk and no one sprouted tentacles from their abdomens—she'd had no idea how good she had it. She took a step backward, and the energy that held her to Elisha Shepherd snapped like a rubber band.

"Brandon, turn around, dammit! Get away from him!"

Elisha's apron glistened in the light of the fire, wet and shiny with recently spilled blood. Whose blood? He stepped toward Brandon.

"I held her arms, you know." Brandon's voice cracked, and when he turned his gaze to Chloe, his eyes shone with tears. "Every day I wish I could take it back."

"Brandon, just run!" Was he fucking stupid? But she couldn't run either—though she had stumbled from Elisha's magnetic field, though she'd found her voice, her feet were once again rooted to the ground.

"This is how it will always be." Brandon nodded to her shirt. "Same night. Just like you."

She looked down at her clothing—gauzy blouse, skirt with pockets. Her clothes had been the same every day since Victor left. Where she awoke was the same, too, no matter where she'd fallen asleep. The air thinned. *You'll be here until you see what you really are.*

What was she? She was...*special*. She looked up in time to see Elisha grab Brandon's shoulders. He shoved.

The shovel clattered to the earth. Brandon grabbed for the edge of the brick, trying to stay upright, but his face and shoulders were already through the opening, and then Elisha was behind him, lifting his feet and heaving him into the fire like a sack of grain. The flames swallowed him, the smoke above went darker, heavier, and Brandon's shrieks were the howls of eternal pain, of a suffering that would never end.

Elisha Shepherd turned to her, bits of flesh and fat glistening on his leather apron in the light of the fire. "Come to me, girl." The kiln's orange flames danced in his eyes. "I can make it stop."

Make it stop. Her muscles were useless. But something in Elisha's gaze spoke of a deep pain, a hunger, a hole he needed her to fill, perhaps even a kindness. Had she been wrong? Was it Lehmann or even Martha who had been trying to trick her? What if Elisha really *could* take pain away?

He killed Helen, and Victor. He killed Martha and Brandon. She should run, she knew she should, but her blood was vibrating, shuddering, her every cell straining toward Elisha's gravity. *God help me, help me.* But she could not say it, could not force her tongue to pray, could not force herself to cast Elisha out.

Shh, shh. Shh, shh.

The sound came from behind her. She drew back from Elisha Shepherd, whipping around to see Lehmann creeping down the hill, his needle-sharp teeth brilliant in the moonlight, his long, lean body shimmering—a snake with arms. Her breath ceased, eyes darting between Lehmann and Elisha. The snake or the Devil? Which fate was worse?

"Come to me, girl."

"Help me." The words spilled from her lips, mingling her breath with the night air around them, and in that one blissful moment, everything was connected and whole—there were no memories, there was no more pain, only a sudden euphoric ignorance as her brain went numb.

Elisha smiled, his irises deepening to the deep crimson of dying coals, and every molecule inside her was pulled, closer, closer, the world disappearing into the red flame of his gaze.

Shh, shh.

Elisha reached for her and she stood there, waiting, his thick fingers getting closer, hands covered in inky stains and—

Lehmann leapt from the darkness between her and Elisha, his entire face unhinged now, the cruel teeth ghastly white even in the dim light. His eyes glittered violet. The energy around them snapped like lightning, and she stumbled back with the force of it as Lehmann lunged for her, her blood singing with electricity. His long, forked tongue launched at her face as if to stab her in the eye. Mucus splattered her arms, so hot it steamed, and Chloe cried out as her flesh sizzled, but she lurched to her feet, trying to scrub it from her arms with her shirt. That thing was going to kill her, it was—

Elisha grabbed the creature, hauled it from the earth, and flipped it over, prying at its soft underbelly with his fingers—Lehmann's blood spurted black in the moonlight. The creature shrieked and squalled so loudly Chloe had to resist holding her ears, but the lizard-thing fought back, clawing at Elisha's face, slashing into his throat, and a torrent of blood erupted over his apron until she couldn't tell which blood was Elisha's and which belonged to Lehmann.

He's trying to save me. Elisha Shepherd is trying to save me.
Of course he is—I'm special.

Her feet tore at the grass as she flew up the hill, the wet sounds of battle at her back, the house closer than it had been even moments before. The world *was* shrinking. She skidded to a halt when motion from the porch caught her attention—a flash of yellow from a lighter. The thin bearded man stood in the shadows looking down over the lawn, smoke curling from his pipe toward the sky. While the rest of the yard was steeped in a thick, murky darkness, the man with the pipe was practically glowing, and the brilliant white emanating from his eyes—but no, that was just the light of the moon against the whites, so unlike Elisha's, Lehmann's…

He's human. Could he get her out of there?

Shh, shh.

Lehmann. He was well behind her, very much alive, and gaining. At the sight of him, the mucus splatters on her arm stung anew, but she focused on the porch ahead and ran as the ghastly thing that had once been her boss gave chase.

"Help!"

The man with the pipe looked at her with the same blank expression he'd had the night she'd seen him on the porch—looked through her, as if she wasn't there at all.

"*Help me!*" She leapt up the porch stairs and grabbed the man's spindly biceps, and when he didn't acknowledge her she clawed at him, scraping at his wrists, at his chest, at the velvet bag he held. But still he did not move, not even when blood welled from the gouges she'd made in his arms. "Help me! Please, help!"

His gaze remained on something at her back. Was he looking at Elisha? Lehmann? What horrors lay behind her? She released him and turned back to the kiln, saw the creature skulking up the hill, dragging an injured foot behind him, coming for her. And…Elisha was just behind it, striding more slowly, though just as determined. Elisha had attacked that creature for her. And he had hurt Helen for her too, peeled her face off with his bare hands because Helen, that fucking bitch, had stolen Victor.

Chloe's heart pumped adrenaline straight into her limbs.

She turned back to the man with the pipe, his sage smoke wafting around her face, into her nose, and from his bag, he yanked...a wriggling animal. A rabbit? The one from the front of the shop, the one she saw every morning, the one she thought of as hers. *Hers.* The bag dangled beside the bunny as the man shoved his other hand back inside, and drew out what appeared to be a wad of green herbs pinched between his fingers. He dropped them along with a handful of something—seeds or stones—that fell with a clatter to the porch.

"It's time to end this. The Light or The Dark?"

It was him. This man—he had summoned Martha and Elisha, and now he'd send the demons back to where they'd come from. She didn't need to do anything at all. *Oh thank you, God.*

Chloe looked around frantically, trying to see what demon he was directing the question to, but...where was Lehmann? No Elisha Shepherd either. They'd just been there, right behind—

"Chloe. Choose."

He was looking at the rabbit in his hand, rubbing a spot between the bunny's eyes, but his words echoed in her head —he was talking to her.

"What...I don't..." She looked behind her again. The creature *was* gone, but she could hear it, hear the gentle *shh, shh* approaching from somewhere, though she had no idea from which direction—she didn't know where to run to escape. And now she could see Elisha as he crested over the top of the hill; up the grass he came in his filthy apron, stocky shoulders set, white hair reflecting the moonlight.

"The Light or The Dark?" The moon played on the smoke at the man's temples, thickening the air around him like a halo. He fell to his knees as if in prayer, and he cried out, wincing, his jaw tightening, but he did not pause, and his arm flashed through the air so fast she thought the glint in his hand was a flicker of moonlight. A knife. He held it to the rabbit's throat.

Scream, Chloe, scream. But she was impotent to do it—her lungs would not even take air, let alone draw in enough for her to use her voice. And then they expanded, and a smooth zippy excitement fluttered through her chest.

The man shook his head as if she'd disappointed him. "Chloe. An answer, or one will be chosen for you."

"The Light! The Light!" That was the correct answer, right? The Dark frightened her as much as it excited her, always had. Always would.

He nodded, and dropped the rabbit along with the silvery blade to the porch, and the thing scampered off, disappearing down the steps. If she had chosen The Dark would he have sacrificed it? Sacrificed her?

God, please. Her knuckles ached—she was clutching her hands together, praying now. "Please, God, help me," she said, so quietly even she couldn't hear it. "Make them all go away. Take the demons away."

Her entire body shook. She could not run from him—could no longer breathe. The man looked right at her, his eyes wide, but not with shock or fear—fury.

"I cast thee out!"

Her chest exploded in pain, a thousand blades piercing her from the inside, and she flew backward onto the porch, writhing, shrieking, howling at the moon, splinters digging into her back, every muscle twitching as if she'd been hit with a stun gun.

"I cast thee into The Light, away from Darkness..."

He was above her, hands extended in midair, nowhere near her skin, but she felt his touch on her forehead, and her flesh sizzled against his phantom fingers. And suddenly she understood this wasn't about Martha, it never had been about Martha. *A trick, a trick.* Her muscles seized. Was he going to say her name? Summon a demon into her body?

Shh, shh. Shh, shh. The lizard was slithering closer.

"Into The Light...find Martha."

Inside her, something popped, and suddenly she had control of her limbs again. Chloe arched her back, flinging the man's invisible touch from her body as she scrambled over the porch to her feet.

Shh, shh. But the creature was still in the grass.

She backed over the wooden planks of the porch—nowhere on that lawn felt safe. "Go away! Go back to where you came from!" Was she talking to the lizard or the bearded man or Elisha? Did it matter? They all needed to leave.

But she didn't have their portals. No one even seemed to hear her. The bearded man stepped from the porch onto the lawn. Would Lehmann eat him instead? Would he be enough to satisfy the demon's hunger? Would they leave her alone after that? But as she moved toward the front door and crept into the shadow under the eaves, she saw Lehmann—right in front of the bearded man now, and still the man didn't move. Then he did, stepping forward—

The bearded man walked through the creature as if it wasn't there, and still the lizard came nearer the porch, *shh, shh*, closer, closer…but it was slowing. *Shh, shh*. Was it afraid of the house? The creature froze on the other side of the railing, put a foot on the porch, stared, but it did not advance. It was waiting, not so much afraid as trying to keep her from going toward the back lawn—herding her. It could leap for her throat at any moment. Chloe pressed her back against the white column, the pressure making her shoulder blades ache.

"I cast thee out, Lehmann, I cast thee out." The whispered words felt foreign on her tongue. "Please, God, make them go away." The creature blinked at her. And stayed.

Elisha stopped at the top of the hill and cocked his head, the side of his face stained black with blood, one eye closed. *Did the lizard scratch it out?* The man with the pipe reached Elisha and stopped; the bearded man could see that demon too. And there was something clenched in the man's hand, dull, metal—the hand drill? Was that Elisha's portal?

The bearded man stilled, raising his palms in the air before the demon, smoke from his pipe shrouding his head.

"I cast thee out!" he bellowed at the sky, and Elisha Shepherd winced, stumbling backward onto the grass.

"I cast thee out!" the man cried again, advancing, and Elisha's face contorted, eyes glittering, furious, as he tried to stand, gripping the lawn with his beefy palms. *Oh thank you, God, thank you.*

"Be gone from this place!" And then the bearded man was whispering something, whispering, and then louder he cried, "I cast thee—"

Elisha Shepherd was on his feet again, almost as if he'd just appeared there, and the bearded man was lifted by some invisible hand and thrown backward over the lawn into the shadows of the house. Elisha remained standing, frowning, on the grass. The bearded man had done it right, he'd tried to banish Elisha Shepherd. But these demons were stronger than he was. Could she get to the portal, send the demons back herself? Was she strong enough? *Great power.* She wheezed in a thin breath, heart throbbing wildly in her temples—the air tasted like sulfur.

Shh, shh.

Beyond the porch railing, the lizard paced. Chloe glanced behind her at the house, where something, a feeling, was oozing from every painted shutter, from every pane of glass, from every plank of the porch. A cool, magnetic pulse throbbed through her veins—she was being drawn toward the lawn by the plasma in her blood. Urged from the safety of the house, as if just beyond the shadowed porch, eternal peace awaited.

The column touched her shoulders again—had she stepped backward? *The porch is shrinking.* Only feet between the column and the railing now, and down the way, the door hinges squealed, and then the front door bowed and exploded outward in a symphony of splintering wood. But the gaping chasm behind the broken oak wasn't safe—the dark interior of that house was full of wickedness, an unbridled hatred that raked at her brain like nails against steel.

The front of her legs pressed into the railing. Her back

was against the column again—the house was going to crush her. Elisha stepped closer over the lawn, teeth gleaming, though smiling or snarling she couldn't tell. The creature looked up at her too, forked tongue splitting the air. What now? The porch was still shrinking. There was no way she'd get to the other side, around to Elisha's portal, before the porch forced her off. But if she went down the stairs and ran over the lawn... *I can outrun the creature, it's hurt.* No time to think—she ran toward the broken door and when she reached the front steps, she jumped, landing hard on the stone, but it wasn't just stone, not anymore; scrubby grass and slick moss crept over the rocks—the moss from beneath the oaks. The ground sighed under her feet.

Shh, shh.

She leapt to standing, but she could no longer see the driveway or the side yard; every path was blocked by densely packed trees, branches twined around one another like lovers refusing to part—hedging her in. She'd have to fight her way through to get to the portal. But one tree stood apart: the oak nearest the house, hulking in the moonlight. And beneath the tree was Martha, arms out as if in offering, the exposed bone in her jaw shining bright white in the light of the moon, though Chloe should not have been able to see that in the shadows. The organ at the girl's knee glittered darkly.

Shh, shh.

Chloe spun around—*shh, shh*—the creature crept toward her along the side of the porch—*shh, shh*—slimy forked tongue flicking between his jack-o-lantern teeth. And beyond him, Elisha Shepherd drew nearer as well, a wall of trees at his back, apron dripping gore onto the dirt. *Shh, shh.* Elisha's shock of white hair shone in the moonlight, his eyes glowed red like the blood of his victims, and his face, his eye—it had healed. She touched her forehead where that bearded man had seared her flesh—nothing there but smooth skin.

Shh, shh. Chloe turned back to the tree, back to the bloody girl from her dreams, Martha with her half a mouth, the organ hanging below the hem of her dress, pulsing, pulsing. The house, the wall of trees, the creature, Elisha…or Martha. There was nowhere else to go. She was trapped.

"Come to me," Elisha whispered, and a cool breeze from his words calmed her heart. But Lehmann was drawing closer between her and the slave master, blocking her, and—

"Do not listen." Martha's alto cut through the cool peace in her chest, the girl's voice filled with a million lifetimes of suffering, but there was something familiar about it, that pain, something that made Chloe feel like she belonged there, with Martha. And then she could hear her mother's voice—"I'll always love you, Chloe, always"—and she'd felt that love, hadn't she, in that moment?

"Come to me," Elisha said, and this time his voice was tighter, more insistent—worried. He was as scared as she was. She didn't want to go to the tree, didn't want to be anywhere near it, but Martha… The girl stood, arms open, her face still and peaceful despite her torn flesh, despite the blood still dripping down her legs. The girl had found peace, maybe even love. Martha knew salvation.

The Light or The Dark. She had to pick between them, and though Elisha's promise remained, tugging at her with its bliss, the calm rang false in the presence of the girl; it was a hollow kind of peace—ignorance but not absolution. Chloe's pain might never heal, not all the way, but she could find better, do better, in spite of it, and Martha wanted to help her. *If you worship just because you're afraid, girl, you'll worship the Devil just as easy, we'll get you right with God.* She ran for the shadow of the oak.

Twenty steps from the girl. Ten. Martha lowered her hand, and something snaked around Chloe's ankle, bringing her to her knees, and then more tentacle-like branches slithered around her legs, wound around her chest, the weight of the wood crushing her rib cage. *Get it off, get it off, get it off!* The world was spinning, a tornado of gray, and a red and orange haze glowed at the edges of her vision. And suddenly

—it stopped. The tree was gone. Martha too. And she was... staring at a ceiling.

Her ceiling. Her and Victor's ceiling. She was on her kitchen floor. Chloe tried to sit but her muscles weren't working right, and she could only lift her head. She gasped in a breath, the tile on her back soothing after the roughness of the wood. Had she passed out? It was...a dream.

She laughed. Glorious, barking, hysterical laugher that brought tears to her eyes and gagged her with giddiness.

How stupid was that? She'd gotten tired and she'd passed out. Maybe she'd been drunk. She burst into another fit of giggles and dropped her head back against the floor, turning it to the side to see the clock on the oven. And stared into another pair of eyes.

Brilliant blue, wide open.

And dead.

Leslie's lips were purple, swollen like the hivey rash marring her cheeks. Chloe had expected the girl's eyes to swell shut, too, but they never had. It had only taken minutes from the time she'd given her the cookie—chocolate chips, coconut, and butter. *Real butter.*

"Chloe?"

Victor was there, and somewhere behind them she heard a door close—was someone else with him? But she could not take her gaze from Victor as his knees hit the floor beside his daughter, his eyes wide as hers. "Oh, Jesus! Oh, God, no!"

"Shh, shh," she said. How had he gotten home so early? Well, fuck, he must have hitched a ride. She pushed herself to sitting. She had to find a way to explain it so he'd stay—he couldn't leave her like her mother had.

"Chloe, what...how did this—"

"It's over now." She heard herself say it, but she didn't feel her lips moving. "An accident, just an accident." But he looked at the counter, at the plate of cookies, and when he turned back, his gaze was wilder, more panicked. "I got us a bottle of wine," she said, "to take the edge off. Maybe in the end it will even be for the best." She hadn't planned on sharing the wine—she'd bought it for her own little celebration—but she'd tear the tag off before she poured it.

Victor's eyes filled with tears as she ran her fingers over his shoulder. *Shit.* She'd intended to get rid of the body before he arrived so she could break it to him slowly, letting him think the girl had run away, or maybe he'd think she'd been kidnapped by someone in Stephanie's family because of the sheer volume of things that had vanished with Leslie. Chloe had used his suitcases because they were bigger, but disposing of the clothes still hadn't gone near quickly enough. Now, even if she could convince him it was accidental, he'd still blame her. And he'd leave.

"It's okay, it's all going to be oka—"

"Okay? What the fuck are you talking about? You can't fix this!" He pulled away from her and clambered over his daughter, lowering his lips to Leslie's as if to give her mouth-to-mouth, but yanked his face back immediately—she'd be cold as ice now, cold as Chloe's heart when she watched Leslie die, the way she'd watched her baby sister die. Hope had squirmed under the blanket when Chloe pressed it over her face, and Chloe had felt nothing but that same coldness. *Little piece of shit. Mom couldn't even take me to the fucking movies.* A righteous rage coursed through her veins.

Victor was sobbing, rocking the girl in his arms. Yes, he'd blame her. Unless she could get him to blame himself.

"We're going to be okay, Victor. I know you couldn't do it yourself, you were too weak, but you might as well have asked me to."

His eyes widened over the top of the girl's head. "Wha—"

"The way you always talked about her, talked like she was ruining your life. You were right. I only wanted to help you."

Victor laid Leslie on the floor, gently, and sat back on his heels. "You fucking bitch. You crazy fucking bitch." Tears streaked his face, his eyes shining with madness—he was hysterical.

Bitch? "Sometimes you have to make hard decisions, Victor. Do you really think magical solutions will fall from the sky and make everything better?" She felt herself saying it this time, saw herself reaching for him again, but it was like watching someone else play her in a movie—disconnected. Numb.

Victor touched Leslie's cheek, trailing a finger from her temple to her swollen lips, and then he climbed over his dead child and grabbed Chloe's ankle and held it tight, squeezing so hard she thought he'd snap the bone.

"I did it for you!" she said.

He jerked her toward him, her ass sliding on the linoleum, head flying back against the floor. Her arm and Leslie's pressed together—the girl was so cold. He wrapped his hands around Chloe's throat, tears staining his cheeks. "She...my child. My *child*."

The past is the past, we only look forward, and nothing else matters.

The world was going black at the edges when he suddenly released her neck and shot to standing, retreating to the island. She gasped in great heaving gulps of air, air that already held the heady odor of decay, though it shouldn't have—the girl was only just dead. But it wasn't coming from the body—it wafted around Chloe as if her soul was the thing that was rotten.

Dizziness pulled at her from all sides. She tried to push herself backward, away from the girl on the floor, but she was dazed, little starbursts of light firing in her peripheral vision from the lack of oxygen. She'd give him a minute, or a few hours—he'd soon realize she was right. He'd understand that he'd simply been too weak to do it himself, that she'd saved him, just like she'd saved her mother. And she'd convinced Victor of many things already: that his band was bullshit, that he was worthless without her, that he was too sick to go it alone. So many hours invested—in the end this would be no different. She'd chosen right this time, chosen him because he was sick, because he was moldable, because he needed her to make decisions for them both. Victor could not leave her no matter what she did.

THE JILTED

Then he was back, knees on either side of her hips, sitting on her thighs. She squinted, working to focus her gaze on his face. He raised his hand—a blade glinted in the overheads.

"Everything will be okay now," she croaked. "I swear."

"Yes." He smiled, but with a manic gleam in his eyes. "The voices at night... I should have known the demon was you." He drove the blade into his wrist. Blood poured from his arm, and she tried to scream, but it was too late—he raised the weapon over his head and brought it down, right toward her heart, intent on breaking it once and for all.

The first prick of the blade burned as it pierced her skin, hot and sharp, and then came a grinding sensation as it sliced through gristle or something more vital in her chest. And in some other dimension, beneath a dark sky, a tree branch stabbed into her heart, unceremonious and swift.

Something was rattling. Then someone was knocking, banging like they wanted to smash the apartment door in, and Victor was yelling something unintelligible. A deafening crash rang through the air, the whoosh of blood in Chloe's ears fading, weakening.

"Police, freeze!" somewhere in the distance. But Victor raised the knife again and plunged it downward, and another bolt of pain seared through her heart. *Bang! Bang!* A stain spread across Victor's chest, but the world was slipping away from her. The air was gone, and with it the desire to breathe. A brilliant, sharp sensation ran through her veins, as if her cells were made of broken glass. The ground was cold beneath her. The tree shuddered overhead—the ceiling had dissolved—and Chloe drew her eyes to the sky, but could see nothing but the branches and Martha, the girl staring down at her, nodding. She tried to cry out Martha's name—failed. Only a gurgle. Something wet dribbled out of her mouth and oozed down her chin.

Then Martha changed, her skin melting and reforming before Chloe's eyes as if she were made of clay. For a moment, she was a black woman, older, cradling a small boy in her arms, both of them with ugly purple slashes around their throats. Then the woman and the boy disintegrated, too, reforming into another child, a baby...

Chloe's little sister, dark bruises around her mouth from where Chloe had held the blanket, and bruises on her thighs, too, from where Chloe had spent the afternoon pinching her, wishing she'd go away, laughing when Hope cried. And then the clay was spreading and expanding: Leslie. Leslie, staring blankly, face swollen and mottled. A smear of chocolate on her chin. Chloe blinked, and in Leslie's place stood Chloe's grandfather, his gray hair combed over his bald spot, his gaze hooded by the fat pockets over his eyes. His belt was wrapped around one beefy forearm.

"We tried to fix you, didn't we, girl? Tried to get you right with God." Tears stained his cheeks. In his hands was the plate with the engraved rabbit.

And as he dropped the plate at her side and bent to wrap his arms around her, she saw the serpent-creature slinking beneath the shadow of the tree, creeping over the dirt toward her, the *shh, shh* of his legs on the grass matching the rhythm of the tree branches overhead. Her grandfather squeezed her once. "I'm sorry," she whispered. Then the serpent opened his mouth wide and lunged for her, his wicked teeth gnashing in the moonlight.

> "Man creates both his god and his devil in his own image.
> His god is himself at his best, and his devil himself at his worst."
> ~Elbert Hubbard and Alice Hubbard,
> An American Bible

EPILOGUE

ABRAM SHEPHERD, PRESENT DAY

The smoke circles my head, then evaporates into the sky above the strip. Ghostly. Delicate. The air feels cooler today, though that might be poor circulation on my part, a growing difficulty regulating even the most basic of bodily functions. Soon it will be worse. One does not need to fear fantastic monsters, flesh and blood creatures lurking beneath the bed. Life is a worthy enough foe.

Last night seemed to pass in a heartbeat, the bloody end to yet another soul. Afterward, the tree unfurled itself to its usual grandeur and kissed the moonlit sky, shuddering as if contented...for the moment. The energy is ever balancing itself, but there will always be a price unpaid. Blood doesn't simply vanish after you clean it off. Some things stick.

When I caught news of the crime on the police scanner, I thought that perhaps Chloe could be the one to end this—the pain was strong in her, the madness, the evil, and the jilted are always easier to summon. Their souls are already seeking something, some salve to heal them from a festering wound that cannot be easily tended. But though I rushed to the scene under the guise of performing the last rites, though I was successful in summoning her here, though I lured The Dark from hiding to take her, The Dark was too strong, and he threw me off before I could banish him. Perhaps I will never purge Elisha's energy from the plantation because there is no single demon ruthless enough to distract The Dark while I exorcise him.

No matter what Chloe chose, her end would have been the same. Hell—though this name is too kind, too simple—would have sucked her away from here; one does not do the things she did and walk away unscathed. But by choosing The Light over her very nature, by refusing The Dark in her final moments, she weakened the vile energy she left behind on Earth—weakened The Darkness itself. Tainted blood will not disappear, but the nastiest clots can be purged before they fester into a greater wound.

And it is that wound I wish to avoid. The stronger The Dark is when I go, the harder it will be for me to choose The Light—my own tainted bloodline will see to that. Self-preservation...I'm no more altruistic than Chloe was. Why I've been chosen to know any of this, I am not sure. But I will summon as many souls as I must for even the slightest chance to ensure my own quiet passage through purgatory—though that is, again, too small a word for this place of revelation and repentance.

A woman approaches from up the street, head cocked as if listening to the cobblestones underfoot, reveling in the cool breeze. Dark hair, dark skin, pressed suit. Off to work, somewhere in the city. She smiles at the ground—happy. Perhaps she is in love.

From the other direction comes a man, a leather jacket even in the heat, a ring through the center cartilage of his nose. I would have recognized him in any clothing—I brought him here. Victor walks far more slowly than the woman, eyeing the shops. He was a sick man in life, but that's not why he's here, though the illness did make him more susceptible. He let a demon control him. They look for that, you know, that vulnerability. He worked hard to silence the voices in his head, especially the one that told him what she was, but Chloe's whispers were surely stronger—what

THE JILTED

lies did she tell him while he slept? That he was weak, that he couldn't do it without her? That no one but her would want him? It matters little now. Because no matter how hard she hit him, no matter how many times the police came to protect him, no matter what she did, he stayed—and Leslie died. While demons believe their sins to be justified, those who stay silent in the face of atrocity allow, by their complicity, sin, injustice, and slaughter. They are the ones who give any demon its power. But all will be held accountable in their own private purgatory—they will experience the pain they've inflicted by neglect. They will feel the pain they ignored.

But Victor doesn't recall his sins just yet. Right now, he's strutting, gaze clear, an excited glint in his eye. Hopeful, though he was surely more so before he met Chloe. Definitely handsome.

No wonder Helen liked him. She only thought she'd drop Victor off that night, but she saw the mess in the apartment and fled, called the police on her way to the station, wrapped her car around a tree doing it. Though I wasn't certain she was tainted, I intervened there too, went to her, summoned her before The Dark could claim her.

The only way to get the demons to pay their penance, to give their energy to The Light, is to prolong their time here —to summon them, and let the demons roam free until they see themselves for what they are. Until they're sorry. And while I am not privy to every nuance in this other world, I understand enough to imagine Helen awoke here in a place that looked like hers, but filled with reminders of things she'd tried to forget in life. Did Martha leave a handwritten note to jog her memory? An article of clothing? What was it that Martha showed Helen to remind her of her sins? What item made Chloe see her own wickedness laid bare? There is always something that reminds us. I touch my rings and watch the street.

The antique shop hulks like a wounded creature emerging from the swamp, blackened and desolate, unassuming. Sandwiched as it is between two newer constructions, one might wonder why it's still there at all.

The woman ignores the burnt facade of the antique store for a beat, her eyes meeting mine, and she nods. I nod in reply, but she follows my gaze back to the shop, maybe wondering when someone will finally fix the blasted thing. It is an eyesore. Those who stride by assume it is part of the history of this place, another sightseer destination, a place for an alleged haunting. Another stop on a ghost tour. Just a farce. But I know this woman feels the energy because she stops before the blackened front door and peeks in. She can feel the eyes she cannot quite see, perhaps, or maybe something in the corner has caught her attention—a glint of light, here then gone.

Walking these streets, we miss far more than we see.

The woman cranes her neck as she peers at something beyond the threshold. Whatever she thinks she saw, she is probably writing off as a figment of her imagination. Perhaps she sees the camera sitting in the dust of the shop, waiting for its owner to come take it away. No one but Victor can claim that camera—even Victor will not remember losing it. Until he does. These items are tools for enlightenment, triggers for understanding, for forward motion. I touch my rings again. If these are my items, when I awaken after death they will be gone. I will need to rediscover them, and knowing they'll be taken and hidden from me makes them all the more precious to me now.

The woman walks on.

The man draws nearer, striding up the street, but he does not see the woman. He does not see the camera either; it is not time yet. He walks with love in his heart, rugged and smiling and optimistic—in the midst of a better time for him, before Chloe showed him who she was. Before she destroyed him. He won't be able to tell the difference in this place at all, not at first, for pain and Hell exist on Earth as surely as they exist in the afterlife—each of us has our own version of damnation. Pain is relative.

When the woman collides with him, neither feels a thing besides a momentary shiver—a chill from the breeze in the damp air, she surely thinks. She does not sense the hot, sharp needles I feel in my flesh when these demons pass me.

Demons and gods never look how we imagine—we'd never trust them if they did. We're no longer impressed by burning bushes, and we care nothing for crowns of thorns. We might see an eight-armed deity and pause only to take photos for social media. And Martha does not show up the same for everyone—she understands what will trigger the humanity in whatever soul she seeks. What they will identify with. What will draw them to her.

Demons do not emerge from the underworld in a puff of black smoke, creatures made of Satan's rib, set to wreak havoc on the living. Demons have no need. Humans are not possessed. Demons are simply born, in hospitals, in bathtubs, to mortal mothers, though they often do not see what they are—I merely draw out their evil, their darkness, exposing the wicked pieces they try to hide even from themselves, for no soul is comprised exclusively of love or hate. Those grotesque hellions that slither from the fiery pits to ravage us have always proven a convenient scapegoat, but our imaginings of them only serve to hide our own guilt beneath a blanket of blame—if demons are responsible, we need not worry, we need not change.

It is simpler to blame demons and allow our own success to be built upon the backs of the oppressed. Humans are the only ones worth fearing, and the demon inside each of us is what we all fear the most—which is why we hide it, refuse to believe it. There is no greater eraser than denial. How many explanations did Chloe disprove before she realized the truth?

They all fight it at first, but the longer any soul is here, the more tricks they discover; perhaps this makes it more satisfying to stay, these small novelties. Perhaps not. Lehmann slinks though this world, finally embodying the serpent he felt like in life. Gregory always wanted to touch more than he was allowed, wanted to suction his victims to him so they could not escape—now he can. Elisha Shepherd craves only power, pulling unsuspecting souls into himself, the evil breeding more of the same, enough to compete with the natural order of things—contaminating even the innocent unlucky enough to share his blood. Though I am not innocent, if he were weaker, perhaps I'd be anticipating a peaceful afterlife instead of preparing for an eternity reliving the atrocities he committed. If I can weaken his hold, I may still earn a good death. For watching it all, our teacher, our agent of enlightenment: Martha, though that is too simple a name —she is all of us. And she alone decides when it is time for things to finally, blissfully end.

The man with the nose ring is outside the antique shop. For a moment the street flickers, and the shop seems warm and welcoming, lit with the pleasant yellow light of the lamps inside. Carved treasures—silver bowls and jade elephants—glint from the front window. His posture straightens. Today is a new day.

He does not know he is here to pay a penance, and from the gleam in his eye, he's unaware of the enormity of his debts. But he will become aware. They always do.

But never soon enough.

∽

Don't miss the next book from Meghan O'Flynn! READ ON FOR A SNEAK PEEK AT *FAMISHED*, the first book in the Ash Park series, then check out *SHADOW'S KEEP* (coming soon) at meghanoflynn.com!

Go to MEGHANOFLYNN.COM to sign up for the newsletter, and get a FREE SHORT STORY! You'll also be first in line for new release information. No spam, and you can opt out anytime.

FAMISHED

AN ASH PARK NOVEL (#1)

Sunday, December 6th

Focus, or she's dead.

Petrosky ground his teeth together, but it didn't stop the panic from swelling hot and frantic within him. After the arrest last week, this crime should have been fucking impossible.

He wished it were a copycat. He knew it wasn't.

Anger knotted his chest as he examined the corpse that lay in the middle of the cavernous living room. Dominic Harwick's intestines spilled onto the white marble floor as though someone had tried to run off with them. His eyes were wide, milky at the edges already, so it had been awhile since someone gutted his sorry ass and turned him into a rag doll in a three-thousand-dollar suit.

That rich prick should have been able to protect her.

Petrosky looked at the couch: luxurious, empty, cold. Last week Hannah had sat on that couch, staring at him with wide green eyes that made her seem older than her twenty-three years. She had been happy, like Julie had been before she was stolen from him. He pictured Hannah as she might have been at eight years old, skirt twirling, dark hair flying, face flushed with sun, like one of the photos of Julie he kept tucked in his wallet.

They all started so innocent, so pure, so...*vulnerable*.

The idea that Hannah was the catalyst in the deaths of eight others, the cornerstone of some serial killer's plan, had not occurred to him when they first met. But it had later. It did now.

Petrosky resisted the urge to kick the body and refocused on the couch. Crimson congealed along the white leather as if marking Hannah's departure.

He wondered if the blood was hers.

The click of a doorknob caught Petrosky's attention. He turned to see Bryant Graves, the lead FBI agent, entering the room from the garage door, followed by four other agents. Petrosky tried not to think about what might be in the garage. Instead, he watched the four men survey the living room from different angles, their movements practically choreographed.

"Damn, does everyone that girl knows get whacked?" one of the agents asked.

"Pretty much," said another.

A plain-clothed agent stooped to inspect a chunk of scalp on the floor. Whitish-blond hair waved, tentacle-like, from the dead skin, beckoning Petrosky to touch it.

"You know this guy?" one of Graves's cronies asked from the doorway.

"Dominic Harwick." Petrosky nearly spat out the bastard's name.

"No signs of forced entry, so one of them knew the killer," Graves said.

"*She* knew the killer," Petrosky said. "Obsession builds over time. This level of obsession indicates it was probably someone she knew well."

But who?

Petrosky turned back to the floor in front of him, where words scrawled in blood had dried sickly brown in the morning light.

> *Ever drifting down the stream—*
> *Lingering in the golden gleam—*
> *Life, what is it but a dream?*

Petrosky's gut clenched. He forced himself to look at Graves. "And, Han—" *Hannah*. Her name caught in his throat, sharp like a razor blade. "The girl?"

"There are bloody drag marks heading out to the back shower and a pile of bloody clothes," Graves said. "He must have cleaned her up before taking her. We've got the techs on it now, but they're working the perimeter first." Graves bent and used a pencil to lift the edge of the scalp, but it was suctioned to the floor with dried blood.

"Hair? That's new," said another voice. Petrosky didn't bother to find out who had spoken. He stared at the coppery stains on the floor, his muscles twitching with anticipation. Someone could be tearing her apart as the agents roped off the room. How long did she have? He wanted to run, to find her, but he had no idea where to look.

"Bag it," Graves said to the agent examining the scalp, then turned to Petrosky. "It's all been connected from the beginning. Either Hannah Montgomery was his target all along or she's just another random victim. I think the fact that she isn't filleted on the floor like the others points to her being the goal, not an extra."

"He's got something special planned for her," Petrosky whispered. He hung his head, hoping it wasn't already too late.

If it was, it was all his fault.

GET *FAMISHED* AT MEGHANOFLYNN.COM

OTHER WORKS BY BESTSELLING AUTHOR MEGHAN O'FLYNN

∾

The Jilted
Shadow's Keep

∾

The Ask Park Series:

Famished
Conviction
Repressed
Hidden
Redemption

∾

"Alien Landscape: A Short Story"
"Crimson Snow: A Short Story"

∾

DON'T MISS ANOTHER RELEASE!
SIGN UP FOR THE NEWSLETTER AT
MEGHANOFLYNN.COM

ABOUT THE AUTHOR

Meghan O'Flynn is the bestselling author of the *The Jilted*, *Shadow's Keep*, and the Ash Park series—which includes *Famished, Conviction, Repressed, Hidden,* and *Redemption*—and has penned a number of short stories including "Crimson Snow" and "Alien Landscape." Her husband thinks she's a little twisted, her children think she's a lot weird, and her dog thinks she's the best human ever, though that beast licks terrible, terrible things and might not be a reliable character witness. You can find out more about that on Meghan's website along with more on her books. (But please leave a book review first, or ghosts might get you. Meghan is 87.56% sure that's how the spirit world works.)

If you want to find out about new releases and freebies, sign up for Meghan's newsletter at meghanoflynn.com, get a **FREE SHORT STORY**, and rest assured that Meghan knows spam sucks even more than creepy ghosts.

Want to connect with Meghan?
www.meghanoflynn.com